THE BOOK OF ILLUSIONS

Paul Auster was born in New Jersey in 1947. After attending Columbia University he lived in France for four years. Since 1974 he has published poems, essays, novels, screenplays and translations. He has also edited the story collection *True Tales of American Life*. *The Book of Illusions* is his tenth novel. He lives in Brooklyn, New York.

WILMA

Also by Paul Auster

Novels
THE NEW YORK TRILOGY
IN THE COUNTRY OF LAST THINGS
MOON PALACE
THE MUSIC OF CHANCE
LEVIATHAN
MR VERTIGO
TIMBUKTU

Non-Fiction
THE INVENTION OF SOLITUDE
THE ART OF HUNGER
HAND TO MOUTH

Screenplays
SMOKE & BLUE IN THE FACE
LULU ON THE BRIDGE

Poetry
SELECTED POEMS

Editor
TRUE TALES OF AMERICAN LIFE

Translation
CHRONICLE OF THE GUAYAKI INDIANS
by Pierre Clastres

THE BOOK OF ILLUSIONS

A NOVEL

PAUL AUSTER

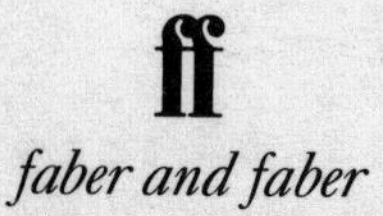

faber and faber

First published in the United States in 2002
by Henry Holt and Company, LLC
115 West 18th Street, New York, New York 10011

First published in the United Kingdom in 2002
by Faber and Faber Limited
3 Queen Square London WC1N 3AU
This paperback edition first published in 2003

Printed in England by Bookmarque Ltd, Croydon

Designed by Victoria Hartman

A CIP record for this book
is available from the British Library

ISBN 0–571–21218–2

2 4 6 8 10 9 7 5 3 1

Man has not one and the same life. He has many lives, placed end to end, and that is the cause of his misery.

–Chateaubriand

THE BOOK OF
ILLUSIONS

1

EVERYONE THOUGHT HE was dead. When my book about his films was published in 1988, Hector Mann had not been heard from in almost sixty years. Except for a handful of historians and old-time movie buffs, few people seemed to know that he had ever existed. *Double or Nothing*, the last of the twelve two-reel comedies he made at the end of the silent era, was released on November 23, 1928. Two months later, without saying good-bye to any of his friends or associates, without leaving behind a letter or informing anyone of his plans, he walked out of his rented house on North Orange Drive and was never seen again. His blue DeSoto was parked in the garage; the lease on the property was good for another three months; the rent had been paid in full. There was food in the kitchen, whiskey in the liquor cabinet, and not a single article of Hector's clothing was missing from the bedroom drawers. According to the *Los Angeles Herald Express* of January 18, 1929, *it looked as though he had stepped out for a short walk and would be returning at any moment.* But he didn't return, and from that point on it was as if Hector Mann had vanished from the face of the earth.

For several years following his disappearance, various stories and rumors circulated about what had happened to him, but none of these conjectures ever amounted to anything. The most plausible ones—that he had committed suicide or fallen victim to foul play—could neither be proved nor disproved, since no body was ever recovered. Other accounts of Hector's fate were more imaginative, more hopeful, more in keeping with the romantic implications of such a case. In one, he had returned to his native Argentina and was now the owner of a small provincial circus. In another, he had joined the Communist Party and was working under an assumed name as an organizer among the dairy workers in Utica, New York. In still another, he was riding the rails as a Depression hobo. If Hector had been a bigger star, the stories no doubt would have persisted. He would have lived on in the things that were said about him, gradually turning into one of those symbolic figures who inhabit the nether zones of collective memory, a representative of youth and hope and the devilish twists of fortune. But none of that happened, for the fact was that Hector was only just beginning to make his mark in Hollywood when his career ended. He had come too late to exploit his talents fully, and he hadn't stayed long enough to leave a lasting impression of who he was or what he could do. A few more years went by, and little by little people stopped thinking about him. By 1932 or 1933, Hector belonged to an extinct universe, and if there were any traces of him left, it was only as a footnote in some obscure book that no one bothered to read anymore. The movies talked now, and the flickering dumb shows of the past were forgotten. No more clowns, no more pantomimists, no more pretty flapper girls dancing to the beat of unheard orchestras. They had been dead for just a few years, but already they felt prehistoric, like creatures who had roamed the earth when men still lived in caves.

I didn't give much information about Hector's life in my book. *The Silent World of Hector Mann* was a study of his films, not a biography, and whatever small facts I threw in about his offscreen activities came directly from the standard sources: film encyclopedias, memoirs, histories of early Hollywood. I wrote the book because I wanted to share my enthusiasm for Hector's work. The story of his life was secondary to me, and rather than speculate on what might or might not have happened to him, I stuck to a close reading of the films themselves. Given that he was born in 1900, and given that he had not been seen since 1929, it never would have occurred to me to suggest that Hector Mann was still alive. Dead men don't crawl out from their graves, and as far as I was concerned, only a dead man could have kept himself hidden for that long.

The book was published by the University of Pennsylvania Press eleven years ago this past March. Three months later, just after the first reviews had started to appear in the film quarterlies and academic journals, a letter turned up in my mailbox. The envelope was larger and squarer than the ones commonly sold in stores, and because it was made of thick, expensive paper, my initial response was to think there might be a wedding invitation or a birth announcement inside. My name and address were written out across the front in an elegant, curling script. If the writing wasn't that of a professional calligrapher, it no doubt came from someone who believed in the virtues of graceful penmanship, a person who had been schooled in the old academies of etiquette and social decorum. The stamp was postmarked Albuquerque, New Mexico, but the return address on the back flap showed that the letter had been written somewhere else—assuming that there was such a place, and assuming that the name of the town was real. Top and bottom, the two lines read: Blue Stone Ranch; Tierra del Sueño, New Mexico. I might have smiled when I saw those words, but I can't remember now. No name was given, and as I opened the envelope to read the message on the card inside, I caught a faint smell of perfume, the subtlest hint of lavender essence.

Dear Professor Zimmer, the note said. *Hector has read your book and would like to meet you. Are you interested in paying us a visit? Yours sincerely, Frieda Spelling (Mrs. Hector Mann).*

I read it six or seven times. Then I put it down, walked to the other end of the room, and came back. When I picked up the letter again, I wasn't sure if the words would still be there. Or, if they were there, if they would still be the same words. I read it six or seven more times, and then, still not sure of anything, dismissed it as a prank. A moment later, I was filled with doubts, and the next moment after that I began to doubt those doubts. To think one thought meant thinking the opposite thought, and no sooner did that second thought destroy the first thought than a third thought rose up to destroy the second. Not knowing what else to do, I got into my car and drove to the post office. Every address in America was listed in the zip code directory, and if Tierra del Sueño wasn't there, I could throw away the card and forget all about it. But it was there. I found it in volume one on page 1933, sitting on the line between Tierra Amarilla and Tijeras, a proper town with a post office and its own five-digit number. That didn't make the letter genuine, of course, but at least it gave it an air of credibility, and by the time I returned home, I knew that I would have to answer it. A letter like that can't be ignored. Once you've read it, you know that if you don't take the trouble to sit down and write back, you'll go on thinking about it for the rest of your life.

I haven't kept a copy of my answer, but I remember that I wrote it by hand and tried to make it as short as possible, limiting what I said to just a few sentences. Without giving it much thought, I found myself adopting the flat, cryptic style of the letter I had received. I felt less exposed that way, less likely to be taken as a fool by the person who had masterminded the prank—if indeed it was a prank. Give or take a word or two, my response went something like this: *Dear Frieda Spelling. Of course I would like to meet Hector Mann. But how can I be sure he's alive? To the best of my knowledge, he hasn't been seen in more than half a century. Please provide details. Respectfully yours, David Zimmer.*

We all want to believe in impossible things, I suppose, to persuade ourselves that miracles can happen. Considering that I was the author of the only book ever written on Hector Mann, it probably made sense that someone would think I'd jump at the chance to believe he was still alive. But I wasn't in the mood to jump. Or at least I didn't think I was. My book had been born out of a great sorrow, and now that the book was behind me, the sorrow was still there. Writing about comedy had been no more than a pretext, an odd form of medicine that I had swallowed every day for over a year on the off chance that it would dull the pain inside me. To some extent, it did. But Frieda Spelling (or whoever was posing as Frieda Spelling) couldn't have known that. She couldn't have known that on June 7, 1985, just one week short of my tenth wedding anniversary, my wife and two sons had been killed in a plane crash. She might have seen that the book was dedicated to them (*For Helen, Todd, and Marco—In Memory*), but those names couldn't have meant anything to her, and even if she had guessed their importance to the author, she couldn't have known that for him those names stood for everything that had any meaning in life—and that when the thirty-six-year-old Helen and the seven-year-old Todd and the four-year-old Marco had died, most of him had died along with them.

They had been on their way to Milwaukee to visit Helen's parents. I had stayed behind in Vermont to correct papers and hand in the final grades for the semester that had just ended. That was my work—professor of comparative literature at Hampton College in Hampton, Vermont—and I had to do it. Normally, we all would have gone together on the twenty-fourth or twenty-fifth, but Helen's father had just been operated on for a tumor in his leg, and the family consensus was that she and the boys should leave as quickly as possible. This entailed some elaborate, last-minute negotiations with Todd's school so that he would be allowed to miss the last two weeks of the second grade. The principal was reluctant but understanding, and in the end she gave in. That was one of the things I kept thinking about after the crash. If only she had turned us down, then Todd would have been forced to stay at home with me, and he wouldn't have been dead. At least one of them would have been spared that way. At least one of them wouldn't have fallen seven miles through the sky, and I wouldn't have been left alone in a house that was supposed to have four people in it. There were other things, of course, other contingencies to brood about and torture myself with, and I never seemed to tire of walking down those same dead-end roads. Everything was part of it, every link in the chain of cause and effect was an essential piece of the horror—from the cancer in my father-in-law's leg to the weather in the Midwest that week to the telephone number of the travel agent who had booked the airline tickets. Worst of all, there was my own insistence on driving them down to Boston so they could be on a direct flight. I hadn't wanted them to leave from Burlington. That would have meant going to New York on an eighteen-seat prop plane to catch a connecting flight to Milwaukee, and I told Helen that I didn't like those small planes. They were too dangerous, I said, and I couldn't stand the idea of letting her and the boys go on one of them without me. So they didn't—in order to appease my worries. They went on a bigger one, and the terrible thing about it was that I rushed to get them there. The traffic was heavy that morning, and when we finally got to Springfield and hit the Mass Pike, I had to drive well over the speed limit to make it to Logan in time.

I remember very little of what happened to me that summer. For several months, I lived in a blur of alcoholic grief and self-pity, rarely stirring from the house, rarely bothering to eat or shave or change my clothes. Most of my colleagues were gone until the middle of August, and therefore I didn't have to put up with many visits, to sit through the agonizing protocols of communal mourning. They meant well, of course, and whenever any of my friends came around, I always invited them in, but their tearful embraces and long, embarrassed silences didn't help. It was better to be left alone, I found, better to gut out the days in the darkness of my own head. When I wasn't drunk or sprawled out on the living room sofa watching television, I spent my time wandering around the house. I would visit the boys' rooms and sit down on the floor, surrounding myself with their things. I wasn't able to think about them directly or summon them up in any conscious way, but as I put together their puzzles and played with their Lego pieces, building ever more complex and baroque structures, I felt that I was temporarily inhabiting them again—carrying on their little phantom lives for them by repeating the gestures they had made when they still had bodies. I read through Todd's fairy-tale books and organized his baseball cards. I classified Marco's stuffed animals according to species, color, and size, changing the system every time I entered the room. Hours vanished in this way, whole days melted into oblivion, and when I couldn't stomach it anymore, I would go back into the living room and pour myself another drink. On those rare nights when I didn't pass out on the sofa, I usually slept in Todd's bed. In my own bed, I always dreamed that Helen was with me, and every time I reached out to take hold of her, I would wake up with a sudden, violent lurch, my hands trembling and my lungs gasping for air, feeling as if I'd been about to drown. I couldn't go into our bedroom after dark, but I spent a lot of time there during the day, standing inside Helen's closet and touching her clothes, rearranging her jackets and sweaters, lifting her dresses off their hangers and spreading them out on the floor. Once, I put one of them on, and another time I got into her underwear and made up my face with her makeup. It was a deeply satisfying experience, but after some additional experimentation, I discovered that perfume was even more effective than lipstick and mascara. It seemed to bring her back more vividly, to evoke her presence for longer periods of time. As luck would have it, I had given her a fresh supply of Chanel No. 5 for her birthday in March. By limiting myself to small doses twice a day, I was able to make the bottle last until the end of the summer.

I took a leave of absence for the fall semester, but rather than go away or look for psychological help, I stayed on in the house and continued to sink. By late September or early October, I was knocking off more than half a bottle of whiskey every night. It kept me from feeling too much, but at the same time it deprived me of any sense of the future, and when a man has nothing to look forward to, he might as well be dead. More than once, I caught myself in the middle of lengthy daydreams about sleeping pills and carbon monoxide gas. I never went far enough to take any action, but whenever I look back on those days now, I understand how close I came to it. The pills were in the medicine cabinet, and I had already taken the bottle off the shelf three or four times; I had already held the loose pills in my hand. If the situation had gone on much longer, I doubt that I would have had the strength to resist.

That was how things stood for me when Hector Mann unexpectedly walked into my life. I had no idea who he was, had never even stumbled across a reference to his name, but one night just before the start of winter, when the trees had finally gone bare and the first snow was threatening to fall, I happened to see a clip from one of his old films on television, and it made me laugh. That might not sound important, but it was the first time I had laughed at anything since June, and when I felt that unexpected spasm rise up through my chest and begin to rattle around in my lungs, I understood that I hadn't hit bottom yet, that there was still some piece of me that wanted to go on living. From start to finish, it couldn't have lasted more than a few seconds. As laughs go, it wasn't especially loud or sustained, but it took me by surprise, and in that I didn't struggle against it, and in that I didn't feel ashamed of myself for having forgotten my unhappiness during those few moments when Hector Mann was on screen, I was forced to conclude that there was something inside me I had not previously imagined, something other than just pure death. I'm not talking about some vague intuition or sentimental yearning for what might have been. I had made an empirical discovery, and it carried all the weight of a mathematical proof. If I had it in me to laugh, then that meant I wasn't entirely numb. It meant that I hadn't walled myself off from the world so thoroughly that nothing could get in anymore.

It must have been a little past ten o'clock. I was anchored to my usual spot on the sofa, holding a glass of whiskey in one hand and the remote-control gadget in the other, mindlessly surfing channels. I came upon the program a few minutes after it started, but it didn't take me long to figure out that it was a documentary about silent-film comedians. All the familiar faces were there—Chaplin, Keaton, Lloyd—but they also included some rare footage of comics I had never heard of before, lesser-known figures such as John Bunny, Larry Semon, Lupino Lane, and Raymond Griffith. I followed the gags with a kind of measured detachment, not really paying attention to them, but absorbed enough not to switch to something else. Hector Mann didn't come on until late in the program, and when he did, they showed only one clip: a two-minute sequence from *The Teller's Tale,* which was set in a bank and featured Hector in the role of a hardworking assistant clerk. I can't explain why it grabbed me, but there he was in his white tropical suit and his thin black mustache, standing at a table and counting out piles of money, and he worked with such furious efficiency, such lightning speed and manic concentration, that I couldn't turn my eyes away from him. Upstairs, repairmen were installing new planks in the floor of the bank manager's office. Across the room, a pretty secretary sat at her desk, buffing her nails behind a large typewriter. At first, it looked as though nothing could distract Hector from completing his task in record time. Then, ever so gradually, little streams of sawdust began to fall on his jacket, and not many seconds after that, he finally caught sight of the girl. One element had suddenly become three elements, and from that point on the action bounced among them in a triangular rhythm of work, vanity, and lust: the struggle to go on counting the money, the effort to protect his beloved suit, and the urge to make eye contact with the girl. Every now and then, Hector's mustache would twitch in consternation, as if to punctuate the proceedings with a faint groan or mumbled aside. It wasn't slapstick and anarchy so much as character and pace, a smoothly orchestrated mixture of objects, bodies, and minds. Each time Hector lost track of the count, he would have to start over again, and that only inspired him to work twice as fast as before. Each time he turned his head up to the ceiling to see where the dust was coming from, he would do it a split second after the workers had filled in the hole with a new plank. Each time he glanced over at the girl, she would be looking in the wrong direction. And yet, through it all, Hector somehow managed to keep his composure, refusing to allow these petty frustrations to thwart his purpose or puncture his good opinion of himself. It might not have been the most extraordinary bit of comedy I had ever seen, but it pulled me in until I was completely caught up in it, and by the second or third twitch of Hector's mustache, I was laughing, actually laughing out loud.

A narrator spoke over the action, but I was too immersed in the scene to catch everything he said. Something about Hector's mysterious exit from the film business, I think, and the fact that he was considered to have been the last of the significant two-reel comedians. By the 1920s, the most successful and innovative clowns had already moved into full-length features, and the quality of short comic films had suffered a drastic decline. Hector Mann did not add anything new to the genre, the narrator said, but he was acknowledged as a talented gagman with exceptional body control, a notable latecomer who might have gone on to achieve important work if his career hadn't ended so abruptly. At that point the scene ended, and I started listening more closely to the narrator's comments. A succession of still photographs of several dozen comic actors rolled across the screen, and the voice lamented the loss of so many films from the silent era. Once sound entered the movies, silent films had been left to rot in vaults, had been destroyed by fires, had been carted away as trash, and hundreds of performances had disappeared forever. But all hope was not dead, the voice added. Old films occasionally turned up, and a number of remarkable discoveries had been made in recent years. Consider the case of Hector Mann, it said. Until 1981, only three of his films had been available anywhere in the world. Vestiges of the other nine were buried in an assortment of secondary materials—press reports, contemporary reviews, production stills, synopses—but the films themselves were presumed to be lost. Then, in December of that year, an anonymous package was delivered to the offices of the Cinémathèque Française in Paris. Apparently mailed from somewhere in central Los Angeles, it contained a nearly pristine copy of *Jumping Jacks,* the seventh of Hector Mann's twelve films. At irregular intervals over the next three years, eight similar packages were sent to major film archives around the world: the Museum of Modern Art in New York, the British Film Institute in London, Eastman House in Rochester, the American Film Institute in Washington, the Pacific Film Archive in Berkeley, and again to the Cinémathèque in Paris. By 1984, Hector Mann's entire output had been dispersed among these six organizations. Each package had emanated from a different city, traveling from places as remote from one another as Cleveland and San Diego, Philadelphia and Austin, New Orleans and Seattle, and because there was never any letter or message included with the films, it was impossible to identify the donor or even to form a hypothesis about who he was or where he might have lived. Another mystery had been added to the life and career of the enigmatic Hector Mann, the narrator said, but a great service had been done, and the film community was grateful.

I wasn't attracted to mysteries or enigmas, but as I sat there watching the final credits of the program, it occurred to me that I might want to see those films. There were twelve of them scattered among six different cities in Europe and the United States, and in order to see them all, a person would have to give up a significant chunk of his time. No less than several weeks, I imagined, but perhaps as long as a month or a month and a half. At that point, the last thing I would have predicted was that I would wind up writing a book about Hector Mann. I was just looking for something to do, something to keep me occupied in a harmless sort of way until I was ready to return to work. I had spent close to half a year watching myself go to the dogs, and I knew that if I let it go on any longer, I was going to die. It didn't matter what the project was or what I hoped to get out of it. Any choice would have been arbitrary by then, but that night an idea had presented itself to me, and on the strength of two minutes of film and one short laugh, I chose to wander around the world looking at silent comedies.

I wasn't a film person. I had started teaching literature as a graduate student in my mid-twenties, and since then all my work had been connected to books, language, the written word. I had translated a number of European poets (Lorca, Éluard, Leopardi, Michaux), had written reviews for magazines and newspapers, and had published two books of criticism. The first one, *Voices in the War Zone,* was a study of politics and literature that examined the work of Hamsun, Céline, and Pound in relation to their pro-Fascist activities during World War II. The second one, *The Road to Abyssinia,* was a book about writers who had given up writing, a meditation on silence. Rimbaud, Dashiell Hammett, Laura Riding, J. D. Salinger, and others—poets and novelists of uncommon brilliance who, for one reason or another, had stopped. When Helen and the boys were killed, I had been planning to write a new book about Stendhal. It wasn't that I had anything against the movies, but they had never been very important to me, and not once in more than fifteen years of teaching and writing had I felt the urge to talk about them. I liked them in the way that everyone else did—as diversions, as animated wallpaper, as fluff. No matter how beautiful or hypnotic the images sometimes were, they never satisfied me as powerfully as words did. Too much was given, I felt, not enough was left to the viewer's imagination, and the paradox was that the closer movies came to simulating reality, the worse they failed at representing the world—which is in us as much as it is around us. That was why I had always instinctively preferred black-and-white pictures to color pictures, silent films to talkies. Cinema was a visual language, a way of telling stories by projecting images onto a two-dimensional screen. The addition of sound and color had created the illusion of a third dimension, but at the same time it had robbed the images of their purity. They no longer had to do all the work, and instead of turning film into the perfect hybrid medium, the best of all possible worlds, sound and color had weakened the language they were supposed to enhance. That night, as I watched Hector and the other comedians go through their paces in my Vermont living room, it struck me that I was witnessing a dead art, a wholly defunct genre that would never be practiced again. And yet, for all the changes that had occurred since then, their work was as fresh and invigorating as it had been when it was first shown. That was because they had understood the language they were speaking. They had invented a syntax of the eye, a grammar of pure kinesis, and except for the costumes and the cars and the quaint furniture in the background, none of it could possibly grow old. It was thought translated into action, human will expressing itself through the human body, and therefore it was for all time. Most silent comedies hardly even bothered to tell stories. They were like poems, like the renderings of dreams, like some intricate choreography of the spirit, and because they were dead, they probably spoke more deeply to us now than they had to the audiences of their time. We watched them across a great chasm of forgetfulness, and the very things that separated them from us were in fact what made them so arresting: their muteness, their absence of color, their fitful, speeded-up rhythms. These were obstacles, and they made viewing difficult for us, but they also relieved the images of the burden of representation. They stood between us and the film, and therefore we no longer had to pretend that we were looking at the real world. The flat screen was the world, and it existed in two dimensions. The third dimension was in our head.

There was nothing to stop me from packing my bags and leaving the next day. I was off for the semester, and the next term wouldn't begin until the middle of January. I was free to do what I wanted, free to go wherever my legs wanted to take me, and the fact was that if I needed more time I could keep on going until I was past January, past September, past all the

Septembers and Januarys for as long as I wished. Such were the ironies of my absurd and miserable life. The moment Helen and the boys were killed, I had been turned into a rich man. The first bit came from a life insurance policy that Helen and I had been talked into buying not long after I started teaching at Hampton—*for peace of mind,* the man said—and because it was attached to the college health plan and didn't cost much, we had been paying in a small amount every month without bothering to think about it. I hadn't even remembered that we owned this insurance when the plane went down, but less than a month later, a man showed up at my house and handed me a check for several hundred thousand dollars. A short time after that, the airline company made a settlement with the families of the victims, and as someone who had lost three people in the crash, I wound up winning the compensation jackpot, the giant booby prize for random death and unforeseen acts of God. Helen and I had always struggled to get by on my academic salary and the occasional fees she earned from freelance writing. At any point along the way, an extra thousand dollars would have made an enormous difference to us. Now I had that thousand many times over, and it didn't mean a thing. When the checks came in, I sent half the money to Helen's parents, but they sent it back by return mail, thanking me for the gesture but assuring me that they didn't want it. I bought new playground equipment for Todd's elementary school, donated two thousand dollars' worth of books and a state-of-the-art sandbox to Marco's day-care center, and prevailed upon my sister and her music-teacher husband in Baltimore to accept a large cash contribution from the Zimmer Death Fund. If there had been more people in my family to give money to, I would have done it, but my parents were no longer alive, and Deborah was the only sibling I had. Instead, I unloaded another sackful by establishing a fellowship at Hampton College in Helen's name: the Helen Markham Traveling Fellowship. The idea was very simple. Every year, a cash award would be given for excellence in the humanities to one graduating senior. The money had to be spent on travel, but other than that there were no rules, no conditions, no requirements to be fulfilled. The winner would be selected by a rotating committee of professors from several different departments (history, philosophy, English, and foreign languages), and as long as the grant was used to finance a trip abroad, the Markham Fellow could do anything with the money that he or she saw fit, no questions asked. A huge outlay was required to set this up, but large as that sum was (the equivalent of four years' salary), it put no more than a small dent in my assets, and even after I had disbursed those various amounts in the various ways that made sense to me, I still had more money than I knew what to do with. It was a grotesque situation, a sickening excess of wealth, and every penny of it had been procured with blood. If not for a sudden change of plans, I probably would have gone on giving away the money until there was nothing left. But one cold night in early November, I got it into my head to do some traveling of my own, and without the resources to pay for it, I never could have followed through on such an impulsive scheme. Until then, the money had been nothing but a torment to me. Now I saw it as a cure, a balm to ward off a terminal collapse of the spirit. Living in hotels and eating in restaurants was going to be an expensive proposition, but for once I didn't have to worry about whether I could afford to do what I wanted. Desperate and unhappy as I was, I was also a free man, and because I had gold in my pockets, I could dictate the conditions of that freedom on my own terms.

• • •

Half of the films were within driving distance of my house. Rochester was about six hours to the west, and New York and Washington were directly to the south—roughly five hours to cover the first leg of the journey, then another five to do the second. I decided to begin with Rochester. Winter was already approaching, and the longer I put off going there, the greater the chances would be of running into storms and icy roads, of bogging down in some northern inclemency. The next morning, I called Eastman House to inquire about seeing the films in their collection. I had no idea how one went about setting up such a thing, and because I didn't want to sound too ignorant when I introduced myself over the phone, I added that I was a professor at Hampton College. I was hoping that would impress them enough to take me for a serious person—and not some crank calling out of the blue, which was what I was. Oh, said the woman on the other end of the line, are you writing something about Hector Mann? She made it sound as if there was only one possible answer to the question, and after a slight pause, I mumbled the words she was expecting to hear. Yes, I said, that's it, that's it exactly. I'm writing a book about him, and I need to see the films for my research.

That was how the project began. It was a good thing it happened so early, because once I had seen the films in Rochester (*The Jockey Club* and *The Snoop*), I understood that I wasn't just wasting my time. Hector was every bit as talented and accomplished as I had hoped he would be, and if the other ten films were up to the standards of those two, then he deserved to have a book written about him, he deserved the chance to be rediscovered. Right from the start, therefore, I didn't only watch Hector's movies, I studied them. If not for my conversation with that woman in Rochester, it never would have occurred to me to take this approach. My original plan had been far simpler, and I doubt that it would have kept me busy much beyond Christmas or the first of the year. As it was, I didn't finish viewing all of Hector's films until the middle of February. The old idea had been to see each film once. Now I saw them many times, and instead of visiting an archive for just a few hours, I stuck around for days, running the films on flatbeds and Moviolas, watching Hector for entire mornings and afternoons at a stretch, winding and rewinding the prints until my eyes wouldn't stay open anymore. I took notes, consulted books, and wrote down exhaustive commentaries, detailing the cuts and camera angles and lighting positions, analyzing all aspects of every scene down to its most peripheral elements, and I never left a place until I was ready, until I had lived with the footage long enough to know every inch of it by heart.

I didn't question whether any of this was worth doing. I had my job, and the only thing that mattered to me was to stick with it and make sure that it got done. I knew that Hector was no more than a minor figure, an addendum to the list of also-rans and luckless contenders, but that didn't stop me from admiring his work and taking pleasure in his company. His films had been knocked off at the rate of one a month for a year, and they were made on budgets so small, so far below the amounts required to stage the spectacular stunts and breathless sequences normally associated with silent comedy, that it was a wonder he had managed to produce anything at all, let alone twelve perfectly watchable films. According to what I read, Hector had started out in Hollywood as a prop man, scenic painter, and sometime extra, had graduated to bit roles in a number of comedies, and had been given his chance to direct and star in his own films by a man named Seymour Hunt. Hunt, a banker from Cincinnati who wanted to break into the movie business, had gone out to California in early 1927 to set up his own production company, Kaleidoscope Pictures. By all accounts a blustering, duplicitous character, Hunt knew nothing about making movies and even less about running a business. (Kaleidoscope shut down after just a year and a half. Hunt, charged with stock fraud and embezzlement, hanged himself before his case ever came to trial.) Underfinanced, understaffed, and plagued by Hunt's constant interference, Hector nevertheless seized his opportunity and tried to make the most of it. There were no scripts, of course, and no prearranged setups. Just Hector and a pair of gagmen named Andrew Murphy and Jules Blaustein improvising as they went along, often shooting at night on borrowed sets with exhausted crews and secondhand equipment. They couldn't afford to wreck a dozen cars or to mount a cattle stampede. Houses couldn't collapse, and buildings couldn't explode. No floods, no hurricanes, and no exotic locations. Extras were at a premium, and if an idea didn't work, they didn't have the luxury of reshooting after the film was over. Everything had to be cranked out on schedule, and there was no time for second thoughts. Gags on command: three laughs a minute, and then put another coin in the meter. For all the drawbacks to the arrangement, Hector seemed to thrive on the limitations that had been imposed on him. The scale of his work was modest, but there was an intimacy to it that held your attention and forced you to respond to him. I understood why film scholars respected his work—and also why no one was terribly excited by it. He hadn't broken any new ground, and now that all his films were available again, it was clear that the history of the period would not have to be rewritten. Hector's films were small contributions to the art, but they weren't negligible, and the more I saw of them, the more I liked them for their grace and subtle wit, for the droll and affecting manner of their star. As I soon discovered, no one had seen all of Hector's films yet. The last ones had turned up too recently, and not one person had taken it upon himself to travel the whole circuit of archives and museums around the world. If I managed to carry out my plan, I would be the first one.

Before leaving Rochester, I called Smits, the dean of faculty at Hampton, and told him that I wanted to extend my leave for another semester. He was a bit put out at first, claiming that my courses had already been announced in the catalogue, but then I lied to him and said that I was undergoing psychiatric treatment, and he apologized. It was a nasty trick, I suppose, but I was fighting for my life at that point, and I didn't have the strength to explain why looking at silent movies had suddenly become so important to me. We wound up having a cordial chat, and in the end he wished me luck, but even though we both pretended that I would be returning in the fall, I think he sensed that I was already slipping away, that my heart was no longer in it.

I saw *Scandal* and *Country Weekend* in New York, then moved on to Washington for *The Teller's Tale* and *Double or Nothing*. I booked reservations for the rest of the trip with a travel agent on Dupont Circle (Amtrak to California, the *QE 2* to Europe), but the next morning, in a sudden burst of blind heroism, I canceled the tickets and opted to go by plane. It was pure folly, but now that I was off to such a promising start, I didn't want to lose my momentum. Never mind that I would have to talk myself into doing the one thing I had resolved never to do again. I couldn't slacken my pace, and if that meant seeking out a pharmacological solution to the problem, then I was prepared to ingest as many knockout pills as necessary. A woman from the American Film Institute gave me the name of a doctor. I figured the appointment would take no more than five or ten minutes. I would tell him why I wanted the pills, he would write out a prescription, and that would be that. Fear of flying was a common complaint, after all, and there would be no need to talk about Helen and the boys, no need to bare my soul to him. All I wanted was to shut down my central nervous system for a few hours, and since you couldn't buy that stuff over the counter, his sole function would be to hand me a slip of paper with his signature on it. But Dr. Singh turned out to be a thorough man, and as he went about the business of taking my blood pressure and listening to my heart, he asked me enough questions to keep me in his office for three-quarters of an hour. He was too intelligent not to want to probe, and little by little the truth came out.

We're all going to die, Mr. Zimmer, he said. What makes you think you're going to die on a plane? If you believe what the statistics tell us, you have a greater chance of dying just by sitting at home.

I didn't say I was afraid of dying, I answered, I said that I was afraid to get on a plane. There's a difference.

But if the plane isn't going to crash, why should you be worried?

Because I don't trust myself anymore. I'm afraid I'll lose control, and I don't want to make a spectacle of myself.

I'm not sure I follow you.

I imagine myself boarding the plane, and before I even get to my seat, I snap.

Snap? In what sense snap? You mean snap mentally?

Yes, I break down in front of four hundred strangers and lose my mind. I go berserk.

And what do you imagine yourself doing?

It depends. Sometimes I scream. Sometimes I punch people in the face. Sometimes I rush into the cockpit and try to strangle the pilot.

Does anyone stop you?

Of course they do. They swarm all over me and wrestle me to the ground. They beat the shit out of me.

When was the last time you were in a fight, Mr. Zimmer?

I can't remember. Back when I was a boy, I suppose. Eleven, twelve years old. School-yard stuff. Defending myself against the class bully.

And what makes you think you'll start fighting now?

Nothing. I just feel it in my bones, that's all. If something rubs me the wrong way, I don't think I'll be able to stop myself. Anything is liable to happen.

But why planes? Why aren't you afraid of losing control of yourself on the ground?

Because planes are safe. Everyone knows that. Planes are safe, fast, and efficient, and once you're up in the air, nothing can happen to you. That's why I'm afraid. Not because I think I'm going to be killed—but because I know I won't.

Have you ever attempted suicide, Mr. Zimmer?

No.

Have you ever thought about it?

Of course I have. I wouldn't be human if I hadn't.

Is that why you're here now? So you can walk off with a

prescription for some nice, powerful drug and do away with yourself?

I'm looking for oblivion, Doctor, not death. The drugs will put me to sleep, and as long as I'm unconscious, I won't have to think about what I'm doing. I'll be there, but I won't be there, and to the degree that I'm not there, I'll be protected.

Protected against what?

Against myself. Against the horror of knowing that nothing is going to happen to me.

You expect to have a smooth, uneventful flight. I still don't see why that should make you afraid.

Because the odds are with me. I'm going to take off and land safely, and once I get to where I'm going, I'll step off the plane alive. Good for me, you say, but once I do that, I spit on everything I believe in. I insult the dead, Doctor. I turn a tragedy into a simple matter of bad luck. Do you understand me now? I tell the dead that they died for nothing.

He understood. I hadn't said it in so many words, but this doctor had a delicate, sophisticated mind, and he was able to figure out the rest for himself. J. M. Singh, graduate of the Royal College of Physicians, resident internist at Georgetown University Hospital, with his precise British accent and prematurely thinning hair, suddenly grasped what I had been trying to tell him in that small cubicle with the fluorescent lights and the shining metal surfaces. I was still on the examining table, buttoning my shirt and looking down at the floor (not wanting to look at him, not wanting to risk the embarrassment of tears), and just then, after what felt like a long and awkward silence, he put his hand on my shoulder. I'm sorry, he said. I'm truly sorry.

It was the first time anyone had touched me in months, and

I found it disturbing, almost repulsive to be turned into an object of such compassion. I don't want your sympathy, Doctor, I said. I just want your pills.

He backed off with a slight grimace, then sat down on a stool in the corner. As I finished tucking in my shirt, I saw him pull out a prescription pad from the pocket of his white coat. I'm willing to do it, he said, but before you get up and leave, I want to ask you to reconsider your decision. I think I have an idea of what you've been through, Mr. Zimmer, and I hesitate to put you in a position that could cause you such torment. There are other methods of travel, you know. Perhaps it would be best if you avoided planes for now.

I've already been down that road, I said, and I've decided against it. The distances are just too big. My next stop is Berkeley, California, and after that I have to go to London and Paris. A train to the West Coast takes three days. Multiply that by two for the return trip, then add on another ten days to cross the Atlantic and come back, and we're talking about a minimum of sixteen lost days. What am I supposed to do with all that time? Stare out the window and soak up the scenery?

Slowing down might not be such a bad thing. It would help to take off some of the pressure.

But pressure is what I need. If I loosened my grip now, I'd fall apart. I'd fly off in a hundred different directions, and I'd never be able to put myself together again.

There was something so intense about the way I delivered those words, something so earnest and crazy in the timbre of my voice, that the doctor almost smiled—or at least appeared to be suppressing a smile. Well, we don't want that to happen, do we? he said. If you're so intent on flying, then go ahead and fly. But let's make sure you do it in only one direction. And with that whimsical comment, he removed a pen from his pocket and scratched out a series of undecipherable marks on the pad. Here it is, he said, tearing off the top sheet and putting it in my hand. Your ticket for Air Xanax.

Never heard of it.

Xanax. A potent, highly dangerous drug. Just use as directed, Mr. Zimmer, and you'll be turned into a zombie, a being without a self, a blotted-out lump of flesh. You can fly across entire continents and oceans on this stuff, and I guarantee that you'll never even know you've left the ground.

By midafternoon the following day, I was in California. Less than twenty-four hours after that, I was walking into a private screening room at the Pacific Film Archive to watch two more Hector Mann comedies. *Tango Tangle* turned out to be one of his wildest, most effervescent productions; *Hearth and Home* was one of the most careful. I spent more than two weeks with these films, returning to the building every morning at ten sharp, and even when the place was closed (on Christmas and New Year's Day), I went on working in my hotel, reading books and consolidating my notes in preparation for the next stage of my travels. On January 7, 1986, I swallowed some more of Dr. Singh's magic pills and flew directly from San Francisco to London—six thousand nonstop miles on the Catatonia Express. A larger dose was required this time, but I was worried that it wouldn't be enough, and just before I boarded the plane, I took an extra pill. I should have known better than to go against the doctor's instructions, but the thought of waking up in the middle of the flight was so terrifying to me, I nearly put myself to sleep forever. There's a stamp in my old passport that proves I entered Great Britain on January eighth, but I have no memory of landing, no memory of going through customs, and no memory of how I got to my hotel. I woke up in an unfamiliar bed on the morning of January ninth, and that was when my life started again. I had never lost track of myself so thoroughly.

There were four films left—*Cowpokes* and *Mr. Nobody* in London; *Jumping Jacks* and *The Prop Man* in Paris—and I realized that this would be my only chance to see them. I could always revisit the American archives if I had to, but a return trip to the BFI and the Cinémathèque was out of the question. I had managed to get myself to Europe, but I didn't have it in me to attempt the impossible more than once. For that reason, I wound up staying in London and Paris much longer than was necessary—almost seven weeks in all, burrowed in for half the winter like some mad, subterranean beast. I had been thorough and conscientious up to that point, but now the project was taken to a new level of intensity, a single-mindedness that verged on obsession. My outward purpose was to study and master the films of Hector Mann, but the truth was that I was teaching myself how to concentrate, training myself how to think about one thing and one thing only. It was the life of a monomaniac, but it was the only way I could live now without crumbling to pieces. When I finally returned to Washington in February, I slept off the effects of the Xanax in an airport hotel, and then, first thing the next morning, collected my car from the long-term parking lot and drove to New York. I wasn't ready to return to Vermont. If I meant to write the book, I would need a place to hole up in, and of all the cities in the world, New York struck me as the one least likely to wear on my nerves. I spent five days looking for an apartment in Manhattan, but nothing turned up. It was the height of the Wall Street boom then, a good twenty months before the '87 crash, and rentals and sublets were in short supply. Eventually, I drove across the bridge to Brooklyn Heights and took the first place I was shown—a one-bedroom apartment on Pierrepont Street that had just come on the market that morning. It was expensive, dingy, and awkwardly designed, but I felt lucky to have it. I bought a mattress for one room, a desk and a chair for the other, and then I moved in. The lease was good for a year. It began on March first, and that was the day I began writing the book.

2

BEFORE THE BODY, there is the face, and before the face there is the thin black line between Hector's nose and upper lip. A twitching filament of anxieties, a metaphysical jump rope, a dancing thread of discombobulation, the mustache is a seismograph of Hector's inner states, and not only does it make you laugh, it tells you what Hector is thinking, actually allows you into the machinery of his thoughts. Other elements are involved—the eyes, the mouth, the finely calibrated lurches and stumbles—but the mustache is the instrument of communication, and even though it speaks a language without words, its wriggles and flutters are as clear and comprehensible as a message tapped out in Morse code.

None of this would be possible without the intervention of the camera. The intimacy of the talking mustache is a creation of the lens. At various moments in each of Hector's films, the angle suddenly changes, and a wide or medium shot is replaced by a close-up. Hector's face fills the screen, and with all references to the environment eliminated, the mustache becomes the center of the world. It begins to move, and because Hector's skill is such that he can control the muscles in the rest of his face, the mustache appears to be moving on its own, like a small animal with an independent consciousness and will. The mouth curls a bit at the corners, the nostrils flare ever so slightly, but as the mustache goes through its antic gyrations, the face is essentially still, and in that stillness one sees oneself as if in a mirror, for it is during those moments that Hector is most fully and convincingly human, a reflection of what we all are when we're alone inside ourselves. These close-up sequences are reserved for the critical passages of a story, the junctures of greatest tension or surprise, and they never last longer than four or five seconds. When they occur, everything else stops. The mustache launches into its soliloquy, and for those few precious moments, action gives way to thought. We can read the content of Hector's mind as though it were spelled out in letters across the screen, and before those letters vanish, they are no less visible than a building, a piano, or a pie in the face.

In motion, the mustache is a tool for expressing the thoughts of all men. In repose, it is little more than an ornament. It marks Hector's place in the world, establishes the type of character he is supposed to represent, and defines who he is in the eyes of others—but it belongs to only one man, and in that it is an absurdly thin and greasy little mustache, there can never be any doubt as to who that man is. He is the South American dandy, the Latin lover, the swarthy rogue with hot blood coursing through his veins. Add in the slicked-back hair and the ever-present white suit, and the result is an unmistakable blend of dash and decorum. Such is the code of images. The meanings are understood at a single glance, and because one thing inevitably follows from another in this booby-trapped universe of missing manhole covers and exploding cigars, the moment you see a man walking down the street in a white suit, you know that suit is going to get him into trouble.

After the mustache, the suit is the most important element in Hector's repertoire. The mustache is the link to his inner self, a metonym of urges, cogitations, and mental storms. The suit embodies his relation to the social world, and with its cue-ball brilliance shining against the grays and blacks that surround it, it serves as a magnet for the eyes. Hector wears the suit in every film, and in every film there is at least one long gag that revolves around the perils of trying to keep it clean. Mud and crankcase oil, spaghetti sauce and molasses, chimney soot and splashing puddles—at one time or another, every dark liquid and every dark substance threaten to smudge the pristine dignity of Hector's suit. That suit is his proudest possession, and he wears it with the dapper, cosmopolitan air of a man out to impress the world. He climbs into it every morning the way a knight climbs into his armor, girding himself for whatever battles society has in store for him that day, and not once does he stop to consider that he is achieving the opposite of what he has intended. He isn't protecting himself against potential blows, he is turning himself into a target, the focal point of every mishap that can possibly occur within a hundred yards of his person. The white suit is a sign of Hector's vulnerability, and it lends a certain pathos to the jokes the world plays on him. Obstinate in his elegance, clinging to the conviction that the suit transforms him into the most attractive and desirable of men, Hector elevates his own vanity into a cause that audiences can sympathize with. Watch him flicking specks of imaginary dust from his jacket as he rings the doorbell of his girlfriend's house in *Double or Nothing*, and you're no longer watching a demonstration of self-love: you're witnessing the torments of self-consciousness. The white suit turns Hector into an underdog. It wins the audience over to his side, and once an actor has achieved that, he can get away with anything.

He was too tall to play an out-and-out clown, too handsome to act the part of innocent bungler as other comics did. With his dark, expressive eyes and elegant nose, Hector looked like a second-rate leading man, an overachieving romantic hero who had wandered onto the set of the wrong film. He was a grown-up, and the very presence of such a person seemed to run counter to the established rules of comedy. Funny men were supposed to be small, misshapen, or fat. They were imps and buffoons, dunces and outcasts, children masquerading as adults or adults with the minds of children. Think of Arbuckle's juvenile rotundity, his simpering shyness and painted, feminized lips. Remember the forefinger that flies into his mouth every time a girl looks at him. Then go down the list of props and accoutrements that shaped the careers of the acknowledged masters: Chaplin's tramp with the floppy shoes and ragged clothes; Lloyd's plucky Milquetoast with the horn-rimmed specs; Keaton's saphead with the pancake hat and frozen face; Langdon's moron with the chalk-white skin. They are all misfits, and because these characters can neither threaten us nor make us envy them, we root for them to triumph over their enemies and win the girl's heart. The only problem is that we aren't quite sure they'll know what to do with the girl once they're alone with her. With Hector, such doubts never enter our mind. When he winks at a girl, there's a better than even chance that she'll wink back. And when she does, it's clear that neither one of them is thinking about marriage.

Laughter, however, is by no means guaranteed. Hector is not what you would call a lovable figure, and he is not someone you necessarily feel sorry for. If he manages to win the viewer's sympathy, it is because he never knows when to quit. Hard-working and convivial, the perfect incarnation of *l'homme moyen sensuel,* he is not out of step with the world so much as a victim of circumstances, a man with an inexhaustible talent for running into bad luck. Hector always has a plan in mind, a purpose for doing what he does, and yet something always seems to come up to thwart him from realizing his goal. His films are fraught with bizarre physical occurrences, outlandish mechanical breakdowns, objects that refuse to behave as they should. A man with less confidence in himself would be defeated by these setbacks, but other than an occasional burst of exasperation (confined to the mustache monologues), Hector never complains. Doors slam on his fingers, bees sting him on the neck, statues fall on his toes, but again and again he shrugs off his misfortunes and continues on his way. You begin to admire him for his steadfastness, for the spiritual calm that comes over him in the face of adversity, but what holds your attention is the way he moves. Hector can charm you with any one of a thousand different gestures. Light-footed and nimble, nonchalant to the point of indifference, he threads himself through the obstacle course of life without the slightest trace of clumsiness or fear, dazzling you with his backpedals and dodges, his sudden torques and lunging pavanes, his double takes and hop-steps and rhumba swivels. Observe the thrums and fidgets of his fingers, his deftly timed exhales, the slight cock of the head when something unexpected catches his eye. These miniature acrobatics are a function of character, but they also give pleasure in and of themselves. Even when flypaper is sticking to the bottom of his shoe and the little boy of the house has just lassoed him with a rope (pinning his arms to his sides),

Hector moves with uncommon grace and composure, never doubting that he'll soon be able to extricate himself from his predicament—even if another one is waiting in the next room. Too bad for Hector, of course, but those are the breaks. What matters is not how well you can avoid trouble, but how you cope with trouble when it comes.

More often than not, Hector finds himself at the bottom of the social ladder. He is married in only two of his films (*Hearth and Home* and *Mr. Nobody*), and except for the private detective he plays in *The Snoop* and his role as traveling magician in *Cowpokes,* he is a working stiff toiling for others in humble, low-salaried jobs. A waiter in *The Jockey Club,* a chauffeur in *Country Weekend,* a door-to-door salesman in *Jumping Jacks,* a dance instructor in *Tango Tangle,* a bank employee in *The Teller's Tale,* Hector is usually presented as a young man just starting out in life. His prospects are far from encouraging, but he never gives the impression of being a loser. He carries himself with too much pride for that, and to watch him go about his business with the sure-handed competence of one who trusts in his own abilities, you understand that he's a person destined for success. Accordingly, most of Hector's films end in one of two ways: either he gets the girl or he performs an act of heroism that captures the attention of his boss. And if the boss is too thick-headed to notice (the wealthy and powerful are mostly portrayed as fools), the girl will see what has happened, and that will be reward enough. Whenever there is a choice between love and money, love always has the last word. Working as a waiter in *The Jockey Club,* for example, Hector manages to nab a jewel thief while serving several tables of drunken guests at a banquet in honor of champion aviatrix Wanda McNoon. With his left hand, he knocks out the thief with a champagne bottle; with his right, he simultaneously serves up dessert to the table, and because the cork flies out of the bottle and the headwaiter is sprayed with a liter's worth of Veuve Clicquot, Hector loses his job. But no matter. The spirited Wanda is an eyewitness to Hector's exploit. She slips him her telephone number, and in the last scene they climb into her plane together and take off for the clouds.

Unpredictable in his behavior, full of contradictory impulses and desires, Hector's character is too complexly delineated for us to feel altogether comfortable in his presence. He is not a type or familiar stock figure, and for every one of his actions that makes sense to us there is another one that confounds us and throws us off balance. He displays all the striving ambitiousness of a hardworking immigrant, a man bent on overcoming the odds and winning a place for himself in the American jungle, and yet one glimpse of a beautiful woman is enough to knock him off course, to scatter his carefully laid plans to the winds. Hector has the same personality in every film, but there is no fixed hierarchy to his preferences, no way of knowing what fancy will strike him next. He is both a populist and an aristocrat, a sensualist and a closet romantic, a man of precise, even punctilious manners who never hesitates to make the grand gesture. He will give his last dime to a beggar on the street, but he will not be motivated by pity or compassion so much as by the poetry of the act itself. No matter how hard he works, no matter how diligently he performs the menial and often absurd tasks that are assigned to him, Hector conveys a sense of detachment, as if he were somehow mocking himself and congratulating himself at the same time. He seems to live in a state of ironical bemusement, at once engaged in the world and observing it from a great distance. In what is perhaps his funniest film, *The Prop Man,* he turns these opposing points of view into a unified principle of mayhem. It was the ninth short of the series, and in it Hector plays the stage manager of a small, down-at-the-heels theater troupe. The company pulls into the town of Wishbone Falls for a three-day run of *Beggars Can't Be Choosers,* a bedroom farce by noted French dramatist Jean-Pierre Saint Jean de la Pierre. When they open the truck to unload the props and carry them into the theater, they discover that the props are missing. What to do? The play can't go on without them. There is an entire living room to furnish, not to speak of replacing several important accessories: a gun, a diamond necklace, and a roasted pig. The curtain is supposed to go up at eight o'clock the next evening, and unless the entire set can be built from scratch, the company will be out of business. The director of the troupe, a pompous blowhard with an ascot wrapped around his neck and a monocle in his left eye, peers into the back of the empty truck and faints dead away. The matter is in Hector's hands. After a few brief but incisive comments from his mustache, he calmly weighs the situation, smooths out the front of his immaculate white suit, and marches off to work. For the next nine and a half minutes, the film becomes an illustration of Proudhon's well-known anarchist dictum: *all property is theft.* In a series of short, frenetic episodes, Hector rushes around town and steals the props. We see him intercepting a furniture delivery to a department store warehouse and walking off with tables, chairs, and lamps—which he packs into his own truck and promptly drives to the theater. He pilfers silverware, drinking glasses, and a full set of china from a hotel kitchen. He bluffs his way into the back room of a butcher shop with a false order form from a local restaurant and trudges out with a pig's carcass slung over his shoulder. That evening, at a private reception for the actors which is attended by the town's most prominent citizens, he manages to remove the sheriff's pistol from its holster. A little while later, he skillfully undoes the latch of a necklace worn by a bulbous, middle-aged woman as she swoons under the seductive power of Hector's charms. He is never more unctuous than in this scene. Contemptible in his simulations, loathsome in the hypocrisy of his ardor, he also comes across as a heroic outlaw, an idealist willing to sacrifice himself for the good of his cause. We recoil from his tactics, but at the same time we pray for him to pull off the theft. The show must go on, and if Hector fails to pocket the jewels, there won't be any show. To complicate the intrigue still further, Hector has just caught sight of the town belle (who happens to be the sheriff's daughter), and even as he continues his amorous assault on the aging battle-axe, he begins making furtive eyes at the young beauty. Fortunately, Hector and his victim are standing behind a velvet curtain. It hangs halfway across an open doorway that separates the entrance hall from the drawing room, and because Hector is positioned on one side of the woman and not the other, he can look into the drawing room by leaning his head slightly to the left. But the woman remains hidden from view, and even though Hector can see the girl and the girl can see Hector, she has no idea that the woman is there. This allows Hector to pursue both of his objectives at once—the false seduction and the true seduction—and because he plays one against the other in a clever mix of cuts and camera angles, each element makes the other one funnier than it would have been on its own. That is the essence of Hector's style. One joke is never enough for him. As soon as a situation has been established, another piece of business must be added to it, and then a third, and possibly even a fourth. Hector's gags unfold like musical compositions, a confluence of contrasting lines and voices, and the more the voices interact with one another, the more precarious and unstable the world becomes. In *The Prop Man,* Hector tickles the neck of the woman behind the curtain, plays peekaboo with the girl in the other room, and finally snags the necklace when a passing waiter slips on the hem of the woman's gown and spills a trayful of drinks down her back—which gives Hector just enough time to undo the clasp. He has achieved what he has set out to do—but only by accident, rescued once again by the mutinous unpredictability of matter.

The curtain goes up the following evening, and the performance is a rousing success. The butcher, the department store owner, the sheriff, and the fat woman are all in the audience, however, and even as the actors are taking their bows and blowing kisses to the enthusiastic crowd, a constable is clamping handcuffs on Hector's wrists and carting him off to jail. But Hector is happy, and he shows not one shred of remorse. He has saved the day, and not even the threat of losing his freedom can diminish his triumph. To anyone familiar with the difficulties Hector encountered while making his films, it is impossible not to read *The Prop Man* as a parable of his life under contract to Seymour Hunt and the struggles of working for Kaleidoscope Pictures. When every card in the deck is stacked against you, the only way to win a hand is to break the rules. You beg, borrow, and steal, as the old adage goes, and if you happen to get caught in the act, at least you've gone down fighting the good fight.

This joyful disregard of consequences takes a darker turn in Hector's eleventh film, *Mr. Nobody.* Time was running out by then, and he must have known that once the contract was fulfilled, his career would be over. Sound was coming. It was an inevitable fact of life, a certainty that would destroy everything that had come before it, and the art that Hector had worked so hard to master would no longer exist. Even if he could reconfigure his ideas to accommodate the new form, it wouldn't do him any good. Hector spoke with a heavy Spanish accent, and the moment he opened his mouth on-screen, American audiences would reject him. In *Mr. Nobody*, he allows himself to indulge in a certain bitterness. The future was grim, and the present was clouded by Hunt's growing financial problems. With each passing month, the damage had spread through every aspect of Kaleidoscope's operations. Budgets were cut, salaries went unpaid, and the high interest charges on short-term loans left Hunt in constant need of ready cash. He borrowed from his distributors against future box-office revenues, and when he reneged on several of these deals, theaters began refusing to show his films. Hector was doing his best work at this point, but the sad fact was that fewer and fewer people were able to see it.

Mr. Nobody is a response to this mounting frustration. The villain of the story is called C. Lester Chase, and once you've figured out the origins of this character's odd and artificial name, it becomes hard not to see him as a metaphorical stand-in for Hunt. Translate *hunt* into French, and the result is *chasse;* drop the second *s* from *chasse*, and you wind up with *chase.* When you further consider that *Seymour* can be read as *see more* and that *Lester* can be abbreviated as *Les,* which turns *C. Lester* into *C. Les*—or *see less*—then the evidence becomes fairly compelling. Chase is the most malevolent character in any of Hector's films. He is out to destroy Hector and rob him of his identity, and he puts his plan into action not by firing a bullet into Hector's back or by plunging a knife into his heart, but by tricking him into swallowing a magic potion that makes him invisible. In effect, this is just what Hunt did to Hector's career in the movies. He put him up on-screen, and then he made it all but impossible for anyone to see him. Hector doesn't vanish in *Mr. Nobody,* but once he drinks the drink, no one can see him anymore. He is still there before our eyes, but the other characters in the film are blind to his presence. He jumps up and down, he flaps his arms, he takes off his clothes on a crowded street corner, but no one notices. When he shouts in people's faces, his voice goes unheard. He is a specter made of flesh and blood, a man who is no longer a man. He still lives in the world, and yet the world has no room for him anymore. He has been murdered, but no one has had the courtesy or the thoughtfulness to kill him. He has simply been erased.

It is the first and only time that Hector presents himself as a rich man. In *Mr. Nobody,* he has everything a person could possibly want: a beautiful wife, two young children, and an enormous house with a full staff of servants. In the opening scene, Hector is eating breakfast with his family. There are some bright slapstick bits that revolve around the buttering of toast and a wasp that lands in a pot of jam, but the narrative purpose of the scene is to present us with a picture of happiness. We are being set up for the losses that are about to occur, and without this glimpse of Hector's private life (perfect marriage, perfect kids, domestic harmony in its most rhapsodic form), the evil business that lies ahead would not have the same impact. As it is, we are devastated by what happens to Hector. He kisses his wife good-bye, and the moment he turns away from her and leaves the house, he plunges headfirst into a nightmare.

Hector is the founder and president of a thriving soft-drink concern, the Fizzy Pop Beverage Corporation. Chase is his vice president and counselor, his supposed best friend. But Chase has accumulated heavy gambling debts and is being harassed by loan sharks to pay up what he owes or else. As Hector arrives at the office in the morning and greets his staff, Chase is in another room talking to a pair of rough-looking men. Don't worry, he says. You'll have your money by the end of the week. I'll be in control of the company by then, and the stock is worth millions. The thugs agree to give him a little more time. But this is your last chance, they tell him. Any more delays, and you'll be swimming with the fishes at the bottom of the river. The men stomp off. Chase wipes the sweat from his forehead and lets out a prolonged sigh. Then he removes a letter from the top drawer of his desk. He looks it over for a moment and appears to be immensely satisfied. With a wicked smirk, he folds it up and slips it into his inside breast pocket. Wheels are obviously turning, but we have no idea where they will take us.

Cut to Hector's office. Chase enters carrying something that resembles a large thermos bottle and asks Hector if he wants to taste the new flavor. What's it called? Hector asks. Jazzmatazz, Chase answers, and Hector nods his approval, impressed by the catchy ring to the word. Suspecting nothing, Hector allows Chase to pour him a hefty sample of the new concoction. As Hector takes hold of the glass, Chase looks on with a glint in his overwatchful eye, waiting for the poisonous brew to do its work. In a medium close-up, Hector lifts the glass to his mouth and takes a small, tentative sip. His nose wrinkles in disapproval; his eyes open wide; his mustache shimmies. The tone is entirely comic, and yet as Chase urges him on and Hector lifts the glass to his mouth for a second go at it, the sinister implications of *Jazzmatazz* become more and more apparent. Hector swallows down another portion of the drink. He smacks his lips, smiles up at Chase, and then shakes his head, as if to suggest that the flavor isn't quite right. Ignoring his boss's criticism, Chase looks down at his watch, spreads out the fingers of his right hand, and begins counting off the seconds from one to five. Hector is baffled. Before he can say anything, however, Chase arrives at the fifth and last second, and just like that, without any warning, Hector pitches forward in his chair and bangs his head against the top of his desk. We assume that the drink has knocked him out, that he is temporarily unconscious, but as Chase stands there watching him with blank and pitiless eyes, Hector begins to disappear. His arms go first, slowly fading from the screen and vanishing, and then his torso, and finally his head. One part of him follows another, and in the end his entire body has dissolved into nothingness. Chase walks out of the room and shuts the door behind him. Pausing in the hallway to savor his triumph, he leans his back against the door and smiles. A title card reads: *So long, Hector. It was nice knowing you.*

Chase walks off. Once he has left the frame, the camera holds on the door for a second or two, and then, very slowly, starts pushing in on the keyhole. It is a lovely shot, full of mystery and anticipation, and as the opening grows larger and larger, taking up more and more of the screen, we are able to look through into Hector's office. An instant later, we are inside the office itself, and because we expect to find it empty, we are not at all prepared for what the camera reveals to us. We see Hector slumped over his desk. He is still unconscious, but he is visible again, and as we try to absorb this sudden and miraculous turnaround, we can come to only one conclusion. The effects of the drink must have worn off. We have just watched Hector disappear, and if we are able to see him now, it can only mean that the drink was less powerful than we thought.

Hector begins to wake up. We feel comforted by this sign of life, back on safe ground. We assume that order has returned to the universe and that Hector will now set about to exact his revenge on Chase and expose him as a scoundrel. For the next twenty-odd seconds, he goes through one of his crispest, most pungent funny-man routines. Like someone trying to fight off a bad hangover, he stands up from his chair, all woozy and disoriented, and begins to stagger about the room. We laugh at this. We believe what our eyes are telling us, and because we are confident that Hector is back to normal, we can be amused by this spectacle of buckling knees and dizzy-headed collapse. But then Hector walks over to the mirror that is hanging on the wall, and everything turns again. He wants to look at himself. He wants to straighten his hair and readjust his tie, but when he peers into the oval of smooth, shining glass, his face isn't there. He has no reflection. He touches himself to make sure that he's real, to confirm the tangibility of his body, but when he looks into the mirror again, he still can't see himself. Hector is perplexed, but he doesn't panic. Maybe there's something wrong with the mirror.

He goes out into the hall. A secretary is walking by, carrying a bundle of papers in her arms. Hector smiles at her and gives a friendly wave, but she appears not to notice. Hector shrugs. Just then, two young clerks approach from the opposite direction. Hector makes a face at them. He growls. He sticks out his tongue. One of the clerks points to the door of Hector's office. Has the boss come in yet? he asks. I don't know, the other one answers. I haven't seen him. When he speaks these words, of course, Hector is standing directly in front of him, no more than six inches from his face.

The scene shifts to the living room of Hector's house. His wife is pacing back and forth, alternately wringing her hands and weeping into a handkerchief. There is no question that she has already heard the news about Hector's disappearance. Chase enters, the ignominious C. Lester Chase, author of the diabolical plot to rob Hector of his soft-drink empire. He pretends to console the poor woman, patting her on the shoulder and shaking his head in false despair. He extracts the mysterious letter from his inside breast pocket and hands it to her, explaining that he found it on Hector's desk that morning. Cut to an insert shot of the letter in extreme close-up. *Dearest Beloved,* it says. *Please forgive me. The doc says I'm suffering from a fatal disease and have only two months to live. To spare you the agony, I've decided to end it now. Don't worry about the business. The company is in good hands with Chase. I will always love you, Hector.* It doesn't take long for these lies and deceptions to do their work. In the next shot, we see the letter slip from the wife's fingers and flutter to the floor. It is all too much for her. The world has been turned upside down, and everything in it has been broken. Less than a second after that, she faints.

The camera follows her down to the floor, and then the image of her inert, recumbent body dissolves into a wide shot of Hector. He has left the office and is wandering the streets, trying to come to terms with the strange and terrible thing that has happened to him. To prove that all hope is really gone, he stops at a crowded intersection and strips down to his underwear. He does a little dance, he walks on his hands, he sticks out his fanny at the passing traffic, and when no one pays any attention to him, he glumly climbs back into his clothes and shuffles off. After that, Hector seems resigned to his fate. He doesn't fight against his condition so much as try to understand it, and rather than look for a way to make himself visible again (by confronting Chase, for example, or by searching for an antidote that would undo the effects of the drink), he embarks on a series of weird and impulsive experiments, an investigation of who he is and what he has become. Unexpectedly—with a sudden, lightning flick of his hand—he knocks off the hat of a passerby. So that's how things are, Hector seems to be saying to himself. A man can be invisible to everyone around him, but his body can still interact with the world. Another pedestrian approaches. Hector sticks out his foot and trips him. Yes, his hypothesis is surely correct, but that doesn't mean that more research isn't required. Warming to his task now, he picks up the hem of a woman's dress and studies her legs. He kisses another woman on the cheek, then a third woman on the mouth. He crosses out the letters on a stop sign, and an instant later a motorcycle slams into a trolley. He sneaks up behind two men, and by tapping each one on the shoulder and kicking them in the shins, he instigates a brawl. There is something cruel and childish about these pranks, but they are also satisfying to watch, and each one adds another fact to the growing body of evidence. Then, as Hector picks up an errant baseball that rolls toward him on the sidewalk, he makes his second important discovery. Once an invisible man takes hold of an object, it disappears from sight. It does not hover in the air; it is sucked into the void, into the same nothingness that encloses the man himself, and the moment it enters that haunted sphere, it is gone. The boy who lost the ball runs to the spot where he thinks it must have landed. The laws of physics dictate that the ball should be there, but it isn't. The boy is mystified. Seeing this, Hector puts the ball on the ground and walks away. The boy looks down, and lo and behold, the ball is there again, lying at his feet. What in the world has happened? The little episode ends with a close-up of the boy's startled face.

Hector rounds the corner and begins walking down the next boulevard. Almost immediately, he is confronted by a repulsive sight, a thing to make one's blood boil. A fat, well-dressed gentleman is stealing a copy of the *Morning Chronicle* from a blind newspaper boy. The man is out of coins, and because he's in a hurry, too rushed to bother breaking a bill, he just takes one of the papers and walks off. Outraged, Hector runs after him, and when the man stops at the corner to wait for a red light, Hector picks his pocket. This is both funny and disturbing. We don't feel the least bit sorry for the victim, but we're dumbfounded by how blithely Hector has taken the law into his own hands. Even when he walks back to the kiosk and turns the money over to the blind boy, we are not fully assuaged. In the first moments after the theft, we are led to believe that Hector will keep the money for himself, and in that small, dark interval we understand that he has not stolen the fat man's wallet in order to correct an injustice but simply because he knew that he could get away with it. His generosity is little more than an afterthought. Everything has become possible for him now, and he no longer has to obey the rules. He can do good if he wants to, but he can also do evil, and at this point we have no idea what decision he will make.

Back at the house, Hector's wife has taken to her bed.

In the office, Chase opens a strongbox and removes a thick pile of stock certificates. He sits down at his desk and begins to count them.

Meanwhile, Hector is about to commit his first major crime. He enters a jewelry store, and in front of half a dozen unseeing witnesses, our expunged and benighted hero empties a glass display case of its contents, calmly loading his pockets with fistfuls of watches, necklaces, and rings. He seems both amused and purposeful, and he goes about his business with a small but noticeable smile creasing the corners of his mouth. It appears to be a cold-blooded and capricious act, and from the evidence before our eyes, we have no choice but to conclude that Hector has been damned.

He leaves the store. Inexplicably, the first thing he does is head straight for a trash bin sitting on the curb. He sticks his arm deep into the rubbish and pulls out a paper bag. He has obviously put it there himself, but although the bag is filled with something, we don't know what it is. When Hector walks back to the front of the store, opens the bag, and begins sprinkling a powdery substance on the sidewalk, we are thoroughly confused. It could be dirt; it could be ashes; it could be gunpowder; but whatever the stuff is, it makes no sense that Hector should be putting it on the ground. In a matter of moments, there is a thin dark line extending from the front of the jewelry store to the edge of the street. Having covered the width of the sidewalk, Hector now advances into the street itself. Dodging cars, sidestepping trolleys, hopping in and out of trouble, he continues to empty the bag as he makes his way across, looking more and more like some mad farmer trying to plant a row of seeds. The line now stretches across the avenue. As Hector steps up onto the opposite curb and extends the line still further, we suddenly catch on. He is making a trail. We still don't know where it leads, but as he opens the door of the building in front of him and disappears through the entrance, we suspect that another trick is about to be played on us. The door closes behind him, and the angle abruptly changes. We are looking at a wide shot of the building Hector has just entered: the headquarters of the Fizzy Pop Beverage Corporation.

The action accelerates after that. In a flurry of quick expository scenes, the jewelry store manager discovers that he has been robbed, rushes out onto the sidewalk and flags down a cop, and then, with urgent, panic-stricken gestures, explains what has happened. The cop glances down, notices the dark line on the pavement, and then follows it with his eyes all the way to the Fizzy Pop building across the street. Looks like a clue, he says. Let's see where it goes, the manager says, and the two of them take off in the direction of the building.

Cut back to Hector. He is walking through a corridor now, carefully putting the finishing touches on his trail. He reaches the door of an office, and as he empties the last of the dirt onto the outer half of the sill, the camera tilts up to show us what is written on the door: C. LESTER CHASE, VICE PRESIDENT. Just then, with Hector still in a crouching position, the door swings open and out steps Chase himself. Hector manages to jump back at the last second—before Chase trips over him—and then, as the door begins to close, he slips in through the opening and waddles ducklike into the office. Even as the melodrama is building toward its climax, Hector continues to pile on the gags. Alone in the office, he sees the stock certificates spread out on Chase's desk. He scoops them up, evens out the edges with a meticulous flourish, and sticks them into his jacket. Then, in a series of rapid, stabbing gestures, he reaches into his side pockets and starts pulling out the jewels, heaping a great mountain of stolen goods onto Chase's blotter. As the last ring is added to the collection, Chase returns, rubbing his hands together and looking inordinately pleased with himself. Hector steps back. His work is finished now, and all that remains is to watch his enemy get what's coming to him.

It happens in a whirl of astonishment and misapprehension, of justice done and justice betrayed. At first, the jewels distract Chase from noticing that the stocks are gone. Time is lost, and when he finally digs under the glittering pile and sees that the certificates aren't there anymore, it is too late. The door bursts open, and in rush the cop and the store manager. The jewels are identified, the crime is solved, and the thief is put under arrest. It doesn't matter that Chase is innocent. The trail has led to his door, and they've caught him red-handed with the merchandise. He protests, of course, tries to escape through the window, begins hurling Fizzy Pop bottles at his attackers, but after some wild business involving a billy club and a bayonet, he is at last overwhelmed. Hector looks on with grim insouciance. Even as Chase is put into handcuffs and led out of the office, Hector does not rejoice in his victory. His plan has worked to perfection, but what good has it done him? The day is drawing to a close now, and he is still invisible.

He goes outside again and starts walking through the streets. The downtown boulevards are deserted, and Hector appears to be the only person left in the city. What has happened to the crowds and commotion that surrounded him before? Where are the cars and trolleys, the masses of people thronging the sidewalk? For a moment we wonder if the spell has not been reversed. Perhaps Hector is visible again, we think, and everyone else has vanished. Then, out of nowhere, a truck drives by, speeding through a puddle. Plumes of water rise up from the pavement, splashing everything in sight. Hector is drenched, but when the camera turns around to show us the damage, the front of his suit is spotless. It should be a funny moment, but it isn't, and in that Hector deliberately makes it *not* funny (a long, doleful look at his suit; the disappointment in his eyes when he sees that he is not splattered with mud), this simple trick alters the mood of the film. As night falls, we see him returning to his house. He goes in, climbs the stairs to the second floor, and enters his children's bedroom. The little girl and the little boy are asleep, each one in a separate bed. He sits down beside the girl, studies her face for a few moments, and then lifts his hand to begin stroking her hair. Just as he is about to touch her, however, he stops himself, suddenly realizing that his hand could wake her, and if she woke up in the darkness and found no one there, she would be frightened. It's an affecting sequence, and Hector plays it with restraint and simplicity. He has lost the right to touch his own daughter, and as we watch him hesitate and then finally withdraw his hand, we experience the full impact of the curse that has been put on him. In that one small gesture—the hand hovering in the air, the open palm no more than an inch from the girl's head—we understand that Hector has been reduced to nothing.

Like a ghost, he stands up and leaves the room. He walks down the hall, opens a door, and goes in. It is his bedroom, and there is his wife, his Dearest Beloved, asleep in their bed. Hector pauses. She is thrashing about, tossing back and forth and kicking off the covers, in the grip of some terrifying dream.

Hector approaches the bed and cautiously rearranges the blankets, props up the pillows, and turns off the lamp on the bedside table. Her fitful movements begin to subside, and before long she has fallen into a sound and tranquil sleep. Hector backs away, blows her a little kiss, and then sits down in a chair near the foot of the bed. It looks as if he intends to stay there for the night, watching over her like some benevolent spirit. Even if he can't touch her or talk to her, he can protect her and feed on the power of her presence. But invisible men are not immune to exhaustion. They have bodies just like everyone else, and like everyone else they have to sleep. Hector's eyelids begin to grow heavy. They flutter and sag, they close and then open again, and even though he jerks himself awake a couple of times, it is clearly a losing battle. A moment later, he succumbs.

The screen fades to black. When the picture returns, it is morning, and daylight is flooding through the curtains. Cut to a shot of Hector's wife, still asleep in bed. Then cut to Hector, asleep in the chair. His body is contorted into an impossible position, a comic tangle of splayed limbs and twisted joints, and because we aren't prepared for the sight of this slumbering pretzel-man, we laugh, and with that laugh the mood of the film changes again. Dearest Beloved wakes first, and as she opens her eyes and sits up in bed, her face tells us everything—moving rapidly from joy to disbelief to guarded optimism. She springs out of bed and rushes over to Hector. She touches his face (which is dangling backward over the arm of the chair), and Hector's body goes into a spasm of high-voltage shocks, jumping around in a flurry of arms and legs that ultimately lands him in an upright position. Then he opens his eyes. Involuntarily, without seeming to remember that he is supposed to be invisible, he smiles at her. They kiss, but just as their lips come into contact, he recoils in confusion. Is he really there? Has the spell been broken, or is he only dreaming it? He touches his face, he runs his hands over his chest, and then he looks his wife in the eyes. Can you see me? he asks. Of course I can see you, she says, and as her eyes fill with tears, she leans forward and kisses him again. But Hector is not convinced. He stands up from his chair and walks over to a mirror hanging on the wall. The proof is in the mirror, and if he is able to see his reflection, he will know that the nightmare is over. That he does see it is a foregone conclusion, but the beautiful thing about that moment is the slowness of his response. For a second or two, the expression on his face remains the same, and as he peers into the eyes of the man staring back at him from the wall, it's as if he's looking at a stranger, encountering the face of a man he has never seen before. Then, as the camera moves in for a closer shot, Hector begins to smile. Coming on the heels of that chilling blankness, the smile suggests something more than a simple rediscovery of himself. He is no longer looking at the old Hector. He is someone else now, and however much he might resemble the person he used to be, he has been reinvented, turned inside-out, and spat forth as a new man. The smile grows larger, more radiant, more satisfied with the face that has been found in the mirror. A circle begins to close around it, and soon we can see nothing but that smiling mouth, the mouth and the mustache above it. The mustache twitches for a few seconds, and then the circle grows smaller, then smaller still. When it finally shuts, the film is over.

In effect, Hector's career ends with that smile. He fulfilled the terms of his contract by producing one more film, but *Double or Nothing* cannot be counted as a new work. Kaleidoscope was all but bankrupt then, and there wasn't enough money left to mount another full-scale production. Instead, Hector pulled out bits of rejected material from previous films and cobbled them together into an anthology of gags, pratfalls, and slapstick improvisations. It was an ingenious salvage operation, but we learn nothing from it except for what it reveals to us about Hector's talents as an editor. To assess his work fairly, we have to look at *Mr. Nobody* as his last film. It is a meditation on his own disappearance, and for all its ambiguity and furtive suggestiveness, for all the moral questions it asks and then refuses to answer, it is essentially a film about the anguish of selfhood. Hector is looking for a way to say good-bye to us, to bid farewell to the world, and in order to do that he must eradicate himself in his own eyes. He becomes invisible, and when the magic finally wears off and he can be seen again, he does not recognize his own face. We are looking at him as he looks at himself, and in this eerie doubling of perspectives, we watch him confront the fact of his own annihilation. Double or nothing. That was the phrase he chose as the title for his next film. Those words are not even remotely connected to anything presented in that eighteen-minute hodgepodge of stunts and gambols. They refer back to the mirror scene in *Mr. Nobody*, and once Hector breaks into that extraordinary smile, we are given a brief glimpse of what the future has in store for him. He allows himself to be born again with that smile, but he is no longer the same person, no longer the Hector Mann who has amused us and entertained us for the past year. We see him transformed into someone we no longer recognize, and before we can absorb who this new Hector might be, he is gone. A circle closes around his face, and he is swallowed up by the blackness. An instant later, for the first and only time in any of his films, the words THE END are written out across the screen, and that is the last anyone ever sees of him.

3

I WROTE THE book in less than nine months. The manuscript came to more than three hundred typed pages, and every one of those pages was a struggle for me. If I managed to finish, it was only because I did nothing else. I worked seven days a week, sitting at the desk from ten to twelve hours a day, and except for my little excursions to Montague Street to stock up on food and paper, ink and typewriter ribbons, I rarely left the apartment. I had no telephone, no radio or TV, no social life of any kind. Once in April and again in August I traveled by subway to Manhattan to consult some books at the public library, but other than that I didn't budge from Brooklyn. But I wasn't really in Brooklyn either. I was in the book, and the book was in my head, and as long as I stayed inside my head, I could go on writing the book. It was like living in a padded cell, but of all the lives I could have lived at that moment, it was the only one that made sense to me. I wasn't capable of being in the world, and I knew that if I tried to go back into it before I was ready, I would be crushed. So I holed up in that small apartment and spent my days writing about Hector Mann. It was slow work, perhaps even meaningless work, but it demanded all my attention for nine straight months, and in that I was too busy to think about anything else, it probably kept me from going insane.

In late April, I wrote to Smits and asked him to extend my leave of absence through the fall semester. I was still undecided about my long-range plans, I said, but unless things changed dramatically for me in the next few months, I was probably finished with teaching—if not for good, then at least for a long while. I hoped he would forgive me. It wasn't that I had lost interest. I just wasn't sure if my legs would hold me when I stood up and tried to talk in front of students.

I was slowly getting used to being without Helen and the boys, but that didn't mean I had made any progress. I didn't know who I was, and I didn't know what I wanted, and until I found a way to live with other people again, I would continue to be something only half human. All through the writing of the book, I intentionally put off thinking about the future. A sensible plan would have been to stay in New York, to buy some furniture for the apartment I had rented and begin a new life there, but when the moment came for me to take the next step, I decided against it and returned to Vermont. I was in the last throes of revising the manuscript then, getting ready to type up the final draft and submit the book for publication, when it suddenly occurred to me that New York was the book, and once the book was over I should leave New York and go somewhere else. Vermont was probably the worst choice I could have made, but it was familiar ground to me, and I knew that if I went back there I would be close to Helen again, that I would be able to breathe the same air we had breathed together when she was still alive. There was comfort in that thought. I couldn't go back to the old house in Hampton, but there were other houses in other towns, and as long as I remained in the general area, I could carry on with my crazed, solitary life without having to turn my back on the past. I wasn't ready to let go yet. It had been only a year and a half, and I wanted my grief to continue. All I needed was another project to work on, another ocean to drown myself in.

I wound up buying a place in the town of West T——, about twenty-five miles south of Hampton. It was a ridiculous little house, a kind of prefab ski chalet with wall-to-wall carpeting and an electric fireplace, but its ugliness was so extreme that it verged on the beautiful. It had no charm or character, no lovingly wrought details to delude one into thinking it could ever become a home. It was a hospital for the living dead, a way station for the mentally afflicted, and to inhabit those blank, depersonalized interiors was to understand that the world was an illusion that had to be reinvented every day. For all the flaws in its design, however, the dimensions of the house struck me as ideal. They weren't so large that you felt lost in them, and they weren't so small that you felt hemmed in. There was a kitchen with skylights in the ceiling; a sunken living room with a picture window and two empty walls high enough to accommodate shelves for my books; a loggia overlooking the living room; and three identically proportioned bedrooms: one for sleeping, one for working, and one for storing the things I no longer had the heart to look at but couldn't bring myself to throw away. It was the right size and shape for a man who meant to live alone, and it had the further advantage of complete isolation. Situated halfway up a mountain and surrounded by thick stands of birch, spruce, and maple trees, it was accessible only by dirt road. If I didn't want to see anyone, I didn't have to. More important, no one would have to see me.

I moved in just after the first of the year, 1987, and for the next six weeks I devoted myself to practical matters: building bookcases, installing a wood-burning stove, selling my car and replacing it with a four-wheel-drive pickup truck. The mountain was treacherous when it snowed, and since it snowed nearly all the time, I needed something that would get me up and down without turning every trip into an adventure. I hired a plumber and an electrician to repair pipes and wires, painted walls, laid in a winter's worth of cordwood, and bought myself a computer, a radio, and a combination telephone–fax machine. Meanwhile, *The Silent World of Hector Mann* was slowly making its way through the circuitous channels of academic-press publication. Unlike other books, scholarly books are not accepted or rejected by a single in-house editor. Copies of the manuscript are sent out to various specialists in the field, and nothing happens until those people have read the submission and mailed in their reports. The fees for such work are minimal (a couple of hundred dollars at best), and since the readers tend to be professors who are busy teaching and writing books of their own, the process often drags. In my case, I waited from the middle of November until the end of March before I had an answer. By then, I was so absorbed in something else that I nearly forgot that I had sent them the manuscript. I was glad that they wanted it, of course, glad that I had something to show for my efforts, but I can't say that it meant that much to me. It was good news for Hector Mann, perhaps, good news for antique-movie hounds and connoisseurs of black mustaches, but now that the experience was behind me, I rarely thought about it anymore. On the few occasions when I did, I felt as if the book had been written by someone else.

In mid-February, I received a letter from a former graduate

school classmate, Alex Kronenberg, who now taught at Columbia. I had last seen him at the memorial service for Helen and the boys, and although we hadn't spoken to each other since, I still considered him to be a solid friend. (His condolence letter had been a model of eloquence and compassion, the best letter I received from anyone.) He started off his new letter by apologizing for not having been in touch sooner. He had been thinking about me a lot, he said, and had heard through the grapevine that I was on leave from Hampton and had spent some months living in New York. He was sorry that I hadn't called. If he had known that I was there, he would have been immensely glad to see me. Those were his precise words—*immensely glad*—a typical Alex locution. In any case, the next paragraph began, he had recently been asked by Columbia University Press to edit a new series of books, the Library of World Classics. A man with the incongruous name of Dexter Feinbaum, a 1927 graduate of the Columbia School of Engineering, had bequeathed them four and a half million dollars for the purpose of starting this collection. The idea was to bring together the acknowledged masterpieces of world literature in one uniform line of books. Everything from Meister Eckhart to Fernando Pessoa would be included, and in cases where the existing translations were deemed inadequate, new translations would be commissioned. *It's a mad enterprise,* Alex wrote, *but they've put me in charge as executive editor, and in spite of all the extra work (I don't sleep anymore), I have to admit that I'm enjoying myself. In his will, Feinbaum made a list of the first one hundred titles he wanted to see published. He got rich by manufacturing aluminum siding, but you can't fault him for his taste in literature. One of the books was Chateaubriand's* Mémoires d'outre-tombe. *I still haven't read the cursed thing, all two thousand pages of it, but I remember what you said to me one night in 1971 somewhere on the Yale campus—it might have been near that little plaza just outside the Beinecke—and I'm going to repeat it to you now. "This," you said (holding up the first volume of the French edition and waving it in the air), "is the best autobiography ever written." I don't know if you still feel that way now, but I probably don't have to tell you that there have been only two complete translations since the book was published in 1848. One in 1849 and one in 1902. It's high time someone did another, don't you think? I have no idea if you're still interested in translating books, but if you are, I would love it if you agreed to do this one for us.*

I had a telephone now. It wasn't that I was hoping anyone would call me, but I figured I should have one put in just in case something went wrong. I had no neighbors up there, and if the roof fell in or the house caught fire, I wanted to be able to ring for help. This was one of my few concessions to reality, a grudging acknowledgment that I was not in fact the only person left in the world. Normally, I would have answered Alex by letter, but I happened to be in the kitchen when I opened the mail that afternoon, and the phone was right there, sitting on the counter not two feet from my hand. Alex had recently moved, and his new address and number were written out just below his signature. It was too tempting not to take advantage of all this, so I picked up the receiver and dialed.

The phone rang four times on the other end, and then an answering machine clicked on. Unexpectedly, the message was spoken by a child. After three or four words, I recognized the voice as that of Alex's son. Jacob must have been around ten at that point, roughly a year and a half older than Todd—or a year and a half older than Todd would have been if he had still been alive. The little boy said: It's the bottom of the ninth. The bases are loaded, and two men are out. The score is four to three, my team is losing, and I'm up. If I get a hit, we win the game. Here comes the pitch. I swing. It's a ground ball. I drop the bat and start running. The second baseman scoops up the grounder, throws to first, and I'm out. Yes, that's right, folks, I'm out. Jacob is out. And so is my father, Alex; my mother, Barbara; and my sister, Julie. The whole family is out right now. Please leave a message after the beep, and we'll call you back just as soon as we round the bases and come home.

It was a cute bit of nonsense, but it rattled me. When the beep sounded after the message was over, I couldn't think of anything to say, and rather than let the tape run on in silence, I hung up. I had never liked talking into those machines. They made me nervous and uncomfortable, but listening to Jacob had spun me around and knocked me off my feet, pushed me into something close to despair. There had been too much happiness in his voice, too much laughter spilling out from the edges of the words. Todd had been a bright and clever little boy, too, but he wasn't eight and a half now, he was seven, and he would go on being seven even after Jacob was a grown man.

I gave myself a few minutes, and then I tried again. I knew what to expect now, and when the message came on for the second time, I held the phone away from my ear so that I wouldn't have to listen to it. The words seemed to go on forever, but when the beep cut them off at last, I brought the phone to my ear again and started to talk. Alex, I said. I've just read your letter, and I want you to know that I'm willing to do the translation. Considering how long the book is, you shouldn't count on seeing a finished manuscript for two or three years. But I assume you're aware of that already. I'm still settling in here, but once I learn how to use the computer I bought last week, I'll get started. Thanks for the invitation. I've been casting about for something to do, and I think I'll enjoy this. Best to Barbara and the kids. Talk to you soon, I hope.

He called back that same evening, both startled and happy that I had accepted. It was just a shot in the dark, he said, but it wouldn't have felt right if I hadn't asked you first. I can't tell you how glad I am.

I'm glad you're glad, I said.

I'll tell them to send you a contract tomorrow. Just to make everything official.

Whatever you say. The fact is, I think I've already figured out how to translate the title.

Mémoires d'outre-tombe. Memoirs from Beyond the Grave.

That feels awkward to me. Too literal, somehow, and yet at the same time difficult to understand.

What do you have in mind?

Memoirs of a Dead Man.

Interesting.

It's not bad, is it?

No, not bad at all. I like it a lot.

The important thing is that it makes sense. It took Chateaubriand thirty-five years to write the book, and he didn't want it to be published until fifty years after his death. It's literally written in the voice of a dead man.

But it didn't take fifty years. The book was published in 1848, the same year he died.

He ran into financial difficulties. After the revolution of 1830, his political career was over, and he fell into debt. Madame Récamier, his mistress of the past dozen years or so—yes, *that* Madame Récamier—talked him into giving some private readings from the *Memoirs* to small, select audiences in her drawing room. The idea was to find a publisher willing to pay Chateaubriand an advance, to give him money for a work that wouldn't be coming out for years. The plan failed, but response to the book was extraordinarily good. The *Memoirs* became the most celebrated unfinished, unpublished, unread book in history. But Chateaubriand was still broke. So Madame Récamier came up with a new scheme, and this one worked—or sort of worked. A stock company was formed, and people bought shares in the manuscript. Word futures, I guess you could call them, in the same way that people from Wall Street gamble on the price of soybeans and corn. In effect, Chateaubriand mortgaged his autobiography to finance his old age. They gave him a nice chunk of money up front, which allowed him to pay off his creditors, and a guaranteed annuity for the rest of his life. It was a brilliant arrangement. The only problem was that Chateaubriand kept on living. The company was formed when he was in his mid-sixties, and he hung on until he was eighty. By then, the shares had changed hands several times, and the friends and admirers who had invested in the beginning were long gone. Chateaubriand was owned by a bunch of strangers. The only thing they were interested in was turning a profit, and the longer he went on living, the more they wanted him to die. Those last years must have been bleak for him. A frail old man crippled with rheumatism, Madame Récamier all but blind, and every one of his friends dead and buried. But he kept on revising the manuscript right up to the end.

What a cheerful story.

Not so funny, I suppose, but let me tell you, the old viscount could write one hell of a good sentence. It's an incredible book, Alex.

So you're saying you don't mind spending the next two or three years of your life with a gloomy Frenchman?

I've just spent a year with a silent-film comedian, and I think I'm ready for a change.

Silent film? I hadn't heard anything about that.

Someone named Hector Mann. I finished writing a book about him in the fall.

You've been busy, then. That's good.

I had to do something. So I decided to do that.

Why haven't I heard of this actor? Not that I know anything about movies, but the name doesn't ring a bell.

No one's heard of him. He's my own private funny man, a court jester who performs only for me. For twelve or thirteen months, I spent every waking moment with him.

You mean you were actually with him? Or is that just a figure of speech?

No one's been with Hector Mann since 1929. He's dead. As dead as Chateaubriand and Madame Récamier. As dead as Dexter What's-His-Name.

Feinbaum.

As dead as Dexter Feinbaum.

So you spent a year watching old movies.

Not exactly. I spent three months watching old movies, and then I locked myself in a room and spent nine months writing about them. It's probably the strangest thing I've ever done. I was writing about things I couldn't see anymore, and I had to present them in purely visual terms. The whole experience was like a hallucination.

And what about the living, David? Do you spend much time with them?

As little as possible.

That's what I thought you'd say.

I had a conversation in Washington last year with a man

named Singh. Dr. J. M. Singh. An excellent person, and I enjoyed the time I spent with him. He did me a great service.

Are you seeing a doctor now?

Of course not. This chat we're having now is the longest talk I've had with anyone since then.

You should have called me when you were in New York.

I couldn't.

You're not even forty, David. Life isn't over, you know.

Actually, I turn forty next month. There's going to be a big bash at Madison Square Garden on the fifteenth, and I hope you and Barbara will be able to come. I'm surprised you haven't received your invitation yet.

Everyone's worried about you, that's all. I don't want to pry, but when someone you care about behaves like this, it's hard just to stand by and watch. I wish you'd give me a chance to help.

You have helped. You've offered me a new job, and I'm grateful to you.

That's work. I'm talking about life.

Is there a difference?

You're a stubborn son-of-a-bitch, aren't you?

Tell me something about Dexter Feinbaum. The man's my benefactor, after all, and I don't even know the first thing about him.

You're not going to talk about this, are you?

As our old friend in the dead-letter office used to say: I would prefer not to.

No one can live without other people, David. It's just not possible.

Maybe not. But no one's ever been me before. Maybe I'm the first one.

• • •

From the introduction to *Memoirs of a Dead Man* (Paris, April 14, 1846; revised July 28):

As it is impossible for me to foresee the moment of my death, and as at my age the days granted to men are only days of grace, or rather of suffering, I feel compelled to offer a few words of explanation.

On September fourth, I will be seventy-eight years old. It is full time for me to leave a world which is fast leaving me, and which I shall not regret. . . .

Sad necessity, which has forever held its foot against my throat, has forced me to sell my Memoirs. *No one can imagine what I have suffered in being obliged to pawn my tomb, but I owed this last sacrifice to my solemn promises and the consistency of my conduct. . . . My plan was to bequeath them to Madame Chateaubriand. She would have sent them out into the world or suppressed them, as she saw fit. Now more than ever, I believe the latter solution would have been preferable. . . .*

These Memoirs *have been composed at different times and in different countries. For that reason, it has been necessary for me to add prologues that describe the places which were before my eyes and the feelings which were in my heart when the thread of my narrative was resumed. The changing forms of my life are thus intermingled with one another. It has sometimes happened to me in my moments of prosperity to have to speak of my days of hardship; and in my times of tribulation to retrace the periods of my happiness. My youth entering into my old age, the gravity of my later years tingeing and saddening the years of my innocence, the rays of my sun crossing and blending together from the moment of its rising to the moment of its setting, have produced in my stories a kind of confusion—or, if you will, a kind of mysterious unity. My cradle recalls something of my tomb, my tomb something of my cradle; my sufferings become pleasures, my pleasures sufferings; and, now that I have completed the perusal of these* Memoirs, *I am no longer certain if they are the product of a youthful mind or a head gray with age.*

I cannot know if this mixture will be pleasing or displeasing to the reader. There is nothing I can do to remedy it. It is the result of my changing fortunes, the inconsistency of my lot. Its storms have often left me with no table to write on but the rock on which I have been shipwrecked.

I have been urged to allow some portions of these Memoirs *to appear in my lifetime, but I prefer to speak from the depths of my tomb. My narrative will thus be accompanied by those voices which have something sacred about them because they come from the sepulchre. If I have suffered enough in this world to be turned into a happy shadow in the next, a ray from the Elysian Fields will throw a protective light on these last pictures of mine. Life sits heavily on me; perhaps death will suit me better.*

These Memoirs *have held a special importance for me. Saint Bonaventure was granted permission to go on writing his book after he was dead. I cannot hope for such a favor, but if nothing else I should like to be resurrected at some midnight hour in order to correct the proofs of mine. . . .*

If any part of my labors has been more satisfying to me than the others, it is that which relates to my youth—the most hidden corner of my life. In it I have had to reawaken a world known only to myself, and as I wandered around in that vanished realm, I have encountered only silence and memories. Of all the people I have known, how many are still alive today?

. . . If I should die outside of France, I request that my body not be brought back to my native country until fifty years have elapsed since its first inhumation. Let my remains be spared a

sacrilegious autopsy; let no one search my lifeless brain and extinguished heart to discover the mystery of my being. Death does not reveal the secrets of life. The idea of a corpse traveling by post fills me with horror, but dry and moldering bones are easily transported. They will be less weary on that final voyage than when I dragged them around this earth, burdened down by the weight of my troubles.

I started working on those pages the morning after my conversation with Alex. I could do that because I owned a copy of the book (the two-volume Pléiade edition compiled by Levaillant and Moulinier, complete with variants, notes, and appendices) and had held it in my hands just three days before Alex's letter arrived. Earlier that week, I had finished installing my new bookcases. For several hours every day, I had been unpacking books and putting them on the shelves, and somewhere in the midst of that tedious operation, I had stumbled across the Chateaubriand. I hadn't looked at the *Memoirs* in years, but that morning, in the chaos of my Vermont living room, surrounded by empty, overturned boxes and towers of unclassified books, I had impulsively opened them again. The first thing my eyes had fallen upon was a short passage in volume one. In it, Chateaubriand tells of accompanying a Breton poet on an outing to Versailles in June of 1789. It was less than a month before the taking of the Bastille, and halfway through their visit they spotted Marie Antoinette walking by with her two children. *Casting a smiling look in my direction, she gave me the same gracious salute that I had received from her on the day of my presentation. I shall never forget that look of hers, which was soon to be no more. When Marie-Antoinette smiled, the shape of her mouth was so clear that (horrible thought!) the memory of that smile enabled me to recognize the jaw of this daughter of kings when the head of the unfortunate woman was discovered in the exhumations of 1815.*

It was a fierce, breathtaking image, and I kept thinking about it long after I had closed the book and put it on the shelf. Marie-Antoinette's severed head, unearthed from a pit of human remains. In three short sentences, Chateaubriand travels twenty-six years. He goes from flesh to bone, from piquant life to anonymous death, and in the chasm between them lies the experience of an entire generation, the unspoken years of terror, brutality, and madness. I was stunned by the passage, moved by it in a way that no words had moved me in a year and a half. Then, just three days after my accidental encounter with those sentences, I received Alex's letter asking me to translate the book. Was it a coincidence? Of course it was, but at the time I felt as though I had willed it to happen—as though Alex's letter had somehow completed a thought I was unable to finish myself. In the past, I had never been one to believe in mystical claptrap of that sort. But when you live as I was living then, all shut up inside yourself and not bothering to look at anything around you, your perspective begins to change. For the fact was that Alex's letter was dated Monday the ninth, and I had received it on Thursday the twelfth, three days later. Which meant that when he was in New York writing to me about the book, I had been in Vermont holding the book in my hands. I don't want to insist on the importance of the connection, but I couldn't help reading it as a sign. It was as if I had asked for something without knowing it, and then suddenly my wish had been granted.

So I settled down and began working again. I forgot about

Hector Mann and thought only about Chateaubriand, burying myself in the massive chronicle of a life that had nothing to do with my life. That was what appealed to me most about the job: the distance, the sheer distance between myself and what I was doing. It had been good to camp out for a year in 1920s America; it was even better to spend my days in eighteenth- and nineteenth-century France. The snow fell on my little mountain in Vermont, but I scarcely paid any attention. I was in Saint-Malo and Paris, in Ohio and Florida, in England, Rome, and Berlin. Much of the work was mechanical, and because I was the servant of the text and not its creator, it demanded a different kind of energy from the one I had put into writing *The Silent World.* Translation is a bit like shoveling coal. You scoop it up and toss it into the furnace. Each lump is a word, and each shovelful is another sentence, and if your back is strong enough and you have the stamina to keep at it for eight or ten hours at a stretch, you can keep the fire hot. With close to a million words in front of me, I was prepared to work as long and as hard as necessary, even if it meant burning down the house.

For most of that first winter, I didn't go anywhere. Once every ten days, I would drive to the Grand Union in Brattleboro to shop for food, but that was the only thing I allowed to interrupt my routine. Brattleboro was a good distance out of my way, but by driving those extra twenty miles I figured I could avoid running into anyone I knew. The Hampton crowd tended to shop at another Grand Union just north of the college, and the chances of any of them turning up in Brattleboro were slim. But that didn't mean it couldn't happen, and in spite of my cautious planning, the strategy eventually backfired on me. One afternoon in March, as I was loading up my cart with toilet paper in aisle six, I found myself cornered by Greg and Mary Tellefson. This led to an invitation to dinner, and even though I did my best to worm out of it, Mary kept juggling the dates until I had run out of imaginary excuses. Twelve nights later, I drove to their house at the edge of the Hampton campus, less than a mile from where I had lived with Helen and the boys. If it had just been the two of them, it might not have been such an ordeal for me, but Greg and Mary had taken it upon themselves to invite twenty other people, and I wasn't prepared for such a crowd. They were all friendly, of course, and most of them were probably glad to see me, but I felt awkward, out of my element, and every time I opened my mouth to say something, I found myself saying the wrong thing. I wasn't up on the Hampton gossip anymore. They all assumed that I would want to hear about the latest intrigues and embarrassments, the divorces and extramarital affairs, the promotions and departmental quarrels, but the truth was that I found it unbearably dull. I would drift away from the conversation, and a moment later I would find myself surrounded by another group of people engaged in a different but similar conversation. No one was tactless enough to mention Helen (academics are too polite for that), and therefore they stuck to supposedly neutral subjects: recent news items, politics, sports. I had no idea what they were talking about. I hadn't looked at a paper in over a year, and as far as I was concerned, they could have been referring to events that had taken place in another world.

The party began with everyone milling around on the ground floor, wandering in and out of rooms, clustering together for a few minutes and then breaking apart to form new clusters in other rooms. I went from the living room to the dining room to the kitchen to the den, and at some point Greg caught up with me and put a scotch and soda in my hand. I took it without thinking, and because I was anxious and ill at ease, I drank it down in about twenty-four seconds. It was the first drop of alcohol I had had in more than a year. I had succumbed to the temptations of various hotel minibars while doing my research on Hector Mann, but I had sworn off liquor after I'd moved to Brooklyn and started writing the book. I didn't particularly crave the stuff when it wasn't around, but I knew that I was only a few weak moments away from creating a bad problem for myself. My behavior after the plane crash had convinced me of that, and if I hadn't picked myself up and left Vermont when I did, I probably wouldn't have lived long enough to be attending Greg and Mary's party—not to speak of being in a position to wonder why the hell I had come back.

After I finished the drink, I went to the bar for a refill, but this time I dispensed with the soda and added only ice to the glass. For the third one, I forgot about the ice and poured it straight.

When dinner was ready, the guests lined up around the dinner table, filled their plates with food, and then scattered into other parts of the house to look for chairs. I wound up on the sofa in the den, wedged between the armrest and Karin Müller, an assistant professor in the German department. My coordination was already a bit wobbly by then, and as I sat there with a plateful of salad and beef stew balanced precariously on my knee, I turned to retrieve my drink from the back of the sofa (where I had placed it before sitting down), and no sooner did I take hold of the glass than it slipped out of my hand. A quadruple shot of Johnnie Walker splashed against Karin's neck, and then, an instant later, the glass clunked against her spine. She jumped—how could she not jump?—

and when she did, she knocked over her own plate of stew and salad, which not only sent my plate crashing to the floor, but landed upside down on my lap.

It was hardly a major catastrophe, but I had drunk too much to know that, and with my pants suddenly drenched in olive oil and my shirt splattered with gravy, I chose to take offense. I don't remember what I said, but it was something cruel and insulting, an utterly uncalled-for remark. *Clumsy cow.* I think that was it. But it also might have been *stupid cow,* or else *stupid, clumsy cow.* Whatever the words were, they expressed an anger that must never be articulated under any circumstances, least of all when they can be overheard by a roomful of edgy, high-strung college professors. There is probably no need to add that Karin was neither stupid nor clumsy; and far from resembling a cow, she was an attractive, slender woman in her late thirties who taught courses on Goethe and Hölderlin and had never shown anything but the greatest respect and kindness toward me. Just seconds before the accident, she had invited me to give a talk to one of her classes, and I was clearing my throat and getting ready to tell her that I would have to think it over when the drink spilled. It was entirely my fault, and yet I immediately turned around and put the blame on her. It was a disgusting outburst, yet one more proof that I wasn't fit to be let out of my cage. Karin had made a friendly overture to me, had in fact been giving off tentative, ever so subtle signs that she was available for more intimate conversations on any number of subjects, and I, who had not touched a woman in almost two years, found myself responding to those nearly imperceptible hints and imagining, in the crude and vulgar way of a man with too much alcohol in his blood, what she would look like without any clothes on. Was that why I snapped at her so viciously? Was my self-loathing so great that I had to punish her for awakening a glimmer of sexual arousal in me? Or did I secretly know that she was doing nothing of the kind and that the whole little drama was my own invention, a moment of lust brought on by the nearness of her warm, perfumed body?

To make matters worse, I wasn't the least bit sorry when she started to cry. We were both standing by then, and when I saw Karin's lower lip begin to tremble and the corners of her eyes fill with tears, I was glad, almost jubilant over the consternation I had caused. There were six or seven other people in the room just then, and they had all turned in our direction after Karin's first yelp of surprise. The noise of clattering plates had brought several more guests to the threshold, and when I came out with my obnoxious remark, there were at least a dozen witnesses who heard it. Everything went silent after that. It was a moment of collective shock, and for the next couple of seconds no one knew what to say or do. In that small interval of breathlessness and uncertainty, Karin's hurt turned to anger.

You have no right to talk to me like that, David, she said. Who do you think you are?

Fortunately, Mary was one of the people who had come to the doorway, and before I could do any further damage, she rushed into the room and took hold of my arm.

David didn't mean it, she said to Karin. Did you, David? It was just one of those things that come flying out on the spur of the moment.

I wanted to say something harsh and contradictory, something that would prove I'd meant every word I'd said, but I held my tongue. It took all my powers of self-control to do that, but Mary had gone out of her way to act as peacemaker, and a part of me knew that I would regret causing her any more trouble. Even so, I didn't apologize, and I didn't try to make nice. Rather than say the thing I wanted to say, I freed my arm from her grasp and left the room, walking out of the den and across the living room as my former colleagues looked on and said nothing.

I went straight upstairs to Greg and Mary's bedroom. My plan was to grab my things and leave, but my parka was buried under a massive pile of coats on the bed, and I couldn't find it. After digging around for a little while, I started tossing the coats onto the floor, eliminating possibilities in order to simplify my search. Just when I had come to the halfway point—more coats off the bed than on—Mary walked into the room. She was a short, round-faced woman with blond frizzy hair and reddish cheeks, and as she stood in the doorway with her hands on her hips, I immediately understood that she'd had it with me. I felt like a child about to be scolded by his mother.

What are you doing? she said.

Looking for my coat.

It's in the downstairs closet. Don't you remember?

I thought it was here.

It's downstairs. Greg put it in the closet when you came. You were the one who found the hanger for him.

All right, I'll look for it downstairs.

But Mary wasn't about to let me off so easily. She took a few more steps into the room, bent down for a coat, and flung it angrily onto the bed. Then she picked up another coat and threw that one onto the bed as well. She went on collecting coats, and each time she thwacked another one down on the bed, she interrupted what she was saying in mid-sentence. The coats were like punctuation marks—sudden dashes, hasty ellipses, violent exclamation points—and each one broke through her words like an axe.

When you go downstairs, she said, I want you to . . . make up with Karin . . . I don't care if you have to get down on your knees . . . and beg for her forgiveness . . . Everyone's talking about it . . . and if you don't do this for me now, David . . . I'm never going to invite you to this house again.

I didn't want to come in the first place, I answered. If you hadn't twisted my arm, I never would have been here to insult your guests. You could have had the same dull and insipid party you always have.

You need help, David . . . I'm not forgetting what you've been through . . . but patience lasts just so long . . . Go and see a doctor before you ruin your life.

I live the life that's possible for me. It doesn't include going to parties at your house.

Mary threw the last coat onto the bed, and then, for no discernible reason, she abruptly sat down and began to cry.

Listen, fuckhead, she said in a quiet voice. I loved her, too. You might have been married to her, but Helen was my best friend.

No she wasn't. She was my best friend. And I was hers. This has nothing to do with you, Mary.

That put an end to the conversation. I had been so hard on her, so absolute in my rejection of her feelings that she couldn't think of anything more to say. When I left the room, she was sitting with her back to me, shaking her head back and forth and looking down at the coats.

Two days after the party, word came from the University of Pennsylvania Press that they wanted to publish my book. I was almost a hundred pages into the Chateaubriand translation at that point, and when *The Silent World of Hector Mann* was released a year later, I had another twelve hundred pages behind me. If I kept working at that pace, I would have a completed draft in seven or eight more months. Add on some extra time for revisions and changes of heart, and in less than a year I would be delivering a finished manuscript to Alex.

As it turned out, that year lasted only three months. I pushed on for another two hundred fifty pages, reaching the chapter about the fall of Napoleon in the twenty-third book (*miseries and wonders are twins, they are born together*), and then, one damp and blustery afternoon at the beginning of summer, I found Frieda Spelling's letter in my mailbox. I admit that I was thrown by it at first, but once I had sent off my response and given the matter a little thought, I managed to persuade myself that it was a hoax. That didn't mean it had been wrong to answer her, but now that I had covered my bets, I assumed that our correspondence would end there.

Nine days later, I heard from her again. She used a full sheet of paper this time, and at the top of the page there was a block of blue embossed type that bore her name and address. I realized how simple it was to produce false personal stationery, but why would anyone go to the trouble of trying to impersonate someone I had never heard of? The name Frieda Spelling meant nothing to me. She might have been Hector Mann's wife, and she might have been a crazy person who lived alone in a desert shack, but it no longer made sense to deny that she was real.

Dear Professor, she wrote. *Your doubts are perfectly understandable, and I am not at all surprised that you are reluctant to believe me. The only way to learn the truth is to accept the invitation I made to you in my last letter. Fly to Tierra del Sueño and meet Hector. If I told you that he wrote and directed a number of feature films after leaving Hollywood in 1929—and that he is willing to screen them for you here at the ranch—perhaps that will entice you to come. Hector is almost ninety years old and in failing health. His will instructs me to destroy the films and the negatives of those films within twenty-four hours of his death, and I don't know how much longer he will last. Please contact me soon. Looking forward to your reply, I remain very truly yours, Frieda Spelling (Mrs. Hector Mann).*

Again, I didn't allow myself to get carried away. My response was concise, formal, perhaps even a bit rude, but before I committed myself to anything, I had to know that she could be trusted. *I want to believe you,* I wrote, *but I must have proof. If you expect me to go all the way to New Mexico, I need to know that your statements are credible and that Hector Mann is indeed alive. Once my doubts have been removed, I will go to the ranch. But I must warn you that I don't travel by plane. Sincerely yours, D. Z.*

There was no question that she would be back in touch—unless I had scared her off. If I had done that, then she would be tacitly admitting that she had deceived me, and the story would be over. I didn't think that was the case, but whatever she was or wasn't up to, it wasn't going to take long for me to find out the truth. The tone of her second letter had been urgent, almost imploring, and if in fact she was who she said she was, she wasn't going to waste any time before writing to me again. Silence would mean that I had called her bluff, but if she answered—and I was fully expecting her to answer—the letter would come quickly. It had taken nine days for the last one to reach me. All things being equal (no delays, no bungles by the post office), I figured the next one would come even faster than that.

I did my best to stay calm, to stick to my routine and forge ahead with the *Memoirs*, but it was no use. I was too distracted, too keyed up to give them the proper attention, and after struggling to meet my quotas for several days in a row, I finally declared a moratorium on the project. Bright and early the next morning, I crawled into the closet in the spare bedroom and pulled out my old research files on Hector, which I had packed away in cardboard boxes after finishing the book. There were six cartons in all. Five of them held the notes, outlines, and drafts of my own manuscript, but the other one was crammed with all sorts of precious material: clippings, photos, microfilmed documents, xeroxed articles, squibs from ancient gossip columns, every scrap of print I had been able to lay my fingers on that referred to Hector Mann. I hadn't looked at those papers in a long time, and with nothing to do now but wait for Frieda Spelling to contact me again, I carried the box into my study and spent the rest of the week combing through it. I don't think I was expecting to learn anything I didn't already know, but the contents of the file had become rather dim to me by then, and I felt that it deserved another look. Most of the information I had collected was unreliable: articles from the tabloid press, junk from the fan magazines, bits of movie reportage rife with hyperbole, erroneous suppositions, and out-and-out falsehoods. Still, as long as I remembered not to believe what I read, I didn't see how the exercise could do any harm.

Hector was the subject of four profiles written between August 1927 and October 1928. The first one appeared in Kaleidoscope's monthly *Bulletin*, the publicity organ of Hunt's newly formed production company. It was essentially a press release to announce the contract they had signed with Hector, and because little was known about him at that point, they were free to invent any story that served their purposes. Those were the last days of the Hollywood Latin Lover, the period just after Valentino's death when dark, exotic foreigners were still drawing large crowds, and Kaleidoscope tried to cash in on the phenomenon by billing Hector as *Señor Slapstick, the South American heart-throb with the comic touch.* To back up this assertion, they fabricated an intriguing list of credits for him, an entire career that supposedly predated his arrival in California: music hall appearances in Buenos Aires, extended vaudeville tours through Argentina and Brazil, a series of smash-hit films produced in Mexico. By presenting Hector as an already established star, Hunt could create a reputation for himself as a man with an eye for talent. He wasn't just a newcomer to the business, he was a clever and enterprising studio boss who had outbid his competitors for the right to import a well-known foreign entertainer and turn him loose on the American public. It was an easy lie to get away with. No one was paying attention to what happened in other countries, after all, and with so many imaginative possibilities to choose from, why be hemmed in by the facts?

Six months later, an article in the February issue of *Photoplay* presented a more sober view of Hector's past. Several of his films had been released by then, and with interest in his work growing around the country, the need to distort his earlier life had no doubt diminished. The story was written by a staff reporter named Brigid O'Fallon, and from her comments in the first paragraph about Hector's *piercing gaze* and *lithe muscularity,* one immediately understands that her only intention is to say flattering things about him. Charmed by his heavy Spanish accent, and yet praising him for the fluency of his English, she asks him why he has a German name. *Ees very simple,* Hector answers. *My parents was born in Germany, and so too*

I. We all emigrate to Argentina when I was a leetle baby. I speak the German with them at home, the Spanish at school. English come later, after I go to America. Steel not so hot. Miss O'Fallon then asks him how long he has been here, and Hector says three years. That, of course, contradicts the information published in the Kaleidoscope *Bulletin,* and when Hector goes on to discuss some of the jobs he held after arriving in California (busboy, vacuum cleaner salesman, ditchdigger), he makes no mention of any previous work in show business. So much for the glorious Latin American career that had turned him into a household name.

It's not hard to dismiss the exaggerations of Hunt's publicity department, but just because they ignored the truth doesn't mean that the *Photoplay* story was any more accurate or believable. In the March issue of the *Picturegoer,* a journalist named Randall Simms writes of visiting Hector on the set of *Tango Tangle* and being altogether astonished to find that *this Argentinian laugh machine speaks flawless English, with scarcely the trace of an accent. If you didn't know where he was from, you would swear that he had been raised in Sandusky, Ohio.* Simms means it as a compliment, but his observation raises disturbing questions about Hector's origins. Even if one accepts Argentina as the place where he spent his childhood, he seems to have left for America much earlier than the other articles suggest. In the next paragraph, Simms reports Hector as saying: *I was a very bad boy. My parents threw me out of the house when I was sixteen, and I never looked back. Eventually, I made my way north and landed in America. Right from the start, I had only one thought in mind: to hit it big in pictures.* The man who speaks those words bears no resemblance to the man who spoke to Brigid O'Fallon one month earlier. Had he put on the heavy accent for *Photoplay* as a gag, or was Simms intentionally mangling the truth, emphasizing Hector's proficiency in English as a way to convince producers of his potential as a sound actor in the months and years ahead? Perhaps the two of them had conspired on the article together, or perhaps a third party had paid Simms off—possibly Hunt, who by then was in deep financial trouble. Could it be that Hunt was trying to increase Hector's market value in order to sell off his services to another production company? It is impossible to know, but whatever Simms's motives were, and however badly O'Fallon might have transcribed Hector's statements, the articles cannot be reconciled, no matter how many excuses one makes for the journalists.

Hector's last published interview appeared in the October issue of *Picture Play*. On the strength of what he said to B. T. Barker—or at least what Barker would have us believe he said—it seems likely that our boy had a hand in creating this confusion himself. This time, his parents are from the city of Stanislav on the eastern edge of the Austro-Hungarian Empire, and Hector's first language is Polish, not German. They leave for Vienna when he is two, stay there for six months, and then go to America, where they spend three years in New York and one year in the Midwest before pulling up stakes again and resettling in Buenos Aires. Barker interrupts to ask where they lived in the Midwest, and Hector calmly replies: Sandusky, Ohio. Just six months earlier, Randall Simms had mentioned Sandusky in his article for the *Picturegoer*—not as a real place but as a metaphor, as a representative American town. Now Hector appropriates that town and puts it in his story, perhaps for no other reason than that he is attracted to the gruff and lilting music of the words. *San-dus-ky, O-hi-o,* has a pleasant sonority to it, and the smart, triple syncopations scan with all the power and precision of a well-turned poetical phrase. His father, he says, was a civil engineer who specialized in the building of bridges. His mother, *the most beautiful woman on earth,* was a dancer, singer, and painter. Hector adored them both, was a well-behaved religious little boy (as opposed to the bad boy of Simms's piece), and until their tragic deaths in a boating accident when he was fourteen, he was planning to follow in his father's footsteps and become an engineer. The sudden loss of his parents changed all that. From the moment he became an orphan, he says, his only dream was to return to America and begin a new life there. It took a long string of miracles before that could happen, but now that he is back, he feels certain that this is the place where he was always meant to be.

Some of these statements could have been true, but not many of them, perhaps not a single one. This is the fourth version he has given of his past, and while they all have certain elements in common (German- or Polish-speaking parents, time spent in Argentina, emigration from the old world to the new), everything else is subject to change. He's hard-nosed and practical in one account; he's cowering and sentimental in the next. He's a troublemaker for one journalist, obedient and pious for another; he grew up rich, he grew up poor; he speaks with a heavy accent, he speaks with no accent at all. Put these contradictions together, and you wind up with nothing, the portrait of a man with so many personalities and family histories that he is reduced to a pile of fragments, a jigsaw puzzle whose pieces no longer connect. Every time he is asked a question, he gives a different answer. Words pour out of him, but he is determined never to say the same thing twice. He appears to be hiding something, to be protecting a secret, and yet he goes about his obfuscations with such grace and sparkling good humor that no one seems to notice. The journalists can't resist him. He makes them laugh, he amuses them with little magic tricks, and after a while they stop pressing him about the facts and give in to the power of the performance. Hector goes on winging it, careening madly from the cobbled boulevards of Vienna to the euphonious flatlands of Ohio, and eventually you begin to ask yourself if this is a game of deception or merely a blundering attempt to fight off boredom. Maybe his lies are innocent. Maybe he isn't trying to fool anyone so much as looking for a way to entertain himself. Interviews can be a dull procedure, after all. If everyone keeps asking you the same questions, maybe you have to come up with new answers just to stay awake.

Nothing was certain, but after sifting through this jumble of fraudulent memories and spurious anecdotes, I felt that I had discovered one minor fact. In the first three interviews, Hector avoids mentioning where he was born. When asked by O'Fallon, he says Germany; when asked by Simms, he says Austria; but in neither instance does he provide any details: no town, no city, no region. It is only when he talks to Barker that he opens up a bit and fills in the blanks. Stanislav had once been part of Austro-Hungary, but after the breakup of the empire at the end of the war, it had been handed over to Poland. Poland is a remote country to Americans, far more remote than Germany, and with Hector doing everything he could to downplay his foreignness, it was an odd admission for him to have named that city as his birthplace. The only possible reason for him to have done that, it seemed to me, was because it was true. I couldn't confirm this suspicion, but it makes no sense for him to have lied about it. Poland didn't help his case, and if he was intent on manufacturing a false background for himself, why bother to mention it at all? It was a mistake, a momentary lapse of attention, and no sooner does Barker hear this slip of the tongue than Hector tries to undo the damage. If he has just made himself too foreign, now he will counteract the error by insisting on his American credentials. He puts himself in New York, the city of immigrants, and then hammers home the point by traveling to the heartland. That's where Sandusky, Ohio, comes into the picture. He plucks the name out of thin air, remembering it from the profile that was written about him six months earlier, and then springs it on the unsuspecting B. T. Barker. It serves his purpose well. The journalist is sidetracked, and instead of asking more questions about Poland, he leans back in his chair and begins reminiscing with Hector about the alfalfa fields of the Midwest.

Stanislav is located just south of the Dniestr River, halfway between Lvov and Czernowitz in the province of Galicia. If that was the terrain of Hector's childhood, then there was every reason to suppose that he was born a Jew. The fact that the area was thick with Jewish settlements was not enough to persuade me, but combine the Jewish population with the fact that his family left the area, and the argument becomes quite convincing. The Jews were the ones who left that part of the world, and beginning with the Russian pogroms in the 1880s, hundreds of thousands of Yiddish-speaking immigrants fanned out across western Europe and the United States. Many of them went to South America as well. In Argentina alone, the Jewish population increased from six thousand to more than one hundred thousand between the turn of the century and the outbreak of World War I. No doubt Hector and his family helped add to those statistics. If they hadn't, then it was scarcely possible for them to have landed in Argentina. At that moment in history, the only people who traveled from Stanislav to Buenos Aires were Jews.

I was proud of my little discovery, but that didn't mean I thought it amounted to much. If Hector was indeed hiding something, and if that something turned out to be the religion he had been born into, then all I had uncovered was the most pedestrian kind of social hypocrisy. It wasn't a crime to be a Jew in Hollywood back then. It was merely something that one chose not to talk about. Jolson had already made *The Jazz Singer* at that point, and Broadway theaters were filled with audiences who paid good money to see Eddie Cantor and Fanny Brice, to listen to Irving Berlin and the Gershwins, to applaud the Marx Brothers. Being Jewish might have been a burden to Hector. He might have suffered from it, and he might have been ashamed of it, but it was difficult for me to imagine that he had been killed for it. There's always a bigot around somewhere with enough hatred in him to murder a Jew, of course, but a person who does that wants his crime to be known, to make use of it as an example to frighten others, and whatever Hector's fate might have been, the one certain fact was that his body was never found.

From the day he signed with Kaleidoscope to the day he disappeared, Hector's run lasted only seventeen months. Short as that time might have been, he achieved a certain measure of recognition for himself, and by early 1928 his name was already beginning to crop up in the Hollywood social columns. I had managed to recover about twenty of those pieces from various microfilm archives during the course of my travels. There must have been many others that I missed, not to speak of others that had been destroyed, but scant and insufficient as those mentions were, they proved that Hector was not someone who tended to sit around at home after dark. He was seen in restaurants and nightclubs, at parties and movie premieres, and nearly every time his name appeared in print, it was accompanied by a descriptive phrase that referred to his *smoldering magnetism*, his *irresistible eyes*, or his *heart-stoppingly handsome face*. This was especially true when the writer was a woman, but there were men who succumbed to his charms as well. One of them, who worked under the name Gordon Fly (the title of his column was *Fly on the Wall*), went so far as to offer the opinion that Hector was wasting his talents in comedy and should switch to drama. *With that profile*, Fly wrote, *it offends one's sense of aesthetic proportion to watch the elegant Señor Mann put his nose at risk by repeatedly bumping into walls and lampposts. The public would be better served if he dropped these stunts and concentrated on kissing beautiful women. Surely there are many young actresses in town who would be willing to take on that role. Sources tell me that Irene Flowers has already had several auditions, but it appears that the dashing hidalgo now has his eye on Constance Hart, the ever-popular Vim and Vigor Girl herself. We eagerly await the results of that screen test.*

Most of the time, however, Hector received no more than a glancing nod from the journalists. He wasn't much of a story yet, nothing more than one promising newcomer among others, and in fully half the columns I had on hand he appears only as a name—usually in the company of a woman, herself only a name as well. Hector Mann was spotted at the Feathered Nest with Sylvia Noonan. Hector Mann stepped out onto the dance floor of the Gibraltar Club last night with Mildred Swain. Hector

Mann shared a laugh with Alice Dwyer, ate oysters with Polly McCracken, held hands with Dolores Saint John, slipped into a gin joint with Fiona Maar. In all, I counted the names of eight different women, but who knows how many others he went out with that year? My information was limited to the articles I had managed to find, and those eight easily could have been twenty, perhaps even more.

When the news of Hector's disappearance broke the following January, little attention was paid to his love life. Seymour Hunt had hanged himself in his bedroom just three days earlier, and instead of trying to dig up evidence of some soured romance or secret affair, the police concentrated their efforts on Hector's troubled relations with the corrupt Cincinnati banker. It was probably too tempting not to make a connection between the two scandals. After Hunt's arrest, Hector had been quoted as saying that he was relieved to know that Americans still had a sense of justice. The anonymous source, described as one of Hector's close personal friends, reported that he had announced within earshot of half a dozen people: *The man is a scoundrel. He cheated me out of thousands of dollars and tried to ruin my career. I'm glad they're locking him up. He's getting what he deserves, and I feel no pity for him.* Rumors began circulating in the press that Hector had been the one who fingered Hunt to the authorities. Advocates of this theory claimed that now that Hunt was dead, his associates had eliminated Hector in order to prevent more revelations from leaking to the public. Some versions went so far as to suggest that Hunt's death had not been a suicide but a murder arranged to look like a suicide—the first step in an elaborate conspiracy by his underworld friends to rub out the traces of their crimes.

It was the gangland reading of events. That must have felt

like a plausible approach in 1920s America, but without a body to back up the hypothesis, the police investigation began to founder. The press played along for the first couple of weeks, running stories about Hunt's business practices and the rise of the criminal element in the motion picture industry, but when no definite connection could be established between Hector's disappearance and the death of his former producer, they began looking for other motives and explanations. Everyone had been tantalized by the proximity of the two events, but it was logically unsound to assume that the one had caused the other. Contiguous facts are not necessarily related facts, even though their nearness to one another would seem to suggest they are linked. Now, as other lines of inquiry began to be pursued, it turned out that many of the trails had already gone cold. Dolores Saint John, named in several of the early articles as Hector's fiancée, quietly skipped town and returned to her parents' house in Kansas. Another month went by before the journalists could find her, and when they did, she refused to talk to them, claiming that she was still too distraught over Hector's disappearance to issue a full statement. Her only comment was *My heart is broken,* and after that she was never heard from again. A fetching young actress who had appeared in half a dozen movies (among them *The Prop Man* and *Mr. Nobody,* in which she had played the sheriff's daughter and Hector's wife), she impulsively abandoned her career and vanished from the world of show business.

Jules Blaustein, the gagman who had worked with Hector on all twelve Kaleidoscope films, told a *Variety* reporter that he and Hector had been collaborating on a series of scripts for sound comedies and that his writing partner had been in *excellent spirits.* He had seen him every day since mid-December, and unlike everyone else who was interviewed about Hector, he continued to talk about him in the present tense. *It's true that things ended rather unpleasantly with Hunt,* Blaustein admitted, *but Hector wasn't the only one who got a bad shake at Kaleidoscope. We all took our knocks there, and even if he got the worst of it, he isn't someone to bear grudges. He has his whole future to look forward to, and the moment his contract with Kaleidoscope was up, he turned his mind to other things. He's been working hard with me, as hard as I've ever seen him work, and his brain has been on fire with new ideas. When he dropped out of sight, our first script was nearly finished—a side-splitter called* Dot and Dash*—and we were about to sign a contract with Harry Cohn at Columbia. Shooting was supposed to begin in March. Hector was going to direct and play a small but hilarious silent role in it, and if that sounds like someone who was planning to kill himself, then you don't know the first thing about Hector. It's absurd to think he would take his own life. Maybe someone took it for him, but that would mean he has enemies, and in all the time I've known him, I've never seen him rub a person the wrong way. The man is a prince, and I love working with him. We can sit here all day musing about what happened, but even money says he's alive somewhere, that he got one of his nutty inspirations in the middle of the night and just took off to be alone for a little while. Everyone keeps saying he's dead, but it wouldn't surprise me if Hector walked through that door right now, tossed his hat on the chair, and said, "Okay, Jules, let's get to work."*

Columbia confirmed that they had been negotiating with Hector and Blaustein on a three-picture contract that included *Dot and Dash* as well as two other feature comedies. Nothing had been signed yet, their spokesman said, but once the terms had been worked out to the satisfaction of both parties, the studio had been looking forward to *welcoming Hector into the family*. Blaustein's remarks, coupled with the statement from Columbia, shot down the idea that Hector's career had come to a dead end, which some of the tabloids had been pushing as a possible motive for suicide. But the facts showed that Hector's prospects had been far from bleak. The mess at Kaleidoscope had not *shattered his spirit*, as the *Los Angeles Record* announced on February 18, 1929, and since no letter or note had turned up to support the contention that Hector had taken his own life, the suicide theory began losing ground to a host of wild speculations and crackpot conjectures: kidnappings gone awry, freakish accidents, supernatural events. Meanwhile, the police were making no progress on the Hunt connection, and although they claimed to be *following up on several promising leads* (the *Los Angeles Daily News*, March 7, 1929), no new suspects were ever brought forward. If Hector had been murdered, there wasn't enough evidence to charge anyone with the crime. If he had killed himself, it wasn't for a reason that anyone could understand. A few cynics suggested that his disappearance was no more than a publicity stunt, a cheap ploy orchestrated by Harry Cohn at Columbia to bring attention to his new star, and that we could expect a miraculous reappearance any day now. That seemed to make a certain kind of cockeyed sense, but as the days passed and Hector still didn't return, that theory proved to be just as wrong as all the others. Everyone had an opinion about what had happened to Hector, but the fact was that no one knew a thing. And if someone did know, that person wasn't talking.

The case made headlines for about a month and a half, but then interest began to drop off. There were no new revelations to report, no new possibilities to examine, and eventually the press turned its attention to other matters. Late in the spring, the *Los Angeles Examiner* ran the first of several stories that appeared intermittently over the next couple of years in which Hector was supposed to have been seen by someone in an unlikely, far-flung place—the so-called Hector sightings—but these were little more than novelty items, small fillers buried at the bottom of the horoscope page, a kind of standing joke for Hollywood insiders. Hector in Utica, New York, working as a labor organizer. Hector on the pampas with his traveling circus. Hector on skid row. In March 1933, Randall Simms, the journalist who had interviewed Hector for the *Picturegoer* five years earlier, published an article in the *Herald-Express* Sunday supplement entitled *Whatever Happened to Hector Mann?* It promised new information about the case, but beyond hinting at a desperate and complicated love triangle that Hector might or might not have been involved in, it was essentially a rehash of the articles that had appeared in the Los Angeles papers in 1929. A similar piece, written by someone named Dabney Strayhorn, cropped up in a 1941 issue of *Collier's,* and a book from 1957 with the trashy title *Hollywood Scandals and Mysteries,* written by Frank C. Klebald, devoted one short chapter to Hector's disappearance, which on closer examination turned out to be an almost word-for-word crib of Strayhorn's magazine article. There might have been other articles and chapters written about Hector over the years, but I wasn't aware of them. I only had what was in the box, and what was in the box was all I had managed to find.

4

TWO WEEKS LATER, I still hadn't heard from Frieda Spelling. I had anticipated calls in the middle of the night, special-delivery letters, telegrams, faxes, desperate pleas to rush to Hector's bedside, but after fourteen days of silence, I stopped giving her the benefit of the doubt. My skepticism returned, and little by little I worked my way back to where I had been before. The box went into the closet again, and after moping around for another week or ten days, I picked up the Chateaubriand manuscript and started hacking away at it again. I had been sidetracked for nearly a month, but other than some residual feelings of disappointment and disgust, I managed to push the thought of Tierra del Sueño out of my mind. Hector was dead again. He had died in 1929, or else he had died the day before yesterday. It didn't matter which death was real. He no longer belonged to this world, and I was never going to have a chance to meet him.

I closed in on myself again. The weather swung back and forth, alternating between good stretches and bad. A day or two of sparkling light followed by furious storms; drenching downpours, then crystal blue skies; wind and no wind, warm and cold, mist dissolving into clarity. It was always five degrees cooler on my mountain than in the town below, but there were afternoons when I was able to walk around in nothing but shorts and a T-shirt. On other afternoons, I had to light a fire and bundle up in three sweaters. June turned into July. I had been working steadily for about ten days then, gradually settling into the old rhythm, digging in for what I thought would be the final push on the job. Just after the holiday weekend, I knocked off early one day and drove into Brattleboro to do my shopping. I spent about forty minutes at the Grand Union, and then, after loading the bags into the cab of the truck, decided to stick around for a while and take in a movie. It was just an impulse, a sudden whim that came over me as I stood in the parking lot, squinting and sweating in the late afternoon sun. My work was finished for the day, and there was no reason not to change my plans, no reason to rush back home if I didn't want to. I got to the Latchis Theatre on Main Street just as the coming attractions for the six o'clock show were about to begin. I bought a Coke and a bag of popcorn, found a seat in the middle of the last row, and sat through one of the *Back to the Future* movies. It turned out to be both ridiculous and enjoyable. After the film was over, I decided to prolong the outing by having dinner at the Korean restaurant across the street. I had eaten there once before, and judging by Vermont standards, the food wasn't half bad.

I had spent two hours sitting in the dark, and by the time I walked out of the theater, the weather had changed again. It was another one of those abrupt shifts: clouds rolling in, the temperature dropping down into the fifties, the wind starting to blow. After a day of intense and brilliant sun, there should have been some light left in the sky at that hour, but the sun had disappeared before dusk, and the long summer day had turned into a wet, chilly evening. It was already raining when I crossed the street and went into the restaurant, and as I sat down at one of the front tables and ordered my food, I watched the storm gathering force outside. A paper bag rose up from the ground and flew into the window of Sam's Army-Navy Store; an empty soda can went clattering down the street toward the river; bullets of rain pelted the sidewalk. I started off with a platter of kimchi, washing down every other bite with a swallow of beer. It was tangy stuff that burned the tongue, and when I moved on to the main course, I kept on dipping the meat into the hot sauce, which meant that I kept on drinking beer. I must have had three bottles in all, perhaps four, and by the time I paid the check, I was a little more juiced than I should have been. Sharp enough to walk a white line, I think, sharp enough to think lucid thoughts about my translation, but probably not sharp enough to drive.

Still, I'm not going to blame the beer for what happened. My reflexes might have been a bit sluggish, but there were other elements involved as well, and I doubt that the result would have been any different if beer had been removed from the equation. The rain was still pounding down when I left the restaurant, and after running several hundred yards to the municipal parking lot, I was soaked through to the skin. It didn't help that I fumbled with the keys as I tried to get them out of my wet pants, and it helped even less that once I caught hold of them and managed to pull them out, I immediately dropped them into a puddle. That meant more lost time as I crouched down to search for them in the darkness, and when I finally stood up and climbed into my truck, I was as wet as someone who had taken a shower with his clothes on. Blame the beer, but also blame those wet clothes and the water dripping into my eyes. Again and again, I had to take one hand off the wheel to wipe my forehead, and when you add that distraction to the inconvenience of a bad defrost system (which meant that when I wasn't wiping my forehead, I was using that same hand to wipe off the fogged-up windshield) and then compound the problem by throwing in defective windshield wipers (when are they not defective?), the conditions that night were hardly ones to guarantee a safe ride home.

The irony was that I was aware of all this. Shivering in my wet clothes, eager to get back and change into something warm, I nevertheless made a conscious effort to drive as slowly as I could. That's what saved me, I suppose, but at the same time it also could have been what caused the accident. If I had been driving faster, I probably would have been more alert, more attuned to the vagaries of the road, but after a while my mind began to wander, and eventually I fell into one of those long, pointless meditations that only seem to occur when you're driving alone in a car. In this case, if I remember correctly, it had to do with quantifying the ephemeral acts of daily life. How much time had I spent in the past forty years lacing up my shoes? How many doors had I opened and closed? How often had I sneezed? How many hours had I lost looking for objects I couldn't find? How many times had I stubbed my toe or banged my head or blinked away something that had crept into my eye? I found it to be a rather pleasant exercise, and I kept adding to the list as I sloshed my way through the darkness. About twenty miles out of Brattleboro, on an open stretch of road between the towns of T—— and West T——, just three miles before the turnoff that would take me up the dirt road to my house, I saw the eyes of an animal gleaming in the headlights. An instant later, I saw that it was a dog. He was twenty or thirty yards ahead, a wet and ragged creature blundering through the night, and contrary to what most dogs do when they're lost, he wasn't traveling on the side of the road but trotting down the center of it—or just to the left of center, which put him smack in the middle of my lane. I swerved to avoid hitting him, and at the same moment I put my foot on the brake. I probably shouldn't have done that, but I had already done it before I could tell myself not to, and because the surface of the road was wet and oily from the rain, the tires didn't hold. I skidded across the yellow line, and before I could swing back the other way, the truck rammed into a utility pole.

I had my seat belt on, but the jolt knocked my left arm against the wheel, and with all the groceries suddenly flying out of their bags, a can of tomato juice sprang up and struck me on the chin. My face hurt like hell, and my forearm was throbbing, but I could still flex my hand, could still open and close my mouth, and I concluded that no bones had been broken. I should have felt relieved, lucky to have escaped without any serious injuries, but I was in no mood to count my blessings and speculate on how much worse it could have been. This was bad enough, and I was furious with myself for having banged up the truck. One headlight was knocked out; the fender was crumpled; the front end was smashed in. The engine was still running, though, but when I tried to back out and drive away, I discovered that the front tires were half submerged in mud. It took me twenty minutes of shoving in the glop and rain to get the thing unstuck, and by then I was too wet and exhausted to bother cleaning up the groceries that had been tossed around the inside of the cab. I just sat down behind the wheel, backed up into the road, and took off. As I later found out, I finished the drive home with a package of frozen peas wedged into the small of my back.

It was already past eleven o'clock when I pulled up in front of my house. I was shivering in my clothes, my jaw and arm were aching, and I was in a foul temper. Expect the unexpected, they say, but once the unexpected happens, the last thing you expect is that it will happen again. My guard was down, and because I was still brooding about the dog and the utility pole, still going over the details of the accident as I climbed out of the truck, I didn't notice the car that was parked to the left of the house. My headlight hadn't swept over in that direction, and when I cut the motor and turned off the light, everything went dark around me. The rain had slackened by then, but it was still drizzling, and there were no lights on in the house. Thinking that I would be back before the sun went down, I hadn't bothered to turn on the light above the front door. The sky was black. The ground was black. I groped my way to the house by memory and feel, but I couldn't see a thing.

It was common practice in southern Vermont to leave your house unlocked, but I didn't do that. I dead-bolted the door every time I went out. It was a stubborn ritual that I refused to break, even if I was going to be gone for only five minutes. Now, as I fumbled with my keys for the second time that night, I understood how stupid these precautions were. I had effectively locked myself out of my own house. The keys were already in my hand, but there were six of them on the chain, and I had no idea which was the right one. I blindly patted the door, trying to locate the lock. Once I had found it, I chose one of the keys at random and maneuvered it into the hole. It went halfway in, and then it got stuck. I would have to try another one, but before I did that, I would have to pull the first one out. That took a good deal more wiggling than I had anticipated. At the last moment, just as I was unjamming the final notch from the hole, the key gave a little jerk, and the key chain slithered out of my hand. It clattered against the wooden steps, then bounced God knows where into the night. And so the journey ended in the same way it had begun: crawling on all fours and cursing under my breath, searching for a set of invisible keys.

I couldn't have been at it for more than two or three seconds when a light went on in the yard. I glanced up, instinctively turning my head toward the light, and before I had a chance to be afraid, before I could even register what was happening, I saw that a car was sitting there—a car that had no business being on my property—and that a woman was getting out of it. She opened a large red umbrella, slammed the door shut behind her, and the light went out. Do you need some help? she said. I scrambled to my feet, and at that instant another light went on. The woman was pointing a flashlight at my face.

Who the fuck are you? I asked.

You don't know me, she answered, but you know the person who sent me.

That's not good enough. Tell me who you are, or I'll call the cops.

My name is Alma Grund. I've been waiting here for over five hours, Mr. Zimmer, and I need to talk to you.

And who's the person who sent you?

Frieda Spelling. Hector's in bad shape. She wants you to know that, and she wanted me to tell you that there isn't much time.

We found the keys with her flashlight, and when I opened the door and stepped into the house, I flicked on the lights in the living room. Alma Grund came in after me—a short woman in her mid- to late thirties, dressed in a blue silk blouse and tailored gray pants. Medium-length brown hair, high heels, crimson lipstick, and a large leather purse slung over her shoulder. When she walked into the light, I saw that there was a birthmark on the left side of her face. It was a purple stain about the size of a man's fist, long enough and broad enough to resemble the map of some imaginary country: a solid mass of discoloration that covered more than half her cheek, starting at the corner of her eye and running down to her jaw. Her hair was cut in such a way as to obscure most of it, and she held her head at an awkward tilt to prevent the hair from moving. It was an ingrained gesture, I supposed, a habit acquired after a lifetime of self-consciousness, and it gave her an air of clumsiness and vulnerability, the demeanor of a shy girl who preferred looking down at the carpet to meeting you in the eye.

On any other night, I probably would have been willing to talk to her—but not that night. I was too annoyed, too put out by what had already happened, and the only thing I wanted was to peel off my wet clothes, take a hot bath, and go to bed. I had shut the door behind me after turning on the living room lights. Now I opened it again and politely asked her to leave.

Just give me five minutes, she said. I can explain everything.

I don't like it when people trespass on my property, I said, and I don't like it when people jump out at me in the middle of the night. You don't want me to have to throw you out of here, do you?

She looked up at me then, surprised by my vehemence, frightened by the undertow of rage in my voice. I thought you wanted to see Hector, she said, and as she spoke those words she took a few more steps into the house, removing herself from the vicinity of the door in case I was planning to carry out my threat. When she turned around and faced me again, I could see only her right side. She looked different from that angle, and I saw that she had a delicate, roundish face, with very smooth skin. Not unattractive, finally; perhaps almost pretty. Her eyes were dark blue, and there was a quick, nervous intelligence in them that reminded me a little of Helen.

I'm not interested in what Frieda Spelling has to say anymore, I said. She kept me waiting for too long, and I had to work too hard to get over it. I'm not going to go there again. Too much hope. Too much disappointment. I don't have the stamina for it. As far as I'm concerned, the story is over.

Before she could answer me, I finished off my little harangue with an aggressive parting shot. I'm going to take a bath, I said. When I'm done with the bath, I expect you to be gone from here. Please be good enough to close the door on your way out.

I turned my back on her and started walking toward the stairs, determined to ignore her now and wash my hands of the whole business. Halfway up the steps, I heard her say: You wrote such a brilliant book, Mr. Zimmer. You have the right to know the real story, and I need your help. If you don't hear me out, terrible things are going to happen. Just listen to me for five minutes. That's all I ask.

She was presenting her case in the most melodramatic terms possible, but I wasn't going to let it affect me. When I reached the top of the stairs, I turned around and spoke to her from the loggia. I'm not going to give you five seconds, I said. If you want to talk to me, call me tomorrow. Better yet, write me a letter. I'm not so good on the phone. And then, not bothering to wait for her reaction, I slipped into the bathroom and locked the door behind me.

I lingered in the tub for fifteen or twenty minutes. Add on

another three or four minutes to dry myself off, two more minutes to examine my chin in the mirror, and then another six or seven to put on a fresh set of clothes, and I must have stayed upstairs for close to half an hour. I wasn't in any rush. I knew that she would still be there when I went downstairs again, and I was still in an ugly humor, still seething with pent-up belligerence and animosity. I wasn't afraid of Alma Grund, but my own anger frightened me, and I had no idea what was in me anymore. There had been that outburst at the Tellefsons' party the previous spring, but I had kept myself hidden since then, and I had lost the habit of talking to strangers. The only person I knew how to be with now was myself—but I wasn't really anyone, and I wasn't really alive. I was just someone who pretended to be alive, a dead man who spent his days translating a dead man's book.

She began with a stream of apologies, looking up at me from the ground floor as I stepped out onto the loggia, asking me to forgive her for her bad manners and explaining how sorry she was to have barged in on me without warning. She wasn't someone who lurked around people's houses at night, she said, and she hadn't meant to scare me. When she knocked on my door at six o'clock, the sun had been shining. She had mistakenly assumed that I would be at home, and if she wound up waiting in the yard for all those hours, it was only because she thought I would be returning at any moment.

As I descended the stairs and made my way into the living room, I saw that she had brushed her hair and put on a new coat of lipstick. She looked more pulled together now—less dowdy, less unsure of herself—and even as I walked toward her and asked her to sit down, I sensed that she wasn't quite as weak or intimidated as I had thought she was.

I'm not going to listen to you until you've answered some questions, I said. If I'm satisfied with what you tell me, I'll give you a chance to talk. If not, I'm going to ask you to leave, and I never want to see you again. Understood?

Do you want long answers or short answers?

Short answers. As short as possible.

Just tell me where to begin, and I'll do my best.

The first thing I want to know is why Frieda Spelling didn't write back to me.

She got your second letter, but just when she sat down to answer you, something happened that prevented her from continuing.

For a whole month?

Hector fell down the stairs. In one part of the house, Frieda was sitting at her desk with a pen in her hand, and in another part of the house Hector was walking toward the stairs. It was eerie how close together those two events were. Frieda wrote three words—*Dear Professor Zimmer*—and at that moment Hector tripped and fell. His leg was broken in two places. Some ribs were cracked. There was a nasty bump on the side of his head. A helicopter came to the ranch, and he was flown to a hospital in Albuquerque. During the operation to set his leg, he suffered a heart attack. They transferred him to the cardiac unit, and then, just when it looked like he was recovering, he came down with pneumonia. It was touch and go for a couple of weeks. Three or four times, we thought we were going to lose him. It just wasn't possible to write, Mr. Zimmer. Too much was happening, and Frieda couldn't think about anything else.

Is he still in the hospital?

He came home yesterday. I took the first plane out this

morning, landed in Boston at around two-thirty, and drove up here in a rented car. It's faster than writing a letter, isn't it? One day instead of three or four, maybe even five. In five days, Hector could be dead.

Why didn't you just pick up the phone and call me?

I didn't want to risk it. It would have been too easy for you to hang up on me.

And why should you care? That's my next question. Who are you, and why are you involved in this?

I've known them all my life. They're very close to me.

You're not telling me you're their daughter, are you?

I'm Charlie Grund's daughter. You might not remember the name, but I'm sure you've come across it. You've probably seen it dozens of times.

The cameraman.

That's right. He shot all of Hector's films at Kaleidoscope. When Hector and Frieda decided to start making movies again, he left California and went to live at the ranch. That was in 1940. He married my mother in 1946. I was born there, I grew up there. It's an important place to me, Mr. Zimmer. Everything I am comes from that place.

And you never left?

I went to boarding school at fifteen. Then to college. After that, I lived in cities. New York, London, Los Angeles. I've been married and divorced, I've worked at jobs, I've done things.

But you live at the ranch now.

I moved back about seven years ago. My mother died, and I went home for the funeral. After that, I decided to stay on. Charlie died a couple of years later, but I'm still there.

Doing what?

Writing Hector's biography. It's taken me six and a half years, but I'm close to finishing now.

Little by little, it begins to make sense.

Of course it makes sense. I wouldn't have come twenty-four hundred miles to hold things back from you, would I?

That's the next question. Why me? Of all the people in the world, why did you choose me?

Because I need a witness. I talk about things in the book that no one else has seen, and my statements won't be credible unless I have another person to back me up.

But that person doesn't have to be me. It could be anyone. In your cautious, roundabout way, you've just told me that those late films exist. If there's more work of Hector's to be seen, you should contact a film scholar and ask him to look at them. You need an authority to vouch for you, someone with a reputation in the field. I'm just an amateur.

You might not be a professional movie critic, but you're an expert on the comedies of Hector Mann. You wrote an extraordinary book, Mr. Zimmer. No one is ever going to write better about those films. It's the definitive work.

Until that moment, she had given me her complete attention. Pacing back and forth in front of her as she sat on the sofa, I had felt like a prosecuting attorney cross-examining a witness. I had held the advantage, and she had looked me straight in the eye as she answered my questions. Now, suddenly, she glanced down at her watch and began to fidget, and I sensed that the mood had been broken.

It's late, she said.

I misread her comment to mean that she was getting tired. That struck me as ridiculous, an altogether absurd thing to say under the circumstances. You're the one who started this, I said. You're not going to bag out on me now, are you? We're just warming up.

It's one-thirty. The plane takes off from Boston at seven-fifteen. If we leave within an hour, we'll probably make it.

What are you talking about?

You don't think I came to Vermont just to chat, do you? I'm taking you back to New Mexico with me. I thought you understood that.

You've got to be kidding.

It's a long trip. If you have more questions to ask, I'll be happy to answer them on the way. By the time we get there, you'll know everything I know. I promise.

You're too smart to think I'd be willing to do that. Not now. Not in the middle of the night.

You have to. Twenty-four hours after Hector dies, those films are going to be destroyed. And he could be dead now. He could have died while I was traveling out here today. Don't you get it, Mr. Zimmer? If we don't leave now, there might not be enough time.

You're forgetting what I told Frieda in my last letter. I don't do planes. They're against my religion.

Without saying a word, Alma Grund reached into her purse and pulled out a small white paper bag. It was marked with a blue and green insignia, and underneath the picture there were a few lines of writing. From where I was standing, I could make out only one word, but that was the only word I needed to know in order to guess what was inside the bag. *Pharmacy*.

I haven't forgotten, she said. I brought along some Xanax to make things easier for you. That's the one you like to use, isn't it?

How do you know about that?

You wrote a magnificent book, but that didn't mean we

could trust you. I had to dig around a little and check you out. I made some calls, I wrote some letters, I read your other work. I know what you've been through, and I'm very sorry—very sorry about what happened to your wife and sons. It must have been horrible for you.

You had no right. It's disgusting to pry into someone's life like that. You crash in here asking for my help, and then you turn around and tell me this? Why should I help you? You make me want to puke.

Frieda and Hector wouldn't have allowed me to invite you unless they knew who you were. I had to do it for them.

I don't accept that. I don't accept a fucking word you're saying.

We're on the same side, Mr. Zimmer. We shouldn't be shouting at each other. We should be working together as friends.

I'm not your friend. I'm not anything to you. You're a phantom who wandered in from the night, and now I want you to go back out there and leave me alone.

I can't do that. I have to take you with me, and we have to go now. Please, don't make me threaten you. It's such a stupid way to handle it.

I had no idea what she was talking about. I was eight inches taller than she was and at least fifty pounds heavier—a good-sized man on the verge of losing his temper, an unknown quantity who could burst into violence at any moment—and there she was talking to me about threats. I stayed where I was, watching her from my position near the woodstove. We were ten or twelve feet apart, and just as she stood up from the sofa, a fresh onslaught of rain came crashing down on the roof, rattling against the shingles like a bombardment of stones. She jumped at the sound, glancing around the room with a skittish, perplexed look in her eyes, and at that moment I knew what was going to happen next. I can't explain where this knowledge came from, but whatever premonition or extrasensory alertness took hold of me when I saw that look in her eyes, I knew that she was carrying a gun in her purse, and I knew that within the next three or four seconds she was going to stick her right hand into the purse and pull out the gun.

It was one of the most sublimely exhilarating moments of my life. I was half a step in front of the real, an inch or two beyond the confines of my own body, and when the thing happened just as I thought it would, I felt as if my skin had become transparent. I wasn't occupying space anymore so much as melting into it. What was around me was also inside me, and I had only to look into myself in order to see the world.

The gun was in her hand. It was a small silver-plated revolver with a pearl handle, no more than half the size of the cap guns I had played with as a boy. As she turned in my direction and lifted her arm, I could see that the hand at the end of her arm was shaking.

This isn't me, she said. I don't do things like this. Ask me to put it away, and I will. But we have to go now.

It was the first time a gun had ever been pointed at me, and I marveled at how comfortable I felt, at how naturally I accepted the possibilities of the moment. One wrong move, one wrong word, and I could die for no reason at all. That thought should have frightened me. It should have made me want to run, but I felt no urge to do that, no inclination to stop what was happening. An immense and horrifying beauty had opened up before me, and all I wanted was to go on looking at it, to go on looking into the eyes of this woman with the strange double face as we stood in that room, listening to the rain pound on top of us like ten thousand drums scaring up the devils of the night.

Go ahead and shoot, I said. You'll be doing me a great service.

The words came out of my mouth before I knew I was going to say them. They sounded harsh and terrible to me, the kind of thing only a deranged person would say, but once I heard them, I realized that I had no intention of taking them back. I liked them. I was pleased with their bluntness and their candor, with their decisive, no-nonsense approach to the dilemma I was facing. For all the courage those words gave me, however, I'm still not sure what they meant. Was I in fact asking her to kill me, or was I looking for a way to talk her out of it and prevent myself from being killed? Did I really want her to pull the trigger, or was I trying to force her hand and trick her into dropping the gun? I've gone over these questions many times in the past eleven years, but I've never been able to come up with a conclusive answer. All I know is that I wasn't afraid. When Alma Grund pulled out that revolver and pointed it at my chest, it didn't strike fear in me so much as fascination. I understood that the bullets in that gun contained a thought that had never occurred to me before. The world was full of holes, tiny apertures of meaninglessness, microscopic rifts that the mind could walk through, and once you were on the other side of one of those holes, you were free of yourself, free of your life, free of your death, free of everything that belonged to you. I had chanced upon one of them in my living room that night. It appeared in the form of a gun, and now that I was inside that gun, I didn't care whether I got out or not. I was perfectly calm and perfectly insane, perfectly prepared to accept what the moment had offered. Indifference of that magnitude is rare, and because it can be achieved only by someone ready to let go of who he is, it demands respect. It inspires awe in those who gaze upon it.

I can remember everything up to that point, everything up to the moment when I spoke those words and a little bit beyond, but after that the sequence becomes rather murky to me. I know that I shouted at her, pounding on my chest and daring her to pull the trigger, but whether I did that before she started to cry or after is not something I can remember. Nor can I remember anything she said. That must mean that I did most of the talking, but the words were rushing out of me so fast by then that I scarcely knew what I was saying. What matters most is that she was frightened. She hadn't expected me to turn the tables on her, and when I glanced up from the gun and looked into her eyes again, I knew that she didn't have the nerve to kill me. She was all bluff and childish desperation, and the moment I started walking toward her, she immediately dropped her arm to her side. A mysterious sound escaped from her throat—a muffled, choked-off stream of breath, an unidentifiable noise that fell somewhere between a moan and a sob—and as I continued to attack her with my taunts and badgering insults, shouting at her to hurry up and get it over with, I knew—and knew absolutely, knew beyond any shadow of a doubt—that the gun wasn't loaded. Again, I don't claim to know where this certainty came from, but the instant I saw her lower her arm, I knew that nothing was going to happen to me, and I wanted to punish her for that, to make her pay for pretending to be something she was not.

I'm talking about a matter of seconds, an entire lifetime reduced to a matter of seconds. I took a step, and then another step, and suddenly I was upon her, twisting her arm and tearing the gun out of her hand. She was no longer the angel of death, but I knew what death tasted like now, and in the madness of the seconds that followed, I did what was surely the wildest, most outlandish thing I have ever done. Just to prove a point. Just to show her that I was stronger than she was. I took the gun from her, backed off a few feet, and then pointed it at my head. There were no bullets in it, of course, but she didn't know that I knew that, and I wanted to use my knowledge to humiliate her, to present her with a picture of a man who wasn't afraid to die. She had started it, and now I was going to finish it. She was screaming by then, I remember, I can still hear how she screamed and begged me not to do it, but nothing was going to stop me now.

I was expecting to hear a click, followed perhaps by a brief percussive echo from the empty chamber. I put my finger around the trigger, gave Alma Grund what must have been a grotesque and nauseating smile, and started to pull. Oh God, she screamed. Oh God, don't do it. I pulled, but the trigger didn't go anywhere. I tried again, and again nothing happened. I assumed the trigger was stuck, but when I lowered the gun to have a proper look at it, I finally saw what the trouble was. The safety catch was on. There were bullets in the gun, and the safety catch was on. She hadn't remembered to release it. If not for that mistake, one of those bullets would have been in my head.

She sat down on the sofa and went on crying into her hands. I didn't know how long it was going to last, but once she pulled herself together, I assumed that she would get up and leave. What other choice did she have? I had nearly blown my brains out because of her, and now that she had lost our sickening contest of wills, I couldn't imagine that she would have the heart to say another word to me.

I put the gun in my pocket. As soon as I was no longer touching it, I could feel the madness start to drain out of my body. Only the horror was left—a kind of hot, tactile afterglow, the memory in my right hand of trying to pull the trigger, of pressing the hard metal against my skull. If there was no hole in that skull now, it was only because I was stupid and lucky, because for once in my life my luck had won out over my stupidity. I had come within an inch of killing myself. A series of accidents had stolen my life from me and then given it back, and in the interval, in the tiny gap between those two moments, my life had become a different life.

When Alma finally lifted her face again, the tears were still running down her cheeks. Her makeup had smudged, leaving a zigzag of black lines across the center of her birthmark, and she looked so disheveled, so undone by the catastrophe she had made for herself, that I almost felt sorry for her.

Go and wash up, I said. You look terrible.

It moved me that she didn't say anything. This was a woman who believed in words, who trusted in her ability to talk her way out of tough corners, but when I gave her that command, she stood up from the sofa in silence and did what I told her to do. Just the wan trace of a smile, the barest hint of a shrug. As she walked off and found her way to the bathroom, I sensed how badly she had been defeated, how mortified she was by what she had done. Inexplicably, the sight of her leaving the room touched something in me. It turned around my thoughts somehow, and in that first little flash of sympathy and fellow feeling, I made a sudden, altogether unexpected decision. To the extent that such things can be quantified, I believe that decision was the beginning of the story I am trying to tell now.

While she was gone, I went into the kitchen to look for a place to hide the gun. After opening and shutting the cupboards above the sink, then casting about in several drawers and aluminum containers, I opted for the freezer compartment of the refrigerator. This was my first experience with a gun, and I wasn't sure if I could unload it without causing more mischief, so I laid it in the freezer as it was, bullets and all, wedging it under a bag of chicken parts and a box of ravioli. I just wanted to get the thing out of sight. After I closed the door, however, I realized that I had no great urge to get rid of it. It wasn't that I had any plans to use the gun again, but I liked the idea of having it near me, and until I thought of a better place to put it, I would let it go on sitting in the freezer. Every time I opened the door, I would remember what had happened to me that night. It would be my secret memorial, a monument to my brush with death.

She was taking a long time in the bathroom. The rain had stopped by then, and rather than sit around waiting for her to come out, I decided to clean up the mess in my truck and bring in the groceries. That took a little under ten minutes. When I had finished putting away the food, Alma was still in the bathroom. I walked over to the door to listen in, beginning to feel some twinges of worry, wondering if she hadn't gone in there with the intention of doing something rash and idiotic. Before I left the house, the water in the sink had been running. I had heard the faucets going at full blast, and when I walked by the door on my way out, I had heard her sobbing under the noise. Now the water was off, and there was no sound at all. That could have meant that her crying fit was over and that she was calmly brushing her hair and putting on her makeup. Or it could have meant that she was out cold on the floor, crumpled up with twenty Xanax pills in her stomach.

I knocked. When she didn't answer, I knocked again and asked if she was all right. She was coming, she said, she would be out in a minute, and then, after a long pause, in a voice that seemed to be struggling for breath, she told me that she was sorry, sorry for every wretched thing that had happened. She would rather die than have to leave the house before I had forgiven her, she said, she was begging me to forgive her, but even if I couldn't do that, she was going now, either way she was going, and she wouldn't trouble me again.

I stood there waiting by the door. When she came out, her eyes had that blotchy, puffed-up look you get after a long weeping jag, but her hair was in place again, and the powder and lipstick managed to hide most of the redness. She was intending to walk on past me, but I put out my hand and stopped her.

It's after two o'clock, I said. We're both exhausted, and we need to get some sleep. You can use my bed. I'll sleep downstairs on the sofa.

She was so ashamed of herself, she couldn't find the courage to lift her head and look at me. I don't understand, she said, addressing her words to the floor, and when I didn't say anything immediately after that, she said it again: I don't understand.

No one's going anywhere tonight, I said. Not me, and not you either. We can talk about tomorrow tomorrow, but for now we both stay put.

What does that mean?

It means that it's a long way to New Mexico. Better to start off fresh in the morning. I know you're in a hurry, but a few hours aren't going to make that much of a difference.

I thought you wanted me to leave.

I did. But now I've changed my mind.

Her head came up a little then, and I could see how thoroughly confused she was. You don't have to be nice to me, she said. I'm not asking for that.

Don't worry. I'm thinking about myself, not you. We have a big day ahead of us tomorrow, and if I don't sack out now, I'm not going to be able to keep my eyes open. I have to be awake to hear what you're going to tell me, don't I?

You're not saying you want to go with me. You can't be saying that. It's not possible for you to be saying that.

I can't think of anything else I have to do tomorrow. Why shouldn't I go?

Don't lie. If you're lying to me now, I don't think I could stand it. You'd be tearing the heart right out of my body.

It took several minutes for me to persuade her that I meant to go. The reversal was simply too stunning for her to comprehend, and I had to repeat myself several times before she was willing to believe me. I didn't tell her everything, of course. I didn't bother to talk about microscopic holes in the universe or the redemptive powers of temporary insanity. That would have been too difficult, and so I confined myself to telling her that my decision was personal and had nothing to do with her. We had both behaved badly, I said, and I was just as responsible for what had happened as she was. No blame, no forgiveness, no keeping score of who did what to whom. Or words to that effect, words that eventually proved to her that I had my own reasons for wanting to meet Hector and that I wasn't going for anyone but myself.

Arduous negotiations ensued. Alma couldn't accept the offer of my bed. She had inconvenienced me enough, and on top of that I was banged up from the road accident earlier that night. I needed rest, and I wasn't going to get it tossing and turning on the sofa. I insisted that I would be all right, but she wouldn't hear of such a thing, and back and forth we went, each one trying to oblige the other in an inane comedy of manners less than an hour after I had ripped a gun out of her hand and come close to firing a bullet into my head. I was too worn out to put up much of an argument, however, and in the end I let her have her way. I fetched some bedding and a spare pillow for her, plopped them down on the sofa, and then showed her where to turn off the lights. That was all. She said she didn't mind putting on the sheets herself, and after she had thanked me for the seventh time in the past three minutes, I went upstairs to my room.

There was no question that I was tired, but once I slipped in under the covers, I had trouble falling asleep. I lay there looking at the shadows on the ceiling, and when that no longer seemed interesting, I turned onto my side and listened to the faint sounds of Alma stirring around on the floor below. Alma, the feminine form of *almus*, meaning nourishing, bountiful. Eventually, the light went out under my door, and I heard the springs in the sofa shift as she settled in for the night. After that, I must have dozed off for a while, since I can't remember anything else that happened until I opened my eyes at three-thirty. I saw the time on the electric clock beside the bed, and because I was groggy, suspended in that half state between sleeping and waking, I only dimly understood that I had opened my eyes because Alma was crawling into the bed beside me and putting her head on my shoulder. It's lonely down there, she said, I can't sleep. That made perfect sense to me. I knew all about not being able to sleep, and before I was awake enough to ask her what she was doing in my bed, I had my arms around her and was kissing her on the mouth.

• • •

We set off the next morning just before noon. Alma wanted to drive, so I rode shotgun and handled the navigation duties, telling her where to turn and which highways to take as she steered her blue rented Dodge toward Boston. There were some traces of the storm left on the ground—fallen branches, wet leaves plastered to the roofs of cars, a toppled flagpole lying on someone's lawn—but the sky was clear again, and we drove through sunlight all the way to the airport.

Neither one of us said anything about what had happened in my bedroom the night before. It sat in the car with us like a secret, like something that belonged to the domain of small rooms and nocturnal thoughts and must not be exposed to the light of day. To name it would have been to risk destroying it, and therefore we didn't go much beyond an occasional sidelong glance, a fleeting smile, a hand placed cautiously on the other's knee. How could I presume to know what Alma was thinking? I was glad that she had crawled into my bed, and I was glad that we had spent those hours together in the darkness. But that was only one night, and I had no idea what was going to happen to us next.

The last time I had driven to Logan Airport, I had been in the car with Helen, Todd, and Marco. The last morning of their lives had been spent on the same roads that Alma and I were traveling now. Turn by turn, they had made the same trip; mile by mile, they had covered the same ground. Route 30 to Interstate 91; 91 to the Mass Pike; the Mass Pike to 93; 93 to the tunnel. A part of me welcomed this grotesque reenactment. It felt like some cunningly devised form of punishment, as if the gods had decided that I wouldn't be allowed to have a future until I returned to the past. Justice therefore dictated that I should spend my first morning with Alma in the same way I had spent my last morning with Helen. I had to get into a car and drive to the airport, and I had to be rushing along at ten and twenty miles over the speed limit to avoid missing a plane.

The boys had been squabbling in the back seat, I remembered, and at one point Todd had hauled off and punched his little brother on the arm. Helen had turned around to remind him that he knew better than to pick on a four-year-old, and our firstborn son had petulantly complained that M. had started it and therefore was only getting what he deserved. If someone hits you, he said, you had the right to hit him back. To which I had answered, making what was to be the last paternal pronouncement of my life, that no one had the right to hit someone smaller than he was. But Marco will always be smaller than I am, Todd said. That means I'll never be able to hit him. Well, I said, impressed by the logic of his argument, sometimes life isn't fair. It was a cretinous thing to say, and I remembered that Helen had burst out laughing when I uttered that dreadful truism. It was her way of telling me that of the four people sitting in the car that morning, Todd was the one with the best set of brains. I agreed with her, of course. They were all smarter than I was, and not for a second did I think I could hold a candle to them.

Alma was a good driver. As I sat there watching her weave in and out of the left and center lanes, passing everything in sight, I told her that she looked beautiful.

That's because you're looking at my good side, she said. If you were sitting over here, you probably wouldn't say that.

Is that why you wanted to drive?

The car's rented in my name. I'm the only one who's supposed to drive it.

And vanity has nothing to do with it.

It's going to take time, David. There's no point in overdoing it when we don't have to.

It doesn't bother me, you know. I'm already getting used to it.

You can't be. Not yet, anyway. You haven't looked at me enough to know what you feel.

You said you were married. It obviously hasn't stopped men from finding you attractive.

I like men. After a while, they come to like me. I might not have been around as much as some girls, but I've had my fair share of experiences. Spend enough time with me, and you won't even see it anymore.

But I like seeing it. It makes you different, someone who doesn't look like anyone else. You're the only person I've ever met who looks only like herself.

That's what my father used to say. He told me it was a special present from God, and it made me more beautiful than all the other girls.

Did you believe him?

Sometimes. And sometimes I felt cursed. It's an ugly thing, after all, and it makes you an easy target when you're a child. I kept thinking that someday I'd be able to get rid of it, that some doctor would perform an operation and make me look normal. Whenever I dreamed about myself at night, both sides of my face were the same. Smooth and white, perfectly symmetrical. That didn't stop until I was about fourteen.

You were learning how to live with it.

Maybe, I don't know. But something happened to me around then, and my thinking started to change. It was a big experience for me, a turning point in my life.

Someone fell in love with you.

No, someone gave me a book. For Christmas that year, my mother bought me an anthology of American short stories. *Classic American Tales,* a huge hardcover book with green cloth binding, and on page forty-six there was a story by Nathaniel Hawthorne. *The Birthmark.* Do you know it?

Dimly. I don't think I've read it since high school.

I read it every day for six months. Hawthorne wrote it for me. It was my story.

A scientist and his young bride. That's the situation, isn't it? He tries to remove the birthmark from her face.

A red birthmark. From the left side of her face.

No wonder you liked it.

Like isn't a strong enough word. I was obsessed by it. That story ate me alive.

The birthmark looks like a human hand, doesn't it? I'm starting to remember now. Hawthorne says that it looks like the imprint of a hand pressed against her cheek.

But small. It's the size of a pygmy's hand, the hand of an infant.

She has that one tiny flaw, but otherwise her face is perfect. She's known as an extraordinary beauty.

Georgiana. Until she marries Aylmer, she doesn't even think of it as a flaw. He's the one who teaches her to hate it, who turns her against herself and makes her want to have it removed. For him, it's not just a defect, not just something that destroys her physical beauty. It's a sign of some inner corruption, a stain on Georgiana's soul, a mark of sin and death and decay.

The stamp of mortality.

Or just simply what we think of as human. That's what

makes it so tragic. Aylmer goes into his laboratory and begins experimenting with elixirs and potions, trying to come up with a formula to erase the dreaded spot, and innocent Georgiana goes along with it. That's what's so terrible. She wants him to love her. That's all she cares about, and if eliminating the birthmark is the price she has to pay for his love, she's willing to risk her life for it.

And he winds up murdering her.

But not before the birthmark disappears. That's very important. At the last second, just as she's about to die, the mark fades from her cheek. It's gone now, entirely gone, and it's only then, at that exact moment, that poor Georgiana dies.

The birthmark is who she is. Make it vanish, and she vanishes along with it.

You have no idea what that story did to me. I kept reading it, kept thinking about it, and little by little I began to see myself as I was. Other people carried their humanity inside them, but I wore mine on my face. That was the difference between me and everyone else. I wasn't allowed to hide who I was. Every time people looked at me, they were looking right into my soul. I wasn't a bad-looking girl—I knew that—but I also knew that I would always be defined by that purple blotch on my face. There was no use in trying to get rid of it. It was the central fact of my life, and to wish it away would have been like asking to destroy myself. I was never going to have an ordinary kind of happiness, but after I read that story, I realized that I had something almost as good. I knew what people were thinking. All I had to do was look at them, study their reactions when they saw the left side of my face, and I could tell whether they could be trusted or not. The birthmark was the test of their humanity. It measured the worth of their souls, and if I worked hard at it, I could see straight into them and know who they were. By the time I was sixteen or seventeen, I had the perfect pitch of a tuning fork. That doesn't mean I haven't made mistakes about people, but most of the time I've known better. I just haven't been able to stop myself.

Like last night.

No, not like last night. That wasn't a mistake.

We nearly killed each other.

It had to be that way. When you run out of time, everything gets speeded up. We couldn't afford the luxury of formal introductions, handshakes, discreet conversation over drinks. It had to be violent. Like two planets colliding at the edge of space.

Don't tell me you weren't scared.

I was scared to death. But I didn't go into this blind, you know. I had to be ready for anything.

They told you I was crazy, didn't they?

No one ever used that word. The strongest thing anyone said was nervous breakdown.

What did your tuning fork tell you when you got there?

You already know the answer to that.

You were spooked, weren't you? I spooked the hell out of you.

It was more than that. I was afraid, but at the same time I was excited, almost trembling with happiness. I looked at you, and for a couple of moments it was almost like looking at myself. That's never happened to me before.

You liked it.

I loved it. I was so lost, I thought I was going to fall to pieces.

And now you trust me.

You're not going to let me down. And I'm not going to let you down. We both know that.

What else do we know?

Nothing. That's why we're sitting together in this car now. Because we're the same, and because we don't know a damn thing other than that.

We made the four o'clock flight to Albuquerque with twenty minutes to spare. Ideally, I should have taken the Xanax by the time we reached Holyoke or Springfield, Worcester at the latest, but I was too wrapped up in talking to Alma to interrupt the conversation, and I kept putting it off. When we drove past the signs for the 495 exit, I realized that there was no point in bothering to take them. The pills were in Alma's bag, but she hadn't read the instructions on the label. She didn't know that they had to be swallowed an hour or two in advance to be effective.

At first, I was glad that I hadn't given in. Every cripple trembles at the thought of abandoning his crutch, but if I could get through the flight without disintegrating into tears or frantic ravings, perhaps I would be better for it in the end. This thought held me for another twenty or thirty minutes. Then, as we approached the outskirts of Boston, I understood that I no longer had a choice. We had been driving for more than three hours, and we still hadn't talked about Hector. I had assumed that we would do that in the car, but we had wound up talking about other things, things that no doubt had to be talked about first, that were no less important than what was waiting for us in New Mexico, and before I knew it, the first leg of the trip was nearly over. I couldn't fall asleep on her now. I had to stay awake to listen to the story she'd promised to tell me.

We sat down in the area next to the departure gate. Alma asked me if I wanted to take a pill, and that was when I told her I wasn't going to use the Xanax. Just hold my hand, I said, and I'll be all right. I'm feeling good.

She held my hand, and for a little while we necked in front of the other passengers. It was pure, adolescent abandon—not my adolescence, perhaps, but the one I had always wished for—and it was such a novel experience to be kissing a woman in public that I didn't have time to dwell on the torture ahead. When we boarded the plane, Alma was rubbing the lipstick off my cheek, and I barely noticed when we crossed the threshold and stepped inside. Walking down the center aisle posed no problem for me, nor did sitting down in my seat. I wasn't even disturbed when I had to fasten my seat belt, and even less so when the engines roared into full throttle and I felt the machine start to vibrate along my skin. We were in first class. The menu said that they would be serving us chicken for dinner. Alma, who was sitting next to the window on my left—and therefore with her right side turned to me again—took my hand in her hand, raised it to her mouth, and kissed it.

The only mistake I made was to close my eyes. When the plane backed up from the terminal and began to taxi down the runway, I didn't want to have to watch us taking off. That was the most dangerous moment, I felt, and if I could survive the transition from earth to sky, simply ignore the fact that we had lost contact with the ground, I figured I might have a chance to survive the rest. But I was wrong to want to block it out, wrong to cut myself off from the event as it unfurled itself in the actuality of the moment. To experience it would have been painful, but much worse was to remove myself from that pain and withdraw into the shell of my thoughts. The world of the present was gone. There was nothing to see, nothing to distract me from succumbing to my fears, and the longer I kept my eyes shut, the more terribly I saw what my fears wanted me to see. I had always wished that I had died with Helen and the boys, but I had never let myself fully imagine what they had lived through in the last moments before the plane went down. Now, with my eyes closed, I heard the boys screaming, and I saw Helen holding them in her arms, telling them that she loved them, whispering through the screams of the one hundred forty-eight other people who were about to die that she would always love them, and when I saw her there with the boys in her arms, I broke down and sobbed. Exactly as I had always imagined I would, I broke down and sobbed.

I put my hands over my face, and for the longest time I went on weeping into my salty, stinking palms, unable to lift my head, unable to open my eyes and stop. Eventually, I felt Alma's hand on the back of my neck. I had no idea how long it had been there, but a moment came when I started to feel it, and after a while I realized that her other hand was going up and down my left arm, stroking it very gently, using the same soft and rhythmical motion that a mother uses to comfort a miserable child. Oddly enough, the instant I became aware of this thought, aware of the fact that I had conjured up this thought about mothers and children, I imagined that I had slipped into the body of Todd, my own son, and that it was Helen who was comforting me and not Alma. That feeling lasted for only a few seconds, but it was extremely powerful, not a thing of the imagination so much as a real thing, an actual transformation that turned me into someone else, and the moment it started to go away, the worst of what had happened to me was suddenly over.

5

HALF AN HOUR later, Alma began to talk. We were seven miles up in the air by then, sailing above some nameless county in Pennsylvania or Ohio, and she went on talking all the way to Albuquerque. There was a brief pause when we landed, and then the story continued after we climbed into her car and began the two-and-a-half-hour trip to Tierra del Sueño. We drove down a series of desert highways as the late afternoon turned to dusk and the dusk then turned to night. As I remember it, the story didn't stop until we came to the gates of the ranch—and even then it wasn't quite finished. She had talked for almost seven hours, but there hadn't been enough time to fit everything in.

She jumped around a lot in the early going, darting back and forth between the past and present, and it took me a while to get my bearings and sort out the chronology of events. It was all in her book, she said, all the names and dates, all the essential facts, and there was no need to rehash the details of Hector's life prior to his disappearance—not that afternoon on the plane, in any case, not when I would be able to read the book myself in the days and weeks ahead. What mattered were the things that bore on Hector's destiny as a hidden man, the years he had spent in the desert writing and directing films that were never shown to the public. Those films were the reason why I was traveling to New Mexico with her now, and interesting as it might have been to know that Hector was born Chaim Mandelbaum—on a Dutch steamship in the middle of the Atlantic—it wasn't terribly important. It didn't matter that his mother died when he was twelve or that his father, a cabinet-maker with no interest in politics, was nearly beaten to death by an anti-Bolshevik, anti-Semitic mob during La Semana Tragica in Buenos Aires in 1919. That led to Hector's departure for America, but his father had been urging him to emigrate for some time before that, and the crisis in Argentina merely accelerated the decision. There was no point in listing the two dozen jobs he held after arriving in New York, and even less urgency to talk about what happened to him after he reached Hollywood in 1925. I knew enough about his early work as an extra, set-builder, and sometime bit player in scores of lost and forgotten films for us to pass over those years, enough about his tangled relations with Hunt not to have to dwell on them again. The experience soured Hector on the movie business, Alma said, but he wasn't ready to give up, and until the night of January 14, 1929, the last thought in his mind was that he would ever have to leave California.

One year before he vanished, he had been interviewed by Brigid O'Fallon for *Photoplay*. She had come to his house on North Orange Drive at three o'clock one Sunday afternoon, and by five o'clock they were on the floor together, rolling around on the carpet and seeking out the holes and crevices in each other's bodies. Hector was wont to behave like that with women, Alma said, and this was hardly the first time he had used his seductive powers to make a swift and decisive conquest. O'Fallon was just twenty-three, a bright Catholic girl from Spokane who had graduated from Smith and come back west to make it in journalism. As it happened, Alma had also graduated from Smith, and she used her connections there to track down a copy of the 1926 yearbook. The head shot of O'Fallon was inconclusive. Her eyes were too close together, Alma said, her chin was too broad, and her bobbed hair was not flattering to her features. Still, there was something effervescent about her, some spark of mischief or humor lurking in her gaze, a bright inner élan. In a photograph of the Drama Society's production of *The Tempest,* O'Fallon had been captured in midperformance, decked out as Miranda in a thin white gown and sporting a single white flower in her hair, and Alma said that she was lovely in that pose, a small slip of a thing shimmering with life and energy—open-mouthed, an arm flung forward, in the act of declaiming a line. As a journalist, O'Fallon wrote in the style of the day. Her sentences were sharp and punchy, and she had a knack for sprinkling her articles with witty asides and deftly turned puns that helped her move up quickly through the ranks of the magazine. The article about Hector was an exception, far more earnest and openly admiring of her subject than any of the other pieces of hers that Alma had read. The heavy accent, however, was only a slight exaggeration. O'Fallon juiced it up a little for comic effect, but that was essentially how Hector spoke at the time. His English improved over the years, but back in the twenties he still sounded like someone who had just stepped off the boat. He might have landed on his feet in Hollywood, but yesterday he was just another bewildered foreigner, standing on the dock with all his earthly possessions crammed into a cardboard suitcase.

In the months that followed the interview, Hector went on

cavorting with any number of beautiful young actresses. He enjoyed being seen in public with them, he enjoyed going to bed with them, but none of those flings lasted. O'Fallon was cleverer than the other women he knew, and once Hector had tired of his latest plaything, he would invariably call up Brigid and ask to see her again. Between early February and late June, he visited her apartment on the average of once or twice a week, and throughout the middle of that period, for most of April and May, he was with her no less than every second or third night. There was no question that he was fond of her. As the months went by, a comfortable intimacy developed between them, but whereas the less experienced Brigid took that as a sign of eternal love, Hector never deluded himself into thinking they were anything more than close friends. He saw her as his pal, as his sexual companion, as his trusted ally, but that didn't mean he had any intention of proposing marriage to her.

She was a reporter, and she must have known what Hector was up to on the nights he didn't sleep in her bed. All she had to do was open the morning paper to follow his exploits, to breathe in the innuendos about his newest crushes and dalliances. Even if most of the stories she read about him were false, there was more than enough evidence to arouse her jealousy. But Brigid wasn't jealous—or at least she didn't appear to be jealous. Every time Hector called, she welcomed him into her arms. She never talked about the other women, and because she didn't accuse him or berate him or ask him to mend his ways, his affection for her only increased. That was Brigid's plan. She had lost her heart to him, and rather than force him to make a premature decision about their life together, she decided to be patient. Sooner or later, Hector would stop running around. The frantic womanizing would lose its appeal to him. He would grow bored; he would work it out of his system;

he would see the light. And when he did, she would be there for him.

So plotted the clear-thinking and resourceful Brigid O'Fallon, and for a time it looked as though she would catch her man. Hector, embroiled in his various disputes with Hunt, struggling against fatigue and the pressures of having to crank out a new film every month, became less inclined to fritter away his nights in jazz clubs and speakeasys, to expend his strength on pointless seductions. O'Fallon's apartment became a refuge for him, and the quiet evenings they spent there together helped keep his head and groin in balance. Brigid was an incisive critic, and because she was savvier about the movie business than he was, he came to rely more and more on her judgment. It was she, in fact, who suggested that he audition Dolores Saint John for the role of the sheriff's daughter in *The Prop Man*, his upcoming two-reeler. Brigid had been studying Saint John's career for the past several months, and in her opinion the twenty-one-year-old actress had the potential to become the next big thing, another Mabel Normand or Gloria Swanson, another Norma Talmadge.

Hector followed her advice. When Saint John walked into his office three days later, he had already watched a couple of her films and was committed to offering her the job. Brigid had been right about Saint John's talent, but nothing she had said and nothing he had seen of Saint John's work on film had prepared Hector for the overwhelming effect her presence would have on him. It was one thing to watch a person act in a silent movie; it was quite another to shake that person's hand and look into her eyes. Other actresses were more impressive on celluloid, perhaps, but in the real world of sound and color, in the fleshed-out, three-dimensional world of the five senses and the four elements and the two sexes, he had never met a creature to compare with this one. It wasn't that Saint John was more beautiful than other women, and it wasn't that she said anything remarkable to him during the twenty-five minutes they spent together that afternoon. To be perfectly honest, she seemed to be a bit on the dull side, of no more than average intelligence, but there was a feral quality to her, an animal energy coursing along her skin and radiating from her gestures that made it impossible for him to stop looking at her. The eyes that looked back at him were of the palest Siberian blue. Her skin was white, and her hair was the darkest shade of red, a red verging on mahogany. Unlike the hair of most American women in June of 1928, it was long, and it hung down to her shoulders. They talked for a while about nothing in particular. Then, without any preamble, Hector told her that the part was hers if she wanted it, and she accepted. She had never worked in physical comedy before, she said, and she was looking forward to the challenge. Then she rose from her chair, shook his hand, and left the office. Ten minutes later, with the image of her face still burning in his head, Hector decided that Dolores Saint John was the woman he was going to marry. She was the woman of his life, and if it turned out that she wouldn't have him, then he would never marry anyone.

She performed ably in *The Prop Man*, doing all that Hector asked of her and even contributing some clever flourishes of her own, but when he tried to sign her up for his next film, she demurred. She had been offered the main role in an Allan Dwan feature, and the opportunity was simply too great for her to turn it down. Hector, who was supposed to have the magic touch with women, was getting nowhere with her. He couldn't find the words to express himself in English, and every time he was on the point of declaring his intentions to her, he would draw back at the last moment. If the words came out wrong, he felt that he would scare her off and ruin his chances forever. Meanwhile, he continued spending several nights a week at Brigid's apartment, and because he had made no promises to her, because he was free to love any person he wanted, he said nothing to her about Saint John. When shooting on *The Prop Man* wrapped in late June, Saint John went off on location to the Tehachapi Mountains. She worked on the Dwan film for four weeks, and during that time Hector wrote her sixty-seven letters. What he hadn't been able to say to her in person, he finally found the courage to put down on paper. He said it again and again, and even though he said it differently each time he wrote, the message was always the same. At first, Saint John was puzzled. Then she was flattered. Then she began to look forward to the letters, and by the end she realized that she couldn't live without them. When she returned to Los Angeles at the beginning of August, she told Hector that the answer was yes. Yes, she loved him. Yes, she would become his wife.

No date was set for the wedding, but they were talking about January or February—time enough for Hector to have fulfilled his contract with Hunt and to have worked out his next move. The moment had come to talk to Brigid, but he kept putting it off, could never quite get around to doing it. He was working late with Blaustein and Murphy, he said, he was in the editing room, he was on a location scout, he was under the weather. Between the beginning of August and the middle of October, he invented dozens of excuses for not seeing her, but still he couldn't bring himself to break it off entirely. Even in the throes of his infatuation with Saint John, he went on visiting Brigid once or twice a week, and every time he walked through the door of the apartment, he slipped back into the same old cozy setup. One could accuse him of being a coward, of course, but one could just as easily assert that he was a man in conflict. Perhaps he was having second thoughts about marrying Saint John. Perhaps he wasn't ready to give up O'Fallon. Perhaps he was torn between the two women and felt that he needed them both. Guilt can cause a man to act against his own best interests, but desire can do that as well, and when guilt and desire are mixed up equally in a man's heart, that man is apt to do strange things.

O'Fallon suspected nothing. In September, when Hector engaged Saint John to play the role of his wife in *Mr. Nobody*, she congratulated him on the intelligence of his choice. Even when rumors filtered back from the set that there was a special *closeness* between Hector and his leading lady, she wasn't unduly alarmed. Hector liked to flirt. He always fell for the actresses he worked with, but once the shooting was finished and everyone went home, he quickly forgot about them. In this case, however, the stories persisted. Hector had already moved on to *Double or Nothing*, his last picture at Kaleidoscope, and Gordon Fly was whispering in his column that wedding bells were about to ring for a certain long-haired siren and her mustachioed, funny-man beau. It was mid-October by then, and O'Fallon, who hadn't heard from Hector in five or six days, called the editing room and asked him to come to her apartment that night. She had never asked him to do anything like that before, and so he canceled his dinner plans with Dolores and went to Brigid's place instead. And there, confronted by the question he had put off answering for the past two months, he finally told her the truth.

Hector had been praying for something decisive, an eruption of female fury that would send him staggering out onto the street and end things once and for all, but Brigid merely looked at him when he broke the news to her, took a deep breath, and said that it wasn't possible for him to love Saint John. It wasn't possible because he loved her. Yes, Hector said, he did love her, he would always love her, but the fact was that he was going to marry Saint John. Brigid started to cry then, but still she didn't accuse him of betrayal, didn't argue for herself or shout out in anger about how terribly he had wronged her. He was wrong about himself, she said, and once he realized that no one would ever love him as she loved him, he would come back to her. Dolores Saint John was a thing, she said, not a person. She was a luminous and intoxicating thing, but underneath her skin she was coarse and shallow and stupid, and she didn't deserve to be his wife. Hector should have said something to her at that point. The occasion demanded that he deliver some brutal, piercing remark that would destroy her hope forever, but Brigid's grief was too strong for him, her devotion was too strong for him, and as he listened to her speak in those small, gasping sentences of hers, he couldn't bring himself to say the words. You're right, he answered. It probably won't last more than a year or two. But I have to go through with it. I have to have her, and once I do, everything else will take care of itself.

He wound up spending the night in Brigid's apartment. Not because he thought it would do them any good, but because she begged him to stay there one last time, and he couldn't say no to her. The next morning, he slipped out before she woke up, and from that moment on, things began to change for him. The contract with Hunt ended; he started working on *Dot and Dash* with Blaustein; his wedding plans took shape. After two and a half months, he still hadn't heard from Brigid. He found her silence a little troublesome, but the truth was that he was too preoccupied with Saint John to give the matter much thought. If Brigid had disappeared, it could only be because she was a person of her word and was too proud to stand in his way. Now that he had made his intentions clear, she had backed off to let him sink or swim on his own. If he swam, he probably wouldn't see her again. If he sank, she would probably turn up at the last minute and try to pull him out of the water.

It must have soothed Hector's conscience to think these things about O'Fallon, to turn her into a form of superior being who felt no pain when knives were stuck into her body, who didn't bleed when she was wounded. But in the absence of any verifiable facts, why not indulge in a little wishful thinking? He wanted to believe that she was doing well, that she was carrying on boldly with her life. He noticed that her articles had stopped appearing in *Photoplay*, but that could have meant that she was out of town or that she had taken another job somewhere else, and for the moment he refused to look at any of the darker possibilities. It wasn't until she finally surfaced again (by slipping a letter under his door on New Year's Eve) that he learned how miserably he had fooled himself. Two days after he had walked out on her in October, she had slit her wrists in the bathtub. If not for the water that had dripped down into the apartment below, the landlady never would have unlocked the door, and Brigid wouldn't have been found until it was too late. An ambulance took her to the hospital. She pulled through after a couple of days, but her mind had crumbled, she wrote, she was incoherent and weeping all the time, and the doctors decided to hold her for observation. That led to a two-month stay in the mental ward. She was prepared to spend the rest of her life there, but that was only because her one purpose in life now was to find a way to kill herself, and it made no difference where she was. Then, just as she was gearing up for her next attempt, a miracle happened. Or rather, she discovered that a miracle had already happened and that she had been living under its spell for the past two months. Once the doctors confirmed that it was a real event and not something she had imagined, she no longer wanted to die. She had lost her faith years ago, she continued. She hadn't been to confession since high school, but when the nurse came in that morning to give her the results of the test, she felt as if God had put his mouth against her mouth and breathed life into her again. She was pregnant. It had happened in the fall, on the last night they had spent together, and now she was carrying Hector's baby inside her.

After they discharged her from the hospital, she had moved out of her apartment. She had a little money saved up, but not enough to go on paying the rent without returning to work—and she couldn't do that now, since she had already quit her job at the magazine. She had found a cheap room somewhere, the letter went on, a place with an iron bedstead and a wooden cross on the wall and a colony of mice living under the floorboards, but she wasn't going to tell him the name of the hotel or even what town it was in. It would be useless for him to go out looking for her. She was registered under a false name, and she meant to lie low until her pregnancy was a little further along, when it would no longer be possible for him to try to talk her into having an abortion. She had made up her mind to let the baby live, and whether Hector was willing to marry her or not, she was determined to become the mother of his child. Her letter concluded: *Fate has brought us together, my darling, and wherever I am now, you will always be with me.*

Then more silence. Another two weeks went by, and Brigid

stuck to her promise and kept herself hidden. Hector said nothing to Saint John about O'Fallon's letter, but he knew that his chances of marrying her were probably dead. He couldn't think about their future life together without also thinking about Brigid, without tormenting himself with images of his pregnant ex-lover lying in a fleabag hotel in some derelict neighborhood, slowly pushing herself into madness as his child grew within her. He didn't want to give up Saint John. He didn't want to let go of the dream of crawling into her bed every night and feeling that smooth, electric body against his naked skin, but men were responsible for their actions, and if the child was going to be born, then there was no escape from what he had done. Hunt killed himself on January eleventh, but Hector was no longer thinking about Hunt, and when he heard the news on January twelfth, he felt nothing. The past was of no importance. Only the future mattered to him, and the future was suddenly in doubt. He was going to have to break off his engagement with Dolores, but he couldn't do that until Brigid surfaced again, and because he didn't know where to find her, he couldn't move, couldn't budge from the spot where the present had stranded him. As time went on, he began to feel like a man whose feet had been nailed to the floor.

On the night of January fourteenth, he knocked off work with Blaustein at seven o'clock. Saint John was expecting him for dinner at her house in Topanga Canyon at eight. Hector would have been there well before then, but he had car trouble along the way, and by the time he finished changing the tire on his blue DeSoto, he had lost three-quarters of an hour. If not for that flat tire, the event that altered the course of his life might never have happened, for it was precisely then, as he crouched down in the darkness just off La Cienega Boulevard and began jacking up the front end of his car, that Brigid O'Fallon knocked on the door of Dolores Saint John's house, and by the time Hector had completed his little task and was back behind the wheel of the car, Saint John had accidentally fired a thirty-two-caliber bullet into O'Fallon's left eye.

That was what she said, in any case, and from the stunned and horrified look that greeted him when he walked through the front door, Hector saw no reason to doubt her. She hadn't known the gun was loaded, she said. Her agent had given it to her when she moved into this isolated house in the canyon three months ago. It was supposed to be for protection, and after Brigid started saying all those crazy things to her, ranting on about Hector's baby and her slit wrists and the bars on the windows of madhouses and the blood from Christ's wounds, Dolores had become frightened and asked her to leave. But Brigid wouldn't go, and a few minutes later she was accusing Dolores of having stolen her man, threatening her with wild ultimatums and calling her a devil, a tramp, and a low-down lousy slut. Just six months ago, Brigid had been that sweet reporter from *Photoplay* with the pretty smile and the sharp sense of humor, but now she was out of her mind, she was dangerous, she was lurching around the room and weeping at the top of her lungs, and Dolores didn't want her there anymore. That was when she thought of the revolver. It was in the middle drawer of the rolltop desk in the living room, less than ten feet from where she was standing, and so she walked over to the desk and opened the middle drawer. She hadn't meant to pull the trigger. Her only thought was that maybe the sight of the gun would be enough to scare off Brigid and get her to leave. But once she took it out of the drawer and pointed it across the room, the thing went off in her hand. There hadn't been much of a sound. Just a kind of small pop, she said, and then Brigid let out a mysterious grunt and fell to the floor.

Dolores wouldn't go into the living room with him (It's too horrible, she said, I can't look at her), and so he went in alone. Brigid was lying facedown on the rug in front of the sofa. Her body was warm, and blood was still leaking from the back of her skull. Hector turned her over, and when he looked into her destroyed face and saw the hole where her left eye had been, he suddenly stopped breathing. He couldn't look at her and breathe at the same time. In order to start breathing again, he had to look away, and once he did that, he couldn't bring himself to look at her anymore. Everything gone. Everything crushed to pieces. And the unborn baby inside her, dead and gone as well. Eventually, he stood up and went into the hall, where he found a blanket in the closet. When he returned to the living room, he looked at her one last time, felt the breath clutch inside him again, and then opened the blanket and spread it over her small, tragic body.

His first impulse was to go to the police, but Dolores was afraid. What would her story sound like when they questioned her about the gun, she said, when they forced her to walk through the improbable sequence of events for the twelfth time and made her explain why a twenty-four-year-old pregnant woman was lying dead on the living room floor? Even if they believed her, even if they were willing to accept that the gun had gone off accidentally, the scandal would ruin her. Her career would be finished, and Hector's career, too, for that matter, and why should they suffer for something that wasn't their fault? They should call Reggie, she said—meaning Reginald Dawes, her agent, the same fool who had given her the gun—and let him handle it. Reggie was smart, he knew all the angles.

If they listened to Reggie, he would figure out a way to save their necks.

But Hector knew that he was already past saving. It was scandal and public humiliation if they talked; it was even worse trouble if they didn't. They could be charged with murder, and once the case was presented in court, not a soul on earth would believe that Brigid's death had been an accident. Choose your poison. Hector had to decide. He had to decide for both of them, and there was no right decision to be made. Forget about Reggie, he said to her. If Dawes got wind of what she had done, he would own her. She would be groveling before him on bloody knees for the rest of her life. There couldn't be anyone else. It was either get on the phone and talk to the cops, or it was talk to no one. And if it was no one, then they would have to take care of the body themselves.

He knew that he would burn in hell for saying that, and he also knew that he would never see Dolores again, but he said it anyway, and then they went ahead and did it. It wasn't a question of good and evil anymore. It was about doing the least harm under the circumstances, about not ruining yet another life for no purpose. They took Dolores's Chrysler sedan and drove up into the mountains about an hour north of Malibu with Brigid's body in the trunk. The corpse was still in the blanket, which in turn was wrapped in the rug, and there was a shovel in the trunk as well. Hector had found it in the garden shed behind Dolores's house, and that was what he used to dig the hole with. If nothing else, he figured he owed her that much. He had betrayed her, after all, and the remarkable thing about it was that she had gone on trusting him. Brigid's stories had had no effect on her. She had dismissed them as ravings, as lunatic lies told by a jealous, unhinged woman, and even when the evidence had been pushed up flat against her beautiful nose, she had refused to accept it. It could have been vanity, of course, a monstrous vanity that saw nothing of the world except what it wanted to see, but at the same time it could have been real love, a love so blind that Hector could scarcely even imagine what he was about to lose. Needless to say, he never learned which one it had been. After they returned from their hideous errand in the hills that night, he drove back to his house in his own car, and he never saw her again.

That was when he disappeared. Except for the clothes on his back and the cash in his wallet, he left everything behind, and by ten o'clock the next morning he was heading north on a train to Seattle. He was fully expecting to be caught. Once Brigid was reported missing, it wouldn't be long before someone made a connection between the two disappearances. The police would want to question him, and at that point they would begin looking for him in earnest. But Hector was wrong about that, just as he had been wrong about everything else. He was the one who was missing, and for the time being no one even knew that Brigid was gone. She had no job anymore, no permanent address, and when she failed to return to her room at the Fitzwilliam Arms in downtown Los Angeles for the rest of that week in early 1929, the desk clerk had her belongings carried down to the basement and rented her room to someone else. There was nothing unusual about that. People disappeared all the time, and you couldn't leave a room empty when a new tenant was willing to pay for it. Even if the desk clerk had felt concerned enough to contact the police, there was nothing they could have done about it anyway. Brigid was registered under a false name, and how could you look for someone who didn't exist?

Two months later, her father called from Spokane and talked to a Los Angeles detective named Reynolds, who continued working on the case until he retired in 1936. Twenty-four years after that, the bones of Mr. O'Fallon's daughter were finally unearthed. A bulldozer dug them up on the construction site of a new housing development at the edge of the Simi Hills. They were sent to the forensic laboratory in Los Angeles, but Reynolds's paperwork was deep in storage by then, and it was no longer possible to identify the person they had belonged to.

Alma knew about those bones because she had made it her business to know about them. Hector had told her where they were buried, and when she visited the housing development in the early eighties, she talked to enough people to confirm that they had been found in that spot.

By then, Saint John was long dead as well. After returning to her parents' house in Wichita following Hector's disappearance, she had issued her statement to the press and gone into seclusion. A year and a half later, she married a local banker named George T. Brinkerhoff. They had two children, Willa and George Junior. In 1934, when the elder child was still under three, Saint John lost control of her car while driving home one night in a hard November rain. She crashed into a telephone pole, and the impact of the collision sent her hurtling through the windshield, which severed the carotid artery in her neck. According to the police autopsy report, she bled to death without regaining consciousness.

Two years later, Brinkerhoff remarried. When Alma wrote to him in 1983 to request an interview, his widow answered that he had died of kidney failure the previous fall. The children were alive, however, and Alma spoke to both of them—one in Dallas, Texas, and the other in Orlando, Florida. Neither one had much to offer. They were so young at the time, they said. They knew their mother from photographs, but they didn't remember her at all.

By the time Hector walked into Central Station on the morning of January fifteenth, his mustache was already gone. He disguised himself by removing his most identifiable feature, transforming his face into another face through a simple act of subtraction. The eyes and eyebrows, the forehead and slicked-back hair would also have said something to a person familiar with his films, but not long after he bought his ticket, Hector found a solution to that problem as well. In the process, Alma said, he also found a new name.

The nine twenty-one for Seattle wouldn't be boarding for another hour. Hector decided to kill the time by going into the station restaurant for a cup of coffee, but no sooner did he sit down at the counter and start breathing in the smells of bacon and eggs frying on the griddle than he was engulfed by a wave of nausea. He wound up in the men's room, locked inside one of the stalls on his hands and knees, retching up the contents of his stomach into the toilet. It all came pouring out of him, the miserable green fluids and the clotted bits of undigested brown food, a trembling purge of shame and fear and revulsion, and when the attack was over, he sank to the floor and lay there for a long while, struggling to catch his breath. His head was pushed up against the back wall, and from that angle he was in a position to see something that otherwise would have escaped his notice. In the elbow of the curved pipe just behind the toilet, someone had left a cap. Hector slid it out from its hiding place and discovered that it was a worker's cap, a sturdy thing made of wool tweed with a short bill jutting from the front—not very different from the cap he had once worn himself, back when he was new in America. Hector turned it over to make sure there was nothing inside it, that it wasn't too dirty or too foul for him to put it on. That was when he saw the owner's name written out in ink along the back of the interior leather band: Herman Loesser. It struck Hector as a good name, perhaps even an excellent name, and in any event a name no worse than any other. He was Herr Mann, was he not? If he took to calling himself Herman, he could change his identity without altogether renouncing who he was. That was the important thing: to get rid of himself for others, but to remember who he was for himself. Not because he wanted to, but precisely because he didn't.

Herman Loesser. Some would pronounce it *Lesser*, and others would read it as *Loser*. Either way, Hector figured that he had found the name he deserved.

The cap fit remarkably well. It was neither too slack nor too snug, and there was just enough give to it for him to pull the brim down over his forehead and obscure the distinctive slant of his eyebrows, to shade the fierce clarity of his eyes. After the subtraction, then, an addition. Hector minus the mustache, and then Hector plus the cap. The two operations canceled him out, and he left the men's room that morning looking like anyone, like no one, like the spitting image of Mr. Nobody himself.

He lived in Seattle for six months, moved down to Portland for a year, and then went back north to Washington, where he stayed until the spring of 1931. At first, he was pushed along by pure terror. Hector felt that he was running for his life, and in the days that followed his disappearance, his ambitions were no different from those of any other criminal: as long as he eluded capture for another day, he considered that day well spent. Every morning and afternoon, he read about himself in the papers, keeping track of the developments in the case to see how close they were to finding him. He was perplexed by what they wrote, appalled by how little effort anyone had made to know him. Hunt was only of the scantest importance, and yet every article began and ended with him: stock manipulations, bogus investments, the business of Hollywood in all its worm-eaten glory. Brigid's name was never mentioned, and until Dolores went back to Kansas, no one even bothered to talk to her. Day by day, the pressure diminished, and after four weeks of no breakthroughs and dwindling coverage in the papers, his panic began to subside. No one suspected him of anything. He could have gone back home if he had wanted to. All he had to do was hop a train for Los Angeles, and he could have picked up his life exactly where he had left it.

But Hector didn't go anywhere. There was nothing he wanted more than to be in his house on North Orange Drive, sitting on the sun porch with Blaustein as they drank their iced teas and put the finishing touches on *Dot and Dash.* Making movies was like living in a delirium. It was the hardest, most demanding work anyone had invented, and the more difficult it became for him, the more exhilarating he found it. He was learning the ropes, slowly mastering the intricacies of the job, and with a little more time he was certain that he would have developed into one of the good ones. That was all he had ever wanted for himself: to be good at that one thing. He had wanted only that, and therefore that was the one thing he would never allow himself to do again. You don't drive an innocent girl insane, and you don't make her pregnant, and you don't bury her dead body eight feet under the ground and expect to go on with your life as before. A man who had done what he had done deserved to be punished. If the world wouldn't do it for him, then he would have to do it himself.

He rented a room in a boardinghouse near the Pike Place Market, and when the money in his wallet finally ran out, he found a job with one of the local fishmongers. Up every morning at four, unloading trucks in the predawn fog, hefting crates and bushels as the damp of Puget Sound stiffened his fingers and worked its way into his bones. Then, after a brief smoke, spreading out crabs and oysters on beds of chipped ice, followed by sundry repetitive daylight occupations: the clank of shells hitting the scale, the brown paper bags, slicing open oysters with his short, lethal scimitar. When he wasn't working, Herman Loesser read books from the public library, kept a journal, and talked to no one unless absolutely compelled to. The object, Alma said, was to squirm under the stringencies he had imposed on himself, to make himself as uncomfortable as possible. When the work became too easy, he moved on to Portland, where he found a job as a night watchman in a barrel factory. After the clamor of the roofed-in market, the silence of his thoughts. There was nothing fixed about his choices, Alma explained. His penance was a continual work in progress, and the punishments he meted out to himself changed according to what he felt were his greatest deficiencies at any given moment. He craved company, he longed to be with a woman again, he wanted bodies and voices around him, and therefore he walled himself up in that vacant factory, struggling to school himself in the finer points of self-abnegation.

The stock market crashed while he was in Portland, and when the Comstock Barrel Company went out of business in mid-1930, Hector lost his job. By then, he had worked his way through several hundred books, beginning with the standard nineteenth-century novels that everyone had always talked about but which he had never taken the trouble to read (Dickens, Flaubert, Stendhal, Tolstoy), and then, once he felt that he had got the hang of it, going back to zero and deciding to educate himself in a systematic manner. Hector knew next to nothing. He had left school at sixteen, and no one had ever bothered to tell him that Socrates and Sophocles were not the same man, that George Eliot was a woman, or that *The Divine Comedy* was a poem about the afterlife and not some boulevard farce in which all the characters wound up marrying the right person. Circumstances had always pressed in on him, and there hadn't been time for Hector to worry about such things. Now, suddenly, there was all the time in the world. Imprisoned in his private Alcatraz, he spent the years of his captivity acquiring a new language to think about the conditions of his survival, to make sense of the constant, merciless ache in his soul. According to Alma, the rigors of this intellectual training gradually turned him into someone else. He learned how to look at himself from a distance, to see himself first of all as a man among other men, then as a collection of random particles of matter, and finally as a single speck of dust—and the farther he traveled from his point of origin, she said, the closer he came to achieving greatness. He had shown her his journals from that period, and fifty years after the fact, Alma had been able to witness the agonies of his conscience firsthand. *Never more lost than now,* she recited to me, quoting a passage from memory, *never more alone and afraid—yet never more alive.* Those words were written less than an hour before he left Portland. Then, almost as an afterthought, he sat down again and added another paragraph at the bottom of the page: *I talk only to the dead now. They are the only ones I trust, the only ones who understand me. Like them, I live without a future.*

The word was that there were jobs in Spokane. The lumber mills were supposedly looking for men, and several logging camps to the east and north were said to be hiring. Hector had no interest in those jobs, but he overheard two fellows talking about the opportunities up there one afternoon not long after the barrel factory shut down, and it gave him an idea, and once he began to think the idea through, he could no longer resist it. Brigid had grown up in Spokane. Her mother was dead, but her father was still around, and there were two younger sisters in the family as well. Of all the tortures Hector could imagine, of all the pains he could possibly inflict on himself, none was worse than the thought of going to the city where they lived. If he caught a glimpse of Mr. O'Fallon and the two girls, then he would know what they looked like, and their faces would be in his mind whenever he thought about the harm he had done to them. He deserved to suffer that much, he felt. He had an obligation to make them real, to make them as real in his memory as Brigid herself.

Still known by the color of his boyhood hair, Patrick O'Fallon had owned and operated Red's Sporting Goods in downtown Spokane for the past twenty years. On the morning of his arrival, Hector found a cheap hotel two blocks west of the train station, paid in advance for one night, and then went out to look for the store. He found it within five minutes. He hadn't thought about what he would do once he got there, but for caution's sake he figured it would be best to stand outside and try to get a look at O'Fallon through the window. Hector had no idea if Brigid had mentioned him in any of her letters home. If she had, the family would have known that he talked with a heavy Spanish accent. More important, they would have paid particular attention to his disappearance in 1929, and with Brigid herself now missing for close to two years, they might have been the only people in America who had figured out the link between the two cases. All he had to do was go into the store and open his mouth. If O'Fallon knew who Hector Mann was, the odds were that his suspicions would be aroused after three or four sentences.

But O'Fallon was nowhere to be seen. As Hector pressed his nose against the glass, pretending to examine a set of golf clubs on display in the window, he had a clear view into the store, and as far as he could make out from that angle, there was no one inside. No customers, no clerk standing behind the counter. It was early yet—just past ten o'clock—but the sign on the door said OPEN, and rather than remain on the crowded street and risk calling attention to himself, Hector scrapped his plan and decided to go in. If they found out who he was, he thought, then so be it.

The door made a tinkling sound when he pulled it open, and the bare wood planks creaked underfoot as he walked toward the counter in back. It wasn't a big place, but the shelves were crammed with merchandise, and there seemed to be everything a sportsman could possibly want: fishing rods and casting reels, rubber fins and swimming goggles, shotguns and hunting rifles, tennis racquets, baseball gloves, footballs, basketballs, shoulder pads and helmets, spiked shoes and cleated shoes, kicking tees and driving tees, duck pins, barbells, and medicine balls. Two lines of regularly spaced support columns ran the length of the store, and on each one there was a framed photograph of Red O'Fallon. He had been young when the pictures were taken, and they all showed him engaged in some form of athletic activity. Wearing a baseball uniform in one, a football uniform in another, but most often running races in the skimpy garb of a track-and-field man. In one photo, the camera had caught him in full stride, both feet off the ground, two yards ahead of his closest competitor. In another, he was shaking hands with a man dressed in top hat and tails, accepting a bronze medal at the 1904 Saint Louis Olympics.

As Hector approached the counter, a young woman emerged from a back room, wiping her hands with a towel. She was looking down, her head tilted to one side, but even though her face was largely obscured from him, there was something about her walk, something about the slope of her shoulders, something about the way she rubbed the towel over her fingers that made him feel that he was looking at Brigid. For the space of several seconds, it was as if the past nineteen months had never happened. Brigid was no longer dead. She had unburied herself, clawed her way out from the dirt he had shoveled over her body, and there she was now, intact and breathing again, with no bullet in her brain and no hole where her eye had been, working as an assistant in her father's store in Spokane, Washington.

The woman kept walking toward him, pausing only to lay the towel on top of an unopened carton, and the uncanny thing about what happened next was that even after she raised her head and looked into his eyes, the illusion persisted. She had Brigid's face, too. It was the same jaw and the same mouth, the same forehead and the same chin. When she smiled at him a moment later, he saw that it was the same smile as well. Only when she had come to within five feet of him did he begin to notice any differences. Her face was covered with freckles, which had not been true of Brigid's face, and her eyes were a deeper shade of green. They were also set more widely apart, ever so slightly farther from the bridge of her nose, and this minute alteration in her features enhanced the overall harmony of her face, making her a notch or two prettier than her sister had been. Hector returned her smile, and by the time she reached the counter and spoke to him in Brigid's voice, asking if he needed help, he no longer felt that he was about to fall to the floor in a dead swoon.

He was looking for Mr. O'Fallon, he said, and he wondered if it would be possible to talk to him. He made no effort to hide his accent, pronouncing the word *Meester* with an exaggerated roll to the final *r,* and then he leaned in closer to her, studying her face for signs of a reaction. Nothing happened, or rather the conversation continued as if nothing had happened, and at that moment Hector knew that Brigid had kept him a secret. She had been raised in a Catholic family, and she must have balked at the idea of letting her father and sisters know that she was bedding down with a man engaged to another woman and that the man, whose penis was circumcised, had no intention of breaking off his engagement to marry her. If that was the case, then they probably hadn't known she was pregnant. Nor that she had slit her wrists in the bathtub; nor that she had spent two months in a hospital dreaming of better and more efficient ways to kill herself. It was even possible that she had stopped writing to them before Saint John had ever appeared on the scene, when she was still confident enough to suppose that everything was going to work out as she hoped it would.

Hector's mind was galloping by then, rushing off in several directions at once, and when the woman behind the counter said that her father was out of town for the week, away on business in California, Hector felt that he knew what that business was. Red O'Fallon had gone down to Los Angeles to talk to the police about his missing daughter. He was urging them to do something about a case that had already dragged on for too many months, and if he wasn't satisfied with their answers, he was going to hire a private detective to begin the search all over again. Damn the expense, he had probably said to his Spokane daughter before he left town. Something had to be done before it was too late.

The Spokane daughter said that she was filling in at the store while her father was gone, but if Hector cared to leave his name and number, she would give him the message when he returned on Friday. No need, Hector said, he would come back on Friday himself, and then, just to be polite, or perhaps because he wanted to make a good impression on her, he asked if she had been left to run things on her own. It looked like too big of an operation to be handled by just one person, he said.

There were supposed to be three people, she answered, but the regular assistant had called in sick that morning, and the stockboy had been fired last week for pilfering baseball gloves and selling them at half price to kids in his neighborhood. The truth was that she was feeling a little lost, she said. It had been ages since she'd helped out at the store, and she couldn't tell the difference between a putter and a wood, could barely even use the cash register without pushing nine wrong buttons and bollixing the sale.

It was all very friendly and direct. She didn't seem to think twice about sharing these confidences with him, and as the conversation continued, Hector learned that she had been away for the past four years, studying to become a teacher at something she called State, which turned out to be the State College of Washington in Pullman. She had graduated in June, and now she was back home living with her father, about to begin her career as a fourth-grade teacher at the Horace Greeley Elementary School. She couldn't believe her luck, she told him.

That was the same school she had attended as a girl, and she and her two older sisters had all had Mrs. Neergaard in the fourth grade. Mrs. N. had taught there for forty-two years, and it struck her as something of a miracle that her old teacher had retired just when she herself had started looking for a job. In less than six weeks, she would be standing in front of the same classroom where she had sat every day as a ten-year-old pupil, and wasn't it strange, she said, wasn't it funny how life worked out sometimes?

Yes, very funny, Hector said, very strange. He knew now that he was talking to Nora, the youngest of the O'Fallon girls, and not to Deirdre, the one who had married at nineteen and gone off to live in San Francisco. After three minutes in her company, Hector decided that Nora was nothing like her dead sister. She might have resembled Brigid, but she had none of her tense, smart-aleck energy, none of her ambition, none of her high-strung, darting intelligence. This one was softer, more comfortable in her own flesh, more naive. He remembered that Brigid had once described herself as the only one of the O'Fallon sisters with real blood running in her veins. Deirdre was made of vinegar, she said, and Nora was composed entirely of warm milk. She was the one who should have been named Brigid, she said, after Saint Brigid, the patron saint of Ireland, for if there was ever a person destined to devote herself to a life of self-sacrifice and good works, it was her baby sister, Nora.

Again, Hector was about to turn around and leave, and once again something held him there. A new idea had entered his head—the maddest of impulses, a thing so risky and self-destructive that it amazed him that he had even thought of it, let alone that he felt he had the nerve to carry it out.

Nothing ventured, nothing gained, he said to Nora, smiling

apologetically and shrugging his shoulders, but the reason why he'd come in this morning was to ask Mr. O'Fallon for a job. He'd heard about that business with the stockboy and wondered if the position was still open. That's odd, Nora said. It happened just the other day, and they hadn't gotten around to placing a notice in the want ads yet. They weren't planning to do that until after her father returned from his trip. Well, word gets around, Hector said. Yes, that was probably true, Nora answered, but why would he want to be a stockboy anyway? That was a job for nobodies, for strong-backed men with dull minds and no ambitions; surely he could do better than that. Not necessarily, Hector said. Times were tough, and any job that paid money these days was a good job. Why not give him a chance? She was all alone in the store, and he knew that she could use some help. If she liked his work, maybe she would put in a good word for him with her father. What did Miss O'Fallon say? Did they have a deal?

He had been in Spokane for less than an hour, and already Herman Loesser was employed again. Nora shook his hand, laughing at the audacity of his proposal, and then Hector removed his jacket (the one decent article of clothing he owned), and started to work. He had turned himself into a moth, and he spent the rest of the day fluttering around a hot, burning candle. He knew that his wings could ignite at any moment, but the closer he came to touching the fire, the more he sensed that he was fulfilling his destiny. As he put it in his journal that night: *If I mean to save my life, then I have to come within an inch of destroying it.*

Against all the odds, Hector held on for close to a year. First as stockboy in the back room, then as chief clerk and assistant manager, working directly under O'Fallon himself. Nora said her father was fifty-three, but when Hector was introduced to him the following Monday, he felt he looked older than that, perhaps as old as sixty, perhaps as old as a hundred. The ex-athlete's hair was no longer red, the once lithe torso was no longer trim, and he limped sporadically from the effects of an arthritic knee. O'Fallon showed up at the store every morning at nine sharp, but the work clearly had no interest to him, and he was generally gone again by eleven or eleven-thirty. If his leg was feeling up to it, he would drive out to the country club and shoot a round of golf with two or three of his cronies. If it wasn't, he would eat a long early lunch at the Bluebell Inn, the restaurant directly across the street, and then go home and spend the afternoon in his bedroom, reading the papers and drinking from the bottles of Jameson's Irish whiskey he had smuggled in from Canada every month.

He never criticized Hector or complained about his work. Nor did he ever compliment him. O'Fallon expressed his satisfaction by saying nothing, and every so often, when he was in one of his more expansive moods, he would greet Hector with a minuscule nod of the head. For several months, there was little more contact between them than that. Hector found it jarring at first, but as time went on he learned not to take it personally. The man lived in a domain of mute inwardness, of unending resistance against the world, and he seemed to float through his days with no other purpose than to use up the hours as painlessly as possible. He never lost his temper, he seldom cracked a smile. He was fair-minded and detached, absent even when present, and he showed no more compassion or sympathy for himself than he did for anyone else.

To the degree that O'Fallon was closed off and indifferent to him, Nora was open and involved. She was the one who had hired Hector, after all, and she continued to feel responsible for him, treating him alternately as her friend, her protégé, and her human reclamation project. After her father returned from Los Angeles and the chief clerk recovered from his bout with the shingles, Nora's services were no longer required at the store. She was busy preparing for the upcoming school year, busy visiting old classmates, busy juggling the attentions of several young men, but for the rest of the summer she always managed to find time to swing by Red's in the early afternoon to see how Hector was getting on. They had worked together for only four days, but in that time they had established a tradition of sharing cheese sandwiches in the stockroom during their half-hour lunch break. Now she continued to show up with the cheese sandwiches, and they continued to spend those half hours talking about books. For Hector, the budding autodidact, it was a chance to learn something. For Nora, fresh out of college and committed to a life of instructing others, it was a chance to impart knowledge to a bright and hungry student. Hector was plowing through Shakespeare that summer, and Nora read the plays along with him, helping him out with the words he didn't understand, explaining this or that point of history or theatrical convention, exploring the psychology and motivations of the characters. During one of their back-room sessions, as Hector stumbled over the pronunciation of the words *Thou ow'st* in the third act of *Lear,* he confessed to her how much his accent embarrassed him. He couldn't learn to speak this bloody language, he said, and he would always sound like a fool when he talked in front of people like her. Nora refused to listen to such pessimism. She had minored in speech therapy at State, she said, and there were concrete remedies, practical exercises, and techniques for improvement. If he was willing to take on the challenge, she promised to get rid of the accent for him, to remove all traces of Spanish from his tongue. Hector reminded her that he was in no position to pay for such lessons. Who said anything about money? Nora answered. If he was willing to work, she was willing to help.

After school opened in September, the new fourth-grade teacher was no longer available for lunch. She and her pupil worked in the evenings instead, getting together every Tuesday and Thursday from seven to nine in the parlor of the O'Fallon house. Hector struggled mightily with the short *i* and *e,* the lisping *th,* the toothless *r.* Silent vowels, interdental plosives, labial inflections, fricatives, palatal occlusions, phonemes. Much of the time, he had no idea what Nora was talking about, but the exercises seemed to have an effect. His tongue began to produce sounds it had never made before, and eventually, after nine months of strain and repetition, he had advanced to the point where it was becoming increasingly difficult to tell where he had been born. He didn't sound like an American, perhaps, but neither did he sound like a raw, uneducated immigrant. Coming to Spokane might have been one of the worst blunders Hector ever made, but of all the things that happened to him there, Nora's pronunciation lessons probably had the deepest and most lasting effect. Every word he spoke for the next fifty years was influenced by them, and they remained in his body for the rest of his life.

O'Fallon tended to stay upstairs in his room on Tuesdays and Thursdays, or else to be out for the evening, playing poker with friends. One night in early October, the telephone rang in the middle of a lesson, and Nora went into the front hall to answer it. She talked to the operator for a few moments, and then, in a tense and excited voice, called up to her father and told him that Stegman was on the line. He was in Los Angeles, she said, and wanted to reverse the charges. Should she accept or not? O'Fallon said that he would be right down. Nora closed the sliding doors between the parlor and the front hall to give her father privacy, but O'Fallon was slightly drunk by then, and he talked in a loud enough voice for Hector to make out some of the things he said. Not every thing, but enough of them to know that the call had not brought good news.

Ten minutes later, the sliding doors opened again, and O'Fallon shuffled into the parlor. He was wearing a pair of worn-out leather slippers, and his suspenders were off his shoulders, hanging down around his knees. Both his tie and collar were gone, and he had to grip the edge of the walnut end table to steady his balance. For the next little while, he talked directly to Nora, who was sitting beside Hector on the davenport in the middle of the room. For all the attention he paid to Hector, his daughter's student might have been invisible. It wasn't that O'Fallon ignored him, and it wasn't that he pretended he wasn't there. He simply didn't notice him. And Hector, who understood every nuance of the conversation that followed, didn't dare get up and leave.

Stegman was throwing in the towel, O'Fallon said. He'd been working on the case for months, and he hadn't turned up a single promising lead. It was getting to him, he said. He didn't want to take any more of their money.

Nora asked her father how he'd responded to that, and O'Fallon said he'd told him that if he felt so bad about taking their money, why the hell did he keep reversing the charges when he called? And then he'd told him he was lousy at his job. If Stegman didn't want the work, he'd look for someone else.

No, Dad, Nora replied, you're wrong. If Stegman couldn't find her, that meant no one could. He was the best private operative on the West Coast. Reynolds said so, and Reynolds was a man they could trust.

To hell with Reynolds, O'Fallon said. To hell with Stegman. They could say whatever they goddamn liked, but he wasn't going to give up.

Nora shook her head back and forth, her eyes filling with tears. It was time to face facts, she said. If Brigid was alive somewhere, she would have written a letter. She would have called. She would have let them know where she was.

The balls she would have, O'Fallon said. She hadn't written a letter in over four years. She'd broken with the family, and that was the fact they had to face.

Not with the family, Nora said. With him. Brigid had been writing to her all along. When she was at school in Pullman, there'd been a letter every three or four weeks.

But O'Fallon didn't want to hear about that. He didn't want to discuss it anymore, and if she wasn't going to stand behind him, then he'd push on alone and damn her and her goddamn opinions. And with those words, O'Fallon let go of the table, wobbled precariously for an instant or two as he tried to regain his footing, and then staggered out of the room.

Hector wasn't supposed to have witnessed this scene. He was just the stockboy, not an intimate friend, and he had no business listening in on private conversations between father and daughter, no right to be sitting in the room as his boss staggered around in a drunken, disheveled state. If Nora had asked him to leave at that moment, the matter would have been closed forever. He wouldn't have heard what he had heard, he wouldn't have seen what he had seen, and the subject never would have been mentioned again. All she had to do was speak one sentence, make one feeble excuse, and Hector would have risen from the davenport and said good night. But Nora had no talent for dissembling. The tears were still in her eyes when O'Fallon left the room, and now that the forbidden subject was finally out in the open, why hold anything back?

Her father hadn't always been like that, she said. When she and her sisters were young, he had been a different person, and it was hard to recognize him now, hard to remember what he'd been like back in the old days. Red O'Fallon, the Northwest Flash. Patrick O'Fallon, the husband of Mary Day. Dad O'Fallon, the emperor of little girls. But think of the past six years, Nora said, think of what he'd been through, and maybe it wasn't so strange that his best friend was a man named Jameson—that grim silent fellow who lived upstairs with him, trapped in all those bottles of amber liquid. The first blow came with the death of her mother, killed by cancer at age forty-four. That had been rough enough, she said, but then bad things kept happening, one family upheaval followed by another, a punch to the stomach and then one to the face, and little by little the stuffing had been knocked out of him. Less than a year after the funeral, Deirdre got herself pregnant, and when she refused to go through with the shotgun wedding O'Fallon had arranged for her, he kicked her out of the house. That turned Brigid against him, too, Nora said. Her oldest sister was in her last year of Smith, living all the way across the country, but when she heard about what happened, she wrote to her father and said that she would never talk to him again unless he welcomed Deirdre back into the house. O'Fallon wouldn't do that. He was paying for Brigid's education, and who did she think she was telling him what to do? She paid her own tuition for the final semester, and then, after her graduation, headed straight out to California to become a writer. She didn't even stop off in Spokane for a visit. She was as stubborn as her father, Nora said, and Deirdre was twice as stubborn as both of them together. It didn't matter that Deirdre was married now and had given birth to another baby. She still wouldn't talk to her father, and neither would Brigid. Meanwhile, Nora went off to attend college in Pullman. She kept in regular contact with both her sisters, but Brigid was the better correspondent, and it was the rare month when Nora didn't receive at least one letter from her. Then, some time at the beginning of Nora's junior year, Brigid stopped writing. At first, it didn't seem like anything to get alarmed about, but after three or four months of continuing silence, Nora wrote to Deirdre and asked if she had had any recent news from Brigid. When Deirdre answered that she hadn't heard from her in six months, Nora began to worry. She talked to her father about it, and poor O'Fallon, desperate to make amends, crushed by guilt over what he had done to his two oldest daughters, immediately contacted the Los Angeles Police Department. A detective named Reynolds was assigned to the case. The investigation took off rapidly, and within several days many of the crucial facts had already been established: that Brigid had quit her job at the magazine, that she had attempted suicide and wound up in the hospital, that she had been pregnant, that she had moved out of her apartment without leaving a forwarding address, that she was indeed missing. Dark as this news was, shattering as it was to contemplate what these facts implied, it looked as though Reynolds was on the brink of discovering what had happened to her. Then, little by little, the trail went cold. A month went by, then three months, then eight months, and Reynolds had nothing new to report. They were talking to everyone who had known her, he said, doing everything they possibly could, but once they'd traced her to the Fitzwilliam Arms, they had run into a brick wall. Frustrated by this lack of progress, O'Fallon decided to push things along by engaging the services of a private detective. Reynolds recommended a man named Frank Stegman, and for a time O'Fallon was filled with new hope. The case was all he lived for, Nora said, and whenever Stegman reported the smallest bit of new information, the tiniest hint of a lead, her father would be on the first train to Los Angeles, traveling through the night if necessary, and then knocking on the door of Stegman's office first thing the next morning. But Stegman had run out of ideas now, and he was ready to give up. Hector had heard it himself. That's what the telephone call had been about, she said, and she couldn't really fault him for wanting to quit. Brigid was dead. She knew that, Reynolds and Stegman knew that, but her father still refused to accept it. He blamed himself for everything, and unless he had some reason to hope, unless he could delude himself into believing that Brigid was going to be found, he wouldn't be able to live with himself. It was that simple, Nora said. Her father would die. The pain would be too much for him, and he would just crumple up and die.

After that night, Nora went on telling him everything. It made sense that she should want to share her troubles with someone, but of all the people in the world, of all the potential candidates she could have chosen from, Hector was the one who got the job. He became Nora's confidant, the repository of information about his own crime, and every Tuesday and Thursday night, as he sat next to her on the davenport and struggled through another one of his lessons, he felt a little more of his brain disintegrate in his head. Life was a fever dream, he discovered, and reality was a groundless world of figments and hallucinations, a place where everything you imagined came true. Did he know who Hector Mann was? Nora actually asked him that question one night. Stegman had come up with a new theory, she said, and after backing out of the affair two months ago, the private eye had called O'Fallon over the weekend and asked for another chance. He'd found out that Brigid had published an article about Hector Mann. Eleven months later, Mann had disappeared, and he wondered if it was just a coincidence that Brigid had disappeared at the same time. What if there was a connection between the two unsolved cases? Stegman couldn't promise any results, but at least he had something to work on now, and with O'Fallon's permission, he wanted to pursue it. If he could establish that Brigid had gone on seeing Mann after she wrote the article, there might be some cause for optimism.

No, Hector said, he'd never heard of him. Who was this Hector Mann? Nora didn't know much about him either. An actor, she said. He'd made some silent comedies a few years ago, but she hadn't seen any of them. There hadn't been enough time to go to the movies when she was in college. No, Hector said, he didn't go very often himself. They cost money, and he'd once read somewhere that movies were bad for your eyes. Nora said that she dimly remembered hearing about the case, but she hadn't followed it too closely at the time. According to Stegman, Mann had been missing for almost two years. And why had he left? Hector wanted to know. No one was sure, Nora said. He'd just vanished one day, and he hadn't been heard from since. It didn't sound too hopeful, Hector said. A man can stay hidden for just so long. If they hadn't found him by now, that probably meant he was dead. Yes, probably, Nora agreed, and Brigid was probably dead, too. But there were rumors, she continued, and Stegman was going to look into them. What kind of rumors? Hector asked. That maybe he'd gone back to South America, Nora said. That was where he was from. Brazil, Argentina, she couldn't remember which country, but it was incredible, wasn't it? How so incredible? Hector asked. That Hector Mann should have been from the same part of the world that he was. What were the odds against that? She was forgetting that South America was a big place, Hector said. South Americans were everywhere. Yes, she knew that, Nora said, but even so, wouldn't it be incredible if Brigid had gone down there with him? It made her happy just to think about it. Two sisters, two South Americans. Brigid in one place with hers, and she in another with hers.

It wouldn't have been so terrible if he hadn't liked her so much, if a part of him hadn't fallen in love with her the first day they met. Hector knew that she was off-limits, that even to contemplate the possibility of touching her would have been an unpardonable sin, and yet he kept returning to her house every Tuesday and Thursday night, dying a little death every time she sat down beside him on the davenport and nestled her twenty-two-year-old body into the burgundy velour cushions. It would have been so simple to reach out and begin stroking her neck, to run his hand down the length of her arm, to turn toward her and begin kissing the freckles on her face. Grotesque as their conversations sometimes were (Brigid and Stegman, her father's deterioration, the pursuit of Hector Mann), tamping down these urges was even harder on him, and it took every ounce of his strength not to cross the line. After two hours of torture, he often found himself heading straight from the lesson toward the river, walking across town until he reached a small neighborhood of collapsing houses and two-story hotels where women could be bought for twenty or thirty minutes of their time. It was a dismal solution, but there were no alternatives. Less than two years before, the most attractive women in Hollywood had been fighting to jump into bed with Hector. Now he was shelling out for it in the back alleys of Spokane, squandering half a day's wages on a few minutes of release.

It never occurred to Hector that Nora might have felt anything for him. He was a lamentable figure, a man not worthy of consideration, and if Nora was willing to give him so much of her time, it was only because she pitied him, because she was a young and passionate person who fancied herself a savior of lost souls. Saint Brigid, as her sister had called her, the martyr of the family. Hector was the naked African tribesman, and Nora was the American missionary who had thrashed her way through the jungle to improve his lot. He had never met anyone so candid, so hopeful, so ignorant of the dark forces at work in the world. At times, he wondered if she wasn't just plain stupid. At other times, she seemed to be possessed of a singular, rarefied wisdom. At still other times, when she turned to him with that intense and stubborn look in her eyes, he thought his heart would break. That was the paradox of the year he spent in Spokane. Nora made life intolerable for him, and yet Nora was the only thing he lived for, the only reason why he didn't pack his bags and leave.

Half the time, he was afraid that he would confess to her. The other half of the time, he was afraid that he would be caught. Stegman followed the Hector Mann angle for three and a half months before giving up again. Where the police had failed, so had the private detective, but that didn't mean that Hector's position was any more secure. O'Fallon had gone to Los Angeles several times in the fall and winter, and it seemed likely to assume that at some point during those visits Stegman had shown him photographs of Hector Mann. What if O'Fallon had noticed the resemblance between his hardworking stock-boy and the missing actor? In early February, not long after he returned from his last trip to California, O'Fallon began looking at Hector in a new way. He seemed more alert, somehow, more curious, and Hector couldn't help wondering if Nora's father wasn't on to him. After months of silence and barely restrained contempt, the old man was suddenly paying attention to the lowly lifter of boxes who toiled in the back room of his store. The indifferent nods were replaced with smiles, and every now and then, for no particular reason, he would pat his employee on the shoulder and ask him how he was doing. Even more remarkable, O'Fallon began opening the door when Hector arrived at the house for his evening lessons. He would shake his hand as though he were a welcomed guest, and then, somewhat awkwardly, but with obvious goodwill, stand around for a moment to comment on the weather before retiring to his room upstairs. With any other man, this behavior would have been seen as normal, the bare minimum required by the rules of etiquette, but in O'Fallon's case it was altogether confounding, and Hector didn't trust it. Too much was at stake to be suckered in by a few polite smiles and friendly words, and the longer this sham amiability went on, the more frightened Hector became. By the middle of February, he sensed that his days in Spokane were numbered. A trap was being set for him, and he had to be prepared to skip town at any moment, to run off into the night and never show his face to them again.

Then the other shoe dropped. Just as Hector was planning to deliver his good-bye speech to Nora, O'Fallon cornered him in the back room of the store one afternoon and asked him if he was interested in a raise. Goines had given notice, he said. The assistant manager was moving to Seattle to run his brother-in-law's print shop, and O'Fallon wanted to fill the position as quickly as possible. He knew that Hector didn't have any experience in sales, but he'd been watching him, he said, he'd been keeping an eye on how he went about his business, and he didn't think it would take him long to catch on to the new job. There would be more responsibility and longer hours, but his salary would be double what it was now. Did he want to think it over, or was he ready to accept? Hector was ready to accept. O'Fallon shook his hand, congratulated him on the promotion, and then gave him the rest of the day off. Just as Hector was about to leave the store, however, O'Fallon called him back. Open the cash register and take out a twenty-dollar bill, the boss said. Then go down the block to Pressler's Haberdashery and buy yourself a new suit, some white shirts, and a couple of bow ties. You're going to be working out front now, and you need to look your best.

In practical terms, O'Fallon had handed over the operation of his business to Hector. He had given him the title of assistant manager, but the fact was that Hector didn't assist anyone. He was in charge of running the store, and O'Fallon, who was officially the manager of his own enterprise, managed nothing. Red spent too little time on the premises to concern himself with petty details, and once he understood that this go-getting foreign upstart could handle the responsibilities of the new post, he scarcely bothered to come around anymore. He was so tired of the business by then, he never even learned the new stockboy's name.

Hector excelled as de facto manager of Red's Sporting Goods. After the yearlong isolation of the Portland barrel factory and the solitary confinement of O'Fallon's stockroom, he welcomed the chance to be among people again. The store was like a small theater, and the role he had been given was essentially the same one he had played in his films: Hector as conscientious underling, as snappy, bow-tie-wearing clerk. The only difference was that his name was Herman Loesser now, and he had to play it straight. No pratfalls or stubbed toes, no slapstick contortions or bumps on the head. His job was to persuade, to oversee the accounts, and to defend the virtues of sport. But no one said that he had to go about it with a glum expression on his face. He had an audience in front of him again and numerous props to work with, and once he figured out the routine, his old actor's instincts came rushing back to him. He charmed the customers with his loquacious spiels, enthralled them with his demonstrations of catcher's gloves and fly-fishing techniques, won their loyalty with his willingness to knock off five, ten, and even fifteen percent from the list price. Wallets were thin in 1931, but games were an inexpensive distraction, a good way not to think about what you couldn't afford, and Red's continued to do a decent business. Boys would play ball no matter what the circumstances, and men would never stop casting lines into rivers and shooting bullets into the bodies of wild animals. And then, not to be forgotten, there was the matter of uniforms. Not just for the teams from the local high schools and colleges, but for the two hundred members of the Rotary Club Bowling League, the ten squads of the Catholic Charities Basketball Association, and the lineups of three dozen amateur softball outfits as well. O'Fallon had locked up that market a decade and a half ago, and every season the orders continued to roll in, as precise and regular as the phases of the moon.

One night in the middle of April, as Hector and Nora came to the end of their Tuesday lesson, Nora turned to him and announced that she had received a proposal of marriage. The statement came out of nowhere, with no reference to anything that had come before it, and for a couple of seconds Hector wasn't sure if he had heard her correctly. An announcement of that sort was usually accompanied by a smile, perhaps even a laugh, but Nora wasn't smiling, and she didn't sound the least bit happy to be sharing this news with him. Hector asked the name of the lucky young man. Nora shook her head, then looked down at the floor and began fidgeting with her blue cotton dress. When she looked up again, there were tears glistening in her eyes. Her lips started to move, but before she managed to say anything, she abruptly rose from her seat, put her hand over her mouth, and rushed out of the parlor.

She was gone before he knew what had happened. There wasn't even enough time for him to call out to her, and when he heard Nora run up the stairs and then bang the door of her room shut, he understood that she wouldn't be coming down again that night. The lesson was over. He should be going, he said to himself, but several minutes went by, and he didn't stir from the davenport. Eventually, O'Fallon drifted into the room. It was just past nine, and Red was in his usual nocturnal condition, but not so far gone that he couldn't keep his balance. He fixed his eyes on Hector, and for the longest time he went on staring at his assistant manager, looking him up and down as a small, crooked smile formed in the lower part of his mouth. Hector couldn't tell if it was a smile of pity or mockery. It looked like both, somehow, a kind of compassionate disdain, if such a thing were possible, and Hector found it disturbing, a sign of some festering hostility that O'Fallon hadn't revealed in months. At last Hector stood up and asked: Is Nora getting married? The boss let out a brief, sarcastic laugh. How the hell should I know? he said. Why don't you ask her yourself? And then, grunting in response to his own laugh, O'Fallon turned and left the room.

Two nights later, Nora apologized for her outburst. She was feeling better now, she said, and the crisis was over. She'd turned him down, and that was that. Case closed; nothing more to worry about. Albert Sweeney was a fine person, but he was just a boy, and she was tired of being with boys, especially rich boys who lived off their fathers' money. If she was ever going to get married, it would be to a man, to someone who knew his way around the world and could take care of himself. Hector said that she couldn't blame Sweeney for having a rich father. It wasn't his fault, and besides, what was so bad about being rich, anyway? Nothing, Nora said. She just didn't want to marry him, that's all. Marriage was forever, and she wasn't going to say yes until the right man came along.

Nora soon recovered her spirits, but Hector's relations with O'Fallon seemed to have entered a new and troubling phase. The turning point had been the showdown in the parlor, with the long stare and the short, derisive laugh, and after that night Hector sensed that he was being watched again. When O'Fallon came into the store now, he took no part in transacting business or dealing with customers. Rather than lend a hand or fill in behind the cash register when things got busy, he would install himself in a chair beside the display case for tennis racquets and golf gloves and quietly read the morning papers, glancing up every now and then with that caustic smile pulling at the lower part of his mouth. It was as though he regarded his assistant as an amusing pet or wind-up toy. Hector was earning good money for him, putting in ten and eleven hours a day so that he could live in quasi retirement, but all these efforts only seemed to make O'Fallon more skeptical of him, more condescending. Wary as Hector was, he pretended not to notice. It was all right to be considered an overzealous fool, he reasoned, and maybe it wasn't even so bad when he started calling you Muchacho and El Señor, but you didn't get close to a man like that, and whenever he entered the room, you made sure that your back was turned to the wall.

When he invited you out to his country club, however, asking you to join him for eighteen holes of golf on a bright Sunday morning in early May, you didn't say no. Nor did you turn him down when he offered to buy you lunch at the Bluebell Inn, not once but twice in the span of a single week, both times insisting that you order the most expensive dishes on the menu. As long as he didn't know your secret, as long as he didn't suspect what you were doing in Spokane, you could tolerate the pressure of his constant scrutiny. You bore up to it precisely because you found it unbearable to be with him, because you pitied him for the wreck he had become, because every time you heard that cynical desolation seeping out from his voice, you knew that you were partly responsible for putting it there.

Their second lunch at the Bluebell Inn took place on a Wednesday afternoon in late May. If Hector had been prepared for what was going to happen, he probably would have reacted differently, but after twenty-five minutes of inconsequential talk, O'Fallon's question caught him by surprise. That evening, when Hector returned to his boardinghouse on the other side of town, he wrote in his journal that the universe had changed shape for him in a single instant. *I have missed everything. I have misunderstood everything. The earth is the sky, the sun is the moon, the rivers are mountains. I have been looking at the wrong world.* Then, with the events of the afternoon still fresh in his mind, he wrote down a word-for-word account of his conversation with O'Fallon:

And so, Loesser, O'Fallon suddenly asked him, tell me what your intentions are.

I do not understand this word, Hector replied. A lovely steak sits in front of me, and I have every intention of eating it up. Is that what you are inquiring about?

You're a sharp fellow, Chico. You know what I mean.

Begging your pardon, sir, but these intentions bewilder me. I do not grasp them.

Long-range intentions.

Oh, yes, now I see. You refer to the future, my thoughts about the future. I can safely say that my only intentions are to go on as I am now. To continue working for you. To do the best I can for the store.

And what else?

There is no else, Mr. O'Fallon. I speak from the heart. You have given me a great opportunity, and I mean to make the most of it.

And who do you think talked me into giving you that opportunity?

I cannot say. I always thought it was your decision, that you were the one who gave me my chance.

It was Nora.

Miss O'Fallon? She never told me. I had no idea that she was responsible. I owe her so much already, and now it seems I am even further in her debt. I am humbled by what you tell me.

Do you enjoy watching her suffer?

Miss Nora suffer? Why on earth should she suffer? She is a remarkable, spirited girl, and everyone admires her. I know that family sorrows weigh on her heart—as they do on yours, sir—but other than the tears she occasionally sheds for her absent sister, I have never seen her in anything but the most lively and buoyant moods.

She's strong. She puts up a good front.

It pains me to hear this.

Albert Sweeney proposed to her last month, and she turned him down. Why do you think she did that? The boy's father is Hiram Sweeney, the state senator, the most powerful Republican in the county. She could have lived off the fat of the land for the next fifty years, and she said no. Why do you think, Loesser?

She told me she did not love him.

That's right. Because she loves someone else. And who do you think that person is?

It is impossible for me to answer that question. I know nothing about Miss Nora's feelings, sir.

You're not a pansy, are you, Herman?

Excuse me, sir?

A pansy. A homo fruit-boy.

Of course not.

Then why don't you do something?

You talk in riddles, Mr. O'Fallon. I cannot grasp.

I'm tired, son. I have nothing to live for now except one thing, and once that thing is taken care of, all I want is to croak in peace. You help me out, and I'm willing to make a bargain with you. Just say the word, amigo, and everything is yours. The store, the business, the whole works.

Are you offering to sell me your business? I have no money. I am in no position to make such bargains.

You drift into the store last summer begging for work, and now you're running the show. You're good at it, Loesser. Nora was right about you, and I'm not going to stand in her way. I'm finished standing in anyone's way. Whatever she wants, that's what she gets.

Why do you keep referring to Miss Nora? I thought you were making a business proposition.

I am. But not unless you oblige me with this one thing. It's not as though I'm asking you for something you don't want yourself. I see the way you two look at each other. All you have to do is make your move.

What are you saying, Mr. O'Fallon?

Figure it out for yourself.

I cannot, sir. I truly cannot.

Nora, stupid. You're the one she's in love with.

But I am nothing, nothing at all. Nora could not love me.

You might think that, and I might think that, but we're both wrong. The girl's heart is breaking, and I'll be damned if I sit by and watch her suffer anymore. I've lost two kids already, and it's not going to happen again.

But I must not marry Nora. I am a Jew, and such things are not permitted.

What kind of a Jew?

A Jew. There is only one kind of Jew.

Do you believe in God?

What difference does that make? I am not like you. I come from another world.

Answer the question. Do you believe in God?

No, I do not. I believe that man is the measure of all things. Both good and bad.

Then we belong to the same religion. We're the same, Loesser. The only difference is that you understand money better than I do. That means you'll be able to take care of her. That's all I want. Take care of Nora, and then I can die a good death.

You put me in a difficult position, sir.

You don't know what difficult is, hombre. You propose to her by the end of the month, or else I'm going to fire you. Do you understand? I'm going to fire you, and then I'm going to kick your ass clear out of the goddamn state.

Hector spared him the trouble. Four hours after leaving the Bluebell Inn, he closed up the store for the last time, then returned to his room and began packing his things. At some point during the evening, he borrowed his landlady's Underwood and typed out a one-page letter to Nora, signing it at the bottom with the initials H. L. He couldn't take the risk of leaving her with a sample of his handwriting, but neither could he walk off without an explanation, without inventing some story to account for his sudden, mysterious departure.

He told her that he was married. It was the biggest lie he could think of, but in the long run it was less cruel than an out-and-out rejection would have been. His wife had fallen ill in New York, and he had to rush back there to deal with the emergency. Nora would be stunned, of course, but once she understood that there had never been any hope for them, that Hector had been unavailable to her from the beginning, she would be able to recover from her disappointment without any lasting scars. O'Fallon would probably see through the deception, but even if the old man figured out the truth for himself, it was doubtful that he would share it with Nora. He was in the business of protecting his daughter's feelings, and why should he object to the removal of this inconvenient nobody who had wormed his way into her affections? He would be glad to be rid of Hector, and little by little, as the dust finally settled, young Sweeney would start coming around again, and Nora would return to her senses. In his letter, Hector thanked her for the many kindnesses she had shown him. He would never forget her, he said. She was a shining spirit, a woman above all other women, and just knowing her for the short time he had been in Spokane had permanently changed his life. All true, and yet all false. Every sentence a lie, and yet every word written with conviction. He waited until three o'clock in the morning, and then he walked to her house and slipped the letter under the front door—just as her dead sister, Brigid, on a similar errand two and a half years ago, had once slipped a letter under the door of his house.

He tried to kill himself in Montana the next day, Alma said, and three days after that he tried again in Chicago. The first time, he stuck the revolver in his mouth; the second time, he pressed the barrel against his left eye—but in neither instance was he able to go through with it. He had checked into a hotel on South Wabash at the fringes of Chinatown, and after the second failed attempt he walked out into the sweltering June night, looking for a place to get drunk. If he could pour enough liquor into his system, he figured it would give him the courage to jump into the river and drown himself before the night was over. That was the plan, in any case, but not long after he went out in search of the bottle, he stumbled onto something better than death, better than the simple damnation he'd been looking for. Her name was Sylvia Meers, and under her guidance Hector learned that he could go on killing himself without having to finish the job. She was the one who taught him how to drink his own blood, who instructed him in the pleasures of devouring his own heart.

He ran into her in a Rush Street gin mill, standing against the bar as he was about to order his second drink. She wasn't much to look at, but the price she quoted was so negligible that Hector found himself agreeing to her terms. He would be dead before the night was out anyway, and what could be more fitting than to spend his last hours on earth with a whore?

She took him across the street to a room in the White House Hotel, and once they had finished their business on the bed, she asked him if he would care to have another go at it. Hector declined, explaining that he didn't have the money for an additional round, but when she told him that there wouldn't be any extra charge, he shrugged and said why not, then proceeded to mount her for a second time. The encore soon ended with another ejaculation, and Sylvia Meers smiled. She complimented Hector on his performance, and then she asked him if he thought he had the stuff to do it again. Not right away, Hector said, but if she gave him half an hour, it probably wouldn't be any trouble. That wasn't good enough, she said. If he could make it in twenty minutes, she would give him another treat, but he would have to get hard again within ten. She looked over at the clock on the bedside table. Ten minutes from now, she said, starting when the second hand swept past the twelve. That was the deal. Ten minutes to get going, and then another ten minutes to finish the job. If he went soft on her at any point along the way, however, he would have to reimburse her for the last time. That was the penalty. Three times for the price of one, or else he coughed up retail for the whole thing. What was it going to be? Did he want to walk away now, or did he think he could come through under pressure?

If she hadn't been smiling when she asked the question, Hector would have thought she was insane. Whores didn't give away their services for free, and they didn't issue challenges to the virility of their clients. That was for the whip specialists and the secret man-haters, the ones who trafficked in suffering and bizarre humiliations, but Meers struck him as a blowsy, lighthearted sort of girl, and she didn't seem to be taunting him so much as trying to coax him into playing a game. No, not a game exactly, but an experiment, a scientific investigation into the copulative staying power of his twice-exhausted member. Could the dead be resurrected, she seemed to be asking him, and if so, how many times? Guesswork wasn't allowed. In order to provide conclusive results, the study had to be conducted under the strictest laboratory conditions.

Hector smiled back at her. Meers was sprawled out on the bed with a cigarette in her hand—confident, relaxed, perfectly at home in her nakedness. What was in it for her? Hector wanted to know. Money, she said. Lots of money. That was a good one, Hector said. There she was offering it for nothing, and in the same breath she was talking about getting rich. How dumb was that? Not dumb, she said, clever. There was money to be made, and if he could get it up again in the next nine minutes, he stood to make it with her.

She put out her cigarette and started running her hands over her body, stroking her breasts and smoothing her palms along her stomach, trailing her fingertips along the insides of her thighs and angling them into contact with her pubic hair, her vulva, and her clitoris, spreading herself open for him as her mouth parted and she slid her tongue over her lips.

Hector was not immune to these classic provocations. Slowly but steadily the dead man inched himself out from his grave, and when Meers saw what was happening, she made a naughty little humming sound in her throat, a single prolonged note that seemed to combine both approval and encouragement. Lazarus was breathing again. She rolled over onto her stomach, muttering a string of four-letter words and moaning in feigned arousal, and then she lifted her ass into the air and told him to go into her. Hector wasn't quite ready, but as he pressed his penis against the scarlet folds of her labia, he stiffened enough to achieve penetration. He didn't have much left by the end, but something came out of him besides sweat, enough to prove the point at any rate, and when he finally slid off her and sank onto the sheets, she turned and kissed him on the mouth. Seventeen minutes, she said. He had done it three times in less than an hour, and that was all she had been looking for. If he wanted in, she was willing to make him her partner.

Hector had no idea what she was talking about. She explained it, and when he still didn't understand what she was trying to tell him, she explained it again. There were men, she said, rich men in Chicago, rich men all over the Midwest who were willing to pay good money to watch people fuck. Oh, Hector said, you mean stag films, blue movies. No, Meers replied, none of that fake stuff. Live performances. Real fucking in front of real people.

She had been doing it for a while, she said, but last month her partner had been arrested on a botched breaking-and-entering job. Poor Al. He drank too much and was having trouble getting it up anyway. Even if he hadn't put himself out of commission, it probably would have been time to start looking for a replacement. In the past couple of weeks, three or four other candidates had survived the test, but none of those fellows could measure up to Hector. She liked his body, she said, she liked the feel of his cock, and she thought he had a terrifically handsome face.

Oh no, Hector said. He would never show his face. If she wanted him to work with her, he would have to wear a mask.

He wasn't being squeamish. His films had been popular in Chicago, and he couldn't take the risk of being recognized. Holding up his end of the bargain would be hard enough, but he didn't see how he could go through with it if he had to perform in a state of fear, if every time he walked in front of an audience he would have to worry that someone was about to call out his name. That was his only condition, he said. Let him hide his face, and she could count him in.

Meers was dubious. Why would he show his dick to the world and then not let anyone see who he was? If she were a man, she said, she'd be proud to have what he had. She'd want everyone to know that it belonged to her.

But they wouldn't be there to look at him, Hector said. She was the star, and the less the audience thought about who he was, the hotter their performances would be. Put a mask on him, and he would have no personality, no distinguishing characteristics, nothing to interfere with the fantasies of the men who were watching them. They didn't want to see him fuck her, he said, they wanted to imagine they were fucking her themselves. Make him anonymous, and he would be turned into an engine of male desire, the representative of every man in the audience. The stiff-boned Sir Stud, banging away at the body of the insatiable Lady Cunt. Every man, and therefore any man. But just one woman, he said, ever and always just one woman, and her name was Sylvia Meers.

Meers bought the argument. It was her first lesson in the tactics of show business, and even if she couldn't follow everything that Hector said to her, she liked the way it sounded, she liked it that he wanted her to be the star. By the time he called her Lady Cunt, she was laughing out loud. Where had he learned to talk like that? she asked him. She'd never known a man who could make something sound so dirty and so beautiful at the same time.

Squalor has its own rewards, Hector said, purposely talking over her head. If a man decides to crawl into his tomb, who better to keep him company than a warm-blooded woman? He dies more slowly that way, and as long as his flesh is joined to her flesh, he can live off the smell of his own corruption.

Meers laughed again, unable to grasp the meaning of Hector's words. It sounded like Bible talk to her, the stuff of preachers and roadside evangelists, but Hector's little poem on death and degeneration was delivered so calmly, with such a kind and friendly smile on his face, that she assumed he was making a joke. Not for a moment did she understand that he had just confessed his innermost secrets to her, that she was looking at a man who four hours earlier had sat down on the bed in his hotel room and pressed a loaded gun against his brain for the second time that week. Hector was glad. When he saw the lack of comprehension in her eyes, he felt lucky to have fallen in with such a dim, lusterless tart. No matter how much time he spent with her, he knew that he would always be alone when they were together.

Meers was in her early twenties, a South Dakota farm girl who had run away from home at sixteen, landed in Chicago a year later, and started working the streets the same month that Lindbergh flew across the Atlantic. There was nothing compelling about her, nothing to set her apart from a thousand other whores in a thousand other hotel rooms at that same moment. A peroxide blonde with a round face, dull gray eyes, and the remnants of acne scars dotting her cheeks, she carried herself with a certain sluttish bravura, but there was no magic in her, no charm to keep one's interest alive for very long. Her neck was too short for the proportions of her body, her small breasts drooped a little, and there was already a slight buildup of flab around her hips and buttocks. As she and Hector worked out the terms of their agreement (a sixty-forty split, which Hector found more than generous), he suddenly turned away, realizing that he wouldn't be able to go through with it if he went on looking at her. What's the matter, Herm, she asked him, ain't you feelin' well? I'm fine, Hector said, his eyes still fixed on a patch of crumbling plaster at the opposite end of the room. I've never felt better in my life. I'm so happy, I could open the window and start screaming like a madman. That's how good I feel, baby. I'm out of my mind, out of my mind with joy.

Six days later, Hector and Sylvia put on their first public performance. Between that initial engagement in early June and their final show in mid-December, Alma calculated that they appeared together some forty-seven times. Most of the work took place in and around Chicago, but some bookings came in from as far away as Minneapolis, Detroit, and Cleveland. The venues ranged from nightclubs to hotel suites, from warehouses and brothels to office buildings and private homes. Their largest audience consisted of about a hundred spectators (at a fraternity party in Normal, Illinois), and the smallest had just one (repeated on ten separate occasions for the same man). The act varied according to the wishes of the clients. Sometimes Hector and Sylvia put on little plays, complete with costumes and dialogue, and at other times they did nothing more than walk in naked and screw in silence. The skits were based on the most conventional erotic daydreams, and they tended to work best in front of small- to medium-sized crowds. The most popular one was the nurse and patient routine. People seemed to like watching Sylvia take off the starched white uniform, and they never failed to applaud when she began unwrapping the gauze bandages from Hector's body. There was also the Confession Box Scandal (which ended with the priest ravishing the nun) and, more elaborately, the tale of the two libertines who meet at a masked ball in pre-revolutionary France. In almost every instance, the spectators were exclusively male. The larger gatherings were usually quite raucous (bachelor parties, birthday celebrations), while the smaller groups rarely made any noise at all. Bankers and lawyers, businessmen and politicians, athletes, stockbrokers, and representatives of the idle rich: they all watched in spellbound fascination. More often than not, at least two or three of them would open their trousers and begin to masturbate. A married couple from Fort Wayne, Indiana, who engaged the duo's services for a private performance in their home, went so far as to undress during the act and begin making love themselves. Meers had been right, Hector discovered. There was good money to be made from daring to give people what they wanted.

He rented a small efficiency apartment on the North Side, and for every dollar he earned, he gave away seventy-five cents of it to charity. He slipped ten- and twenty-dollar bills into the collection box at Saint Anthony's Church, sent in anonymous donations to Congregation B'nai Avraham, and dispensed untold quantities of loose change to the blind and crippled beggars he encountered on the sidewalks of his neighborhood. Forty-seven performances averaged out to just under two performances a week. That left five days free, and Hector spent most of them in seclusion, holed up in his apartment reading books. His world had split in two, Alma said, and his mind and body were no longer talking to each other. He was an exhibitionist and a hermit, a mad debauchee and a solitary monk, and if he managed to survive these contradictions in himself for as long as he did, it was only because he willed his mind to go numb. No more struggles to be good, no more pretending to believe in the virtues of self-denial. His body had taken control of him, and the less he thought about what his body was doing, the more successfully he was able to do it. Alma noted that he stopped writing in his journal during this period. The only entries were dry little jottings that recorded the times and places of his jobs with Sylvia—a page and a half in six months. She took it as a sign that he was afraid to look at himself, that he was acting like a man who had covered up all the mirrors in his house.

The only time he had any trouble was the first time, or just before the first time, when he still didn't know if he would be up to the job. Fortunately, Sylvia booked their first performance for an audience of just one man. That made it bearable somehow—to go public in a private sort of way, with just one pair of eyes on him and not twenty or fifty or a hundred. In this case, the eyes belonged to Archibald Pierson, a seventy-year-old retired judge who lived alone in a three-story Tudor house in Highland Park. Sylvia had already been there once with Al, and as she and Hector climbed into a taxi on the appointed night and headed toward their destination in the suburbs, she warned him that they would probably have to go through the act twice, perhaps even three times. The coot was stuck on her, she said. He'd been calling for weeks now, desperate to know when she'd be coming back, and little by little she'd bargained the price up to two and a half C's per shot, double what it had been the last time. I ain't no slouch when it comes to talkin' bread, she announced proudly. If we play this goon right, Hermie boy, he could become our meal ticket.

Pierson turned out to be a shy and jittery old man—thin as a shoemaker's awl, with a full head of neatly combed white hair and enormous blue eyes. He had put on a green velvet smoking jacket for the occasion, and as he led Hector and Sylvia into the living room, he kept clearing his throat and smoothing down the front of the jacket, as if he felt uncomfortable in that foppish attire. He offered them cigarettes, offered them drinks (which they both declined), and then announced that he was planning to accompany their performance by playing a phonograph record of the String Sextet Number One in B flat by Brahms. Sylvia giggled when she heard the word *sextet,* failing to realize that it referred to the number of instruments in the piece, but the judge made no comment. Pierson then complimented Hector on his mask—which Hector had slipped over his face before entering the house—and said that he found it tantalizing, a clever touch. I think I'm going to enjoy this, he said. I salute you on your choice of partner, Sylvia. This one is infinitely more dashing than Al.

The judge liked to keep things simple. He wasn't interested in provocative costumes, sultry dialogue, or artificially dramatic scenes. All he wanted was to look at their bodies, he said, and once the preliminary conversation was over, he instructed them to go into the kitchen and remove their clothes.

While they were gone, he put on the music, turned off the lamps, and lit candles in half a dozen spots around the room. It was theater without theatrics, a raw enactment of life itself. Hector and Sylvia were supposed to walk into the room naked, then get down to business on the Persian rug. That was the extent of it. Hector would make love to Sylvia, and when the climactic moment was upon him, he would withdraw from her and ejaculate on her breasts. Everything came down to that, the judge said. The spurt was crucial, and the farther it traveled through the air, the happier it was going to make him.

After they had taken off their clothes in the kitchen, Sylvia walked up to Hector and started running her hands over his body. She kissed him on the neck, pulled back the mask and kissed him on the face, and then cupped his flaccid penis in her hand and stroked it until it became hard. Hector was glad he had thought of the mask. It made him feel less vulnerable, less ashamed of exposing himself to the old man, but still he was nervous, and he welcomed the warmth of Sylvia's touch, appreciated that she was trying to work the butterflies out of his system. She might have been the star, but she knew that the burden of proof rested with him. Hector couldn't fake it as she could; he couldn't just go through the motions of simulated pleasure and pretend that he was enjoying it. He had to deliver something real at the end of the performance, and unless he went about it with genuine conviction, he wouldn't have a chance of getting there.

They walked into the living room holding hands, two naked savages in a jungle of gilt-edged mirrors and Louis the Fifteenth escritoires. Pierson was already installed in his seat at the far end of the room: a vast leather wing chair that seemed to swallow him up, making him look even thinner and more desiccated than he was. To his right was the phonograph machine, with the Brahms sextet revolving on the turntable. To his left was a low mahogany stand, covered with lacquered boxes, jade statuettes, and other bits of costly chinoiserie. It was a room full of nouns and unmovable objects, an enclave of thoughts. Nothing could have been more incongruous in those surroundings than the erection Hector carried in with him—than the spectacle of verbs that suddenly began to unfold not ten feet from the judge's chair.

If the old man enjoyed what he saw, he displayed no outward signs of pleasure. He stood up twice during the performance to change the record, but other than those brief, mechanical interruptions, he remained in the same position throughout, sitting on his leather throne with one leg crossed over the other and his hands in his lap. He didn't touch himself, he didn't unbutton his trousers, he didn't smile, he didn't make a sound. It was only at the end, at the moment when Hector pulled out of Sylvia and the desired eruption occurred, that a small shuddering noise seemed to catch in the judge's throat. Almost like a sob, Hector thought—and then again, almost like nothing at all.

That was the first time, Alma said, but it was also the fifth time and the eleventh time and the eighteenth time and six other times as well. Pierson became their most devoted customer, and again and again they returned to the house in Highland Park to roll around on the rug and collect their money. Nothing made Sylvia happier than that money, Hector realized, and within a couple of months she had earned enough from the act to quit peddling her wares at the White House Hotel. Not all of it went into her own pocket, but even after she turned over fifty percent to the man she called her protector, her income was two or three times greater than it had been before. Sylvia was an uneducated hick, a semi-illiterate vulgarian who spoke in a blur of double negatives and mind-bending malapropisms, but she proved to have a decent head for business. She was the one who arranged the bookings, negotiated with the clients, and took care of all practical matters: transportation to and from jobs, costume rentals, the scaring up of new work. Hector never had to concern himself with any of these details. Sylvia would call to tell him when and where they would be appearing next, and all he had to do was wait for her to swing by in a taxi to pick him up at his apartment. Those were the unspoken rules, the boundaries of their relationship. They worked together, they fucked together, they made money together, but they never bothered to become friends, and except for the times when they had to rehearse a new skit, they saw each other only when they performed.

All along, Hector assumed that he was safe with her. She didn't ask questions or pry into his past, and in the six and a half months they worked together, he never saw her look at a paper, let alone talk about the news. Once, in an oblique sort of way, he made a passing reference to that silent comedian who had disappeared a few years back. What was his name? he asked, snapping his fingers and pretending to search for the answer, but when Sylvia responded with one of those blank, indifferent looks of hers, Hector took it to mean that she wasn't familiar with the case. Somewhere along the line, however, someone must have talked to her. Hector never knew who it was, but he suspected that it was Sylvia's boyfriend—her so-called protector, Biggie Lowe, a two-hundred-forty-pound hulk who had started out in Chicago as a dance-hall bouncer and now worked as the night manager of the White House Hotel.

Maybe Biggie put her up to it, filling her head with talk of quick money and foolproof extortion schemes, or maybe Sylvia was acting on her own, trying to squeeze a few extra dollars out of Hector for herself. One way or the other, greed got the better of her, and once Hector caught on to what she was planning, the only thing he could do was run.

It happened in Cleveland, less than a week before Christmas. They had gone there by train at the invitation of a wealthy tire manufacturer, had finished doing their French libertine act in front of three dozen men and women (who had gathered at the industrialist's house to participate in a semi-annual private orgy), and were now sitting in the back seat of their host's limousine, on the way to the hotel where they would be stopping for a few hours' sleep before returning to Chicago the next afternoon. They had just been paid a record amount for their work: one thousand dollars for a single, forty-minute performance. Hector's share was supposed to be four hundred dollars, but when Sylvia counted out the tire magnate's money, she gave her partner only two hundred fifty.

That's twenty-five percent, Hector said. You still owe me the other fifteen.

I don't think so, Meers replied. That's what you're gettin', Herm, and if I was you, I'd thank my lucky cards.

Oh? And to what do I owe this sudden change in fiscal policy, dear Sylvia?

It ain't physical, boyo. It's dollars and cents. I got the goods on a certain party now, and unless you want me blabbin' my trap all over town, you'll go down to twenty-five. No more forty. Them days is dead and gone.

You screw like a princess, darling. You understand sex better than any woman I have ever known, but you lack much in the thought department, don't you? You want to work out a new arrangement, fine. Sit down and talk to me about it. But you don't change the rules without consulting me first.

Okay, Mr. Hollywood. Then stop using the mask. If you do that, maybe I'll reconsider.

I see. So this is what we're driving at.

When a guy don't want to show his face, he's got a secret, don't he? And when a girl gets wind of what that secret is, it's a whole new ballgame. I shook hands on a deal with Herm. But there ain't no Herm, is there? His name is Hector, and now we got to start all over again.

She could start all over again as many times as she liked, but it wasn't going to be with him. When the limousine pulled up in front of the Hotel Cuyahoga a few seconds later, Hector told her that they would go on talking about it in the morning. He wanted to sleep on it, he said, to think it over for a while before coming to a decision, but he was sure they could come up with a solution that would satisfy them both. Then he kissed her on the hand, just as he always did when he said good-bye to her after a performance—the half-mocking, half-chivalrous gesture that had become their standard farewell. From the triumphant smirk that spread across Sylvia's face as he lifted her hand to his mouth, Hector realized that she had no idea what she had done. She hadn't blackmailed him into giving her a greater share of the profits, she had just broken up the act.

He went to his room on the seventh floor, and for the next twenty minutes he stood in front of the mirror, pressing the barrel of the gun against his right temple. He came close to pulling the trigger, Alma said, closer than he had the other two times, but when his will failed him once again, he put the gun down on the table and left the hotel. It was four-thirty in the morning. He walked to the Greyhound depot twelve blocks to the north and bought himself a ticket on the next bus out—or the next but one. The six o'clock was headed for Youngstown and points east, and the six-oh-five was going in the opposite direction. The ninth stop on the westbound coach was Sandusky. That was the town where he had never spent his childhood, and remembering how beautiful that word had once sounded to him, Hector decided to go there now—just to see what his imaginary past looked like.

It was the morning of December 21, 1931. Sandusky was sixty miles away, and he slept through most of the ride, not waking until the bus reached the terminal two and a half hours later. He had just over three hundred dollars in his pocket: the two hundred fifty from Meers, another fifty he had slipped into his wallet before leaving Chicago on the twentieth, and change from the ten he had broken for his bus ticket. He went into the depot luncheonette and ordered the breakfast special: ham and eggs, toast, home fries, orange juice, and all the coffee you could drink. Halfway through his third cup, he asked the counterman if there was anything to see in town. He was just passing through, he said, and he doubted he would ever be back this way again. Sandusky ain't much, the counterman said. It's just a little burg, you know, but if I was you, I'd go and check out Cedar Point. That's where the amusement park is. You've got your roller coasters and fun rides, the Leapfrog Railway, the Hotel Breakers, all kinds of things. That's where Knute Rockne invented the forward pass, by the way, in case you're a football fan. It's shut down for the winter now, but it might be worth a look.

The counterman drew a little diagram for him on the paper napkin, but instead of turning right out of the depot, Hector went left. That took him to Camp Street instead of Columbus Avenue, and then, to compound the error, he turned west on West Monroe instead of east. He went all the way to King Street before it dawned on him that he was walking in the wrong direction. The peninsula was nowhere in sight, and instead of cyclones and Ferris wheels, he found himself looking at a dreary expanse of broken-down factories and empty warehouses. Cold, gray weather, a threat of snow in the air, and a mangy, three-legged dog the only living creature within a hundred yards.

Hector turned around and began to retrace his steps, and the moment he turned, Alma said, he was gripped by a feeling of nullity, an exhaustion so great, so relentless, that he had to lean against the wall of a building to prevent himself from falling down. A frigid wind was blowing in off Lake Erie, and even as he felt it rush against his face, he couldn't tell if the wind was real or something he had imagined. He didn't know what month it was, what year. He couldn't remember his name. Bricks and cobblestones, his breath gusting into the air in front of it, and the three-legged dog limping around the corner and vanishing from sight. It was a picture of his own death, he later realized, the portrait of a soul in ruins, and long after he had pulled himself together and moved on, a part of him was still there, standing on that empty street in Sandusky, Ohio, gasping for breath as his existence dribbled out of him.

By ten-thirty, he was on Columbus Avenue, threading his way among a crowd of Christmas shoppers. He passed the Warner Bros. Theater, Ester Ging's manicure salon, and Capozzi's Shoe Repair, saw people going in and out of Kresge's, Montgomery Ward, and Woolworth's, heard a lone Salvation Army Santa Claus ringing a brass bell. When he came to the Commercial Banking and Trust Company, he decided to go in and convert a couple of his fifties into a stack of fives and tens and ones. It was a meaningless transaction, but he couldn't think of anything else to do just then, and rather than go on wandering in circles, he figured it might not be such a bad idea to get in out of the cold, even if only for a few minutes.

Unexpectedly, the bank was full of customers. Men and women were lined up eight and ten deep in front of the four barred tellers' windows arrayed along the west wall. Hector went to the end of the longest line, which happened to be the second one from the door. A moment after he took his spot, a young woman joined the line immediately to his left. She appeared to be in her early twenties, and she was wearing a thick woolen coat with a fur collar. Because he had nothing better to do at that moment, Hector began studying her out of the corner of his eye. She had an admirable, interesting face, he found, with high cheekbones and a gracefully defined chin, and he liked the pensive, self-sufficient look he detected in her eyes. In the old days, he would have started talking to her immediately, but now he was content simply to watch, to muse upon the flesh that was hidden beneath the coat and to imagine the thoughts churning inside that lovely, striking head of hers. At one point, she inadvertently glanced over at him, and when she saw how avidly he was staring at her, she returned his look with a brief, enigmatic smile. Hector nodded, acknowledging her smile with a brief smile of his own, and an instant later her expression changed. She narrowed her eyes into a puzzled, searching frown, and Hector knew that she had recognized him. There was no doubt about it: the woman had seen his movies.

She was familiar with his face, and although she still couldn't remember who he was, it wasn't going to take her more than thirty seconds to come up with the answer.

It had happened to him several times in the past three years, and each time he had managed to slip away before the person could start asking him questions. Just as he was about to do it again, however, all hell broke loose in the bank. The young woman was standing in the line closest to the entrance, and because she had turned slightly in Hector's direction, she failed to notice that the door had opened behind her and that a man had rushed in with a red-and-white bandana tied around his face. He was carrying an empty duffel bag in one hand and a loaded pistol in the other. It was easy to tell that the pistol was loaded, Alma said, because the first thing the bank robber did was fire a shot into the ceiling. Down on the floor, he shouted, everybody down on the floor, and as the terrified customers did what the man instructed them to do, he reached out and grabbed hold of the person directly in front of him. It was all a matter of layout, architecture, topography. The young woman to Hector's left was the person closest to the entrance, and therefore she was the one who was grabbed, who wound up having the gun pointed at her head. Nobody move, the man warned, nobody move or this bird gets her brains blowed out. With a brusque and violent gesture, he yanked her off her feet and began half-pushing, half-dragging her toward the tellers' windows. His left arm was wrapped around her shoulders from behind, the duffel bag was dangling from his clenched fist, and the eyes above the bandana were crazed, out of focus, incandescent with fear. It wasn't that Hector made any conscious decision to do what he did next, but the moment his knee touched the floor, he found himself standing up again. He wasn't intending to be heroic, and he certainly wasn't intending to get himself killed, but whatever else he might have been feeling at that moment, he wasn't afraid. Angry, perhaps, and more than a little worried that he was about to put the girl at risk, but not afraid for himself. The important thing was the angle of approach. Once he made his move, there wouldn't be time to stop or change direction, but if he rushed the man at full speed, and if he came at him from the right side—the duffel-bag side—there was no way that the man wouldn't turn from the girl and point the gun at him. It was the only natural response. If a wild beast comes charging at you out of nowhere, you forget about everything but the beast.

That was as far as Hector could take the story, Alma said. He could talk about what happened up to that moment, up to the moment when he started running toward the man, but he had no memory of hearing the gun go off, no memory of the bullet that tore into his chest and knocked him to the ground, no memory of seeing Frieda break loose from the man. Frieda was in a better position to see what happened, but because she was so busy twisting herself out of the man's arms, she missed many of the subsequent events as well. She saw Hector drop to the floor, she saw the hole that opened in his overcoat and the blood that came spurting out of it, but she lost track of the man and didn't see him trying to escape. The shot was still ringing in her ears, and with so many people shrieking and howling around her, she didn't hear the three additional shots that the bank guard fired into the man's back.

They were both certain of the date, however. That was fixed in their minds, and when Alma visited the microfilm vaults of the *Sandusky Evening Herald*, the Cleveland *Plain Dealer*, and several other defunct and surviving local papers, she was able to piece together the rest of the story for herself. BLOODBATH ON COLUMBUS AVENUE, BANK ROBBER DIES IN SHOOTOUT, HERO RUSHED TO HOSPITAL read some of the headlines. The man who almost killed Hector was named Darryl Knox, a.k.a. Nutso Knox, a twenty-seven-year-old ex–auto mechanic wanted in four states for a series of bank robberies and armed holdups. The journalists all celebrated his demise, calling special attention to the nifty gunwork of the guard—who managed to deliver the conclusive shot just as Knox was slipping out the door—but what interested them most was Hector's bravery, which they extolled as the finest demonstration of courage to have been seen in those parts in many years. *The girl was a goner,* one eyewitness was quoted as saying. *If that fellow hadn't taken the bull by the horns, I'd hate to think where she'd be now.* The girl was Frieda Spelling, age twenty-two, variously described as a painter, a recent graduate of Bernard College (sic), and the daughter of the late Thaddeus P. Spelling, prominent Sandusky banker and philanthropist. In article after article, she expressed her thanks to the man who had saved her life. She had been so scared, she said, so certain that she was going to die. She prayed that he would recover from his wounds.

The Spelling family offered to cover the man's medical expenses, but for the first seventy-two hours it seemed doubtful that he would pull through. He was unconscious when he arrived at the hospital, and after so much trauma and loss of blood, he was given no more than an outside chance of warding off the dangers of shock and infection, of walking out of there alive. The doctors removed his destroyed left lung, picked out the bits of exploded metal that had lodged in the tissue around his heart, and then they sewed him up again. For better or worse, Hector had found his bullet. He hadn't meant for it to happen that way, Alma said, but what he hadn't been able to do himself someone else did for him, and the irony was that Knox bungled the job. Hector didn't die from his encounter with death. He simply went to sleep, and when he woke up after his long slumber, he forgot that he had ever wanted to kill himself. The pain was too excruciating to dwell on anything as complicated as that. His insides were on fire, and all he could think about now was how to draw his next breath, how to go on breathing without bursting into flames.

At first, they had only the sketchiest idea of who he was. They emptied his pockets and examined the contents of his wallet, but they found no driver's license, no passport, no identification papers of any kind. The only thing with a name on it was a membership card for a North Side branch of the Chicago Public Library. H. Loesser, it said, but there was no address or telephone number, nothing to pinpoint where he lived. According to the newspaper articles published after the shooting, the Sandusky police were making every effort to uncover more information about him.

But Frieda knew who he was—or at least she thought she knew. She had gone to college in New York, and as a nineteen-year-old sophomore in 1928 she had managed to see six or seven of the twelve Hector Mann comedies. It wasn't that she had any interest in slapstick, but his films had been playing along with other films, part of the program of cartoons and newsreels than ran before the featured attraction, and she had become familiar enough with his looks to know who he was when she saw him. When she spotted Hector in the bank three years later, the absence of the mustache momentarily confused her. She recognized the face, but she couldn't attach a name to it, and before she could figure out who the man was, Knox rushed in behind her and pointed the gun at her head. Twenty-four hours went by before she was able to think about it again, but once the horror of her near death had begun to recede a little, the solution came to her in a flash of sudden, overpowering certainty. It didn't matter that the man's name was supposed to be Loesser. She had followed the news of Hector's disappearance in 1929, and if he wasn't dead, as most people seemed to think he was, then he had to be living under another name. What made no sense was that he had popped up in Sandusky, Ohio, but the truth was that most things made no sense, and if the laws of physics stipulated that every person in the world occupied a certain amount of space—which meant that everyone was necessarily somewhere—then why couldn't that somewhere have been Sandusky, Ohio? Three days later, when Hector emerged from his coma and started talking to the doctors, Frieda visited the hospital to thank him for what he had done. He couldn't say much, but the little he did say bore the irrefutable marks of a foreign accent. The voice clinched it for her, and when she bent over and kissed him on the forehead just before she left the hospital, she knew beyond a shadow of a doubt that her life had been saved by Hector Mann.

6

LANDING TURNED OUT to be less difficult for me than taking off. I had prepared myself to be afraid, to be thrown into another frenzy of slobbering incompetence and spiritual malfunction, but when the captain told us that we were about to go into our descent, I felt curiously stable, unperturbed. There must have been a difference between going up and going down, I decided, between losing touch with the earth and returning to solid ground. One was a farewell, the other was a salutation, and perhaps beginnings were more bearable than endings, I thought, or perhaps I had discovered (quite simply) that the dead were not allowed to scream in you more than once a day. I turned toward Alma and gripped her arm. She was just getting into the early stages of Hector's romance with Frieda, moving past the night when he broke down and confessed to her and then going on to describe Frieda's startling response to that confession (The bullet absolves you, she said; you gave my life back to me, now I'm giving your life back to you), but when I put my hand on Alma's arm, she suddenly stopped talking, breaking off in mid-sentence, in mid-thought. She smiled, then leaned forward and kissed me—first on the cheek, then on the ear, and then square on the mouth. They fell hard for each other, she said. If we don't watch out, the same thing is going to happen to us.

Hearing those words must have made a difference, too—helped me to be less afraid, less prone to inner meltdown—but how apt, finally, that the word *fall* should have been the verb in the two sentences that summed up my history of the past three years. A plane falls from the sky, and all the passengers are killed. A woman falls in love, and a man falls with her, and not for an instant as the plane goes down does either one of them think about death. In midair, with the land revolving below us as we banked into our final turn, I understood that Alma was giving me the possibility of a second life, that something was still in front of me if I had the courage to walk toward it. I listened to the music of the engines as they shifted key. The noise inside the cabin grew louder, the walls shook, and then, almost as an afterthought, the wheels of the plane touched the ground.

It took a while for us to get going again. There was the opening of the hydraulic door, the walk through the terminal, the stopping in at the men's room and the women's room, the search for a telephone to call the ranch, the buying of water for the trip to Tierra del Sueño (Drink as much as you can, Alma said; the altitudes are deceiving here, and you don't want to get dehydrated), the combing of the long-term parking lot for Alma's Subaru station wagon, and then a final pause to fill up with gas before we hit the road. It was the first time I had been to New Mexico. Under normal circumstances, I would have gawked at the landscape, pointing to rock formations and demented-looking cacti, asking the name of this mountain or that gnarled shrub, but I was too caught up in Hector's story to bother with that now. Alma and I were passing through some of the most impressive country in North America, but for all the effect it had on us we could have been sitting in a room with the lights out and the shades drawn. I would travel that road several more times in the days to come, but I remember almost nothing of what I saw on that first trip. Whenever I think about riding in Alma's banged-up yellow car, the only thing that comes back to me is the sound of our voices—her voice and my voice, my voice and her voice—and the sweetness of the air rushing in on me through a crack in the window. But the land itself is invisible. It had to have been there, but I wonder now if I ever bothered to look at it. Or, if I did, if I wasn't too distracted to register what I was seeing.

They kept him in the hospital until early February, Alma said. Frieda went to visit him every day, and when the doctors finally said that he was strong enough to go, she talked her mother into letting him recuperate at their house. He was still in bad shape. It took another six months before he could move around very well.

And Frieda's mother was okay with that? Six months is an awfully long time.

She was thrilled. Frieda was a wild thing back then, one of those liberated bohemian girls who'd grown up in the late twenties, and she had nothing but contempt for Sandusky, Ohio. The Spellings had survived the crash with eighty percent of their wealth intact—which meant that they still belonged to what Frieda liked to call *the inner circle of the midwestern haute booboisie.* It was a narrow world of Republican stick-in-the-muds and foggy-headed women, and the principle entertainments consisted of joyless country club dances and long, stultifying dinner parties. Once a year, Frieda would grit her teeth and come home for the Christmas holidays, enduring those gruesome events for the sake of her mother and her married brother, Frederick, who still lived in town with his wife and two children. By the second or third of January, she'd rush back to New York, vowing never to return again. That year, of course, she didn't attend any parties—and she didn't go back to New York. She fell in love with Hector instead. As far as her mother was concerned, anything that kept Frieda in Sandusky was a good thing.

You're saying she had no objections to the marriage either?

Frieda had been in open rebellion for a long time. Just one day before the shooting, she'd told her mother that she was planning to move to Paris and would probably never set foot in America again. That's why she was in the bank that morning—to withdraw money from her account to buy the ticket. The last thing Mrs. Spelling ever expected to hear from her daughter's lips was the word *marriage.* In the light of this miraculous turnaround, how not to embrace Hector and welcome him into the family? Not only did Frieda's mother not object, she organized the wedding herself.

So Hector's life begins in Sandusky, after all. He plucks the name of a town out of thin air, tells a bunch of lies about it, and then he makes those lies come true. It's pretty bizarre, don't you think? Chaim Mandelbaum becomes Hector Mann, Hector Mann becomes Herman Loesser, and then what? Who does Herman Loesser become? Did he even know who he was anymore?

He went back to being Hector. That's what Frieda called him. That's what we all called him. After they were married, Hector became Hector again.

But not Hector Mann. He wouldn't have been that reckless, would he?

Hector Spelling. He took Frieda's last name.

Wow.

Not wow. Just practical. He didn't want to be Loesser anymore. That name represented everything that had gone wrong with his life, and if he was going to start calling himself something else, why not use the name of the woman he loved? It's not as if he ever went back on that. He's been Hector Spelling for more than fifty years.

How did they wind up in New Mexico?

They drove out West on their honeymoon and decided to stay. Hector had a lot of respiratory problems, and the dry air turned out to be good for him.

There were dozens of artists out there by then. The Mabel Dodge crowd in Taos, D. H. Lawrence, Georgia O'Keeffe. Did that have anything to do with it?

Nothing at all. Hector and Frieda lived in another part of the state. They never even met those people.

They moved there in 1932. Yesterday, you said that Hector started making movies again in 1940. That's eight years. What happened in the interval?

They bought four hundred acres of land. Prices were incredibly low at the time, and I don't think they paid more than a few thousand dollars for the whole property. Frieda came from a rich family, but she didn't have much money of her own. A small inheritance from her grandmother—ten or fifteen thousand dollars, something like that. Her mother kept offering to pay her bills, but Frieda wouldn't accept her help. Too proud, too stubborn, too independent. She didn't want to think of herself as a sponge. So she and Hector weren't in a position to hire large crews of workers to build a house for them. No architect, no contractor—they couldn't afford those things. Luckily, Hector knew what he was doing. He had learned carpentry from his father, had built sets for the movies, and all that experience allowed them to keep costs to a minimum. He designed the house himself, and then he and Frieda more or less built it with their own hands. It was a very simple place. A six-room adobe cottage. Just one story, and the only help they got with it came from a team of three Mexican brothers, unemployed day laborers who lived on the outskirts of town. For the first few years, they didn't even have electricity. They had water, of course, they had to have water, but it took a couple of months before they were able to find it and start digging the well. That was the first step. After that, they chose the site for the house. Then they drew up the plans and started construction. All that took time. They didn't just move there and settle in. It was blank and savage space, and they had to build everything from the ground up.

And then what? Once the house was ready, what did they do with themselves?

Frieda was a painter, and so she went back to being a painter. Hector read books and kept up with his journal, but mostly he planted trees. That became his major occupation, his work of the next few years. He cleared several acres of land around the house, and then, bit by bit, he installed an elaborate system of underground irrigation pipes. That made gardening possible, and once the garden was under way, he got busy with the trees. I've never counted them all, but there must be two or three hundred of them. Cottonwoods and junipers, willows and aspens, pinyons and white oaks. There used to be nothing but yucca and sagebrush growing there. Hector turned it into a little forest. You'll see it for yourself in a few hours, but for me it's one of the most beautiful places on earth.

That's the last thing I would have expected from him. Hector Mann, horticulturalist.

He was happy. Probably happier than at any other time in his life, but with that happiness came a total lack of ambition. The only thing that concerned him was taking care of Frieda and tending to his patch of ground. After all he'd been through in the past years, that felt like enough, like more than enough. He was still doing penance, you understand. It's just that he was no longer trying to destroy himself. Even now, he still talks about those trees as his greatest accomplishment. Better than his films, he says, better than anything else he's ever done.

What did they do for money? If things were so tight, how did they manage to get by?

Frieda had friends in New York, and many of those friends had contacts. They found jobs for her. Illustrating children's books, drawing for magazines, freelance work of one kind or another. It didn't bring in much, but it helped keep them afloat.

She must have had some talent, then.

We're talking about Frieda, David, not some upper-crust poseur. She had enormous gifts, a real passion for making art. She once told me that she didn't think she had the stuff to be a great painter, but then she added that if she hadn't met Hector when she did, she probably would have spent her life trying to become one. She hasn't painted in years, but she still draws like a demon. Fluid, sinuous lines, a terrific sense of composition. When Hector started making movies again, she did the storyboards, designed the sets and costumes, and helped establish the look of the films. She was an integral part of the whole enterprise.

I still don't understand. They were living this bare-bones existence out in the desert. Where did they come up with the money to start making movies?

Frieda's mother died. The estate was worth over three million dollars. Frieda inherited half of it, and the other half went to her brother, Frederick.

That would account for the financing, wouldn't it?

It was a lot of money back then.

It's still a lot of money today, but there's more to the story than just money. Hector made a promise never to work in films again. You told me that a few hours ago, and now he's suddenly back directing films. What made him change his mind?

Frieda and Hector had a son. Thaddeus Spelling II, named after Frieda's father. Taddy for short, or Tad, or Tadpole—they called him all sorts of things. He was born in 1935 and died in 1938. Stung by a bee one morning in his father's garden. They found him lying on the ground, all puffed up and swollen, and by the time they drove him to the doctor thirty miles away, he was already dead. Imagine the effect it had on them.

I can imagine it. If there's one thing I can imagine, I can imagine that.

I'm sorry. It was a stupid thing for me to say.

Don't be sorry. It's just that I know what you're talking about. No mental gymnastics required to understand the situation. Tad and Todd. It can't get any closer than that, can it?

Still . . .

No still. Just go on talking . . .

Hector collapsed. Months went by, and he didn't do anything at all. He sat in the house; he looked at the sky through the bedroom window; he studied the backs of his hands. It wasn't that Frieda didn't have a hard time of it, too, but he was so much more fragile than she was, so unprotected. She was tough enough to know that the boy's death was an accident, that he'd died because he was allergic to bees, but Hector saw it as a form of divine punishment. He had been too happy. Life had been too good to him, and now the fates had taught him a lesson.

The films were Frieda's idea, weren't they? After she inherited the money, she talked Hector into going back to work.

More or less. He was headed for a nervous breakdown, and she knew that she had to step in and take action. Not just to save him, but to save her marriage, to save her own life.

And Hector went along with it.

Not at first. But then she threatened to leave him, and he finally gave in. Not with any great reluctance, I should add. He was desperate to get back into it. For ten years, he'd been dreaming about camera angles, lighting setups, story ideas. It was the one thing he wanted to do, the one thing in the world that made sense to him.

But what about his promise? How did he justify breaking his word? From all you've told me about him, I don't see how he could have done that.

He did it by splitting hairs—and then he made a pact with the devil. If a tree falls in the forest and no one hears it fall, does it make a sound or not? Hector had read a lot of books by then, he knew all the tricks and arguments of the philosophers. If someone makes a movie and no one sees it, does the movie exist or not? That's how he justified what he did. He would make movies that would never be shown to audiences, make movies for the pure pleasure of making movies. It was an act of breathtaking nihilism, and yet he's stuck to the bargain ever since. Imagine knowing that you're good at something, so good that the world would be in awe of you if they could see your work, and then keeping yourself a secret from the world. It took great concentration and rigor to do what Hector did—and also a touch of madness. Hector and Frieda are both a bit mad, I suppose, but they've achieved something remarkable. Emily Dickinson wrote in obscurity, but she tried to publish her poems. Van Gogh tried to sell his paintings. As far as I know, Hector is the first artist to make his work with the conscious, premeditated intention of destroying it. There's Kafka, of course, who told Max Brod to burn his manuscripts, but when it came to the decisive moment, Brod couldn't go through with it. But Frieda will. There's no question about that. The day after Hector dies, she'll take his films into the garden and burn them all—every print, every negative, every frame he ever shot. That's guaranteed. And you and I will be the only witnesses.

How many films are we talking about?

Fourteen. Eleven features of ninety minutes or more, and three others that run under an hour.

I don't imagine he was still into comedies, was he?

Report from the Anti-World, The Ballad of Mary White, Travels in the Scriptorium, Ambush at Standing Rock. Those are some of the titles. They don't sound very funny, do they?

No, not what you'd call your standard laugh-a-thons. But not too grim, I hope.

It depends on how you define the word. I don't find them grim. Serious, yes, and often quite strange, but not grim.

How do you define strange?

Hector's films are extremely intimate, low to the ground, unflamboyant in tone. But there's always this fantastical element running through them, a weird kind of poetry. He broke a lot of rules. He did things film directors aren't supposed to do.

Like what?

Voice-overs, for one thing. Narration is considered a weakness in movies, a sign that the images aren't working, but Hector relied on it heavily in a number of his films. One of them, *The History of Light*, doesn't have a word of dialogue. It's wall-to-wall narration from start to finish.

What else did he do wrong? Wrong on purpose, I mean.

He was out of the commercial loop, and that meant he could work without constraints. Hector used his freedom to explore things other filmmakers weren't allowed to touch, especially in the forties and fifties. Naked bodies. Down-to-earth sex. Childbirth. Urination, defecation. Those scenes are a bit shocking at first, but the shock wears off rather quickly. They're a natural part of life, after all, but we're not used to seeing them presented on film, so we sit up for a couple of seconds and take notice. Hector didn't make a big point of it. Once you come to understand what's possible in his work, these so-called taboos and moments of explicitness blend into the overall texture of the stories. In a way, those scenes were a form of protection for him—just in case someone tried to walk off with one of the prints. He had to make sure that his films would be unreleaseable.

And your parents went along with this.

It was a hands-on, do-it-yourself operation. Hector wrote, directed, and edited the films. My father lit them and shot them, and after the shooting was done, he and my mother did all the lab work. They processed the footage, cut the negatives, mixed the sound, and saw everything through until the final prints were in the can.

Right there at the ranch?

Hector and Frieda turned their property into a small movie studio. They began construction in May 1939 and finished in March 1940, and what they wound up with was a self-contained universe, a private compound for making films. There was a double sound stage in one building, along with additional areas for a carpentry shop, a seamstress shop, dressing rooms, and separate storage spaces for sets and costumes. Another building was for post production. They couldn't risk sending out their films to a commercial lab, so they built their own lab. That took up one wing. In the other half was the editing facility, the projection room, and an underground storage vault for prints and negatives.

All that equipment couldn't have come cheap.

It cost them over a hundred fifty thousand dollars to set the place up. But they could afford it, and most things had to be bought only once. Several cameras, but only one editing machine, one pair of projectors, and one optical printer. After they had what they needed, they worked within tightly controlled budgets. Frieda's inheritance was drawing interest, and they dipped into the principal as sparingly as they could. They worked on a small scale. They had to if they meant to stretch out the money and make it last.

And Frieda was in charge of sets and costumes.

Among other things. She was also Hector's assistant editor, and when films were in production, she handled any one of several different jobs. Script supervisor, boom operator, focus puller—whatever needed doing on that day, at that moment.

And your mother?

My Faye. My beautiful, beloved Faye. She was an actress. She came to the ranch in 1945 to do a role in a film and fell in love with my father. She was still in her early twenties then. She performed in every film they made after that, mostly as the female lead, but she helped out on other fronts as well. Sewing costumes, painting scenery, advising Hector on his scripts, working with Charlie in the lab. That was the adventure of it.

No one did just one thing there. They were all involved, and they all put in incredibly long hours. Months and months of laborious prep work, months and months in post production. Making films is a slow, intricate business, and with so few of them trying to do so much, they pushed along by inches. It generally took them about two years to finish a project.

I understand why Hector and Frieda wanted to be there—or partly understand it, am struggling to understand it—but your mother and father still baffle me. Charlie Grund was a gifted cameraman. I've studied his work, I know what he did with Hector in 1928, and it makes no sense that he would have walked away from his career.

My father had just been through a divorce. He was thirty-five, going on thirty-six, and he still hadn't made it into the top echelon of Hollywood DP's. After fifteen years in the business, he was working on B pictures—when he had work at all. Westerns, Boston Blackie movies, kids' serials. He had immense talent, Charlie did, but he was a quiet person, someone who never appeared to be very comfortable with himself, and people often mistook that shyness for arrogance. He kept losing out on the good jobs, and after a while it started to get to him, to eat away at his confidence. When his first wife left him, he went to hell for a few months. Drinking too much, feeling sorry for himself, not keeping up with his work. And that's when Hector called—just when he was down in that hole.

That still doesn't explain why he agreed to do it. No one makes pictures without wanting others to see them. It just isn't done. What's the point of putting film in the camera, then?

He didn't care. I know it's hard for you to believe, but the work was all that mattered to him. The results were secondary, almost of no importance. A lot of film people are like that—

especially the ones below the line, the blue-collar guys, the grunts. They enjoy figuring things out. They like putting their hands on the equipment and getting it to do things for them. It's not about art or ideas. It's about working at something and making it come out right. My father had his ups and downs in the film business, but he was good at making films, and Hector gave him the opportunity to make films without having to worry about the business. If it had been anyone else, I doubt that he would have gone. But my father loved Hector. He always said that working for him at Kaleidoscope was the happiest year of his life.

He must have been shocked when Hector called. More than ten years go by, and suddenly there's a dead man on the other end of the line.

He thought someone was playing a prank on him. The only other possibility was that he was talking to a ghost, and since my father didn't believe in ghosts, he told Hector to go fuck himself and hung up the phone. Hector had to call back three more times before he was willing to accept it.

When was this?

Late thirty-nine. November or December, just after the Germans invaded Poland. By early February, my father was living at the ranch. Hector and Frieda's new house was ready by then, and he moved into the old one, the little cottage they'd built when they first got there. That's where I lived with my parents when I was growing up, and that's where I live now—in that six-room adobe house, under the shade of Hector's trees, writing my insane and endless book.

But what about the other people who came to the ranch? Actors were brought in, you said, and your father must have had some technical help. It's not possible to make a film with just four people. Even I know that. Maybe they could handle pre production and post production on their own, but not production itself. And once you have people coming in from the outside, how do you get away with it? How do you stop them from talking?

You tell them you're working for someone else. You pretend you've been hired by an eccentric millionaire from Mexico City, a man so in love with American movies that he's built his own studio in the American wilderness and commissioned you to make movies for him—movies that will never be seen by anyone but the man himself. That's the arrangement. If you come to the Blue Stone Ranch to work on a film, you do so with the understanding that your work will be seen by an audience of just one person.

That's preposterous.

Maybe so, but a lot of people swallowed the story.

You'd have to be pretty desperate to believe a thing like that.

You haven't spent much time with actors, have you? They're the most desperate people in the world. Ninety percent of them are unemployed, and if you offer them a job with a decent salary, they're not going to ask many questions. All they want is the chance to work. Hector didn't go after big names. He wasn't interested in stars. He just wanted competent professionals, and since he wrote his screenplays for small casts—sometimes just two or three roles—it wasn't difficult to find them. By the time he finished one film and was ready to go on to the next, there was a new crop of actors to choose from. Except for my mother, he never used the same actor twice.

All right, forget about everyone else. What about you? When did you first hear the name Hector Mann? You knew him as

Hector Spelling. How old were you when you realized that Hector Spelling and Hector Mann were the same person?

I always knew that. We had a complete set of the Kaleidoscope films at the ranch, and I must have seen them fifty times when I was a child. The moment I learned how to read, I noticed that Hector was Mann, not Spelling. I asked my father about it, and he said that Hector had acted under a stage name when he was young, but now that he wasn't acting anymore, he'd stopped using it. It felt like a perfectly plausible explanation to me.

I thought those films were lost.

They almost were. By all rights, they should have been. But just when Hunt was about to declare bankruptcy, a day or two before the marshals came to seize his goods and padlock the door, Hector and my father broke into the Kaleidoscope offices and stole the films. The negatives weren't there, but they marched off with prints of all twelve comedies. Hector gave them to my father for safekeeping, and two months later Hector was gone. When my father moved to the ranch in 1940, he brought the the films with him.

How did Hector feel about that?

I don't understand. How should he have felt?

That's what I'm asking you. Was he pleased or displeased?

Pleased. Of course he was pleased. He was proud of those little films, and he was glad to have them back.

Then why did he wait so long before sending them out into the world again?

What makes you think he did that?

I don't know, I assumed . . .

I thought you understood. It was me. I was the one who did it.

I suspected as much.

Then why didn't you say something?

I didn't think I had the right to. In case it was supposed to be a secret.

I don't have any secrets from you, David. Whatever I know, I want you to know, too. Don't you get it? I sent out those films blind, and you were the one who found them. You're the only person in the world who found them all. That makes us old friends, doesn't it? We might not have met until yesterday, but we've been working together for years.

It was an incredible stunt you pulled. I talked to curators everywhere I went, and not one of them had any idea who you were. When I was in California, I had lunch with Tom Luddy, the head of the Pacific Film Archive. They were the last place to receive one of the Hector Mann mystery boxes. By the time theirs came, you'd already been at it for a few years, and the word was out. Tom said that he didn't even bother to open the package. He took it straight to the FBI to have it checked for fingerprints, but they couldn't find any in the box—not a single one. You didn't leave a trace.

I wore gloves. If I was going to go to the trouble of keeping a secret, I certainly wasn't going to slip up on a detail like that.

You're a clever girl, Alma.

You bet I'm clever. I'm the cleverest girl in this car, and I dare you to prove I'm not.

But how could you justify going behind Hector's back? It was his decision to make, not yours.

I talked to him about it first. It was my idea, but I didn't go ahead with it until he gave me the green light.

What did he say?

He shrugged. And then he gave me a little smile. It doesn't matter, he said. Do whatever you want, Alma.

So he didn't stop you, but he didn't help you, either. He didn't do anything.

It was November eighty-one, almost seven years ago. I'd just come back to the ranch for my mother's funeral, and it was a bad time for all of us, the beginning of the end, somehow. I didn't take it well. I admit that. She was only fifty-nine when we put her in the ground, and I hadn't been prepared for it. Pulverizing. That's the only word I can think of: a pulverizing sorrow. As if everything inside me had turned to dust. The others were so old by then. I looked up and suddenly realized that they were finished, that the great experiment was over. My father was eighty, Hector was eighty-one, and the next time I looked up, they'd all be gone. It had a tremendous effect on me. Every morning, I went into the screening room to watch my mother in her old films, and by the time I came out again, it would be dark outside and I'd be sobbing my guts out. After two weeks of that, I decided to go home. I was living in L.A. then. I had a job with an independent production company, and they needed me back at work. I was all set to go. I'd already called the airline and booked my ticket, but at the last minute—literally, on my last night at the ranch—Hector asked me to stay.

Did he give a reason?

He said he was ready to talk, and he needed someone to help him. He couldn't do it on his own.

You mean the book was his idea?

It all came from him. I never would have thought of it myself. And even if I had, I wouldn't have talked to him about it. I wouldn't have dared.

He lost his courage. That's the only explanation. Either he lost his courage or he went senile.

That's what I thought, too. But I was wrong, and you're wrong now. Hector changed his mind because of me. He told me I had a right to know the truth, and if I was willing to stay there and listen to him, he promised to tell me the whole story.

Okay, I'll accept that. You're part of the family, and now that you're an adult, you deserve to know the family secrets. But how does a private confession turn into a book? It's one thing for him to unburden himself to you, but a book is for the world, and as soon as he tells his story to the world, his life becomes meaningless.

Only if he's still alive when it's published. But he won't be. I've promised not to show it to anyone until after he's dead. He promised me the truth, and I promised him that.

And it's never occurred to you that he might be using you? You get to write your book, yes, and if all goes well, it's acknowledged as an important book, but at the same time Hector gets to live on through you. Not because of his films—which won't even exist anymore—but because of what you've written about him.

It's possible, anything is possible. But his motives don't really concern me. He could be acting out of fear, out of vanity, out of some last-minute surge of regret, but he's told me the truth. That's the only thing that counts. Telling the truth is hard, David, and Hector and I have lived through a lot together these past seven years. He's made everything available to me—all his journals, all his letters, every document he's been able to lay his hands on. At this point, I'm not even thinking about publication. Whether it comes out or not, writing this book has been the biggest experience of my life.

Where does Frieda fit into all this? Has she been helping the two of you or not?

It's been rough on her, but she's done her best to go along with us. I don't think she agrees with Hector, but she doesn't want to stand in his way. It's complicated. Everything with Frieda is complicated.

How long did it take before you decided to send out Hector's old films?

That happened right at the beginning. I still didn't know if I could trust him, and I proposed it as a test, to see if he was being honest with me. If he'd turned me down, I don't think I would have stayed. I needed him to sacrifice something, to give me a sign of good faith. He understood that. We never talked about it in so many words, but he understood. That's why he didn't do anything to stop it.

That still doesn't prove he's been honest with you. You put his old films back in circulation. Where's the harm in that? People remember him now. A crazy professor from Vermont even wrote a book about him. But none of that changes the story.

Every time he's told me something, I've gone and checked it out. I've been to Buenos Aires, I've followed the trail of Brigid O'Fallon's bones, I've dug up the old newspaper articles about the Sandusky bank shooting, I've talked to more than a dozen actors who worked at the ranch in the forties and fifties. There aren't any discrepancies. Some people couldn't be found, of course, and others turned out to be dead. Jules Blaustein, for example. And I still don't have anything on Sylvia Meers. But I did go to Spokane and talk to Nora.

She's still alive?

Very much so. At least she was three years ago.

And?

She married a man named Faraday in 1933 and had four

children. Those children produced eleven grandchildren, and right around the time of my visit, one of those grandchildren was about to make them great-grandparents.

Good. I don't know why I say that, but I'm glad to hear it.

She taught the fourth grade for fifteen years, and then they made her principal of the school. She went on doing that until she retired in 1976.

In other words, Nora went on being Nora.

She was seventy-something years old when I went out there, but she still felt like the same person Hector had described to me.

And what about Herman Loesser? Did she remember him?

She cried when I mentioned his name.

What do you mean *cried*?

I mean her eyes filled up with tears, and the tears rolled down her cheeks. She cried. In the same way you and I cry. In the same way every person cries.

Good Lord.

She was so startled and embarrassed, she had to get up and leave the room. When she came back, she took hold of my hand and said that she was sorry. She'd known him a long time ago, she said, but she'd never been able to stop thinking about him. He'd been in her thoughts every day for the past fifty-four years.

You're making this up.

I don't make things up. If I hadn't been there, I wouldn't have believed it myself. But it happened. It all happened, just as Hector said it did. Every time I think he's lied to me, it turns out that he's been telling the truth. That's what makes his story so impossible, David. Because he's told me the truth.

7

THERE WAS NO moon in the sky that night. When I stepped out of the car and put my feet on the ground, I remember saying to myself: Alma is wearing red lipstick, the car is yellow, and there is no moon in the sky tonight. In the darkness behind the main house, I could dimly make out the contours of Hector's trees—great hulks of shadow stirring in the wind.

Memoirs of a Dead Man opens with a passage about trees. I found myself thinking about that as we approached the front door, trying to remember my translation of the third paragraph of Chateaubriand's two-thousand-page book, the one that begins with the words *Ce lieu me plaît; il a remplacé pour moi les champs paternels* and concludes with the following sentences: *I am attached to my trees. I have addressed elegies, sonnets, and odes to them. There is not one amongst them that I have not tended with my own hands, that I have not freed from the worm that had attacked its root or the caterpillar that had clung to its leaves. I know them all by their names, as if they were my children. They are my family. I have no other, and I hope to be near them when I die.*

I wasn't expecting to see him that night. When Alma called

from the airport, Frieda had told her that Hector would probably be asleep by the time we made it to the ranch. He was still hanging on, she said, but she didn't think he'd be up to talking to me until tomorrow morning—assuming he managed to last that long.

Eleven years later, I still wonder what would have happened if I had stopped and turned around before we reached the door. What if, instead of putting my arm around Alma's shoulder and walking straight toward the house, I had stopped for a moment, looked at the other half of the sky, and discovered a large round moon shining down on us? Would it still be true to say that there was no moon in the sky that night? If I didn't take the trouble to turn around and look behind me, then yes, it would still be true. If I never saw the moon, then the moon was never there.

I'm not suggesting that I didn't take the trouble. I kept my eyes open, I tried to absorb everything that was happening around me, but no doubt there was much that I missed as well. Like it or not, I can only write about what I saw and heard—not about what I didn't. This is not an admission of failure so much as a declaration of methodology, a statement of principles. If I never saw the moon, then the moon was never there.

Less than a minute after we entered the house, Frieda was taking me up to Hector's room on the second floor. There was no time for anything but the most cursory look around, the briefest of first impressions—her close-cropped white hair, the firmness of her grip when she shook my hand, the weariness in her eyes—and before I could say any of the things I was supposed to say (thank you for having me, I hope he's feeling better), she informed me that Hector was awake. He'd like to see you now, she said, and suddenly I was looking at her back as she led me up the stairs. No time to make any observations about the house, then—except to note that it was large and simply furnished, with many drawings and paintings hanging on the walls (perhaps Frieda's, perhaps not)—nor to think about the unlikely person who had opened the door, a man so diminutive that I didn't even notice him until Alma bent down and kissed him on the cheek. Frieda entered the room an instant later, and although I remember that the two women hugged, I can't recall if Alma was beside me when I walked up the stairs. I always seem to lose track of her at that point. I look for her in my mind, but I never manage to locate her. By the time I get to the top of the stairs, Frieda is inevitably gone as well. It couldn't have happened that way, but that's how I remember it. Whenever I see myself walking into Hector's room, I always go in alone.

What astonished me most, I think, was the simple fact that he had a body. Until I saw him lying there in the bed, I'm not sure that I ever fully believed in him. Not as an authentic person, at any rate, not in the way I believed in Alma or myself, not in the way I believed in Helen or even Chateaubriand. It stunned me to acknowledge that Hector had hands and eyes, fingernails and shoulders, a neck and a left ear—that he was tangible, that he wasn't an imaginary being. He had been inside my head for so long, it seemed doubtful that he could exist anywhere else.

The bony, liver-spotted hands; the gnarled fingers and thick, protruding veins; the collapsed flesh under his chin; the half-open mouth. He was lying on his back with his arms out over the covers when I entered the room, awake but still, looking up at the ceiling in a kind of trance. When he turned in my direction, however, I saw that his eyes were Hector's eyes. Furrowed cheeks, grooved forehead, wattled throat, tufted white hair—and yet I recognized the face as Hector's face. It had been sixty years since he'd worn the mustache and the white suit, but he hadn't altogether vanished. He'd grown old, he'd grown infinitely old, but a part of him was still there.

Zimmer, he said. Sit down beside me, Zimmer, and turn off the light.

His voice was weak and clogged with phlegm, a soft rumbling of sighs and demi-articulations, but it was loud enough for me to make out what he said. The *r* at the end of my name had a slight roll to it, and as I reached over and turned off the lamp on the bedside table, I wondered if it wouldn't be easier for him if we continued in Spanish. After the light was off, however, I saw that a second lamp was on in the far corner of the room—a standing lamp with a broad vellum shade—and that a woman was sitting in a chair beside the lamp. She stood up the moment I glanced over at her, and I must have jumped a little when she did that—not only because I was startled, but because she was tiny, as tiny as the man who had opened the door downstairs. Neither one of them could have been more than four feet tall. I thought I heard Hector laugh behind me (a faint wheeze, the merest whisper of a laugh), and then the woman nodded at me in silence and walked out of the room.

Who was that? I said.

Don't be alarmed, Hector said. Her name is Conchita. She is part of the family.

I didn't see her, that's all. It surprised me.

Her brother Juan lives here, too. They are little people. Strange little people who cannot talk. We depend on them.

Do you want me to turn off the other light?

No, this is good. Not so hard on the eyes. I am content.

I sat down on the chair beside the bed and leaned forward, trying to position myself as close to his mouth as possible. The light from the other side of the room was no stronger than the light of a candle, but the illumination was sufficient for me to see Hector's face, to look into his eyes. A pale glow hovered over the bed, a yellowish air mixed with shadows and dark.

It is always too soon, Hector said, but I am not afraid. A man like me has to be crushed. Thank you for being here, Zimmer. I did not expect you to come.

Alma was very convincing. You should have sent her to me a long time ago.

You shook up my bones, sir. At first, I could not accept what you did. Now I think I am glad.

I didn't do anything.

You wrote a book. Again and again, I have read that book, and again and again I have asked myself: why did you choose me? What was your purpose, Zimmer?

You made me laugh. That was all it ever was. You cracked open something inside me, and after that you became my excuse to go on living.

Your book does not say that. It does honor to my old work with the mustache, but you do not talk about yourself.

I'm not in the habit of talking about myself. It makes me uncomfortable.

Alma has mentioned great sorrows, unspeakable pain. If I have helped you to bear that pain, it is perhaps the greatest good I have done.

I wanted to be dead. After listening to what Alma told me this afternoon, I gather you've been to that place yourself.

Alma was right to tell you those things. I am a ridiculous man. God has played many jokes on me, and the more you know about them, the better you will understand my films. I look forward to hearing what you say about them, Zimmer. Your opinion is very important to me.

I know nothing about films.

But you study the works of others. I have read those books, too. Your translations, your writings on the poets. It is no accident that you have spent years on the question of Rimbaud. You understand what it means to turn your back on something. I admire a man who can think like that. It makes your opinion important to me.

You've managed without anyone's opinion until now. Why this sudden need to know what others think?

Because I am not alone. Others live here, too, and I must not think only of myself.

From what I've been told, you and your wife have always worked together.

Yes, that is true. But there is Alma to consider as well.

The biography?

Yes, the book she is writing. After her mother's death, I understood that I owed her that. Alma has so little, and it seemed worth it to abandon some of my ideas about myself in order to give her a chance at life. I have begun to act like a father. It is not the worst thing that could have happened to me.

I thought Charlie Grund was her father.

He was. But I am her father, too. Alma is the child of this place. If she can turn my life into a book, then perhaps things will begin to go well for her. If nothing else, it is an interesting story. A stupid story, perhaps, but not without its interesting moments.

You're saying that you don't care about yourself anymore, that you've given up.

I have never cared about myself. Why should it bother me to turn myself into an example for others? Perhaps it will make them laugh. That would be a good outcome—to make people laugh again. You laughed, Zimmer. Perhaps others will begin to laugh with you.

We were just warming up, just beginning to get into the swing of the conversation, but before I could think of a response to Hector's last comment, Frieda walked into the room and touched me on the shoulder.

I think we should let him rest now, she said. You can go on talking in the morning.

It was demoralizing to be cut off like that, but I wasn't in a position to object. Frieda had given me less than five minutes with him, and already he had won me over, already he had made me like him more than I would have thought possible. If a dying man could exert that power, I remarked to myself, imagine what he must have been like at full strength.

I know that he said something to me before I left the room, but I can't remember what it was. Something simple and polite, but the precise words escape me now. *To be continued,* I think it was, or else *Until tomorrow, Zimmer,* a banal phrase that signified nothing of any great importance—except, perhaps, that he still believed he had a future, however short that future might have been. As I stood up from the chair, he reached out and grabbed my arm. That I do remember. I remember the cold, clawlike feel of his hand, and I remember thinking to myself: this is happening. Hector Mann is alive, and his hand is touching me now. Then I remember telling myself to remember what that hand felt like. If he didn't live until morning, it would be the only proof that I had seen him alive.

After those first hectic minutes, there was a stretch of calm that lasted for several hours. Frieda remained on the second floor, sitting in the chair I had occupied during my visit with Hector, and Alma and I went downstairs to the kitchen, which turned out to be a large, brightly lit room with stone walls, a fireplace, and a number of old appliances that seemed to have been built in the early sixties. I liked being there, and I liked sitting down at the long wooden table next to Alma and feeling her touch my arm in the same spot where Hector had touched me only a moment before. Two different gestures, two different memories—one on top of the other. My skin had become a palimpsest of fleeting sensations, and each layer bore the imprint of who I was.

Dinner was a random collection of hot and cold dishes: lentil soup, hard sausage, cheese, salad, and a bottle of red wine. The food was served to us by Juan and Conchita, the *strange little people who couldn't talk,* and while I won't deny that I was somewhat unnerved by them, I was too preoccupied with other things to give them any real attention. They were twins, Alma said, and they had started working for Hector and Frieda when they were eighteen, more than twenty years ago. I noted their perfectly formed miniature bodies, their crude peasant faces, their effervescent smiles and apparent goodwill, but I was more interested in watching Alma talk to them with her hands than I was in watching them talk to her. It intrigued me that Alma was so fluent in sign language, that she could flick off sentences with a few rapid twirls and swoops of her fingers, and because they were Alma's fingers, those were the fingers I wanted to watch. It was getting late, after all, and before long we would be going to bed. In spite of everything else that was happening just then, that was the subject I preferred to think about.

Remember the three Mexican brothers? Alma said.

The ones who helped build the original house.

The Lopez brothers. There were four girls in the family as well, and Juan and Conchita are the youngest children of the third sister. The Lopez brothers built most of the sets for Hector's films. They had eleven sons among them, and my father trained six or seven of the boys as film technicians. They were the crew. The fathers constructed the sets, and the sons worked as camera loaders and dolly operators, sound recorders and propmen, grips and gaffers. This went on for years. I used to play with Juan and Conchita when we were kids. They were the first friends I had in the world.

Eventually, Frieda came downstairs and joined us at the kitchen table. Conchita was washing a plate at the sink (standing on a footstool, working with grown-up efficiency in her seven-year-old's body), and the moment she caught sight of Frieda, she gave her a long, searching look, as if waiting for instructions. Frieda nodded, and Conchita put down the plate, dried off her hands with a dish towel, and left the room. Nothing had been said, but it was clear that she was going upstairs to sit with Hector, that they were watching over him in shifts.

By my reckoning, Frieda Spelling was seventy-nine years old. After listening to Alma's descriptions of her, I was prepared for someone ferocious—a blunt, intimidating woman, a larger-than-life character—but the person who sat down with us that evening was subdued, soft-spoken, almost reserved in her manner. No lipstick or makeup, no effort to do anything with her hair, but still feminine, still beautiful in some pared-down, incorporeal way. As I continued to look at her, I began to sense that she was one of those rare people in whom mind ultimately wins out over matter. Age doesn't diminish these people. It makes them old, but it doesn't alter who they are, and the longer they go on living, the more fully and implacably they incarnate themselves.

Forgive the confusion, Professor Zimmer, she said. You've come at a difficult time. Hector had a bad morning, but when I told him that you and Alma were on your way, he insisted on staying up. I hope it wasn't too much for him.

We had a good talk, I said. I think he's happy I came.

Happy might not be the word for it, but he's something, something very intense. You've created quite a stir in this house, Professor. I'm sure you're aware of that.

Before I could answer her, Alma broke in and changed the subject. Have you been in touch with Huyler? she asked. His breathing doesn't sound good, you know. It's much worse than it was yesterday.

Frieda sighed, then rubbed her hands over her face—exhausted from too little sleep, from too much agitation and worry. I'm not going to call Huyler, she said (talking more to herself than to Alma, as if repeating an argument she had gone through a dozen times before), because the only thing Huyler will say is *Bring him to the hospital,* and Hector won't go to the hospital. He's sick of hospitals. He made me promise, and I gave him my word. No more hospitals, Alma. So what's the point in calling Huyler?

Hector has pneumonia, Alma said. He has one lung, and he can barely breathe anymore. That's why you have to call Huyler.

He wants to die in the house, Frieda said. He's been telling me that every hour for the past two days, and I'm not going to go against him. I gave him my word.

I'll drive him to Saint Joseph's myself if you're too tired, Alma said.

Not without his permission, Frieda said. And we can't talk to him now because he's asleep. We'll try in the morning, if you like, but I'm not going to do it without his permission.

As the two women went on talking, I looked up and saw that Juan was perched on a footstool in front of the stove, scrambling eggs in a frying pan. When the food was ready, he transferred it onto a plate and carried it over to where Frieda was sitting. The eggs were hot and yellow, steaming up from the blue china in a swirl of vapor—as if the smell of those eggs had become visible. Frieda looked at them for a moment, but she didn't seem to understand what they were. They could have been a pile of rocks, or an ectoplasm that had dropped down from outer space, but they weren't food, and even if she did recognize them as food, she had no intention of putting them in her mouth. She poured herself a glass of wine instead, but after one small sip, she put the glass down again. Very delicately, she pushed the glass away from her, and then, using her other hand, she pushed away the eggs.

Bad timing, she said to me. I was hoping to be able to talk to you, to get to know you a little bit, but it doesn't look like that's going to be possible.

There's always tomorrow, I said.

Maybe, she said. Right now, I'm only thinking about now.

You should lie down, Frieda, Alma said. When was the last time you slept?

I can't remember. The day before yesterday, I think. The night before you left.

Well, I'm back now, Alma said, and David's here, too. You don't have to take on everything yourself.

I don't, Frieda said, I haven't. The little people have been an enormous help, but I have to be there to talk to him. He's too weak to sign anymore.

Get some rest, Alma said. I'll stay with him myself. David and I can do it together.

I hope you don't mind, Frieda said, but I'd feel much better if you stayed here in the house tonight. Professor Zimmer can sleep in the cottage, but I'd rather have you upstairs with me. Just in case something happens. Is that all right? I've already had Conchita make up the bed in the big guest room.

That's fine, Alma said, but David doesn't have to sleep in the cottage. He can stay with me.

Oh? Frieda said, utterly caught off guard. And what does Professor Zimmer say about that?

Professor Zimmer approves of the plan, I said.

Oh? she said again, and for the first time since she'd entered the kitchen, Frieda smiled. It was a terrific smile, I felt, full of amazement and stupefaction, and as she looked back and forth from Alma's face to my face, the smile continued to grow. My God, she said, you two work fast, don't you? Who would have expected *that*?

No one, I was about to say, but before I could get the words out of my mouth, the telephone rang. It was a bizarre interruption, and because it came so quickly after Frieda said the word *that,* there seemed to be a connection between the two events, as if the telephone had sounded in direct response to the word. It broke the mood entirely, extinguished the gleam of mirth that had been spreading across her face. Frieda stood up, and as I watched her walk to the phone (which was hanging on the wall beside the open doorway, five or six steps to her right), it occurred to me that the purpose of the call was to tell her that she wasn't allowed to smile, that smiling wasn't permitted in a house of death. It was a crazy thought, but that didn't mean my intuition was wrong. I had been on the point of saying *No one,* and when Frieda picked up the phone and asked who it was, it turned out that no one was there. Hello, she said, who is this?

and when no one answered her question, she asked it again and then hung up. She turned to us with an anguished look on her face. No one, she said. Goddamn bloody no one.

Hector died a few hours later, sometime between three and four in the morning. Alma and I were asleep when it happened, naked under the covers in the guest room bed. We had made love, talked, made love again, and I can't be sure when our bodies finally gave out on us. Alma had traveled across the country twice in two days, had driven hundreds of miles to and from airports, and still she was able to rouse herself from the depths of sleep when Juan knocked on our door. I wasn't. I slept through all the noise and commotion and wound up missing everything. After years of insomnia and restless nights, I had finally slept soundly, and it happened on the one night when I should have been awake.

I didn't open my eyes until ten o'clock. Alma was sitting on the edge of the bed, stroking my cheek with her hand, whispering my name in a calm but urgent voice, and even after I had brushed out the cobwebs and lifted myself onto my elbow, she didn't tell me the news for another ten or fifteen minutes. There were kisses first, followed by some very intimate talk about the state of our feelings, and then she handed me a mug of coffee, which she allowed me to drink all the way to the bottom before starting in. I have always admired her for having the strength and the discipline to do that. By not talking about Hector right away, she was telling me that she wasn't going to let us drown in the rest of the story. We had begun our own story now, and it was just as important to her as the other—which was her life, her whole life up to the moment she had met me.

She was glad that I'd slept through it, she said. It had given her a chance to be alone for a while and to shed some tears, to get the worst of it behind her before the day started. It was going to be a rough day, she continued, a rough and eventful day for both of us. Frieda was on the warpath—charging forward on all fronts, getting ready to burn everything as quickly as she could.

I thought we had twenty-four hours, I said.

That's what I thought, too. But Frieda says it has to be *within* twenty-four hours. We had a big fight about that before she left.

Left? You mean she's not at the ranch?

It was an incredible scene. Ten minutes after Hector died, Frieda was on the phone, talking to someone at the Vista Verde Mortuary in Albuquerque. She asked them to send out a car as soon as possible. They got here at around seven, seven-thirty, which means they should almost be there by now. She plans to have Hector cremated today.

Can she do that? Don't you have to go through a lot of formalities first?

All she needs is a death certificate. Once the doctor examines the body and says that Hector died of natural causes, she'll be free to do what she wants.

She must have had this in mind all along. She just didn't tell you.

It's grotesque. We'll be out in the screening room watching Hector's films, and Hector's body will be in an oven, turning into a mound of ashes.

And then she'll come back, and the films will turn into ashes, too.

We have only a few hours. There isn't going to be enough time to watch them all, but we might be able to get through two or three if we start now.

It's not much, is it?

She was ready to burn them all this morning. At least I managed to talk her out of that.

You make it sound as if she's lost her mind.

Her husband is dead, and the first thing she has to do is destroy his work, destroy everything they made together. If she stopped to think, she wouldn't be able to go ahead with it. Of course she's out of her mind. She made this promise almost fifty years ago, and today's the day she has to carry it out. If I were in her shoes, I'd want to get it over with as fast as I could. Get it over with—and then collapse. That's why Hector gave her only twenty-four hours. He didn't want there to be any time for second thoughts.

Alma stood up then, and as she walked around the room opening the venetian blinds, I slid out of bed and put on my clothes. There were a hundred more things to say, but we would have to put them off until after we had watched the films. Sunlight rushed through the windows as Alma yanked up the blinds, filling the room with a dazzle of midmorning brightness. She was wearing blue jeans, I remember, and a white cotton sweater. No shoes or socks, and the tips of her splendid little toes were painted red. It wasn't supposed to have worked out like this. I had been counting on Hector to keep himself alive for me, to give me a string of slow, contemplative days at the ranch with nothing to do but watch his films and sit with him in the darkness of his old man's room. It was hard to choose between disappointments, to decide which frustration was worse: never to be able to talk to him again—or to know that those films would be burned before I'd had a chance to see them all.

We passed Hector's room on the way downstairs, and when

I looked inside I saw the little people stripping the sheets off the bed. The room was entirely bare now. The objects that had cluttered the surfaces of the bureau and the bedside table were gone (pill bottles, drinking glasses, books, thermometers, towels), and except for the blankets and pillows strewn about the floor, there was nothing to suggest that a man had died in there only seven hours ago. I caught them just as they were about to remove the bottom sheet. They were standing on opposite sides of the bed, hands poised in midair, getting ready to pull down from the two top corners in unison. The effort had to be coordinated because they were so small (their heads barely came above the mattress), and as the sheet momentarily billowed up from the bed, I saw that it was smudged with various stains and discolorations, the last intimate signs of Hector's presence in the world. We all die leaking out piss and blood, shitting ourselves like newborn children, suffocating in our own mucus. A second later, the sheet flattened out again, and the deaf-and-dumb servants began walking the length of the bed, moving from top to bottom as the sheet doubled over itself and then silently fell to the floor.

Alma had prepared sandwiches and drinks for us to carry over to the screening room. As she went into the kitchen to load up the picnic basket, I wandered around downstairs, looking at the art on the walls. There must have been three dozen paintings and drawings in the living room alone, another dozen in the hall: bright, undulating abstractions, landscapes, portraits, sketches in pen and ink. Nothing was signed, but they all seemed to be the work of one person, which meant that Frieda must have been the artist. I stopped in front of a small drawing that was hanging above the record cabinet. There wasn't going to be enough time to look at everything, so I decided to concentrate on that one and ignore the rest. It was an overhead view of a young child: a two-year-old sprawled out on his back with his eyes closed, evidently asleep in his crib. The paper had turned yellow and was crumbling a bit around the edges, and when I saw how old it was, I felt certain that the child in the picture was Tad, Hector and Frieda's dead son. Naked, loose-jointed arms and legs; naked torso; a bunched-up cotton diaper held together with a safety pin; a suggestion of the crib bars just beyond the crown of the head. The lines had a swift, spur-of-the-moment feel to them—a whirl of pulsing, confident strokes that had probably been executed in under five minutes. I tried to imagine the scene, to work my way back into the moment when the point of the pencil had first touched the paper. A mother is sitting next to her child as he takes his afternoon nap. She is reading a book, but when she glances up and sees him in that unguarded pose—head flung back and lolling to one side—she digs a pencil out of her pocket and begins to draw him. Since she has no paper, she uses the last page of the book, which happens to be blank. When the drawing is finished, she tears the page out of the book and puts it away—or else she leaves it there and forgets all about it. And if she forgets, years will go by before she opens the book again and rediscovers the lost drawing. Only then will she clip the brittle sheet from the binding, frame it, and hang it on the wall. There was no way for me to know when this might have happened. It could have been forty years ago, and it could have been last month, but whenever she had stumbled across that drawing of her son, the boy was already dead—perhaps long dead, perhaps dead for more years than I had been alive.

After Alma returned from the kitchen, she took my hand and led me out of the living room into an adjoining corridor with whitewashed stucco walls and a red slate floor. There's something I want you to see, she said. I know we're pressed for time, but it won't take more than a minute.

We walked to the end of the hall, passing two or three doors along the way, and then stopped in front of the last door. Alma put down the lunch basket and pulled out a fistful of keys from her pocket. There must have been fifteen or twenty keys on that ring, but she went straight to the one she wanted and slipped it into the lock. Hector's study, she said. He spent more time in here than anywhere else. The ranch was his world, but this was the center of that world.

It was filled with books. That was the first thing I noticed when I went in—how many books there were. Three of the four walls were lined with shelves from the floor to the ceiling, and every inch of those shelves was crammed with books. There were further clusters and piles of them on chairs and tables, on the rug, on the desk. Hardcovers and paperbacks, new books and old books, books in English, Spanish, French, and Italian. The desk was a long wooden table in the middle of the room—a twin to the table that stood in the kitchen—and among the titles I remember seeing there was *My Last Sigh*, by Luis Buñuel. Because the book was lying facedown and open just in front of the chair, I wondered if Hector hadn't been reading it on the day he fell and broke his leg—which was the last day he had spent any time in his study. I was about to pick it up to see where he had left off, but Alma took my hand again and led me over to the shelves in the back corner of the room. I think you'll find this interesting, she said. She pointed to a row of books several inches above her head (but exactly at my eye level), and I saw that all of them had been written by French authors: Baudelaire, Balzac, Proust, La Fontaine. A little to the left, Alma said, and as I moved my eyes to the left, scanning the spines for whatever it was she wanted to show me, I suddenly spotted the familiar green and gold of the two-volume Pléiade edition of Chateaubriand's *Mémoires d'outre-tombe*.

It shouldn't have made any difference to me, but it did. Chateaubriand wasn't an obscure writer, but it moved me to know that Hector had read the book, that he had entered the same labyrinth of memories that I had been wandering in for the past eighteen months. It was another point of contact, somehow, another link in the chain of accidental encounters and curious sympathies that had drawn me to him from the beginning. I pulled the first volume from the shelf and opened the book. I knew that Alma and I had to be on our way, but I couldn't resist the urge to run my hands over a couple of pages, to touch some of the words that Hector had read in the quiet of this room. The book fell open somewhere in the middle, and I saw that one of the sentences had been underlined faintly in pencil. *Les moments de crise produisent un redoublement de vie chez les hommes.* Moments of crisis produce a redoubled vitality in men. Or, more succinctly perhaps: Men don't begin to live fully until their backs are against the wall.

We hurried out into the hot summer morning with our sandwiches and cold drinks. One day earlier, we had been driving through the wreckage of a New England rainstorm. Now we were in the desert, walking under a sky without clouds, breathing in the thin, juniper-scented air. I saw Hector's trees off to the right, and as we maneuvered our way around the edge of the garden, cicadas clanged in the tall grass. Splashes of yarrow, fleabane, and bedstraw. I felt hyper-alert, filled with a kind of mad resolve, a jumbled-up state of fear, expectation, and happiness—as if I had three minds, and they were all working at once. A giant wall of mountains stood in the remote distance; a hawk circled overhead; a blue butterfly landed on a stone. Less than a hundred yards after setting out from the house, I could already feel sweat gathering on my forehead. Alma pointed to a long, one-story adobe building with cracked cement steps and weeds growing in front of it. The actors and technicians had slept there while films were in production, she said, but the windows were boarded up now and the water and electricity had been turned off. The post-production complex was another fifty yards ahead, but it was the building beyond that one that caught my attention. The soundstage was an enormous structure, a sprawling cube of whiteness glinting in the sun, and it looked odd to me in those surroundings, more like an airplane hangar or a truck depot than a place for shooting films. On an impulse, I squeezed Alma's hand, then shoved my fingers in with hers and laced them together. What are we going to watch first? I asked.

The Inner Life of Martin Frost.

Why that one and not another?

Because it's the shortest. We'll be able to see it through to the end, and if Frieda still isn't back when we've finished, we'll go on to the next shortest one. I couldn't think of any other way to go about it.

It's my fault. I should have come out here a month ago. You can't believe how stupid I feel.

Frieda's letters weren't very forthcoming. If I'd been in your position, I would have hesitated, too.

I couldn't accept that Hector was alive. And then, once I did accept it, I couldn't accept that he was dying. Those films have been sitting around for years. If I'd acted right away, I could have seen them all. I could have watched them two or three times, learned them by heart, digested them. Now we're scrambling to watch just one. It's absurd.

Don't beat yourself up, David. It took me months to convince them that you should come to the ranch. If it's anyone's fault, it's mine. I'm the one who was slow. I'm the one who feels stupid.

Alma opened the door with another one of her keys, and the moment we stepped across the threshold and entered the building, the temperature dropped by ten degrees. The air-conditioning was on, and unless they kept it running all the time (which I doubted), that meant Alma had already come out here earlier in the morning. It seemed like an insignificant fact, but once I'd thought about it for a couple of moments, I felt an immense surge of pity for her. She had watched Frieda drive away with Hector's body at seven or seven-thirty, and then, instead of going upstairs and waking me, she had gone over to the post-production building and turned on the air conditioner. For the next two and a half hours, she had sat in here alone, mourning Hector as the building gradually cooled off, unable to face me again until she had cried herself out. We could have spent those hours watching a movie, but she hadn't been ready to begin, and so a part of the day had slipped through our fingers. Alma wasn't tough. She was braver than I'd thought she was, but she wasn't tough, and as I followed her down the chilly hallway toward the screening room, I finally understood how terrible this day was going to be for her, how terrible it had already been.

Doors to the left, doors to the right, but no time to open any of them, no time to go in and browse around the editing suite or the sound-mixing studio, no time even to ask if the equipment was still there. At the end of the corridor, we turned left, walked down another corridor with bare cinder-block walls (pale blue, I remember), and then went through a set of double doors into the little theater. There were three rows of cushioned chairs with fold-up seats—approximately eight to ten per row—and a slight downward incline to the floor. The screen was bolted to the wall, with no stage or curtain in front of it, a rectangle of opaque white plastic with tiny perforations and a glossy oxide sheen. Behind us was the projection booth, jutting out from the back wall. The lights were on in there, and when I turned around and looked up, the first thing I noticed was that there were two projectors—and that each one was loaded with a reel of film.

Except for a few dates and numbers, Alma didn't tell me much about the movie. *The Inner Life of Martin Frost* was the fourth film Hector had made at the ranch, she said, and after completion of photography in March 1946, he had worked on it for another five months before unveiling the final version at a private screening on August twelfth. The running time was forty-one minutes. As with all of Hector's films, it had been shot in black-and-white, but *Martin Frost* was somewhat different from the others in that it could be described as a comedy (or a film with comic elements in it) and therefore was the only one of his late works with any connection to the slapstick two-reelers of the twenties. She had chosen it because of its length, she said, but that didn't mean it wasn't a good place to begin. Her mother had played her first role for Hector in this film, and if it wasn't the most ambitious work they did together, it was probably the most charming. Alma looked away for a moment. Then, after drawing in a deep breath, she turned back to me and added: Faye was so alive then, so vivid. I never get tired of watching her.

I waited for her to go on, but that was the only comment she made, the only remark that came close to offering a subjective opinion. After another short silence, she opened the picnic basket and pulled out a notebook and a ballpoint pen—which was equipped with a flashlight for writing in the dark. Just in case you want to jot something down, she said. As I took the objects from her, she leaned forward and kissed me on the cheek—a little peck, a schoolgirl's kiss—and then turned and headed for the door. Twenty seconds later, I heard a tapping sound. I looked up, and there she was again, waving at me from the glassed-in projection booth. I waved back—perhaps I even blew her a kiss—and then, just as I was installing myself in the middle seat of the front row, Alma dimmed the lights. She didn't come down again until the film was over.

It took me a while to settle into it, to figure out what was going on. The action was filmed with such deadpan realism, such scrupulous attention to the particulars of everyday life, that I failed to perceive the magic embedded in the heart of the story. The movie began like any other love comedy, and for the first twelve or fifteen minutes Hector stuck to the time-worn conventions of the genre: the accidental meeting between the man and the woman, the misunderstanding that pushes them apart, the sudden turnaround and explosion of desire, the plunge into delirium, the emergence of difficulties, the grappling with doubt and the overcoming of doubt—all of which would lead (or so I thought) to a triumphant resolution. But then, about a third of the way into the narrative, I understood that I had it wrong. In spite of appearances, the setting of the film was not Tierra del Sueño or the grounds of the Blue Stone Ranch. It was the inside of a man's head—and the woman who had walked into that head was not a real woman. She was a spirit, a figure born of the man's imagination, an ephemeral being sent to become his muse.

If the film had been shot anywhere else, I might not have been so slow to catch on. The immediacy of the landscape disconcerted me, and for the first couple of minutes I had to struggle against the impression that I was watching some kind of elaborate, highly skilled home movie. The house in the film was Hector and Frieda's house; the garden was their garden; the road was their road. Even Hector's trees were there—looking younger and scrawnier than they were now, perhaps, but still, they were the same trees I had passed on my way to the post-production building not ten minutes earlier. There was the bedroom I had slept in the night before, the rock on which I had seen the butterfly land, the kitchen table that Frieda had stood up from to answer the phone. Until the film began to play out on the screen in front of me, all those things had been real. Now, in the black-and-white images of Charlie Grund's camera, they had been turned into the elements of a fictional world. I was supposed to read them as shadows, but my mind was slow to make the adjustment. Again and again, I saw them as they were, not as they were meant to be.

The credits came on in silence, with no music playing in the background, no auditory signals to prepare the viewer for what was to come. A progression of white-on-black cards announced the salient facts. The Inner Life of Martin Frost. Story and Direction: Hector Spelling. Cast: Norbert Steinhaus and Faye Morrison. Camera: C. P. Grund. Sets and Costumes:

Frieda Spelling. The name Steinhaus meant nothing to me, and when the actor appeared on-screen a few moments later, I felt certain that I had never seen him before. He was a tall, lanky fellow in his mid-thirties with sharp, observant eyes and slightly thinning hair. Not especially handsome or heroic, but sympathetic, human, with enough going on in his face to suggest a certain activity of mind. I felt comfortable watching him and didn't resist believing in his performance, but it was harder for me to do that with Alma's mother. Not because she wasn't a good actress, and not because I felt let down (she was lovely to look at, excellent in her role), but simply because she was Alma's mother. No doubt that added to the dislocation and confusion I experienced at the start of the film. There was Alma's mother—but Alma's mother young, fifteen years younger than Alma was now—and I couldn't help looking for signs of her daughter in her, for traces of resemblance between them. Faye Morrison was darker and taller than Alma, undeniably more beautiful than Alma, but their bodies had a similar shape, and the look in their eyes, the tilt of their heads, and the tone in their voices bore similarities as well. I don't mean to imply that they were the same, but there were enough parallels, enough genetic echoes for me to imagine that I was watching Alma without the birthmark, Alma before I had met her, Alma as a girl of twenty-two or twenty-three—living through her mother in some alternate version of her own life.

The film begins with a slow, methodical tracking shot through the interior of the house. The camera skims along the walls, floats above the furniture in the living room, and eventually comes to a stop in front of the door. *The house was empty*, an offscreen voice tells us, and a moment later the door opens and in steps Martin Frost, carrying a suitcase in one hand and a bag of groceries in the other. As he kicks the door shut behind him, the voice-over narration continues. *I had just spent three years writing a novel, and I was feeling tired, in need of a rest. When the Spellings decided to go to Mexico for the winter, they offered me the use of their place. Hector and Frieda were close friends, and they both knew how much the book had taken out of me. I figured that a couple of weeks in the desert might do me some good, and so one morning I climbed into my car and drove from San Francisco to Tierra del Sueño. I had no plans. All I wanted was to be there and do nothing, to live the life of a stone.*

As we listen to Martin's narration, we see him wandering around in various parts of the house. He carries the groceries into the kitchen, but the moment the bag touches the counter, the scene cuts to the living room, where we find him inspecting the books on the shelves. As his hand reaches for one of the books, we jump upstairs to the bedroom, where Martin is opening and closing the drawers of the bureau, putting away his things. A drawer bangs shut, and an instant later he is sitting on the bed, testing the bounce of the mattress. It is a jagged, efficiently orchestrated montage, combining close and medium shots in a succession of slightly off-kilter angles, varied tempos, and small visual surprises. Normally, one would expect music to be playing under such a sequence, but Hector dispenses with instruments in favor of natural sound: the creaking bedsprings, Martin's footsteps on the tile floor, the rustling of the paper bag. The camera fixes on the hands of a clock, and as we listen to the last words of the opening monologue (*All I wanted was to be there and do nothing, to live the life of a stone*), the image begins to blur. Silence follows. For a beat or two, it is as if everything has stopped—the voice, the sounds, the images—and then, very abruptly, the scene shifts to the outdoors. Martin is walking in the garden. A long shot is followed by a close shot; Martin's face, and then a languid perusal of the things around him: trees and scrub, sky, a crow settling onto the branch of a cottonwood. When the camera finds him again, Martin is crouching down to observe a procession of ants. We hear the wind rush through the trees—a prolonged sibilance, roaring like the sound of surf. Martin looks up, shielding his eyes from the sun, and again we cut away from him to another part of the landscape: a rock with a lizard crawling over it. The camera tilts up an inch or two, and at the top of the frame we see a cloud floating past the rock. *But what did I know?* Martin says. *A few hours of silence, a few gulps of desert air, and all of a sudden an idea for a story was turning around in my head. That's how it always seems to work with stories. One minute there's nothing. And the next minute it's there, already sitting inside you.*

The camera pans from a close-up of Martin's face to a wide shot of the trees. The wind is blowing again, and as the leaves and branches tremble under the assault, the sound amplifies into a pulsing, breathlike wave of percussiveness, an airborne clamor of sighs. The shot lasts three or four seconds longer than we think it will. It has a strangely ethereal effect, but just when we are about to ask ourselves what this curious emphasis could signify, we are thrown back into the house. It is a harsh, sudden transition. Martin is sitting at a desk in one of the upstairs rooms, pounding away at a typewriter. We listen to the clatter of the keys, watch him work on his story from a variety of angles and distances. *It wasn't going to be long,* he says. *Twenty-five or thirty pages, forty at the most. I didn't know how much time I would need to write it, but I decided to stay in the house until it was finished. That was the new plan. I would write the story, and I wouldn't leave until it was finished.*

The picture fades to black. When the action resumes, it is morning. A tight shot of Martin's face shows him to be asleep, his head resting on a pillow. Sunlight pours through the slatted shutters, and as we watch him open his eyes and struggle to wake up, the camera pulls back to reveal something that cannot be true, that defies the laws of common sense. Martin has not spent the night alone. There is a woman in bed with him, and as the camera continues dollying back into the room, we see that she is asleep under the covers, curled up on her side and turned toward Martin—her left arm flung casually across his chest, her long dark hair spilling out over the adjacent pillow. As Martin gradually emerges from his torpor, he notices the bare arm lying across his chest, then realizes that the arm is attached to a body, and then sits up straight in bed, looking like someone who's just been given an electric shock.

Jostled by these sudden movements, the young woman groans, buries her head in the pillow, and then opens her eyes. At first, she doesn't seem to notice that Martin is there. Still groggy, still fighting her way into consciousness, she rolls onto her back and yawns. As her arms stretch out, her right hand brushes against Martin's body. Nothing happens for a second or two, and then, very slowly, she sits up, looks into Martin's confused and horrified face, and shrieks. An instant later, she flings back the covers and bounds from the bed, rushing across the room in a frenzy of fear and embarrassment. She has nothing on. Not a stitch, not a shred, not even the hint of an obscuring shadow. Stunning in her nakedness, with her bare breasts and bare belly in full view of the camera, she charges toward the lens, snatches her bathrobe from the back of a chair, and hastily thrusts her arms into the sleeves.

It takes a while to clear up the misunderstanding. Martin, no less vexed and agitated than his mysterious bed partner, slides out of bed and puts on his pants, then asks her who she is and what she's doing there. The question seems to offend her. No, she says, who is *he*, and what is *he* doing there? Martin is incredulous. What are you talking about? he says. I'm Martin Frost—not that it's any of your business—and unless you tell me who you are right now, I'm going to call the police. Inexplicably, his statement astonishes her. You're Martin Frost? she says. The real Martin Frost? That's what I just said, Martin says, growing more peevish by the second, do I have to say it again? It's just that I know you, the young woman replies. Not that I really know you, but I know who you are. You're Hector and Frieda's friend.

How is she connected to Hector and Frieda? Martin wants to know, and when she informs him that she's Frieda's niece, he asks her for the third time what her name is. Claire, she finally says. Claire what? She hesitates for a moment and then says, Claire . . . Claire Martin. Martin snorts with disgust. What is this, he says, some kind of joke? I can't help it, Claire says. That's my name.

And what are you doing here, Claire *Martin*?

Frieda invited me.

When Martin responds with a disbelieving look, she picks up her purse from the chair. After fumbling through its contents for several seconds, she pulls out a key and holds it up to Martin. You see? she says. Frieda sent it to me. It's the key to the front door.

With growing irritation, Martin digs into his pocket and

pulls out an identical key, which he angrily holds up to Claire—jabbing it right under her nose. Then why would Hector send me this one? he says.

Because . . . Claire answers, backing away from him, because . . . he's Hector. And Frieda sent me this one because she's Frieda. They're always doing things like that.

There is an irrefutable logic to Claire's statement. Martin knows his friends well enough to understand that they're perfectly capable of getting their signals crossed. Inviting two people to the house at the same time is just the sort of thing the Spellings are apt to do.

With a defeated look, Martin begins to pace around the room. I don't like it, he says. I came here to be alone. I have work to do, and having you around is . . . well, it's not being alone, is it?

Don't worry, Claire says. I won't get in your way. I'm here to work, too.

It turns out that Claire is a student. She's preparing for a philosophy exam, she says, and has many books to read, a semester's worth of assignments to cram into a couple of weeks. Martin is skeptical. What do pretty girls have to do with philosophy? his look seems to say, and then he grills her about her studies, asking her what college she attends, the name of the professor who is giving the course, the titles of the books she has to read, and so on. Claire pretends not to notice the insult buried in these questions. She goes to Cal Berkeley, she says. Her professor's name is Norbert Steinhaus, and the course is called From Descartes to Kant: The Foundations of Modern Philosophical Inquiry.

I promise to be very quiet, Claire says. I'll move my things into another bedroom, and you won't even know I'm here.

Martin has run out of arguments. All right, he says, reluctantly giving in to her, I'll stay out of your way, and you'll stay out of mine. Do we have a deal?

They do. They even shake hands on it, and as Martin clomps out of the room to begin working on his story, the camera swings around and slowly pushes in on Claire's face. It is a simple but compelling shot, our first serious look at her in repose, and because it is accomplished with such patience and fluidity, we sense that the camera isn't trying to reveal Claire to us so much as to get inside her and read her thoughts, to caress her. She follows Martin with her eyes, watching him as he leaves the room, and an instant after the camera comes to rest in front of her, we hear the latch of the door click shut. The expression on Claire's face doesn't change. Good-bye, Martin, she says. Her voice is low, barely more than a whisper.

For the rest of the day, Martin and Claire work in their separate rooms. Martin sits at the desk in the study, typing, looking out the window, typing again, muttering to himself as he reads back the words he has written. Claire, looking like a college student in her blue jeans and sweatshirt, is sprawled out on the bed with *The Principles of Human Knowledge*, by George Berkeley. At some point, we notice that the philosopher's name is written out in block letters across the front of the sweatshirt: BERKELEY—which also happens to be the name of her school. Is this supposed to mean something, or is it simply a kind of visual pun? As the camera cuts back and forth from one room to the other, we hear Claire reading out loud to herself: *And it seems no less evident that the various sensations or ideas imprinted on the sense, however blended or combined together, cannot exist otherwise than in a mind perceiving them.* And again: *Secondly, it will be objected that there is a great difference betwixt real fire and the idea of fire, between dreaming or imagining oneself burnt, and actually being so.*

Late in the afternoon, a knock is heard at the door. Claire goes on reading, but when a second, louder knock follows the first, she puts down her book and tells Martin to come in. The door opens a few inches, and Martin pokes his head into the room. I'm sorry, he says. I wasn't very nice to you this morning. I shouldn't have acted that way. It is a stiff and bumbling apology, but delivered with such awkwardness and hesitation that Claire can't help smiling with amusement, perhaps even a trace of pity. She has one more chapter to go, she says. Why don't they meet in the living room in half an hour and have a drink? Good idea, Martin says. As long as they're stuck with each other, they might as well act like civilized people.

The action cuts to the living room. Martin and Claire have opened a bottle of wine, but Martin still seems nervous, not quite sure what to make of this strange and attractive reader of philosophy. In a clumsy stab at humor, he points to her sweatshirt and says, Does it say Berkeley because you're reading Berkeley? When you start reading Hume, will you wear one that says Hume?

Claire laughs. No, no, she says, the words are pronounced differently. *Berk*-ley and *Bark*-ley. The first one is a college, the other is a man. You know that. Everyone knows that.

It's the same spelling, Martin says. Therefore, it's the same word.

It's the same spelling, Claire says, but it's two different words.

Claire is about to go on, but then she stops, suddenly realizing that Martin is pulling her leg. She breaks into a broad smile. Holding out her glass, she asks Martin to pour her another drink. You wrote a short story about two characters with the same name, she says, and here I am lecturing you on the principles of nominalism. It must be the wine. I'm not thinking clearly anymore.

So you read that story, Martin says. You must be one of six people in the universe who knows about it.

I've read all your work, Claire answers. Both novels and the collection of stories.

But I've published only one novel.

You've just finished your second, haven't you? You gave a copy of the manuscript to Hector and Frieda. Frieda lent it to me, and I read it last week. *Travels in the Scriptorium.* I think it's the best thing you've done.

By now, whatever reservations Martin might have felt toward her have all but crumbled away. Not only is Claire a spirited and intelligent person, not only is she pleasant to look at, but she knows and understands his work. He pours himself another glass of wine. Claire discourses on the structure of his latest novel, and as Martin listens to her incisive but flattering comments, he leans back in his chair and smiles. It is the first time since the opening of the film that the brooding, ever-serious Martin Frost has let down his guard. In other words, he says, Miss Martin approves. Oh yes, Claire says, most definitely. Miss Martin approves of Martin. This play on their names leads them back to the Berk-ley/Bark-ley conundrum, and once again Martin asks Claire to explain the word on the sweatshirt. Which one is it? he says. The man or the college? It's both, Claire answers. It says whatever you want it to say.

At that moment, a small glint of mischief flashes in her eyes. Something has occurred to her—a thought, an impulse, a sudden inspiration. Or, Claire says, putting her glass on the table and standing up from the couch, it doesn't mean anything at all.

By way of demonstration, she peels off the sweatshirt and calmly tosses it onto the floor. She has nothing on underneath but a lacy black bra—hardly the kind of garment one would expect to discover on such an earnest student of ideas. But this is an idea, too, of course, and now that she has put it into action with such a bold and decisive gesture, Martin can only gape. Not in his wildest dreams could he have imagined that things would happen so fast.

Well, he finally says, that's one way of eliminating the confusion.

Simple logic, Claire replies. A philosophical proof.

And yet, Martin continues, speaking after another long pause, by eliminating one kind of confusion, you only create another.

Oh Martin, Claire says. Don't be confused. I'm trying to be as clear as I can.

There is a fine line between charm and aggression, between throwing yourself at someone and letting nature take its course. In this scene, which ends with the words just spoken (*I'm trying to be as clear as I can*), Claire manages to straddle both sides of the argument at once. She seduces Martin, but she goes about it in such a clever, lighthearted way that it never occurs to us to question her motives. She wants him because she wants him. That is the tautology of desire, and rather than go on discussing the endless nuances of such a proposition, she cuts directly to the chase. Removing the sweatshirt is not a vulgar announcement of her intentions. It is a moment of sublimely achieved wit, and from that moment on, Martin knows that he has met his match.

They wind up in bed. It is the same bed where they encountered each other that morning, but this time they are in no rush to separate, to fly apart on contact and scramble into their clothes. They come crashing through the door, walking and embracing at the same time, and as they fall to the bed in an awkward tangle of arms and legs and mouths, we have no doubt where all this groping and heavy breathing is going to take them. In 1946, the conventions of moviemaking would have required the scene to end there. Once the man and the woman started to kiss, the director was supposed to cut away from the bedroom to a shot of sparrows taking flight, to surf pounding against the shore, to a train speeding through a tunnel—any of several stock images to stand in for carnal passion, the fulfillment of lust—but New Mexico wasn't Hollywood, and Hector could let the camera go on rolling for as long as he liked. Clothes come off, bare flesh is seen, and Martin and Claire begin to make love. Alma had been right to warn me about the erotic moments in Hector's films, but she had been wrong to think that I would be shocked by them. I found the scene to be rather subdued, almost poignant in the banality of its intentions. The lighting is dim, the bodies are flecked with shadows, and the whole thing lasts no more than ninety or a hundred seconds. Hector doesn't want to arouse or titillate so much as to make us forget that we are watching a film, and by the time Martin starts running his mouth down Claire's body (over her breasts and along the curve of her right hip, across her pubic hair and into the soft inner part of her leg), we want to believe that we have. Again, not a note of music is played. The only sounds we hear are the sounds of breath, of rustling sheets and blankets, of bedsprings, of wind gusting through the branches of the trees in the unseen darkness outside.

The next morning, Martin begins talking to us again. Over

a montage that denotes the passage of five or six days, he tells us about the progress of his story and his growing love for Claire. We see him alone at his typewriter, see Claire alone with her books, see them together in a number of different places around the house. They cook dinner in the kitchen, kiss on the living room sofa, walk in the garden. At one point, Martin is crouching on the floor beside his desk, dipping a brush into a bucket of paint and slowly writing out the letters H-U-M-E on a white T-shirt. Later on, Claire is dressed in that T-shirt, sitting Indian-style on the bed and reading a book by the next philosopher on her list, David Hume. These small vignettes are interspersed with random close-ups of objects, abstract details that have no apparent connection to what Martin is saying: a pot of boiling water, a puff of cigarette smoke, a pair of white curtains fluttering in the embrasure of a half-open window. Steam, smoke, and wind—a catalogue of formless, insubstantial things. Martin is describing an idyll, a moment of sustained and perfect happiness, and yet as this procession of dreamlike images continues to march across the screen, the camera is telling us not to trust in the surfaces of things, to doubt the evidence of our own eyes.

One afternoon, Martin and Claire are eating lunch in the kitchen. Martin is in the middle of telling her a story (*And then I said to him, If you don't believe me, I'll show you. And then I reached into my pocket and*—) when the telephone rings. Martin gets up to answer it, and as soon as he exits the frame, the camera reverses angle and dollies in on Claire. We see her expression change from one of joyful camaraderie to concern, perhaps even alarm. It is Hector, calling long-distance from Cuernavaca, and although we can't hear his end of the conversation, Martin's comments are clear enough for us to understand what Hector is saying. It seems that a cold front is headed toward the desert. The furnace has been on the blink, and if the temperatures drop as low as they are expected to, then Martin will need to have it checked out. If anything goes wrong, the man to call is Jim, Jim Fortunato of Fortunato Plumbing and Heat.

It's no more than a mundane point of business, but Claire grows increasingly upset as she listens to the exchange. When Martin finally mentions her name to Hector (*I was just telling Claire about that bet we made the last time I was here*), Claire stands up and rushes out of the room. Martin is surprised by her sudden departure, but that surprise is nothing compared to the one that follows an instant later. *What do you mean, Who's Claire?* he says to Hector. *Claire Martin, Frieda's niece.* We don't have to listen to Hector's answer to know what he says. One look at Martin's face and we understand that Hector has just told him that he's never heard of her, that he has no idea who Claire is.

By then, Claire is already outside, running away from the house. In a series of rapid, pinpoint cuts, we see Martin burst through the door and chase after her. He calls out to Claire, but Claire keeps on running, and another ten seconds go by before he manages to catch up with her. Reaching out and grabbing her elbow from behind, he spins her around and forces her to stop. They are both out of breath. Chests heaving, lungs gasping for air, neither one of them able to talk.

At last Martin says: What's going on, Claire? Tell me, what's going on? When Claire doesn't answer him, he leans forward and shouts in her face: You have to tell me!

I can hear you, Claire says, speaking in a calm voice. You don't have to shout, Martin.

I've just been told that Frieda has one brother, Martin says.

He has two children, and both of them happen to be boys. That makes two nephews, Claire, but no niece.

I didn't know what else to do, Claire says. I had to find a way to make you trust me. After a day or two, I thought you'd figure it out on your own—and then it wouldn't matter anymore.

Figure out what?

Until now, Claire has looked embarrassed, more or less contrite, not so much ashamed of her deception as disappointed that she's been found out. Once Martin confesses to his ignorance, however, the look changes. She seems genuinely astonished. Don't you get it, Martin? she says. We've been together for a week, and you're telling me you still don't get it?

It goes without saying that he doesn't—and neither do we. The bright and beautiful Claire has turned into an enigma, and the more she says, the less we are able to follow her.

Who are you? Martin asks. What the hell are you doing here?

Oh Martin, Claire says, suddenly on the verge of tears. It doesn't matter who I am.

Of course it does. It matters very much.

No, my darling, it doesn't.

How can you say that?

It doesn't matter because you love me. Because you want me. *That's* what matters. All the rest is nothing.

The picture fades out on a close-up of Claire, and before another image succeeds it, we hear the faint sounds of Martin's typewriter clicking away in the distance. A slow fade-in begins, and as the screen gradually brightens, the sounds of the typewriter seem to draw closer to us, as if we were moving from the outside to the inside of the house, walking up the stairs, and approaching the door of Martin's room. When the new image settles into focus, the entire screen is filled with an immense, tightly framed shot of Martin's eyes. The camera holds in that position for a couple of beats, and then, as the voice-over narration continues, it starts to pull back, revealing Martin's face, Martin's shoulders, Martin's hands on the keys of the typewriter, and finally Martin sitting at his desk. With no halt in its backward progress, the camera leaves the room and begins traveling down the corridor. *Unfortunately*, Martin says, *Claire was right. I did love her, and I did want her. But how can you love someone you don't trust?* The camera stops in front of Claire's door. As if by telepathic command, the door swings open—and then we are inside, moving in on Claire as she sits in front of a dressing-table mirror applying makeup to her face. Her body is sheathed in a black satin slip, her hair is swept up in a loosely knotted chignon, the back of her neck is exposed. *Claire was like no other woman*, Martin says. *She was stronger than everyone else, wilder than everyone else, smarter than everyone else. I had been waiting to meet her all my life, and yet now that we were together, I was scared. What was she hiding from me? What terrible secret was she refusing to tell? A part of me thought I should get out of there—just pack up my things and leave before it was too late. And another part of me thought: she's testing me. If I fail the test, I'll lose her.*

Eyebrow pencil, mascara, cheek rouge, powder, lipstick. As Martin delivers his confused, soul-searching monologue, Claire goes on working in front of the mirror, transforming herself from one kind of woman into another. The impulsive tomboy disappears, and in her place emerges a glamorous, sophisticated, movie-star temptress. Claire stands up from the table and wriggles into a narrow black cocktail dress, slips her feet into a pair of three-inch heels, and we scarcely recognize her anymore. She cuts a ravishing figure: self-possessed, confident, the very picture of feminine power. With a faint smile on her lips, she checks herself in the mirror one last time and then walks out of the room.

Cut to the hallway. Claire knocks on Martin's door and says: Dinner's ready, Martin. I'll be waiting for you downstairs.

Cut to the dining room. Claire is sitting at the table, waiting for Martin. She has already set out the appetizers; the wine has been uncorked; the candles have been lit. Martin enters the room in silence. Claire greets him with a warm, friendly smile, but Martin pays no attention to it. He seems wary, out of sorts, not at all sure of how he should act.

Eyeing Claire with suspicion, he walks over to the place that has been set for him, pulls out the chair, and begins to sit down. The chair appears to be solid, but no sooner does he lower his weight onto it than it splinters into a dozen pieces. Martin goes tumbling to the floor.

It is a hilarious, wholly unexpected turn of events. Claire bursts out laughing, but Martin is not at all amused. Sprawled out on his rear end, he smolders in a funk of injured pride and resentment, and the longer Claire goes on laughing at him (she can't help herself; it's simply too funny), the more ridiculous he is made to look. Without saying a word, Martin slowly climbs to his feet, kicks aside the bits of broken chair, and puts another chair in its place. He sits down cautiously this time, and when he is at last assured that the seat is strong enough to hold him, he turns his attention to the food. Looks good, he says. It is a desperate attempt to maintain his dignity, to swallow his embarrassment.

Claire seems inordinately pleased by his comment. With another smile brightening her face, she leans toward him and asks: How's your story going, Martin?

By now, Martin is holding a lemon wedge in his left hand,

about to squeeze it onto his asparagus. Instead of answering Claire's question right away, he presses the lemon between his thumb and middle finger—and the juice squirts into his eye. Martin yelps in pain. Once again, Claire bursts out laughing, and once again our grumpy hero is not the least bit amused. He dips his napkin into his water glass and begins patting his eye, trying to get rid of the sting. He looks defeated, utterly humiliated by this fresh display of clumsiness. When he finally puts down the napkin, Claire repeats the question.

And so, Martin, she says, how's your story going?

Martin can barely stand it anymore. Refusing to answer Claire's question, he looks her straight in the eye and says: Who are you, Claire? What are you doing here?

Unruffled, Claire smiles back at him. No, she says, you answer my question first. How's your story going?

Martin looks as if he's about to snap. Maddened by her evasions, he just stares at her and says nothing.

Please, Martin, Claire says. It's very important.

Struggling to control his temper, Martin mumbles a sarcastic aside—not addressing Claire so much as thinking out loud, talking to himself: You really want to know?

Yes, I really want to know.

All right . . . All right, I'll tell you how it's going. It's . . . (he reflects for a moment) . . . it's (continuing to think) . . . Actually, it's going quite well.

Quite well . . . or very well?

Um . . . (thinking) . . . very well. I'd say it's going very well.

You see?

See what?

Oh, Martin. Of course you do.

No, Claire, I don't. I don't see anything. If you want to know the truth, I'm completely lost.

Poor Martin. You shouldn't be so hard on yourself.

Martin gives her a lame smile. They have reached a kind of standoff, and for the moment there is nothing more to be said. Claire digs into her food. She eats with obvious enjoyment, savoring the taste of her concoction with small tentative bites. Mmm, she says. Not bad. What do you think, Martin?

Martin lifts his fork to take a bite, but just as he is about to put the food in his mouth, he glances over at Claire, distracted by the soft moans of pleasure emanating from her throat, and with his attention briefly diverted from the matter at hand, his wrist turns downward by a few degrees. As the fork continues its journey toward his mouth, a thin trail of salad dressing comes dripping off the utensil and slides down the front of his shirt. At first, Martin doesn't notice, but as his mouth opens and his eyes return to the looming morsel of asparagus, he suddenly sees what is happening. He jumps back and lets go of the fork. Christ! he says. I've done it again!

The camera cuts to Claire (who bursts out laughing for the third time) and then dollies in on her for a close-up. The shot is similar to the one that ended the scene in the bedroom at the beginning of the film, but whereas Claire's face was motionless as she watched Martin make his exit, now it is animated, brimming with delight, expressing what seems to be an almost transcendent joy. *She was so alive then,* Alma had said, *so vivid.* No moment in the story captures that sense of fullness and life better than this one. For a few seconds, Claire is turned into something indestructible, an embodiment of pure human radiance. Then the picture begins to dissolve, breaking apart against a background of solid blackness, and although Claire's laughter goes on for several more beats, it begins to break apart as well—fading into a series of echoes, of disjointed breaths, of ever more distant reverberations.

A long stillness follows, and for the next twenty seconds the screen is dominated by a single nocturnal image: the moon in the sky. Clouds drift past, the wind rustles through the trees below, but essentially there is nothing before us but that moon. It is a stark and purposeful transition, and within moments we have forgotten the comic high jinks of the previous scene. *That night,* Martin says, *I made one of the most important decisions of my life. I decided that I wasn't going to ask any more questions. Claire was asking me to make a leap of faith, and rather than go on pressing her, I decided to close my eyes and jump. I had no idea what was waiting for me at the bottom, but that didn't mean it wasn't worth the risk. And so I kept on falling . . . and a week later, just when I was beginning to think that nothing could ever go wrong, Claire went out for a walk.*

Martin is sitting at the desk in his second-floor study. He turns from the typewriter to look out the window, and as the angle reverses to record his point of view, we see a long overhead shot of Claire walking alone in the garden. The cold front has apparently arrived. She is wearing a scarf and overcoat, her hands are in her pockets, and a light snowfall has dusted the ground. When the camera cuts back to Martin, he is still looking through the window, unable to tear his eyes away from her. Another reverse, and then another shot of Claire, alone in the garden. She takes a few more steps, and then, without warning, she collapses to the ground. It is a terrifyingly effective fall. No tottering or dizziness, no gradual buckling of the knees. Between one step and the next, Claire plunges into total unconsciousness, and from the sudden, merciless way her strength gives out on her, it looks as if she's dead.

The camera zooms in from the window, bringing Claire's inert body into the foreground. Martin enters the frame: running, out of breath, frantic. He falls to his knees and cradles her head in his hands, looking for a sign of life. We no longer know what to expect. The story has shifted into another register, and one minute after laughing our heads off, we find ourselves in the middle of a tense, melodramatic scene. Claire eventually opens her eyes, but enough time passes for us to know that it isn't a recovery so much as a stay of execution, an augur of things to come. She looks up at Martin and smiles. It is a spiritual smile, somehow, an inward smile, the smile of someone who no longer believes in the future. Martin kisses her, and then he bends down, gathers Claire into his arms, and begins carrying her toward the house. *She seemed to be all right,* he says. *Just a little fainting spell, we thought. But the next morning, Claire woke up with a high fever.*

We cut to a shot of Claire in bed. Hovering around her like a nurse, Martin takes her temperature, plies her with aspirins, dabs her forehead with a wet towel, feeds her broth with a spoon. *She didn't complain,* he continues. *Her skin was hot to the touch, but she seemed to be in good spirits. After a while, she pushed me out of the room. Go back to your story, she said. I'd rather sit here with you, I told her, but then Claire laughed, and with a funny, pouting expression on her face, she said that if I didn't go back to work this instant, she was going to jump out of bed, rip off her clothes, and run outside with nothing on. And that wasn't going to make her well, was it?*

A moment later, Martin is sitting at his desk, typing another page of his story. The sound is particularly intense here—keys clattering at a furious rhythm, great staccato bursts of activity—but then the volume diminishes, falls off into near silence, and Martin's voice returns. We go back to the bedroom. One by one, we see a succession of highly detailed close-ups, still-life renderings of the tiny world around Claire's sickbed: a glass of water, the edge of a closed book, a thermometer, the knob on the night-table drawer. *But the next morning,* Martin says, *the fever was worse. I told her that I was taking the day off, whether she liked it or not. I sat beside her for several hours, and by the middle of the afternoon, she seemed to take a turn for the better.*

The camera jumps back to a wide shot of the room, and there she is, sitting up in bed, looking like the old vivacious Claire. In a mock-serious voice, she is reading a passage from Kant out loud to Martin: . . . *things which we see are not by themselves what we see . . . so that, if we drop our subject or the subjective form of our senses, all qualities, all relations of objects in space and time, nay space and time themselves, would vanish.*

Things seem to be returning to normal. With Claire on the mend, Martin goes back to his story the next day. He works steadily for two or three hours, and then he breaks off to check in on Claire. When he enters the bedroom, she is fast asleep, bundled up under a pile of quilts and blankets. It is cold in the room—cold enough for Martin to see his own breath in front of him when he exhales. Hector warned him about the furnace, but Martin has clearly forgotten to attend to it. Too many crazy things happened after that phone call, and Fortunato's name must have slipped his mind.

There is a fireplace in the room, however, and a small stack of wood on the hearth. Martin begins preparing a fire, working as quietly as he can so as not to disturb Claire. Once the flames catch hold, he adjusts the logs with a poker, and one of them inadvertently slips out from under the others. The noise breaks in on Claire's sleep. She stirs, groaning softly as she thrashes about under the covers, and then she opens her eyes. Martin swivels around from his spot in front of the fire. I didn't mean to wake you, he says. I'm sorry.

Claire smiles. She looks weak, drained of physical

resources, barely conscious. Hello, Martin, she whispers. How's my beautiful man?

Martin walks over to the bed, sits down, and puts his hand on Claire's forehead. You're burning up, he says.

I'm all right, she answers. I feel fine.

This is the third day, Claire. I think we should call a doctor.

No need for that. Just give me some more of those aspirins. In half an hour I'll be good as new.

Martin shakes out three aspirins from the bottle and hands them to her with a glass of water. As Claire swallows the pills, Martin says: This isn't good. I really think a doctor should take a look at you.

Claire gives Martin the empty glass, and he puts it back on the table. Tell me what's happening in the story, she says. That will make me feel better.

You should rest.

Please, Martin. Just a little bit.

Not wanting to disappoint her, and yet not wanting to tax her strength, Martin confines his summary to just a few sentences. It's dark now, he says. Nordstrum has left the house. Anna is on her way, but he doesn't know that. If she doesn't get there soon, he's going to walk into the trap.

Will she make it?

It doesn't matter. The important thing is that she's going to him.

She's fallen in love with him, hasn't she?

In her own way, yes. She's putting her life in danger for him. That's a form of love, isn't it?

Claire doesn't answer. Martin's question has overwhelmed her, and she is too moved to give a response. Her eyes fill up with tears; her mouth trembles; a look of rapturous intensity shines forth from her face. It's as if she has reached some new understanding of herself, as if her whole body were suddenly giving off light. How much more to go? she asks.

Two or three pages, Martin says. I'm almost at the end.

Write them now.

They can wait. I'll do them tomorrow.

No, Martin, do them now. You must do them now.

The camera lingers on Claire's face for a moment or two—and then, as if propelled by the force of her command, Martin is at his desk again, typing. This initiates a sequence of cross-cuts between the two characters. We go from Martin back to Claire, from Claire back to Martin, and in the space of ten simple shots, we finally get it, we finally understand what's been happening. Then Martin returns to the bedroom, and in ten more shots he finally understands as well.

1. Claire is writhing around on the bed, in acute pain, struggling not to call out for help.

2. Martin comes to the bottom of a page, pulls it out of the machine, and rolls in another. He begins typing again.

3. We see the fireplace. The fire has nearly gone out.

4. A close-up of Martin's fingers, typing.

5. A close-up of Claire's face. She is weaker than before, no longer struggling.

6. A close-up of Martin's face. At his desk, typing.

7. A close-up of the fireplace. Just a few glowing embers.

8. A medium shot of Martin. He types the last word of his story. A brief pause. Then he pulls the page out of the machine.

9. A medium shot of Claire. She shudders slightly—and then appears to die.

10. Martin is standing beside his desk, gathering up the pages of the manuscript. He walks out of the study, holding the finished story in his hand.

11. Martin enters the room, smiling. He glances at the bed, and an instant later the smile is gone.

12. A medium shot of Claire. Martin sits down beside her, puts his hand on her forehead, and gets no response. He presses his ear against her chest—still no response. In a mounting panic, he tosses aside the manuscript and begins rubbing her body with both hands, desperately trying to warm her up. She is limp; her skin is cold; she has stopped breathing.

13. A shot of the fireplace. We see the dying embers. There are no more logs on the hearth.

14. Martin jumps off the bed. Snatching the manuscript as he goes, he wheels around and rushes toward the fireplace. He looks possessed, out of his mind with fear. There is only one thing left to be done—and it must be done now. Without hesitation, Martin crumples up the first page of his story and throws it into the fire.

15. A close-up of the fire. The ball of paper lands in the ashes and bursts into flame. We hear Martin crumpling up another page. A moment later, the second ball lands in the ashes and ignites.

16. Cut to a close-up of Claire's face. Her eyelids begin to flutter.

17. A medium shot of Martin, crouched in front of the fire. He grabs hold of the next sheet, crumples it up, and throws it in as well. Another sudden burst of flame.

18. Claire opens her eyes.

19. Working as fast as he can now, Martin goes on bunching up pages and throwing them into the fire. One by one, they all begin to burn, each one lighting the other as the flames intensify.

20. Claire sits up. Blinking in confusion; yawning; stretching out her arms; showing no traces of illness. She has been brought back from the dead.

Gradually coming to her senses, Claire begins to glance around the room, and when she sees Martin in front of the fireplace, madly crumpling up his manuscript and throwing it into the fire, she looks stricken. What are you doing? she says. My God, Martin, what are you doing?

I'm buying you back, he says. Thirty-seven pages for your life, Claire. It's the best bargain I've ever made.

But you can't do that. It's not allowed.

Maybe not. But I'm doing it, aren't I? I've changed the rules.

Claire is overwrought, about to break down in tears. Oh Martin, she says. You don't know what you've done.

Undaunted by Claire's objections, Martin goes on feeding his story to the flames. When he comes to the last page, he turns to her with a triumphant look in his eyes. You see, Claire? he says. It's only words. Thirty-seven pages—and nothing but words.

He sits down on the bed, and Claire throws her arms around him. It is a surprisingly fierce and passionate gesture, and for the first time since the beginning of the film, Claire looks afraid. She wants him, and she doesn't want him. She is ecstatic; she is horrified. She has always been the strong one, the one with all the courage and confidence, but now that Martin has solved the riddle of his enchantment, she seems lost. What are you going to do? she says. Tell me, Martin, what on earth are we going to do?

Before Martin can answer her, the scene shifts to the outside. We see the house from a distance of about fifty feet, sitting in the middle of nowhere. The camera tilts upward, pans to the right, and comes to rest on the boughs of a large cottonwood. Everything is still. No wind is blowing; no air is rushing through the branches; not a single leaf moves. Ten seconds go by, fifteen seconds go by, and then, very abruptly, the screen goes black and the film is over.

8

LATER THAT SAME day, the print of *Martin Frost* was destroyed. I should probably consider myself lucky to have seen it, to have been there for the last showing of a film at the Blue Stone Ranch, but a part of me wishes that Alma had never turned on the projector that morning, that I had never been exposed to a frame of that elegant and haunting little movie. It wouldn't have mattered if I hadn't liked it, if I had been able to dismiss it as a bad or incompetent piece of storytelling, but this was manifestly not bad, manifestly not incompetent, and now that I knew what was about to be lost, I realized that I had traveled over two thousand miles to participate in a crime. When *The Inner Life* went up in flames with the rest of Hector's work that July afternoon, it felt like a tragedy to me, like the end of the goddamn bloody world.

That was the only movie I saw. There wasn't enough time to watch another, and given that I sat through *Martin Frost* only once, it was a good thing Alma thought to provide me with the notebook and the pen. There is no contradiction in that statement. I might wish that I had never seen the film, but the fact was that I did see it, and now that the words and images had insinuated themselves inside me, I was thankful that there was a way to hold on to them. The notes I took that morning have helped me to remember details that otherwise would have slipped away from me, to keep the film alive in my head after so many years. I scarcely looked down at the page as I wrote—scribbling in the mad telegraphic shorthand I developed as a student—and if much of my writing bordered on the illegible, I eventually managed to decipher about ninety or ninety-five percent of it. It took weeks of painstaking effort to make the transcription, but once I had a fair copy of the dialogue and had broken down the story into numbered scenes, it became possible to reestablish contact with the film. I have to go into a kind of trance in order to do that (which means that it doesn't always work), but if I concentrate hard enough and get myself into the right mood, the words can actually conjure up the images for me, and it's as if I'm watching *The Inner Life of Martin Frost* again—or little flashes of it, in any case, locked in the projection room of my skull. Last year, when I began toying with the idea of writing this book, I went in for several consultations with a hypnotist. Nothing much happened the first time, but the next three visits produced astonishing results. By listening to the tape recordings of those sessions, I have been able to fill in certain blanks, to bring back a number of things that were beginning to vanish. For better or worse, it seems that the philosophers were right. Nothing that happens to us is ever lost.

The screening ended a few minutes past noon. Alma and I were both hungry by then, both in need of a short break, and so instead of plunging directly into another film, we went out into the hall with our basket lunch. It was a strange spot for a picnic—camped out on the dusty linoleum floor, digging into our cheese sandwiches under a row of blinking fluorescent lights—but we didn't want to lose any time by looking for a better place outdoors. We talked about Alma's mother, about Hector's other work, about the oddly satisfying mixture of whimsy and seriousness in the film that had just ended. Movies could trick us into believing any kind of nonsense, I said, but this time I had fallen for it. When Claire came back to life in the final scene, I had shuddered, had felt that I was watching an authentic miracle. Martin burned his story in order to rescue Claire from the dead, but it was also Hector rescuing Brigid O'Fallon, also Hector burning his own movies, and the more things had doubled back on themselves like that, the more deeply I had entered the film. Too bad we couldn't watch it again, I said. I wasn't sure if I had watched the wind closely enough, if I had paid enough attention to the trees.

I must have rattled on longer than I should have, for no sooner did Alma announce the title of the next movie we were going to see (*Report from the Anti-World*) than a door slammed somewhere in the building. We were just climbing to our feet at that point—brushing the crumbs off our clothes, taking a last swig of iced tea from the thermos, getting ready to go back inside. We heard the sound of tennis shoes flapping against the linoleum. A couple of moments later, Juan appeared at the end of the hall, and when he started coming toward us at a half trot—more running than walking—we both knew that Frieda had returned.

For the next little while, it was as if I wasn't there anymore. Juan and Alma talked to each other in silence, communicating in a flurry of hand signals, sweeping arm movements, and emphatic shakes and nods of the head. I didn't understand what they were saying, but as the remarks flew back and forth between them, I could see that Alma was becoming more and more upset. Her gestures turned harsh, truculent, almost aggressive in their denial of what Juan was telling her. Juan threw up his hands in a pose of surrender (Don't blame me, he seemed to be saying, I'm only the messenger), but Alma lashed out at him again, and his eyes clouded over with hostility. He pounded his fist in his palm, then turned and pointed a finger at my face. It wasn't a conversation anymore. It was an argument, and the argument was suddenly about me.

I kept on watching, kept on trying to understand what they were talking about, but I couldn't penetrate the code, couldn't make sense of what I was seeing. Then Juan left, and as he marched down the hall on his stocky, diminutive legs, Alma explained what had happened. Frieda got back ten minutes ago, she said. She wants to start in right away.

That was awfully fast, I said.

Hector won't be cremated until five this afternoon. She didn't want to hang around Albuquerque that long, so she decided to come home. She plans to pick up the ashes tomorrow morning.

What were you and Juan arguing about, then? I had no idea what was going on, but he pointed his finger at me. I don't like it when people point their finger at me.

We were talking about you.

So I gathered. But what do I have to do with Frieda's plans? I'm just a visitor.

I thought you understood.

I don't understand sign language, Alma.

But you saw that I was angry.

Of course I did. But I still don't know why.

Frieda doesn't want you around. It's all too private, she says, and it isn't a good time for strangers.

You mean she's booting me off the ranch?

Not in so many words. But that's the gist of it. She wants you to leave tomorrow. The plan is to drop you off at the airport on our way to Albuquerque in the morning.

But she's the one who invited me. Doesn't she remember that?

Hector was alive then. Now he's not. Circumstances have changed.

Well, maybe she has a point. I came here to watch movies, didn't I? If there aren't any movies to watch, there's probably no reason for me to stay. I got to see one of them. Now I can watch the others burn up in the fire, and then I'll be on my way.

That's just it. She doesn't want you to see that either. According to what Juan just told me, it's none of your business.

Oh. Now I see why you lost your temper.

It has nothing to do with you, David. It's about me. She knows I want you there. We talked about it this morning, and now she's broken her promise. I'm so pissed off, I could punch her in the face.

And where am I supposed to hide myself while everyone's at the barbecue?

In my house. She said you could stay in my house. But I'm going to talk to her. I'll make her change her mind.

Don't bother. If she doesn't want me there, I can't stand on my rights and make a fuss, can I? I don't have any rights. It's Frieda's land, and I have to do what she says.

Then I won't go either. She can burn the damn films with Juan and Conchita.

Of course you'll go. It's the last chapter of your book, Alma, and you have to be there to see it happen. You have to stick it out to the end.

I wanted you to be there, too. It won't be the same if you're not with me.

Fourteen prints and negatives are going to make a hell of a fire. Lots of smoke, lots of flame. With any luck, I'll be able to see it from the window of your house.

As it turned out, I did see the fire, but I saw more smoke than flame, and because the windows were open in Alma's little house, I smelled more than I saw. The burning celluloid had an acrid, stinging odor, and the airborne chemicals hovered in the atmosphere long after the smoke had drifted away. According to what Alma told me that evening, it took the four of them over an hour to haul the films out of the underground storage room. Then they strapped the cans onto hand trucks and wheeled them over the rocky ground to an area just behind the sound stage. With the help of newspapers and kerosene, they lit fires in two oil drums—one for the prints and the other for the negatives. The old nitrate stock burned easily, but the films from after 1951, which had been printed on tougher, less flammable triacetate-based stocks, had trouble igniting. They had to unspool the films from their reels and feed them into the fire one by one, Alma said, and that took time, much longer than anyone had anticipated. They had guessed that they would be finished at around three o'clock, but in point of fact they kept on working until six.

I spent those hours alone in her house, trying not to resent my exile. I had put a good face on it in front of Alma, but the truth was that I was just as angry as she was. Frieda's behavior had been unforgivable. You don't ask someone to your house and then disinvite him once he's there. And if you do, at least you offer an explanation, and not through the intermediary of a deaf-and-dumb servant, who delivers the message to someone else while pointing a finger at your face. I knew that Frieda was distraught, that she was living through a day of storms and cataclysmic sorrows, but much as I wanted to make excuses for her, I couldn't help feeling hurt. What was I doing there? Why had Alma been sent to Vermont to drag me back at gunpoint if they didn't want to see me? Frieda was the one who had written the letters, after all. She was the one who had asked me to come to New Mexico and watch Hector's films. According to Alma, it had taken her months to persuade them to invite me. I had assumed that Hector had resisted the idea and that Alma and Frieda had eventually talked him into it. Now, after eighteen hours at the ranch, I was beginning to suspect that I had been wrong.

If not for the insulting way I was treated, I probably wouldn't have given these matters a second thought. After Alma and I finished our conversation in the post-production building, we packed up the remains of our lunch and walked over to her adobe cottage, which was set on a small rise of land about three hundred yards from the main house. Alma opened the door, and sitting at our feet, just beyond the edge of the sill, was my travel bag. I had left it in the guest room of the other house that morning, and now someone (probably Conchita) had carried it over on Frieda's orders and deposited it on the floor of Alma's place. It struck me as an arrogant, imperious gesture. Again, I pretended to laugh it off (Well, I said, at least that spares me the trouble of having to do it myself), but underneath my flippant remark, I was boiling with rage. Alma left to join the others, and for the next fifteen or twenty minutes I wandered around the house, going in and out of rooms, trying to control my temper. Presently, I heard the sound of the hand trucks clattering in the distance, the clang of metal scraping against stone, the intermittent noise of stacked-up film cans clicking and vibrating against one another. The auto-da-fé was about to begin. I went into the bathroom, stripped off my clothes, and turned on the faucets of the tub at full blast.

Soaking in the warm water, I let my mind drift for a while, slowly rehearsing the facts as I understood them. Then, turning them around and looking at them from a different angle, I tried to accommodate those facts to the events that had taken place in the past hour: Juan's belligerent dialogue with Alma, Alma's vituperative response to Frieda's message (*she's broken her promise . . . I could punch her in the face*), my expulsion from the ranch. It was a purely speculative line of reasoning, but when I thought back to what had happened the night before (the graciousness of Hector's welcome, his eagerness to show me his films) and then compared it to what had happened since, I began to wonder if Frieda had not been opposed to my visit all along. I wasn't forgetting that she was the one who had invited me to Tierra del Sueño, but perhaps she had written those letters against her better judgment, buckling in to Hector's demands after months of quarrels and disagreements. If that was so, then ordering me off her land did not represent a sudden change of heart. It was merely something she could get away with now that Hector was dead.

Until then, I had thought of them as equal partners. Alma had talked about their marriage at some length, and not once had it occurred to me that their motives might have been different, that their thinking had not been in perfect harmony. They had made a pact in 1939 to produce films that would never be shown to the public, and they had both embraced the idea that the work they did together should ultimately be destroyed. Those were the conditions of Hector's return to filmmaking. It was a brutal interdiction, and yet only by sacrificing the one thing that would have given his work meaning—the pleasure of sharing it with others—could he justify his decision to do that work in the first place. The films, then, were a form of penance, an acknowledgment that his role in the accidental murder of Brigid O'Fallon was a sin that could never be pardoned. *I am a ridiculous man. God has played many jokes on me.* One form of punishment had given way to another, and in the tangled, self-torturing logic of his decision, Hector had continued to pay off his debts to a God he refused to believe in. The bullet that tore apart his chest in the Sandusky bank had made it possible for him to marry Frieda. The death of his son had made it possible for him to return to filmmaking. In neither instance, however, had he been absolved of his responsibility for what had happened on the night of January 14, 1929. Neither the physical suffering caused by Knox's gun nor the mental suffering caused by Taddy's death had been terrible enough to set him free. Make films, yes. Pour every ounce of your talents and energies into making them. Make them as though your life depended on it, and then, once your life is over, see to it that they are destroyed. You are forbidden to leave any traces behind you.

Frieda had gone along with all this, but it couldn't have been the same for her. She hadn't committed a crime; she wasn't dragged down by the weight of a guilty conscience; she wasn't pursued by the memory of putting a dead girl into the trunk of a car and burying her body in the California mountains. Frieda was innocent, and yet she accepted Hector's terms, putting aside her own ambitions to devote herself to the creation of work whose central aim was nothingness. It would have been understandable to me if she had watched him from a distance—indulging Hector in his obsessions, perhaps, pitying him for his mania, yet refusing to get involved in the mechanics of the enterprise itself. But Frieda was his accomplice, his staunchest defender, and she was up to her elbows in it from the start. Not only did she talk Hector into making films again (threatening to leave him if he didn't), but it was her money that financed the operation. She sewed costumes, drew storyboards, cut film, designed sets. You don't work that hard at something unless you enjoy it, unless you feel that your efforts have some value—but what possible joy could she have found from spending all those years in the service of nothing? At least Hector, trapped in his psycho-religious battle between desire and self-abnegation, could comfort himself with the thought that there was a purpose to what he was doing. He didn't make films in order to destroy them—but in spite of it. They were two separate actions, and the best part of it was that he wouldn't have to be around to see the second one happen. He would already be dead by the time his films went into the fire, and it would no longer make any difference to him. For Frieda, however, the actions must have been one and the same, two steps in a single, unified process of creation and destruction. All along, she was the one who had been destined to light the match and bring their work to an end, and that thought must have grown in her as the years went by until it overpowered everything else. Little by little, it had become an aesthetic principle in its own right. Even as she continued working on the films with Hector, she must have felt that the work was no longer about making films. It was about making something in order to destroy it. That was the work, and until all evidence of the work had been destroyed, the work would not exist. It would come into being only at the moment of its annihilation—and then, as the smoke rose up into the hot New Mexican day, it would be gone.

There was something chilling and beautiful about this idea. I understood how seductive it must have been for her, and yet once I allowed myself to look at it through Frieda's eyes, to experience the full power of that ecstatic negation, I also understood why she wanted to get rid of me. My presence tainted the purity of the moment. The films were supposed to die a virgin death, unseen by anyone from the outside world. It was bad enough that I had been allowed to see one of them, but now that the articles of Hector's will were about to go into effect, she could insist that the ceremony be conducted in the way she had always imagined it. The films had been born in secrecy, and they were supposed to vanish in secrecy as well. Strangers weren't permitted to watch, and although Alma and Hector had mounted a last-minute effort to bring me into the inner circle, Frieda had never viewed me as anything but a stranger. Alma was part of the family, and therefore she had been anointed as the official witness. She was the court historian, so to speak, and after the last member of her parents' generation was dead, the only memories to survive of them would be the ones recorded in her book. I was supposed to have been the witness of the witness, the independent observer brought in to confirm the accuracy of the witness's statements. It was a small role to play in such a large drama, and Frieda had cut me out of the script. As far as she was concerned, I had been unnecessary from the start.

I sat in the tub until the water grew cold, then wrapped myself in a couple of towels and lingered for another twenty or thirty minutes—shaving, dressing, combing my hair. I found it pleasant to be in Alma's bathroom, standing among the tubes and jars that lined the shelves of the medicine cabinet, that crowded the top of the small wooden chest by the window. The red toothbrush in its slot above the sink, the lipsticks in their gold and plastic containers, the mascara brush and eyeliner pencil, the box of tampons, the aspirins, the dental floss, the Chanel No. 5 eau de cologne, the prescription bottle of antimicrobial cleanser. Each one was a sign of intimacy, a mark of solitude and self-reflection. She put the pills into her mouth, rubbed the creams into her skin, ran the combs and brushes through her hair, and every morning she came into this room and stood in front of the same mirror I was looking into now. What did I know about her? Almost nothing, and yet I was certain that I didn't want to lose her, that I was ready to put up a fight in order to see her again after I left the ranch in the morning. My problem was ignorance. I had no doubt that there was trouble in the household, but I didn't know Alma well enough to be able to measure the true extent of her anger against Frieda, and because I couldn't do that, I didn't know to what degree I should be worried about what was happening. The night before, I had watched them together at the kitchen table, and there had been no trace of conflict then. I remembered the solicitude in Alma's voice, the delicate request from Frieda for Alma to spend the night in the main house, the sense of a familial bond. It wasn't unusual for people that close to lash out at each other, to say things in the heat of the moment they would later come to regret—but Alma's outburst had been particularly intense, simmering with threats of violence that were rare (in my experience) among women. *I'm so pissed off, I could punch her in the face.* How often had she said that kind of thing? Was she prone to delivering such rash, hyperbolic statements, or did this represent a new turn in her relations with Frieda, a sudden break after years of silent animosity? Had I known more, I wouldn't have had to ask the question. I would have understood that Alma's words were meant to be taken seriously, that their very extravagance proved that things were already beginning to fly out of control.

I finished up in the bathroom, then continued my aimless travels around the house. It was a small, compact place, sturdily built, somewhat clumsy in design, but in spite of the narrow dimensions, Alma seemed to live in only part of it. One room in the back was given over entirely to storage. Cardboard boxes were stacked up along one wall and half of another, and a dozen or so discarded objects were strewn about the floor: a chair with a missing leg, a rusted tricycle, a fifty-year-old manual typewriter, a black-and-white portable TV with snapped-off rabbit ears, a pile of stuffed animals, a Dictaphone, and several partially used cans of paint. Another room had nothing in it at all. No furniture, no mattress, not even a lightbulb. A large, intricate cobweb dangled from a corner of the ceiling. Three or four dead flies were trapped inside, but their bodies were so desiccated, so nearly reduced to weightless flecks of dust, that I figured the spider had abandoned her web and set up shop somewhere else.

That left the kitchen, the living room, the bedroom, and the study. I wanted to sit down and read Alma's book, but I didn't feel I had the right to do that without her permission. She had written more than six hundred pages by then, but those pages were still in rough-draft form, and unless a writer specifically asks you to comment on a work in progress, you aren't allowed to peek. Alma had pointed to the manuscript earlier (*There's the monster*, she had said), but she hadn't mentioned anything

about reading it, a
betraying a trust. In
else in the four room
refrigerator, the clothe
tions of books, records,
that she drank skim milk
butter, favored the color b
wide-ranging tastes in liter
own heart. Dashiell Hammett
Mingus; Verdi, Wittgenstein, a … und
all the books I had published w … alive—the
two volumes of criticism, the fou … translated poems—
and I realized that I had never seen all six of them together outside of my own house. On another shelf, there were books by Hawthorne, Melville, Emerson, and Thoreau. I pulled out a paperback selection of Hawthorne's stories and found "The Birthmark," which I read in front of the bookcase on the cold tile floor, trying to imagine what Alma must have felt when she'd read it as a young girl. Just as I was coming to the end (*The momentary circumstance was too strong for him; he failed to look beyond the shadowy scope of time . . .*), I caught my first whiff of kerosene wafting in through a window at the back of the house.

The smell drove me a little crazy, and I immediately climbed to my feet and started walking again. I went into the kitchen, drank a glass of water, and then continued on into Alma's study, where I paced around in circles for ten or fifteen minutes, fighting off the urge to read her manuscript. If I couldn't do anything to prevent Hector's films from being destroyed, at least I could try to understand why it was happening. None of the answers given to me so far had come close my best to follow the argument, to that had led them to such a grim and , but now that the fires had been lit, it suddenly me as absurd, pointless, horrible. The answers the book, the reasons were in the book, the origins of idea that had led to this moment were in the book. I sat down at Alma's desk. The manuscript was just to the left of the computer—an immense pile of pages with a stone resting on top to keep the pages from blowing away. I removed the stone, and the words underneath it read: *The Afterlife of Hector Mann*, by Alma Grund. I turned the page, and the next thing I came upon was an epigraph written by Luis Buñuel. The passage was from *My Last Sigh*, the same book I had stumbled across in Hector's study that morning. *A while later*, the quotation began, *I suggested that we burn the negative on the place du Tertre in Montmartre, something I would have done without hesitation had the group agreed. In fact, I'd still do it today; I can imagine a huge pyre in my own little garden where all my negatives and all the copies of my films go up in flames. It wouldn't make the slightest difference. (Curiously, however, the surrealists vetoed my suggestion.)*

That broke the spell somewhat. I had seen some of Buñuel's films in the sixties and seventies, but I wasn't familiar with his autobiography, and it took me a few moments to ponder what I had just read. I glanced up, and by turning my attention away from Alma's manuscript—however briefly—I was given time to regroup, to stop myself before I went any further. I put the first page back where it had been, then covered up the title with the stone. As I did so, I edged forward in my chair, changing my position enough to be able to see something I hadn't noticed before: a small green notebook lying on the desk, midway between the manuscript and the wall. It was the size of a school composition book, and from the battered state of the cover and the nicks and tears along the cloth spine, I gathered that it was quite old. Old enough to be one of Hector's journals, I said to myself—which was exactly what it turned out to be.

I spent the next four hours in the living room, sitting in an ancient club chair with the notebook on my lap, reading through it twice from beginning to end. There were ninety-six pages in all, and they covered approximately a year and a half—from the autumn of 1930 to the spring of 1932—starting with an entry that described one of Hector's English lessons with Nora and concluding with a passage about a nighttime walk in Sandusky several days after he confessed his guilt to Frieda. If I had been harboring any doubts about the story Alma had told me, they were dispelled by what I read in that journal. Hector in his own words was the same Hector she had talked about on the plane, the same tortured soul who had run from the Northwest, had come close to killing himself in Montana, Chicago, and Cleveland, had succumbed to the degradations of a six-month alliance with Sylvia Meers, had been shot in a Sandusky bank and had lived. He wrote in a small, spidery hand, often crossing out phrases and writing over them in pencil, misspelling words, smearing ink, and because he wrote on both sides of the page, it wasn't always easy to make out what he had written. But I managed. Little by little, I think I got most of it, and each time I deciphered another paragraph, the facts tallied with the ones in Alma's account, the details matched. Using the notebook she had given me, I copied out a few of the significant entries, transcribing them in full so as to have a record of Hector's exact words. Among them were his last conversation with Red O'Fallon at the Bluebell Inn, the dismal showdown with Meers in the back seat of the chauffeured car, and this one from the time he spent in Sandusky (living in the Spellings' house after his release from the hospital), which brought the notebook to a close:

3/31/32. Walked F.'s dog tonight. A wiggly black thing named Arp, after the artist. Dada man. The street was deserted. Mist everywhere, almost impossible to see where I was. Perhaps rain as well, but drops so fine they felt like vapor. A sense of no longer being on the ground, of walking through clouds. We approached a streetlamp, and suddenly everything began to shimmer, to gleam in the murk. A world of dots, a hundred million dots of refracted light. Very strange, very beautiful: statues of illuminated fog. Arp was pulling on the leash, sniffing. We walked on, came to the end of the block, rounded the corner. Another streetlamp, and then, stopping for a moment as Arp lifted his leg, something caught my eye. A glow on the sidewalk, a burst of brightness blinking out from the shadows. It had a bluish tint to it—rich blue, the blue of F.'s eyes. I crouched down to have a better look and saw that it was a stone, perhaps a jewel of some kind. A moonstone, I thought, or a sapphire, or maybe just a piece of cut glass. Small enough for a ring, or else a pendant that had fallen off a necklace or bracelet, a lost earring. My first thought was to give it to F.'s niece, Dorothea, Fred's four-year-old daughter. Little Dotty. She comes to the house often. Loves her grandma, loves to play with Arp, loves F. A charming sprite, crazy for baubles and ornaments, always dressing up in wild costumes. I said to myself: I'll give the stone to Dotty. So I started to pick it up, but the moment my fingers came into contact with the stone, I discovered that it wasn't what I'd thought it was. It was soft, and it broke apart when I touched it, disintegrating into a wet, slithery ooze. The thing I had taken for a stone was a gob of human spit. Someone had walked by, had emptied his mouth onto the sidewalk, and the saliva had gathered into a ball, a smooth, multifaceted sphere of bubbles. With the light shining through it, and with the reflections of the light turning it that lustrous shade of blue, it had looked like a hard and solid object. The moment I realized my mistake, my hand shot back as if I'd been burned. I felt sickened, overwhelmed by disgust. My fingers were covered in saliva. Not so bad when it's your own, perhaps, but revolting when it comes from the mouth of a stranger. I took out my handkerchief and wiped off my fingers as best I could. When I was finished, I couldn't bring myself to put the handkerchief back in my pocket. Carrying it at arm's length, I walked to the end of the street and dropped it into the first garbage can I saw.

Three months after those words were written, Hector and Frieda were married in the living room of Mrs. Spelling's house. They drove out to New Mexico on their honeymoon, bought some land, and decided to settle there. Now I understood why they had chosen to call their place the Blue Stone Ranch. Hector had already seen that stone, and he knew that it didn't exist, that the life they were about to build for themselves was founded on an illusion.

The burning ended at around six o'clock, but Alma didn't get back to the cottage until almost seven. It was still light out, but the sun was starting to go down, and I remember how the house filled up with brightness just before she came through the door: huge shafts of light plunging through the windows, an inundation of glowing golds and purples that spread into every corner of the room. It was only my second desert sunset, and I wasn't prepared for an attack of such radiance. I moved to the sofa, turning in the opposite direction to get the dazzle out of my eyes, but a few minutes after I settled into that new spot, I heard the latch turn in the door behind me. More light poured into the room: streams of red, liquefied sun, a tidal wave of luminosity. I wheeled around, shielding my eyes for protection, and there was Alma in the open doorway, almost invisible, a spectral outline with light shooting through the tips of her hair, a being on fire.

Then she closed the door, and I was able to see her face, to look into her eyes as she crossed the living room and came toward the sofa. I don't know what I was expecting from her just then. Tears, perhaps, or anger, or some excessive display of emotion, but Alma looked remarkably calm, not in turmoil anymore so much as exhausted, drained of energy. She walked around the sofa from the right, apparently unconcerned that she was showing me the birthmark on the left side of her face, and I realized that this was the first time she had done that. I wasn't sure if I should consider it a breakthrough, however, or credit it to a lapse of attention, a symptom of fatigue. She sat down next to me without saying a word, then leaned her head against my shoulder. Her hands were dirty; her T-shirt was smudged with soot. I put both arms around her and held her for a while, not wanting to press her with questions, to force her into talking when she didn't want to. Eventually, I asked her if she was all right, and when she answered yes, I'm all right, I understood that she had no desire to go into it. She was sorry it had taken so long, she said, but other than offering some explanations for the delay (which was how I heard about the oil drums, the hand trucks, and so on), we barely touched on the subject for the rest of the night. After it was over, she said, she had walked Frieda back to the main house. They had discussed tomorrow's arrangements, and then she had put

Frieda to bed with a sleeping pill. She would have come straight back at that point, but the phone in the cottage was on the blink (sometimes it worked, sometimes it didn't), and rather than take a chance with it, she had called from the phone in the main house to book a ticket for me on the morning flight to Boston. The plane would be leaving Albuquerque at eight forty-seven. It was a two-and-a-half-hour drive to the airport, and because it wasn't going to be possible for Frieda to wake up early enough to get us there in time, the only solution had been to order a van to come for me instead. She had wanted to take me there herself, to see me off in person, but she and Frieda were due at the funeral home at eleven, and how could she make two runs to Albuquerque before eleven o'clock? The math didn't compute. Even if she left with me as early as five, she wouldn't be able to go back and forth and back again in under seven and a half hours. How can I do what I can't do? she said. It wasn't a rhetorical question. It was a statement about herself, a declaration of misery. How the hell can I do what I can't do? And then, turning her face in to my chest, she suddenly broke down and cried.

I got her into the bath, and for the next half hour I sat beside her on the floor, washing her back, her arms and legs, her breasts and face and hands, her hair. It took a while before she stopped crying, but little by little the treatment seemed to produce the desired effect. Close your eyes, I said to her, don't move, don't say a word, just melt into the water and let yourself drift away. I was impressed by how willingly she gave in to my commands, by how unembarrassed she was by her own nakedness. It was the first time I had seen her body in the light, but Alma acted as though it already belonged to me, as though we had already passed beyond the stage where such things needed to be questioned anymore. She went limp in my arms, surrendered to the warmth of the water, surrendered unconditionally to the idea that I was the one who was taking care of her. There was no one else. She had been living alone in this cottage for the past seven years, and we both knew that it was time for her to move on. You'll come to Vermont, I said. You'll live there with me until you finish your book, and every day I'll give you another bath. I'll work on my Chateaubriand, you'll work on your biography, and when we aren't working, we'll fuck. We'll fuck in every corner of the house. We'll hold three-day fuck-fests in the backyard and the woods. We'll fuck until we can't stand up anymore, and then we'll go back to work, and when our work is finished, we'll leave Vermont and go somewhere else. Anywhere you say, Alma. I'm willing to entertain all possibilities. Nothing is out of the question.

It was a rash thing to say under the circumstances, a supremely vulgar and outrageous proposition, but time was short, and I didn't want to leave New Mexico without knowing where we stood. So I took a risk and decided to force the issue, presenting my case in the crudest, most graphic terms I could think of. To Alma's credit, she didn't flinch. Her eyes were closed when I began, and she kept them closed until the end of the speech, but at a certain point I noticed that a smile was tugging at the corners of her mouth (I believe it started when I used the word *fuck* for the first time), and the longer I went on talking to her, the bigger that smile seemed to become. When I was finished, however, she didn't say anything, and her eyes remained closed. Well? I said. What do you think? What I think, she answered slowly, is that if I opened my eyes now, you might not be there.

Yes, I said, I see what you mean. On the other hand, if you don't open them, you'll never know if I am or not, will you?

I don't think I'm brave enough.

Of course you are. And besides, you're forgetting that my hands are in the tub. I'm touching your spine and the small of your back. If I wasn't there, I wouldn't be able to do that, would I?

Anything is possible. You could be someone else, someone who's only pretending to be David. An impostor.

And what would an impostor be doing with you here in this bathroom?

Filling my head with wicked fantasies, making me believe I can have what I want. It isn't often that someone says exactly what you want them to say. Maybe I said those words myself.

Maybe. Or maybe someone said them because the thing he wants is the same thing you want.

But not exactly. It's never *exactly*, is it? How could he say the *exact* words that were in my mind?

With his mouth. That's where words come from. From someone's mouth.

Where is that mouth, then? Let me feel it. Press that mouth against mine, mister. If it feels the way it's supposed to feel, then I'll know it's your mouth and not my mouth. Then maybe I'll start to believe you.

With her eyes still closed, Alma lifted her arms into the air, reaching up in the way small children do—asking to be hugged, asking to be carried—and I leaned over and kissed her, crushing my mouth against her mouth and parting her lips with my tongue. I was on my knees—arms in the water, hands resting on her back, elbows pinned against the side of the tub—and as Alma grabbed the back of my neck and pulled me toward her, I lost my balance and splashed down on top of her. Our heads went under the water for a moment, and when we came up again, Alma's eyes were open. Water was sloshing over the rim of the tub, we were both gasping, and yet without pausing to take in more than a gulp of air, we repositioned ourselves and started kissing in earnest. That was the first of several kisses, the first of many kisses. I can't account for the manipulations that followed, the complex maneuvers that enabled me to pull Alma out of the bath while keeping my lips planted on her lips, while managing not to lose contact with her tongue, but a moment came when she was out of the water and I was rubbing down her body with a towel. I remember that. I also remember that after she was dry, she peeled off my wet shirt and unbuckled the belt that was holding up my pants. I can see her doing that, and I can also see myself kissing her again, can see the two of us lowering ourselves onto a pile of towels and making love on the floor.

It was dark in the house when we left the bathroom. A few glimmers of light in the front windows, a thin burnished cloud stretching along the horizon, residues of dusk. We put on our clothes, drank a couple of shots of tequila in the living room, and then went into the kitchen to rustle up some dinner. Frozen tacos, frozen peas, mashed potatoes—another ad hoc assemblage, making do with what there was. It didn't matter. The food disappeared in nine minutes, and then we returned to the living room and poured ourselves another round of drinks. From that point on, Alma and I talked only about the future, and when we crawled into bed at ten o'clock, we were still making plans, still discussing what life would be like for us when she joined me on my little hill in Vermont. We didn't know when she would be able to get there, but we figured it wouldn't take longer than a week or two to wrap things up at the ranch, three at the outside limit. In the meantime, we would talk on the phone, and whenever it was too late or too early to call, we would send each other faxes. Come hell or high water, we said, we would be in touch every day.

I left New Mexico without seeing Frieda again. Alma had been hoping she would walk down to the cottage to say good-bye to me, but I wasn't expecting it. She had already crossed me off her list, and given the early hour of my departure (the van was scheduled to come at five-thirty), it seemed unlikely that she would go to the trouble of losing any sleep on my account. When she failed to show up, Alma blamed it on the pill she had taken before going to bed. That felt rather optimistic to me. According to my reading of the situation, Frieda wouldn't have been there under any circumstances—not even if the van had left at noon.

At the time, none of this seemed terribly important. The alarm went off at five, and with only half an hour to get myself ready and out the door, I wouldn't have given Frieda a single thought if her name hadn't been mentioned. What mattered to me that morning was waking up with Alma, drinking coffee with her on the front steps of the house, being able to touch her again. All groggy and tousled, all stupid with happiness, all bleary with sex and skin and thoughts about my new life. If I had been more alert, I would have understood what I was walking away from, but I was too tired and too rushed for anything but the simplest gestures: a last hug, a last kiss, and then the van pulled up in front of the cottage, and it was time for me to go. We went back into the house to retrieve my bag, and as we were walking out again, Alma plucked a book from the table near the door and handed it to me (To look at on the plane, she said), and then there was a last last hug, a last last kiss, and I was off to the airport. It wasn't until I was halfway there that I realized that Alma had forgotten to give me the Xanax.

On any other day, I would have told the driver to turn around and go back to the ranch. I almost did it then, but after thinking through the humiliations that would follow from that decision—missing the plane, exposing myself as a coward, reaffirming my status as neurotic weakling—I managed to curb my panic. I had already made one drugless flight with Alma. Now the trick was to see if I could do it alone. To the extent that distractions were necessary, the book she had given me proved to be an enormous help. It was over six hundred pages long, weighed almost three pounds, and kept me company the whole time I was in the air. A compendium of wildflowers with the blunt, no-nonsense title *Weeds of the West,* it had been put together by a team of seven authors (six of whom were described as Extension Weed Specialists; the seventh was a Wyoming-based Herbarium Manager) and published, aptly enough, by something called the Western Society of Weed Science, in association with the Western United States Land Grant Universities Cooperative Extension Services. In general, I didn't take much interest in botany. I couldn't have named more than a few dozen plants and trees, but this reference book, with its nine hundred color photographs and precise prose descriptions of the habitats and characteristics of over four hundred species, held my attention for several hours. I don't know why I found it so absorbing, but perhaps it was because I had just come from that land of prickly, water-starved vegetation and wanted to see more of it, had not quite had my fill. Most of the photographs had been shot in extreme close-up, with nothing in the background but blank sky. Occasionally, the picture would include some surrounding grass, a patch of dirt, or, even more rarely, a distant rock or mountain. Noticeably absent were people, the smallest reference to human activity. New Mexico had been inhabited for thousands of years, but to look at the photos in that book was to feel that nothing had ever happened there, that its entire history had been erased. No more ancient cliff dwellers, no more archaeological ruins, no more Spanish conquerors, no more Jesuit priests, no more Pat Garrett and Billy the Kid, no more Indian pueblos, no more builders of the atomic bomb. There was only the land and what covered the land, the meager growths of stems and stalks and spiny little flowers that sprang up from the parched soil: a civilization reduced to a smattering of weeds. In themselves, the plants weren't much to look at, but their names had an impressive music, and after I had studied the pictures and read the words that accompanied them (*Leaf blade ovate to lanceolate in outline. . . . Achenes are flattened, ribbed and rugose, with pappus of capillary bristles*), I took a brief pause to write down some of those names in my notebook. I started on a fresh verso, immediately after the pages I had used to record the extracts from Hector's journal, which in turn had followed the description of *The Inner Life of Martin Frost*. The words had a chewy Saxon thickness to them, and I took pleasure in sounding them out to myself, in feeling their stolid, clanging resonances on my tongue. As I look at the list now, it strikes me as near gibberish, a random collection of syllables from a dead language—perhaps from the language once spoken on Mars.

Bur chervil. Spreading dogbane. Labriform milkweed. Skeletonleaf bursage. Common sagewort. Nodding beggarsticks. Plumeless thistle. Squarerrose knapweed. Hairy fleabane. Bristly hawksbeard. Curlycup gunweed. Spotted catsear. Tansy ragwort. Riddell groundsel. Blessed milkthistle. Poverty sumpweed. Spineless horsebrush. Spiny cocklebur. Western sticktight. Smallseed falseflax. Flixwood tansymustard. Dyer's woad. Clasping pepperweed. Bladder campion. Nettleleaf goosefoot. Dodder. Prostrate spurge. Twogrooved milkvetch. Everlasting peavine. Silky crazyweed. Toad rush. Henbit. Purple deadnettle. Spurred anoda. Panicle willowweed. Velvety gaura. Ripgut brome. Mexican sprangletop. Fall panicum. Rattail fescue. Sharppoint fluvellin. Dalmatian toadflax. Bilobed speedwell. Sacred datura.

Vermont looked different to me after I returned. I had been gone for only three days and two nights, but everything had become smaller in my absence: closed in on itself, dark, clammy. The greenness of the woods around my house felt unnatural, impossibly lush in comparison to the tans and browns of the desert. The air was thick with moisture, the ground was soft underfoot, and everywhere I turned I saw wild proliferations of plant life, startling instances of decay: the over-saturated twigs and bark fragments moldering on the trails, the ladders of fungus on the trees, the mildew stains on the walls of the house. After a while, I understood that I was looking at these things through Alma's eyes, trying to see them with a new clarity in order to prepare myself for the day when she moved in with me. The flight to Boston had gone well, much better than I had dared to hope it would, and I had walked off the plane feeling that I had accomplished something important. In the big scheme of things, it probably wasn't much, but in the small scheme of things, in the microscopic place where private battles are won and lost, it counted as a singular victory. I felt stronger than I had felt at any time in the past three years. Almost whole, I said to myself, almost ready to become real again.

For the next several days, I kept as busy as I could, tackling chores on several fronts at once. I worked on the Chateaubriand translation, took my banged-up truck to the body shop for repairs, and cleaned the house to within an inch of its life—scrubbing floors, waxing furniture, dusting books. I knew that nothing could hide the essential ugliness of the architecture, but at least I could make the rooms presentable, give them a sheen they hadn't had before. The only difficulty was deciding what to do with the boxes in the spare bedroom—which I intended to convert into a study for Alma. She would need to have a place to finish her book, a place to go to when she needed to be alone, and that room was the only one available. Storage space in the rest of the house was limited, however, and with no attic and no garage at my disposal, the only area I could think of was the cellar. The problem with that solution was the dirt floor. Every time it rained, the cellar would fill up with water, and any cardboard box left down there was certain to be drenched. To avoid that calamity, I bought ninety-six cinder blocks and eight large rectangles of plywood. By stacking the cinder blocks three high, I managed to construct a platform that was well above the waterline of the worst flood that had visited me. For extra security against the effects of dampness, I wrapped each box in a thick plastic garbage bag and sealed up the opening with tape. That should have been satisfactory, but it took another two days for me to build up the courage to carry them downstairs. Everything that remained of my family was in those boxes. Helen's dresses and skirts. Her hairbrush and stockings. Her big winter coat with the fur hood. Todd's baseball glove and comic books. Marco's jigsaw puzzles and plastic men. The gold compact with the cracked mirror. Hooty Tooty the stuffed bear. The Walter Mondale campaign button. I had no use for these things anymore, but I had never been able to throw them away, had never even considered giving them to charity. I didn't want Helen's clothes to be worn by another woman, and I didn't want the boys' Red Sox caps to sit on the heads of other boys. Taking those things down to the cellar was like burying them in the ground. It wasn't the end, perhaps, but it was the beginning of the end, the first milestone on the road to forgetfulness. Hard to do, but not half as hard as getting on that plane to Boston had been. After I finished emptying the room, I went to Brattleboro and picked out furniture for Alma. I bought her a mahogany desk, a leather chair that rocked back and forth when you pushed a button under the seat, an oak filing cabinet, and a nifty, multicolored throw rug. It was the best stuff in the store, top-of-the-line office equipment. The bill came to more than three thousand dollars, and I paid in cash.

I missed her. However impetuous our plan might have been, I never had any doubts or second thoughts about it. I pushed on in a state of blind happiness, waiting for the moment when she would finally be able to come east, and whenever I started to miss her too much, I would open the freezer door and look at the gun. The gun proved that Alma had already been there—and if she had been there once, there was no reason to believe she wouldn't return. At first, I didn't dwell on the fact that the gun was still loaded, but after two or three days it started to bother me. I hadn't touched it in all that time, but one afternoon, just to be safe, I lifted it out of the refrigerator and carried it into the woods, where I fired all six bullets into the ground. They made a noise like a string of Chinese firecrackers, like bursting paper bags. When I returned to the house, I put the gun in the top drawer of the bedside table. It couldn't kill anymore, but that didn't mean it was any less potent, any less dangerous. It embodied the power of a thought, and every time I looked at it, I remembered how close that thought had come to destroying me.

The phone in Alma's cottage was temperamental, and I couldn't always get through to her when I called. Faulty wiring, she said, a loose connection somewhere in the system, which meant that even after I dialed her number and heard the rapid little clicks and beeps that suggested the call was going through, the bell on her end didn't ring. More often than not, however, that phone could be counted on for outgoing calls. On the day I returned to Vermont, I made several unsuccessful attempts to reach her, and when Alma finally called at eleven (nine o'clock mountain time), we decided to stick to that arrangement in the future. She would call me rather than the other way around. Every time we talked after that, we ended the conversation by fixing the time of the next call, and for three nights running the routine worked as smoothly as a trick in a magic show. We would say seven o'clock, for example, and at ten minutes to seven I would install myself in the kitchen, pour myself a straight shot of tequila (we went on drinking tequila together, even long-distance), and at seven sharp, just as the second hand on the wall clock was sweeping up to mark the hour, the telephone would ring. I came to depend on the precision of those calls. Alma's punctuality was a sign of faith, a commitment to the principle that two people in two different parts of the world could nevertheless be of one mind about nearly everything.

Then, on the fourth night (the fifth night after I had left Tierra del Sueño), Alma didn't call. I suspected that she was having trouble with her phone, and therefore I didn't act right away. I went on sitting in my spot, patiently waiting for the phone to ring, but when the silence stretched on for another twenty minutes, then thirty minutes, I began to worry. If the phone was out of order, she would have sent a fax to explain why I hadn't heard from her. Alma's fax machine was hooked up to another line, and there had never been any glitches with that number. I knew it was useless, but I picked up my own phone and called her anyway—with the expected negative result. Then, thinking that she might have been caught up in some business with Frieda, I called the number at the main house, but the result was the same. I called again, just to make sure I had dialed correctly, but again there was no answer. As a last resort, I sent a brief note by fax. *Where are you, Alma? Is everything all right? Puzzled. Please write (fax) if phone is out of order. I love you, David.*

There was only one phone in my house, and it was in the kitchen. If I went upstairs to the bedroom, I was afraid I wouldn't hear it ringing if Alma called later in the night—or, if I did, that I wouldn't be able to get downstairs in time to answer it. I had no idea what to do with myself. I waited around in the kitchen for several hours, hoping that something would happen, and then, when it finally got to be past one in the morning, I went into the living room and stretched out on the sofa. It was the same lumpy ensemble of springs and cushions that I had turned into a makeshift bed for Alma the first night we were together—a good place for thinking morbid thoughts. I kept at it until dawn, torturing myself with imagined car crashes, fires, medical emergencies, deadly stumbles down flights of stairs. At some point, the birds woke up and started singing in the branches outside. Not long after that, I unexpectedly fell asleep.

I had never thought that Frieda would do to Alma what she had done to me. Hector had wanted me to stay at the ranch and watch his films; then he died, and Frieda had prevented it from happening. Hector had wanted Alma to write his biography. Now that he was dead, why hadn't it occurred to me that Frieda would take it upon herself to prevent the book from being published? The situations were almost identical, and yet I hadn't seen the resemblance, had utterly failed to notice the similarities between them. Perhaps it was because the numbers were so far apart. Watching the films would have taken me no more than four or five days; Alma had been working on her book for close to seven years. It never crossed my mind that anyone could be cruel enough to take seven years of a person's work and rip it to shreds. I simply lacked the courage to think that thought.

If I had seen what was coming, I wouldn't have left Alma alone at the ranch. I would have forced her to pack her manuscript, pushed her into the van, and taken her with me to the airport on that last morning. Even if I hadn't acted then, it still might have been possible to do something before it was too late. We had had four telephone conversations since my return to Vermont, and Frieda's name had come up in every one of them. But I hadn't wanted to talk about Frieda. That part of the story was over for me now, and I was only interested in talking about the future. I rattled on to Alma about the house, about the room I was preparing for her, about the furniture I had ordered. I should have been asking her questions, pressing her for details about Frieda's state of mind, but Alma seemed to enjoy hearing me talk about these domestic matters. She was in the early stages of moving—filling up cardboard boxes with her clothes, deciding what to take and what to leave behind, asking me which books in my library duplicated hers—and the last thing she was expecting was trouble.

Three hours after I left for the airport, Alma and Frieda had driven to the funeral parlor in Albuquerque to collect the urn. Later that day, in a windless corner of the garden, they had scattered Hector's ashes among the rosebushes and tulip beds. It was the same spot where Taddy had been stung by the bee, and Frieda had been quite shaky throughout the ceremony, holding her own for a minute or two and then giving in to prolonged fits of silent crying. When Alma and I talked on the phone that night, she told me that Frieda had never looked so vulnerable to her, so dangerously close to collapse. Early the next morning, however, she walked over to the main house and discovered that Frieda was already awake—sitting on the floor in Hector's study, combing through mountains of papers, photographs, and drawings that were spread out in a circle around her. The screenplays were next, she told Alma, and after that she was going to make a systematic search for every other document linked to the production of the films: storyboard folios, costume sketches, set-design blueprints, lighting diagrams, notes for the actors. It would all have to be burned, she said, not a single scrap of material could be spared.

Already, then, just one day after I left the ranch, the limits of the destruction had been changed, pushed back to accommodate a broader interpretation of Hector's will. It wasn't just the movies anymore. It was every piece of evidence that could prove those movies had ever existed.

There were fires on each of the next two days, but Alma took no part in them, letting Juan and Conchita serve as helpers as she went about her own business. On the third day, scenery was dragged out from the back rooms of the sound stage and burned. Props were burned, costumes were burned, Hector's journals were burned. Even the notebook I had read in Alma's house was burned, and still we were unable to grasp where things were headed. That notebook had been written in the early thirties, long before Hector went back to making films. Its only value was as a source of information for Alma's biography. Destroy that source, and even if the book was eventually published, the story it told would no longer be credible. We should have understood that, but when we talked on the phone that night, Alma mentioned it only in passing. The big news of the day had to do with Hector's silent films. Copies of those films were already in circulation, of course, but Frieda was worried that if they were discovered on the ranch, someone would make the connection between Hector Spelling and Hector Mann, and so she had decided to burn them as well. It was a gruesome job, Alma reported her as saying, but it had to be done thoroughly. If one part of the job was left unfinished, then all the other parts would become meaningless.

We arranged to talk again at nine o'clock the next evening (seven her time). Alma was going to be in Sorocco for most of the afternoon—shopping at the supermarket, taking care of personal errands—but even though it was an hour-and-a-half drive back to Tierra del Sueño, we figured that she would return to the cottage by six. When her call didn't come, my imagination immediately started filling in the blanks, and by the time I stretched out on the sofa at one o'clock, I was convinced that Alma had never made it home, that something monstrous had happened to her.

It turned out that I was both right and wrong. Wrong that she hadn't made it home, but right about everything else—although not in any of the ways I had imagined. Alma pulled up in front of her house a few minutes after six. She never locked the door, so she wasn't unduly alarmed to discover that the door of the cottage was open, but smoke was rising from the chimney, and that struck her as bizarre, altogether incomprehensible. It was a hot day in the middle of July, and even if Juan and Conchita had come to deliver fresh laundry or were taking out the trash, why on earth had they lit a fire? Alma left her groceries in the back of her car and went straight into the house. Crouched in front of the hearth in the living room, Frieda was crumpling up sheets of paper and throwing them into the fire. Gesture for gesture, it was a precise reenactment of the final scene of *Martin Frost:* Norbert Steinhaus burning the manuscript of his story in a desperate attempt to bring Alma's mother back to life. Bits of paper ash floated out into the room, hovering around Frieda like injured black butterflies. The edges of the wings glowed orange for an instant, then turned whitish gray. Hector's widow was so absorbed in her work, so intent on finishing the job she had started, that she never even looked up when Alma walked through the door. The unburned pages were spread out across her knees, a small pile of eight-and-a-half-by-eleven sheets, perhaps twenty or thirty of them, perhaps forty. If that was all there was left, then the other six hundred pages were already gone.

In her own words, Alma *went into a frenzy, a vicious tirade, an insane burst of shouting and screaming.* She charged across the living room, and when Frieda stood up to defend herself, Alma shoved her aside. That was all she could remember, she said. One violent shove, and then she was already past Frieda, running toward her study and the computer at the back of the house. The burned manuscript was only a printout. The book was in the computer, and if Frieda hadn't tampered with the hard drive or found any of the backup disks, then nothing would be lost.

Hope for an instant, a brief surge of optimism as she crossed the threshold of the room, and then no hope. Alma entered the study, and the first thing she saw was a blank space where the computer had been. The desk was bare: no more monitor, no more keyboard, no more printer, no more blue plastic box with the twenty-one labeled floppy disks and the fifty-three different research files. Frieda had carted away the whole lot. No doubt Juan had been in on it with her, and if Alma understood the situation correctly, then it was already too late to do anything about it. The computer would be smashed; the disks would be cut into little pieces. And even if that hadn't happened yet, where was she going to start looking for them? The ranch spread out over four hundred acres. All you had to do was pick a spot somewhere, dig a hole, and the book would disappear forever.

She wasn't sure how long she remained in the study. Several minutes, she thought, but it could have been longer than that, perhaps as long as a quarter of an hour. She remembered sitting down at the desk and putting her hands over her face. She wanted to cry, she said, to let loose in a jag of uninterrupted screaming and sobbing, but she was still too stunned to cry, and so she didn't do anything but sit there and listen to herself breathe through her hands. At a certain point, she began to notice how quiet it had become in the house. She assumed that meant Frieda had already left—that she had simply walked out and gone back to the other house. That was just as well, Alma thought. No amount of arguing or explaining would ever undo what had happened, and the fact was that she never wanted to talk to Frieda again. Was that true? Yes, she decided, it was true. If that was the case, then the time had come to get out of there. She could pack a bag, get into her car, and drive to a motel somewhere near the airport. First thing in the morning, she could be on the plane to Boston.

That was when Alma stood up from the desk and left the

study. It wasn't yet seven o'clock, but she knew me well enough to be certain that I would be in my house—hovering around the phone in the kitchen, pouring myself a tequila in anticipation of her call. She wasn't going to wait until the appointed time. Years of her life had just been stolen from her, the world was blowing up in her head, and she had to talk to me now, had to start talking to someone before the tears came and she couldn't get the words out of her mouth. The phone was in the bedroom, the next room over from the study. All she had to do was turn right when she went out the door, and ten seconds later she would have been sitting on her bed dialing my number. When she came to the threshold of the study, however, she hesitated for a moment and turned left instead. Sparks had been flying all over the living room, and before she settled in to a long conversation with me, she had to make sure that the fire was out. It was a reasonable decision, the correct thing to do under the circumstances. So she took that detour to the other side of the house, and a moment later the story of that night turned into a different story, the night became a different night. That's the horror for me: not just being unable to prevent what happened, but knowing that if Alma had called me first, it might not have happened at all. Frieda would still have been lying dead on the living room floor, but none of Alma's responses would have been the same, none of the things that happened after she discovered the body would have played out as they did. Talking to me would have made her feel a little stronger, a little less crazy, a little better prepared to absorb the shock. If she had told me about the shove, for example, had described to me how she had pushed Frieda in the chest with the flat of her hand before running past her into the study, I might have been able to warn her about the possible consequences. People lose their balance, I would have told her, they stumble backward, they fall, they hit their heads against hard objects. Go into the living room and check. Find out if Frieda is still there, and Alma would have gone into the living room without hanging up the phone. I would have been able to talk to her immediately after she discovered the body, and that would have calmed her down, given her a chance to think more clearly, made her stop and reconsider before going ahead with the terrible thing she was proposing to do. But Alma hesitated in the doorway, turned left rather than right, and when she found Frieda's body lying crumpled up on the floor, she forgot about calling me. No, I don't think she forgot, I don't mean to suggest that she forgot—but the idea was already taking shape in her head, and she couldn't bring herself to pick up the phone. Instead, she went into the kitchen, sat down with a bottle of tequila and a ballpoint pen, and spent the rest of the night writing me a letter.

I was asleep on the sofa when the fax started coming through. It was six in the morning in Vermont, but still night in New Mexico, and the machine woke me up on the third or fourth ring. I had been out for less than an hour, sunk in a coma of exhaustion, and the first rings didn't register with me except to alter the dream I was having at the moment—a nightmare about alarm clocks and deadlines and having to wake up to deliver a lecture entitled The Metaphors of Love. I don't often remember my dreams, but I remember that one, just as I remember everything else that happened to me after I opened my eyes. I sat up, understanding now that the noise wasn't coming from the alarm clock in my bedroom. The phone was ringing in the kitchen, but by the time I got to my feet and staggered across the living room, the ringing had stopped. I heard a little click in the machine, signaling that a fax transmission was about to begin, and when I finally made it to the kitchen, the first bits of the letter were curling through the slot. There were no plain-paper fax machines in 1988. The paper came in scrolls—flimsy parchment with a special electronic coating—and when you received a letter, it looked like something that had been sent from the ancient past: half of a Torah, or a message delivered from some Etruscan battlefield. Alma had spent more than eight hours composing her letter, intermittently stopping and starting, picking up the pen and putting it down again, growing steadily drunker as the night wore on, and the final accumulation ran to over twenty pages. I read it all standing on my feet, pulling on the scroll as it inched its way out of the machine. The first part recounted the things I have just summarized: the burning of Alma's book, the disappearance of the computer, the discovery of Frieda's body in the living room. The last part ended with these paragraphs:

I can't help it. I'm not strong enough to carry around a thing like this. I keep trying to get my arms around it, but it's too big for me, David, it's too heavy, and I can't even lift it off the ground.

That's why I'm not going to call you tonight. You'll tell me it was an accident, that it wasn't my fault, and I'll start to believe you. I'll want to believe you, but the truth is that I pushed her hard, much harder than you can push an eighty-year-old woman, and I killed her. It doesn't matter what she did to me. I killed her, and if I let you talk me out of it now, it would only destroy us later. There's no way around this. In order to stop myself, I would have to give up the truth, and once I did that, every good thing in me would start to die. I have to act now, you see, while I still have the courage. Thank God for alcohol. Guinness Gives You Strength, as the London billboards used to say. Tequila gives you courage.

You start from somewhere, and no matter how far you think you've traveled from that place, you always wind up there in the end. I thought you could rescue me, that I could make myself belong to you, but I've never belonged to anyone but them. Thank you for the dream, David. Ugly Alma found a man, and he made her feel beautiful. If you could do that for me, just think what you could do for a girl with only one face.

Feel lucky. It's good that it's ending before you find out who I really am. I came to your house that first night with a gun, didn't I? Don't ever forget what that means. Only a crazy person would do something like that, and crazy people can't be trusted. They snoop into other people's lives, they write books about things that don't concern them, they buy pills. Thank God for pills. Was it really an accident that you left them behind the other day? They were in my purse the whole time you were here. I kept meaning to give them to you, and I kept forgetting to do it—right up to the moment when you climbed into the van. Don't blame me. It turns out that I need them more than you do. My twenty-five little purple friends. Maximum-strength Xanax, guaranteed to provide a night of unbroken sleep.

Forgive. Forgive. Forgive. Forgive. Forgive.

I tried calling her after that, but she didn't answer the phone. I got through this time—I could hear the phone ringing on the other end—but Alma never picked up the receiver. I held on for forty or fifty rings, stubbornly hoping that the noise would break her concentration, distract her into thinking about something other than the pills. Would five more rings have made a difference? Would ten more rings have stopped her from going ahead with it? Eventually, I decided to hang up, found a piece of paper, and sent her a fax of my own. *Please talk to me,* I wrote. *Please, Alma, pick up the phone and talk to me.* I called her again a second later, but this time the line went dead after six or seven rings. I didn't understand at first, but then I realized that she must have pulled the cord out of the wall.

9

LATER THAT WEEK, I buried her next to her parents in a Catholic cemetery twenty-five miles north of Tierra del Sueño. Alma had never mentioned any relatives to me, and since no Grunds or Morrisons turned up to claim her body, I covered the costs of the funeral myself. There were grim decisions to be made, grotesque choices that revolved around the relative merits of embalming and cremation, the durability of various woods, the price of caskets. Then, having opted for burial, further questions about clothing, shades of lipstick, fingernail polish, hair style. I don't know how I managed to do those things, but I suspect that I went about them in the same way that everyone else does: half there and half not, half in my mind and half out. All I can remember is saying no to the idea of cremation. No more fires, I said, no more ashes. They had already cut her up to perform their autopsy, but I wasn't going to let them burn her.

On the night of Alma's suicide, I had called the sheriff's office from my house in Vermont. A deputy named Victor Guzman had been sent out to the ranch to investigate, but even though he arrived there before six A.M., Juan and Conchita had already vanished. Alma and Frieda were both dead, the letter that had been faxed to me was still in the machine, but the little people had gone missing. When I left New Mexico five days later, Guzman and the other deputies were still looking for them.

Frieda's remains were disposed of by her lawyer, according to the instructions of her will. The service was held in the arbor of the Blue Stone Ranch—just behind the main house, in Hector's little forest of willows and aspens—but I made a point of not being there. I felt too much hatred for Frieda now, and the thought of going to that ceremony turned my stomach. I never met the lawyer, but Guzman had told him about me, and when he called my motel to invite me to Frieda's funeral, I simply told him that I was busy. He rambled on for a few minutes after that, talking about poor Mrs. Spelling and poor Alma and how ghastly the whole thing had been, and then, *in strictest confidence,* barely pausing between sentences, he informed me that the estate was worth over nine million dollars. The ranch would be going up for sale once the will cleared probate, he said, and those proceeds, along with all monies acquired from the divestiture of Mrs. Spelling's stocks and bonds, would be given to a nonprofit organization in New York City. Which one? I asked. The Museum of Modern Art, he said. The entire nine million was going to be put in an anonymous fund for the preservation of old films. Pretty strange, he said, don't you think? No, I said, not strange. Cruel and sickening, maybe, but not strange. If you liked bad jokes, this one could keep you laughing for years.

I wanted to go back to the ranch one last time, but when I pulled up in front of the gate, I didn't have the heart to drive through. I had been hoping to find some photographs of Alma, to look around the cottage for some odds and ends that I could take back to Vermont with me, but the police had put up one of those crime-scene barriers with the yellow tape, and I suddenly lost my nerve. No cop was standing there to block my way, and it wouldn't have been any trouble to slip past the fence and enter the property—but I couldn't, I couldn't—and so I turned the car around and drove on. I spent my last hours in Albuquerque ordering a headstone for Alma's grave. At first, I thought I would keep the inscription to the bare minimum: ALMA GRUND 1950–1988. But then, after I had signed the contract and paid the man for the work, I went back into the office and told him that I had changed my mind. I wanted to add another word, I said. The inscription should read: ALMA GRUND 1950–1988 WRITER. Except for the twenty-page suicide note she sent me on the last night of her life, I had never read a word she had written. But Alma had died because of a book, and justice demanded that she be remembered as the author of that book.

I went home. Nothing happened on the flight back to Boston. We ran into turbulence over the Midwest, I ate some chicken and drank a glass of wine, I looked out the window—but nothing happened. White clouds, silver wing, blue sky. Nothing.

The liquor cabinet was empty when I walked into my house, and it was too late to go out and buy a new bottle. I don't know if that's what saved me, but I had forgotten that I'd finished off the tequila on my last night there, and with no hope of obliteration within thirty miles of boarded-up West T——, I had to go to bed sober. In the morning, I drank two cups of coffee and went back to work. I had been planning to fall apart, to slip into my old routine of hapless sorrow and alcoholic ruin, but in the light of that summer morning in Vermont, something in me resisted the urge to destroy myself. Chateaubriand was just coming to the end of his long meditation on the life of Napoleon, and I rejoined him in the twenty-fourth book of the memoirs, on the island of Saint Helena with the deposed emperor. *He had already been in exile for six years; he had needed less time to conquer Europe. He rarely left the house anymore and spent his days reading Ossian in Casarotti's Italian translation. . . . When Bonaparte went out, he walked along rugged paths flanked by aloes and scented broom . . . or hid himself in the thick clouds that rolled along the ground. . . . At this moment in history, everything withers in a day; whoever lives too long dies alive. As we move through life, we leave behind three or four images of ourselves, each one different from the others; we see them through the fog of the past, like portraits of our different ages.*

I wasn't sure if I had tricked myself into believing that I was strong enough to go on working—or if I had simply gone numb. For the rest of the summer I felt as though I were living in a different dimension, awake to the things around me and yet removed from them at the same time, as if my body had been wrapped in transparent gauze. I put in long hours with the Chateaubriand, rising early and going to bed late, and I made steady progress as the weeks went on, gradually increasing my daily quota from three finished pages of the Pléiade edition to four. It looked like progress, it felt like progress, but that was also the period when I became prone to curious lapses of attention, fits of absentmindedness that seemed to dog me whenever I wandered from my desk. I forgot to pay the phone bill for three months in a row, ignored every threatening notice that arrived in the mail, and didn't settle the account until a man appeared in my yard one day to disconnect the service. Two weeks later, on a shopping expedition to Brattleboro that included a visit to the post office and a visit to the bank, I managed to throw my wallet into the mailbox, thinking it was a pile of letters. These incidents confounded me, but not once did I stop to consider why they were happening. To ask that question would have meant getting down on my knees and opening the trap door under the rug, and I couldn't afford to look into the darkness of that place. Most nights, after I had knocked off work and finished eating my dinner, I would sit up late in the kitchen, transcribing the notes I had taken at the screening of *The Inner Life of Martin Frost.*

I had known Alma for only eight days. For five of those days we had been apart, and when I calculated how much time we had spent together during the other three, it came to a grand total of fifty-four hours. Eighteen of those hours had been lost in sleep. Another seven had been squandered in separations of one kind or another: the six hours I spent alone in the cottage, the five or ten minutes I spent with Hector, the forty-one minutes I spent watching the film. That left a mere twenty-nine hours when I was actually able to see her and touch her, to enclose myself in the circle of her presence. We made love five times. We ate six meals together. I gave her one bath. Alma had walked in and out of my life so quickly, I sometimes felt that I had only imagined her. That was the worst part of facing her death. There weren't enough things for me to remember, and so I kept going over the same ground again and again, kept adding up the same figures and arriving at the same paltry sums. Two cars, one jet plane, six glasses of tequila. Three beds in three houses on three different nights. Four telephone conversations. I was so befuddled, I didn't know how to mourn her except by keeping myself alive. Months later, when I finished the translation and moved away from Vermont, I understood that Alma had done that for me. In eight short days, she had brought me back from the dead.

It doesn't matter what happened to me after that. This is a book of fragments, a compilation of sorrows and half-remembered dreams, and in order to tell the story, I have to confine myself to the events of the story itself. I will simply say that I live in a large city now, somewhere between Boston and Washington, D.C., and that this is the first piece of writing I have attempted since *The Silent World of Hector Mann.* I taught for a while again, found other work that was more satisfying to me, then quit teaching for good. I should also say (for those who care about such things) that I no longer live alone.

It has been eleven years since I returned from New Mexico, and in all that time I have never talked to anyone about what happened to me there. Not a word about Alma, not a word about Hector and Frieda, not a word about the Blue Stone Ranch. Who would have believed such a story if I had tried to tell it? I had no proof, no evidence to support my case. Hector's films had been destroyed, Alma's book had been destroyed, and the only thing I could have shown anyone was my pathetic little collection of notes, my trilogy of desert jottings: the breakdown of *Martin Frost,* the snippets from Hector's journal, and an inventory of extraterrestrial plants that had nothing to do with anything. Better to keep my mouth shut, I decided, and let the mystery of Hector Mann remain unsolved. Other people were writing about his work now, and when the silent comedies were put out on video in 1992 (a boxed collection of three tapes), the man in the white suit slowly began to acquire a following. It was a small comeback, of course, a minuscule event in the land of industrial entertainments and billion-dollar marketing budgets, but satisfying nevertheless, and I took pleasure in stumbling across articles that referred to Hector as a minor master of the genre or (to quote from Stanley Vaubel's piece in *Sight and Sound*) *the last great practitioner of the art of silent slapstick*. Perhaps that was enough. When a fan club was established in 1994, I was invited to become an honorary member. As the person responsible for the first and only full-length study of Hector's work, I was seen as the founding spirit of the movement, and they hoped I would give them my blessing. At last count, there were over three hundred dues-paying members of the International Brotherhood of Hector Manniacs, some of them living in such far-flung places as Sweden and Japan. Every year, the president invites me to attend their annual meeting in Chicago, and when I finally accepted in 1997, I was given a standing ovation at the end of my talk. In the question-and-answer period that followed, someone asked if I had uncovered any information relating to Hector's disappearance while conducting the research for my book. No, I said, unfortunately not. I had looked for months, but I hadn't been able to turn up a single fresh clue.

I turned fifty-one in March 1998. Six months later, on the first day of fall, just one week after I participated in a panel discussion on silent movies at the American Film Institute in Washington, I had my first heart attack. The second one came on November twenty-sixth, in the middle of Thanksgiving dinner at my sister's house in Baltimore. The first one had been fairly gentle, a so-called mild infarction, the equivalent of a short solo for unaccompanied voice. The second one ripped through my body like a choral symphony for two hundred singers and full brass orchestra, and it nearly killed me. Until then,

I had refused to think of fifty-one as old. It might not have been particularly young, but neither was it the age when a man was supposed to prepare himself for the end and make his peace with the world. They kept me in the hospital for several weeks, and the news from the doctors was sufficiently discouraging for me to revise that opinion. To use a phrase I have always been fond of, I discovered that I was living on borrowed time.

I don't think I was wrong to have held on to my secrets for all those years, and I don't think I was wrong to have told them now. Circumstances changed, and once they changed, I changed my mind as well. They sent me home from the hospital in mid-December, and by early January I was writing the first pages of this book. It is late October now, and as I come to the end of my project, I note with a certain grim satisfaction that we are also closing in on the last weeks of the century—Hector's century, the century that began eighteen days before he was born and which no one in his right mind will be sorry to see end. Following Chateaubriand's model, I will make no attempt to publish what I have written now. I have left a letter of instruction for my lawyer, and he will know where to find the manuscript and what to do with it after I am gone. I have every intention of living to a hundred, but on the off chance I don't get that far, all the necessary arrangements have been made. If and when this book is published, dear reader, you can be certain that the man who wrote it is long dead.

There are thoughts that break the mind, thoughts of such power and ugliness that they corrupt you as soon as you begin to think them. I was afraid of what I knew, afraid of falling into the horror of what I knew, and therefore I didn't put the thought into words until it was too late for the words to do me any good. I have no facts to offer, no concrete evidence that would hold up in a court of law, but after playing out the events of that night again and again for the past eleven years, I am almost certain that Hector did not die a natural death. He was weak when I saw him, yes, weak and no doubt within days of dying, but his thoughts were lucid, and when he gripped my arm at the end of our conversation, he pressed his fingers into my skin. It was the grip of a man who meant to go on living. He was going to keep himself alive until we had concluded our business, and when I went downstairs after Frieda told me to leave the room, I fully expected to see him again in the morning. Think of the timing—think of how quickly the disasters accumulated after that. Alma and I went to bed, and once we fell asleep, Frieda tiptoed down the hall, went into Hector's room, and smothered him with a pillow. I'm convinced that she did it out of love. There was no anger in her, no sense of betrayal or revenge—simply a fanatic's devotion to a just and holy cause. Hector couldn't have put up much resistance. She was stronger than he was, and by cutting his life short by just a few days, she would be rescuing him from the folly of having invited me to the ranch. After years of steadfast courage, Hector had buckled in to doubts and indecision, had wound up questioning everything he had done with his life in New Mexico, and the moment I arrived in Tierra del Sueño, the beautiful thing he had made with Frieda would be smashed to bits. The craziness didn't begin until I set foot on the ranch. I was the catalyst for everything that happened while I was there, the final ingredient that triggered the fatal explosion. Frieda had to get rid of me, and the only way she could do that was by getting rid of Hector.

I often think about what happened the next day. So much of it turns on what was never said, on little gaps and silences, on the curious passivity that seemed to radiate from Alma at certain critical junctures. When I woke up in the morning, she was sitting beside me on the bed, stroking my face with her hand. It was ten o'clock—long past the time when we should have been in the screening room watching Hector's films—and yet she didn't rush me. I drank the cup of coffee she had put on the bedside table, we talked for a while, we put our arms around each other and kissed. Later on, when she returned to the cottage after the films had been destroyed, she seemed relatively unfazed by the scene she had witnessed. I'm not forgetting that she broke down and cried, but her reaction was far less intense that I had thought it would be. She didn't rant, she didn't lose her temper, she didn't curse Frieda for having lit the fires before she was compelled to do so by Hector's will. We had talked enough in the past two days for me to know that Alma was against burning the films. She was awed by the magnitude of Hector's renunciation, I think, but she also believed that it was wrong, and she'd told me that she had argued with him about it many times over the years. If that was so, then why didn't she become more upset when the films were finally destroyed? Her mother was in those films, her father had shot those films, and yet she barely said a word about them after the fires went out. I have thought about her silence for many years, and the only theory that makes sense to me, the only one that fully accounts for the indifference she displayed that evening, is that she knew the films hadn't been destroyed. Alma was a deeply clever and resourceful person. She had already made copies of Hector's early films and sent them out to half a dozen archives around the world. Why couldn't she have made copies of his late films as well? She had done a fair amount of traveling while working on her book. What would have prevented her from smuggling out a couple of negatives each time she left the ranch and taking them to a lab somewhere to strike new prints? The vault was unguarded, she had keys to all the doors, and she wouldn't have had any trouble getting the material in and out without being noticed. If that was what she had done, then she would have hidden the prints somewhere and waited for Frieda to die before making them public. It would have taken years, perhaps, but Alma was patient, and how could she have known that her life would end on the same night that Frieda's did? One could argue that she would have let me in on the secret, that she wouldn't have kept such a thing to herself, but perhaps she was planning to tell me about it when she came to Vermont. She didn't refer to the films in her long, disjointed suicide letter, but Alma was in a state of anguish that night, trembling in a delirium of terror and apocalyptic self-judgments, and I don't think she was truly in this world anymore when she sat down to write me the letter. She forgot to tell me. She meant to tell me, but then she forgot. If that was the case, then Hector's films haven't been lost. They're only missing, and sooner or later a person will come along who accidentally opens the door of the room where Alma hid them, and the story will start all over again.

I live with that hope.